C000147953

A Violet Death

by

Joanna Sheen & Julia Wherrell

Victoria Farm Press Ltd.

This edition published 2014 by Victoria Farm Press Ltd,
Stokeinteignhead, Devon TQ12 4QH
www.victoriafarmpress.co.uk
ISBN 978-0-9926844-2-6

Printed and bound in Great Britain by:
Maslands Printers Ltd of Tiverton, Devon.

Set in Minion Pro.

To Richard, with love, and thank you for all the support
Joanna

For Greg, Rosie and Tilly
Julia

Acknowledgements

Joanna and Julia would like to thank Pippa, Judy and Jo
for their input and suggestions.

Special thanks to Sue Viccars our editor.

Chapter 1

Victoria lay back in the bath, closed her eyes and sighed, not from pleasure but from frustration. She hated baths, and this one in particular. It was so large and took so long to fill that the water always seemed to be tepid before she'd even got into it. And it was horribly stained around the taps. She opened one eye just to remind herself how bad it was, and closed it again. A power shower, that was what she wanted.

Of course her aunt, who'd died and left her the cottage earlier in the year, had never worried about such niceties as luxurious bathrooms. Victoria had always thought of her as a strictly 'soap-and-flannel' person, far too busy to lie around in baths or care about how much water pressure a shower had. In fact, she hadn't wasted much time or effort on the cottage at all as she'd got into her seventies, and now it needed redecorating and some serious TLC. And the bathroom, in particular, deserved a major overhaul.

Victoria shivered and, quickly rinsing the conditioner from her hair, reached for the bath plug chain and pulled, but nothing happened. Muttering, she hauled herself into a squatting position and tugged with all her might. The chain broke and it, and the metal plug, shot out of the water and sailed over Victoria's head. As she fell backwards she heard the crash of shattered glass as the plug made its way resolutely though the window and down into the garden.

Chapter 1

Her collapse back into the bath created a large tidal wave which rolled from the tap end back towards her, slapping her full in the face before cascading impressively over the end of the bath and soaking the bathroom floor.

"Damn, damn and triple damn," she muttered, trying to wipe hair and water from her eyes and ignoring the excessive gurgling noises coming from the plughole as the bath emptied, sounding just a little too much like laughter.

Once dressed, she stomped downstairs and stopped as she saw a pool of water in the middle of the kitchen floor. "Moss!" she cried, looking round for the puppy. Seeing him safely shut in his puppy crate, she realised the water must have come through the ceiling from the bathroom and that he was innocent. She sighed, let him out then rummaged around under the sink for a floor cloth to wipe up the bath water.

Albert had offered his DIY skills to fix her bathroom but she felt a qualified plumber would be wiser so she could keep business and friendship well apart. And to be honest, she wasn't entirely sure the mix of Albert, his toolbox and the mains water supply was really such a good idea.

She had grown really fond of Albert during the three months since she had moved down but, fond or not, he could be endlessly frustrating when he tackled something that he should have left to someone better qualified. Her bedroom window currently wouldn't open at all since he had 'mended' it for her. The brackets for the hanging baskets that he had put up for her were upside down and the picture he'd hung in the hallway was distinctly off centre. He worked better on a bigger scale with tractors, chainsaws and diggers. But he had given her Moss and that, and their deepening friendship, meant the world to her.

Shaking herself out of her reverie, she picked up the local

parish magazine, a treasure trove of information, and looked again at the advert for KDC Bathroom Contractors. She'd left a message with them the previous day and hoped she might get a response sooner rather than later.

Moments later, Victoria almost leapt out of her chair as there was a loud thump on the back door and a male voice yelled: "Hello? Miss West – you home?"

Moss raced across the kitchen floor but didn't have enough grip on the lino to stop himself skidding into the door, yelping in surprise. Victoria crossed the kitchen rather more successfully and opened the back door. "Hello, can I help you?"

Standing on the step was a tall skinny man, probably in his mid-thirties but sporting a gold earring and blond streaks in his hair that would have been kinder on a younger man. His blue eyes were bright and distinctly cheeky, the crinkles around them telling of a life full of parties and good times rather than dedicated ambition.

"Kev Wilks, of KDC, you rang yesterday."

Victoria tried hard not to look surprised by this 1990s throwback. "Ah, so you found out where I live – and here you are! Right, well, would you like to come in?"

"I think everyone in the village knows where you live Miss West, doesn't take many visits to the Arms to know what's what!"

"Oh the Swaddle Arms – the pub you mean, yes of course." She would get used to everyone knowing everyone else one day; it was just taking a bit of adjustment. In London, you probably didn't even know your next-door neighbour.

"Now then, what can I do you for? Miss… can I call you Victoria?"

Victoria felt this was somewhat forward, but didn't want to offend him. "Of course. So, do you want to look at the bathroom

I'm hoping to modernise?"

"Be delighted to Victoria, be delighted, know what I mean?"

Victoria wasn't completely sure she did know what he meant, but he seemed harmless – and how bad could someone who advertised in the parish magazine be, for heaven's sake?

"Well, come in – leave the door open as Albert should be here any minute." She was lying, but it seemed a sensible precaution when she had never met 'Kev' before.

Taking him upstairs to the bathroom she pondered just how expensive this project might be. She had the money from renting out her flat in London, and some savings, but they weren't going to go very far and she had lots of essential works to do on the cottage. Well, one thing at a time.

"Just in here." She stood back while he gazed around the room.

"Blimey, you been mopping the floors? And did you know there's a hole in your window? I wondered what that glass was outside."

"Erm, just a minor accident this morning, nothing to worry about." Victoria folded her arms defensively and smiled blandly at him (at the same time making a mental note to clear up the debris as soon as he had left).

Kev whistled and shook his head. "Flippin' time capsule this bathroom, innit? You get a lot of that in these old places down 'ere, know what I mean?"

Victoria decided this time it was fairly simple to know what he meant and agreed. The bathroom was old, but not old enough to be classed as shabby chic, just practical fitments from forty years ago and all very utilitarian. "What I'd like is a completely new suite, a wonderfully powerful shower and new decor, tiles, flooring and so on." She waved her hands expansively, knowing she was being vague.

Kev sucked in a breath and winked at her. "Nice big shower, fit two people in, know what I mean! All possible but not going to be cheap, take a decent pump to get a head of water up 'ere, if you know what I mean."

Victoria sighed, partly worried about how expensive it might be but also about how many 'you know what I means' she'd have to endure before the project was completed.

"Luckily I just did a job for the big house down the other end of the village so I've got quite a few brochures knocking about at home and some rough ideas on prices, so I can get back to you PDQ. I'll just measure up. Wouldn't be any chance of a cuppa would there? Would go down a treat, know what I mean!" He produced a steel retracting rule from his back pocket and began whistling, pausing to add "I take three sugars in mine love."

Biting back a feminist retort, Victoria disappeared meekly to the kitchen to boil a kettle. After all, she could always say no to his estimate if it was way out of her budget. As she had a tin with some of Albert's cake in it she put that out on the table too.

"Blimey love, you know how to spoil a bloke, lucky old Albert I say, know what I mean," said Kev, as he strolled into the kitchen, ogling the cake like a starving child.

"I, er…" Lost for words Victoria sat down and pushed his tea towards him. "So, you'd like some cake?"

"Me? Cake? Does the pope wear a funny 'at? Too true I'd like some!"

Victoria waited for the 'know what I mean' but was spared this time. "So what do you think about the bathroom? Is it a job you could do?"

"Me? Oh yeah, doddle, just a case of getting the right kit. I've got a mate that 'elps with the tiling and the lifting and shifting." He took a big bite and nodded vigorously, presumably indicating his appreciation of the cake. "Coo, you feed me like that while I'm 'ere and the missus'll get mad if the old Armanis get too tight for a Saturday night, know what I mean?"

She decided she most definitely did not want to know what he meant on this occasion. "So, er, Kev… may I call you Kev? Do you need a day or two to prepare an estimate, or…?" Her voice tailed off and she looked at him expectantly.

"Well I can give you an estimate for the labour and the basic works, but of course, the final price will depend on your choice of shower and tiles and flooring and all that. Young Albert will vouch that I am honest geezer – it really depends on your budget. I can do you a bathroom for one and a half, or five or even ten if you want to push the boat out. Know what I mean?"

Victoria thought about her ever-dwindling bank account. But then she had always promised herself a really wonderful bathroom and maybe this was the time to get it. "I think, above all else, I really want a quality power shower, it's something I love so there will need to be a substantial pump, as you say. Plus all the rest of it," she finished rather lamely.

"No problem love, we can do that." Kev stood up and held out his hand and Victoria realised she had agreed, sort of, without asking anyone else to quote. "Oh, and by the way, I stuck some tape over that hole in your window, just to keep the breeze out for now. I'll glaze it proper like when we get started. OK?"

"Thank you, that's great." Moss had been angelic all through their discussion but had at some point got bored and when she looked down she saw he had been entertaining himself by chewing a handle on one of the dresser's bottom cupboards. "Oh Moss no!" Victoria rushed over to stop him. She tried to open the cupboard with only the sharp splintered remains of the handle. As the door jerked open a jumble of old kitchen gadgets cascaded onto the floor.

"'Ere let me give you an 'and." Kev knelt down to retrieve the assorted bits and pieces off the floor.

"I must get round to turning out everything here, there's so much old stuff I really won't use." Victoria said regretfully, looking at yet another pile of junk she'd have to dispose of.

"You should have a word with Albert about that lot: eBay, that's your answer. Bet you'd get a mint for it." Kev crawled under the table and reached for an old-fashioned hand whisk.

"Really? Are you sure? For this tat? I can't think it's something Albert would do, surely?"

"Yes it is – my Kelly, the missus – she's mad keen and she often talks to young Albert about what they're bidding on."

Shows how little I still know about him, thought Victoria as she stretched across the floor for an errant skewer with a decorative handle that had rolled under the table.

"Oh my word, have we disturbed you?" said a voice from the doorway.

Victoria sat up suddenly and banged her head on the table, adding to her confusion. In the sunlight stood a short, scrawny man wearing horn-rimmed spectacles, a flat cap and a grubby trench coat. Too-long grey hair spilled greasily out from under his cap and Victoria took an instant dislike to her caller. Next to her, she felt Moss stiffen and heard the slightest growl start in his throat.

"A lovely sunny day, wouldn't you say?"

"I'm sorry, can I help you?" Victoria clambered to her feet, clutching the skewer. "Have we met before?"

"Not as such, no, but the door was open. I don't mean to disturb you with your gentleman caller, but I feel I already know you as I was acquainted with your late aunt." So was most of Devon, apparently, thought Victoria.

Kev also emerged from under the table. "Look Percy what do

y'want? Surely you can't claim I've left the van on double yellow lines in a farmyard, mate?"

"I actually came to call on Miss West." Percy turned towards Victoria and bowed slightly. "Percy, Percy Shooter, Head of the Swaddlecombe Neighbourhood Watch scheme."

"Really? I didn't think there would be a need for anything like that around here!" said Victoria, grabbing a wriggling pup. "It's one of the things I love about this area, everyone is so friendly and the crime rate seems tiny, compared to where I lived in London." She stroked Moss's ears as the puppy, his whole body taught and quivering, stared fixedly at Percy.

"Ah well, there you'd be surprised Miss West, yes, very surprised! There's all sorts goes on around here, I should know! There's not much I miss!" He tutted, rolled his eyes and puffed out his chest. I'll bet, thought Victoria, a right nosy parker. Kev shot her a meaningful look, confirming her suspicions.

"You might be interested to know that one of my other roles is to submit regular round ups to the local paper, the Herald – I assume you know it?"

"Well, yes, I've seen it, but…"

"I produce a monthly report about what's been happening on my patch, bit of a roving reporter, you could say." He was fingering something inside his mac and Victoria was relieved to see it was nothing more a small digital camera, hanging from a strap slung around his neck.

"As you can see, I submit photos too." He beamed, obviously very pleased with his important role in village life.

Victoria wondered if he knew what she did for a living and was waiting for her to compare notes with a fellow professional. She decided to be mean, so just smiled and said "Gosh, do you really? Well done you!"

Kev moved over to the back door and edged around their unwelcome visitor. He looked over to Victoria. "I'll get back to you later and bring some brochures in, let you choose, know what I mean?" – and with a wave disappeared out to the yard.

There was an uncomfortable pause, then Victoria noticed a movement behind Percy's right leg. A small white dog was peering round the side of his trousers. "Hello, who are you?" she smiled and the dog trotted around her owner and wagged her tail.

"This is my faithful news hound!" Percy made a strange sort of hissing and hiccupping noise that Victoria assumed was meant to be a laugh. "She's called Mitzi."

"Is she friendly? Moss is only four months old and he's a bit boisterous at the moment."

"Oh Mitzi won't mind, she's gentle enough."

Victoria put Moss down on the floor again and he stared at the Westie. There was a moment of calm – then he launched himself at the older dog and began playing in true puppy style, tumbling over his own feet, getting up, bouncing off Mitzi, rolling over, running off a short distance and then charging back. The older dog took it in her stride, wearing the resigned expression of an old timer who has seen it all before, and endured the bombardment with good grace.

"Sorry about this," said Victoria as Moss continued to circle and jump and ricochet off everything. "He'll probably fall asleep in a few minutes, exhausted."

"Mitzi is placid for a Westie, I'm pleased to say. One of my bêtes noires, Miss West, is unattended dogs that are left to bark. I detest yappy dogs in particular. That, and people who don't clear up after their dogs, of course. A real menace. And then there's the lack of street lighting in the community." He folded his arms and looked positively pleased that there was so much he could complain about.

"Of course," nodded Victoria, although, in truth, she felt

the lack of streetlights was fantastic but wasn't going to give him ammunition by saying so. She had only recently discovered the wonderful inky blackness of a Devon night, when you could see the Milky Way stretching high above you. Albert had pointed it out to her one evening as they had sat in one of his fields listening to the owls and the foxes crying in the distance...

"Miss West?"

"I'm sorry – what did you say?" She realised this irritating little man had been whining on and on about yet more things he didn't like about Swaddlecombe while she had drifted off into a reverie. She couldn't understand why, if he wanted to change the village so much, he had come to live here in the first place.

"I said could I come in and show you some of our Neighbourhood Watch literature? You might want to display some of it in your windows?"

"Oh, I don't think so. No one comes past here to see it – we're not exactly on the beaten track, and I can't imagine a burglar reading it and deciding he'd best try somewhere else. Moss – no, don't do that! Leave Mr Shooter's trousers alone!" Victoria rushed forward to shoo the puppy away and successfully backed the unpleasant little man out into the garden.

"I see, well..." said Percy, shuffling bits of paper and scowling at her over his glasses. "Perhaps if I could just..."

"Actually, I'm sort of in the middle of something right now," said Victoria.

"Really?" He said, rocking back and forth on his heels. What a ridiculous little man he was, she thought; his very tone and body language put her teeth on edge. And how rude!

"Yes, really. I'm researching an article and I have a deadline to meet."

"Ah, a fellow scribe. What is your article about, if you don't mind me asking?"

Well I do, she thought, but now I've given the game away I can't very well not say. "It's a feature on a successful local business, Ansome Violets."

"Is it now. Well, well – goodness me," said Percy, and shook his head.

Victoria was taken aback – this was not the response she'd expected. "What do you mean by that?"

"Oh nothing. Just interesting. Successful local business you say. Hmmm… but how long for?"

"Well, they've been going for years, won awards and…"

"Oh yes, we all know the history, but what of the future? Those brothers, they're chalk and cheese. Can't imagine they'll maintain the status quo for much longer. Fight like cat and dog, so I'm told."

As if on cue Moss, who had been slowly stalking the long-suffering Mitzi from afar, suddenly pounced and a fracas ensued. "Moss! For goodness sake!" cried Victoria as the puppy bounced into the flowerbed. "I am sorry Mr Shooter, I did say he was rather boisterous."

"Indeed. Now look, if I could just…"

"'Ello my lover!" cried Albert appearing, as if by magic, around the side of the cottage. "I thought you'd be head down over your computer keyboard today with that deadline looming, not standing in the garden gossiping?"

Thank goodness, thought Victoria. My knight in shining armour – yet again. "Yes, I was just trying to say to Mr Shooter that I needed to get on," she said, smiling warmly at him.

Albert strode up and stood beside Victoria and put his arm very firmly round her. He was a tall man and loomed over Percy.

"Ah, I see…I'd better leave you to yet another gentleman caller!" said Percy, in an annoyingly suggestive manner.

Moss had recovered himself and now came hurtling across the lawn to fling himself at Albert. "'Ere, steady on pup!" he said. "Where's the fire?" Gathering Moss in his arms, he patiently endured enthusiastic licking of first his ears and then his chin. "Daft bugger," he said, and smiled at Percy. "Be seeing you then."

Percy cleared his throat and said. "Right, well, I expect I shall see you again before too long, Miss West. Our paths are sure to cross even if not, sadly, in the pursuit of a safer rural community."

"Her's quite safe with me as her neighbour!" beamed Albert.

"That I doubt very much," muttered Percy, and turned on his heel. "Come on Mitzi, we don't want to play gooseberry do we?" The little Westie glanced at Moss, now lying back in Albert's arms like a contented baby, and trotted after her master as he marched off like a drill sergeant.

"What did he mean by that? Cheeky bugger," said Albert. "Sorry maid, but I could see through the kitchen window that you'd been stuck with that little weasel for some time and I thought you needed rescuing."

"You were quite right, thank you, but we did rather send him packing. He strikes me as the sort who'll take offence."

Albert carried Moss into the kitchen, flung himself into a chair and rearranged the pup in his arms. "I s'pect you're right, he's a nasty busy body, but I can't say I'm going to lose a wink of sleep over it."

Moss was almost asleep in Albert's arms, lying on his back, all four paws in the air, fat little pink belly on show. "Look at that dog, he just adores you!"

"Are you surprised?" Albert twinkled at her. "It's my animal magnetism!" and she slapped his arm lightly.

"Tea?"

"Need you ask?"

"Cake?"

"Ah! Now that reminds me! Here, take this little bundle of mischief and I'll be back in a tick." He passed the snoozing puppy to Victoria and headed back out of the door to his own cottage on the other side of the barn. Victoria kissed the puppy's head, breathing in his yeasty 'freshly baked puppy' scent and stroked his velvet-soft ears. She placed him in his basket under the table and got on with making a pot of tea.

"Now then, I want you to try this," said Albert as he returned, clutching a cake tin.

"Ooh, exciting! What is it?" Victoria put the tea things on the table and sat down.

"This," said Albert opening the lid slowly, "might just be the winning recipe in the specialty cake class at the Swaddlecombe Show!"

She smiled. "Modest as ever!"

The annual Swaddlecombe Show was one of many rural shows that popped up on calendars throughout the summer months in this part of the world. Victoria had first heard talk of it almost from the moment she'd moved in. Entry forms for produce and preserves classes had been littering the counter in the village shop for weeks. She'd overheard various conversations about it in the pub, dark mutterings about the best compost mix for ensuring huge marrows and heated debates about unethical rhubarb forcing. She had no idea such events still took place. She remembered a village carnival from her childhood in Buckinghamshire, all fancy floats and beauty queens, but that had petered out years ago. This show seemed rooted in tradition and the countryside itself with livestock and produce and traditional games and competitions.

Clearing his throat and looking slightly wounded, Albert continued. "Well now, the theme this year is a vegetable cake, as I have already mentioned. Now don't you go making a face like that Victoria West, you know full well how delicious my carrot cake is."

"True. But what a weird idea – a vegetable cake!"

"Not at all, it's something that's been done for years, a very economical way of making the most of what you've got in your garden, Anyway, you damned townie you, this is my way of thinking. As you and I have agreed to continue the little subterfuge started by your Aunt Edith and yours truly many years ago…"

"You mean the downright cheating where Edith pretended she baked the cakes when it was you all the time?"

"Well yes, you could see it like that. But who's being cheated? That's what I'd like to know. They are home made, fair and square, I just don't claim all the glory."

"Because you don't want to be seen as a man who bakes cakes." She grinned and watched him shift a little furtively in his chair. "Well, yes, that's true, but…" He put the lid back on the tin and his shoulders slumped.

"Oh get on with it. I've said I'll pretend I baked it even though I've never even made so much as a scone!"

"Well that's it you see, I thought as it was supposed to be you baking it now, and not Edith, I thought we ought to be a bit more exotic, you being a toffee-nosed townie, and all that." Before she could protest he whipped off the lid and slid the cake under her nose.

"Ooh Albert. That looks nice!"

"That's what all the ladies say!" Victoria felt herself go a little pink – how did he manage to make her do that? She was forty-three and had never blushed when she lived in London. Never, ever.

"It looks like a chocolate cake – which, as you know, is my favourite. Well, that or a Victoria sponge, I can never quite decide, but anyway, it looks splendid."

Albert was cutting a small slice and lifting it from the tin. It looked rich and moist and utterly divine. "Well, you're sort of right, it is a chocolate cake, but it's actually a chocolate and beetroot cake." As she opened her mouth to protest, he popped a piece into her mouth.

"Mmmmmmmm!!" said Victoria, struggling to speak and eat at the same time.

Albert cut himself a large slice, frowning as he chewed slowly.

Victoria rolled her eyes and licked her lips. "Wow, I'll never say I don't like beetroot again! That is amazing, rich and chocolatey, but with a sort of velvety earthiness. Can I say that?"

"You just did." He was still chewing and frowning.

"You're frowning, don't you like it?"

He cut another slice and peered at it from all angles, before taking another bite. "It's OK for a first effort, but I reckon I can improve on it."

"Really? I don't know if I could stand anything more delicious, I might faint!"

He grinned. "Don't be daft. But you think this is a recipe we could press on with then?"

"Of course, but you're the one doing all the work! All I do is the tasting and the barefaced lying!"

"Ah well, I've been thinking about that and I reckon you ought to bake it a few times yourself, just in case anyone asks you about it."

"Me? I can't bake! I've never baked in my life."

"You're never too old to start. I'll get this recipe fine-tuned and then I'll print you out a copy and you can have a go."

"It will be a disaster, believe me. But perhaps if you guided me through it the first time, maybe I could get the hang of it?" She quite fancied the idea of him standing over her and helping as she whisked and kneaded. (No, hang on – that was bread, wasn't it? You don't knead cake…)

But Albert was shaking his head. "No, I reckon you should have a go on your own, it's not rocket science woman. I'll supply all the tins and the ingredients and we can fire up the Rayburn."

"What, in this weather? You must be joking, the kitchen will be 100 degrees."

"Well you can't cook on that there nasty little electric cooker thing you've installed," he said, jerking his head in the direction of the shiny new electric oven in the corner.

"That's not rocket science either – millions of people cook perfectly well on 'nasty little electric cookers' like that all over the world."

"They must be mad," he sighed. "Well, this autumn, I am definitely getting you to understand the workings of that there Rayburn. It isn't right this house not having warmth at its heart. Edith always had it running, well 'cept when the weather was really hot, otherwise, it was running all the time. Anyway, I shall need it for me sickly lambs come February so you'd better have got the gist of it by then!"

She frowned. "What do you mean, 'sickly' lambs – surely you mean 'roast'?"

Albert sighed and shook his head. "I despair sometimes, really I do. In spring, when we have sickly lambs, or orphans or whatever, we often pop them in the warming oven – leaving the door open of course – as it's a lovely gentle warmth to keep the poor little beggars alive. Your aunt was a dab hand at it, and bottle-feeding them too. I have high hopes for you in that area, Victoria."

"Me? You must be joking! I'm not good with baby anythings – apart from puppies of course." She smiled at Moss. How could anyone not love him?

"You ever held a newborn lamb?"

She frowned. "No, of course not, but…"

Albert smiled knowingly. "Well, just you wait and see maid, that's all I can say."

"Oh for goodness sake! Look, if it makes you happy, I will have a go at the cake recipe, but don't hold your breath."

He grinned and helped himself to a cup of tea. "Can't stop long, got to go and check the cows in Ten Acres." He slurped his tea, prodded the cake again and sat back. "Do all your fields have such interesting names?" she asked, pouring herself a cup.

"I don't rightly know. There's Eight Acres and Five Acres and then there's Upper Field, Middle Field and Lower Field and…"

She grinned. "That's what I mean! They are all so, well, utilitarian. Aren't any of them called romantic names like Long Meadow or Primrose Hill, or Grassy Bottom or something?"

Albert sipped his tea and contemplated. "Nope. Well, there's Pond Field and The Marshy Bit. Is that any good?"

"Not really – it won't make an interesting blog writing about 'walking across Ten Acres and into The Marshy Bit'!"

"Well, there you are then. Sorry my lover, but I can't go around renaming me fields to suit your whims! Bit like those daft paint charts you're always wafting about the place with names for colours like Donkey's Breath and London Smog and Rose-tinted Lino. Why you can't have proper names that people can identify like grass green, sky blue and cow-shit brown, I don't know!"

Victoria was trying to hide her laughter as she drank her tea. He shook his head, "I dunno, you townies, you're a proper sample and that's a fact."

"By the way," she said, "I had a visit from Kev of KDC Bathrooms earlier. Nice chap, he seemed to know you quite well – is he good at what he does?"

"That would have to depend on who you asked!" smiled Albert.

"No seriously!" said Victoria, "I can see he's a bit of a lad, but is he a good plumber?"

Albert sat and thought for a moment, "So you really don't want me to sort out the bathroom for you?"

Victoria felt awkward but quickly said, "No Albert I don't. You have a lot to do on the farm and to be honest I would like a shower installed as soon as possible. I miss it terribly." She smiled, hoping that her words had been gentle enough so that he wouldn't be offended.

"Well OK. If you can't have yours truly do it then I guess Kev would be second best. Good bloke Kev, knows his stuff and nice missus too, that Kelly." He nodded emphatically.

"That's good then, he's going to get me some catalogues to look through. What are you doing this evening?" she asked as she put down her mug.

"Funny you should ask." He leant across the table and, meeting her eyes with his own piercing blue ones said, "I was going to ask you to come to the pub for a meal... was that what you had in mind too?"

"Ah, no, damn, not exactly. Moss and I have got our first puppy class this evening and I wondered if you wanted to come along?"

Albert slumped back in his chair, deflated. "No thank you, I do not! My dogs are working dogs, none of this 'heel' nonsense and walking on a lead. Can't think of nothing worse than listening to that dog woman Bunty Wotsit-Doodah shouting 'Sit!' at me all evening!"

"It's Bunty Beacham-Brown and she'd be shouting at the dog, not you. But I do agree, I'm finding the prospect quite daunting. Oh dear, we'll just have to brave it on our own, Moss." She glanced under the table at the sleeping puppy. "But I think I'll be back home before eight o'clock." She too leaned forward and, touching the back of Albert's hand, playfully added, "So I expect I could be persuaded to spruce myself up a little and accompany you to the Swaddle Arms shortly after that."

He grinned. "You could come out with me as tatty as you like and I wouldn't mind! Right, that's a date then. I'd best go and check my boring old brown cows in boring old Ten Acres and live with the fact that they aren't sky blue pink and grazing in a flower-strewn meadow, or the like." He stood up. "I'll see you at eight o'clock maid." Ducking under the table he said, "And you be good young 'un" to Moss, who twitched the end of his tail in his sleep.

"You know I'm heading off to Ansome Violets this afternoon to get the article underway?"

"I think you mentioned it. Know where you're going?"

"I think so…"

"Well, it's easy. Look, you go left out of the drive, right at the bottom, over the narrow bridge, when you get to Jim's place you…"

"Albert stop! I can never follow your directions! I am going armed with an old-fashioned Ordnance Survey map and my sat nav, and between the three of us I think we'll be fine."

Victoria's sense of direction was not good and the Devon signposts were somewhat erratic, so getting lost had become quite a regular pastime since she'd arrived in Swaddlecombe. Fortunately, she couldn't think of a lovelier place for it to happen; the wildflowers lining the lanes and the profusion of wildlife made every trip, no matter how wayward, an adventure. She was also fortunate still to be bowling round in Gloria, Albert's beautiful old primrose-yellow MGB sports car, lent to her when her own car had been written off and which, she was ashamed to admit, she still had not replaced.

He grinned. "I reckon you'll manage to get there, somehow." He stood up and paused. "Don't you be put off by George Ansome's gruff ways, mind. He's a softie underneath, good honest chap. Just comes across as a bit of a bear with a sore head most of the time." He paused. "And you watch out for that younger one, Samuel. He's a bit of a wastrel if you ask me. Head in the clouds, all sorts of daft green ideas and environmental bollocks, if you know what I mean."

She sighed. "Yes, I do know what you mean. Your 'typical farmer' side is coming out now, you old grump! There are lots of good green initiatives and ideas that are very beneficial for the environment, as you well know, so I may find what Samuel has to say quite interesting."

Albert harrumphed. "Hmmm, well, you just watch him anyway, slippery bugger." With that he, gave her a peck on the cheek and strode off to inspect his cows. Victoria smiled at his retreating back. What was all that about, she wondered? He was such a funny man, quite complex in some ways, and yet marvellously simple in others!

Taking a deep breath, she gathered her thoughts. She needed to find her notebook, the map and all her camera gear and get them stowed in the MGB's tiny boot, then she had to put Moss into the puppy crate where he could snuggle down contentedly into his bedding.

At first, she'd thought the idea of a crate, or cage, seemed cruel, but he loved it from the outset and clearly felt secure. He slept in it contentedly every night, enabling Victoria to sleep peacefully upstairs, spared any random acts of vandalism at which puppies were so skilled. In his first few days, before she had bought the crate, Moss had ruined her wellingtons, chewed the legs of three kitchen chairs and peed copiously on a silk blouse. According to Bunty Beacham-Brown, she'd escaped quite lightly and she had recommended the portable puppy crate as the simplest way to ensure domestic harmony. She had been right.

Chapter 2

Victoria stared at the very good-looking man who opened the door – he was nothing like the ruddy faced nurseryman she had imagined. Sandy-haired, green-eyed and tanned, he smiled at her and his eyes held a distinctly mischievous expression. Her mind went blank and she completely forgot what she had been about to say.

"Can I help you?" said the man, patiently.

"If it's they bloomin' sales people tell them to bugger off!" A gruff voice barked from inside the house.

"I rather think it might be someone more interesting than a sales person George, believe me." With that he turned his attention to Victoria again and she found her voice.

"Oh do excuse me, I'm Victoria West, I rang earlier about interviewing Mr Ansome as I would like to write an article about the business."

"Aha, far from an unwanted sales person then! I'm Sam, Sam Ansome, the attractive half of Ansome Violets. Do come in and meet the far less appealing other half, my older brother George."

Sam ushered her through the hallway, gently resting his hand against her back in a somewhat proprietary manner. "George! GEORGE!" he shouted, as a scruffy man appeared in the kitchen nursing a mug of something hot between his hands.

"I bloody heard you the first time," replied George. "It's not all of us that leap to attention the minute a pretty young thing crosses the threshold."

"Please forgive my brother's surliness," Sam said turning to Victoria. "His bark is possibly worse than his bite. But then again..."

Victoria struggled to regain her composure. She felt wrong-footed by the welcome and none of the words she had prepared for her arrival at Ansome Violets seemed quite right now. The drive over had been as adventurous as most of her forays into uncharted parts of Devon tended to be. She had found herself in the midst of an entire flock of sheep – being moved from one field to another and shepherded by two incredibly capable collies – confronted by a lone cow, chewing cud happily in the middle of a lane and unfazed by her car or anything else – and a dead end, thanks to a complete lack of signposting. But anyway, she was here now.

Remembering her mission she smiled at George and Sam. It had to be said that Sam was not hard to smile at, whereas George's entire body language seemed to discourage it. "Thank you so much for letting me come over and chat, I do feel this will make a fascinating article for my country magazine."

"So do we get any money for this then young lady? I'm not for buying anything, told you that." George – his mug of tea now safely stowed on the kitchen table – folded his arms and scowled.

"As I said on the phone, this is editorial, it's free publicity for you. Our readership is pretty huge so you'll get lots of free coverage and we will of course print all the details of your website and mail order address, upcoming shows and anything like that which may be beneficial to the nursery." Victoria tried to smile at George as she talked to him but he remained stony-faced. She tried to see a resemblance between the two brothers, and failed.

"Well we don't do that computer malarkey and we don't want hordes of unwanted visitors tramping over the place, but mentioning the shows, that might be a useful touch. We always do the Devon County – good money to be made there and Chelsea as well, obviously, but I doubt any of your flibbertigibbet readers will go to a proper gardening show."

Victoria stopped herself saying that in fact many of her readers went to Chelsea and were actually keen and talented gardeners, and decided to take the line of least resistance. "Well you just let me know anything you want in the way of contact or future show information and that can definitely be organised."

"Hmmm," replied George and glowered into his mug of tea.

"Let me get you a cup of tea," said Sam, trying to cover the awkward silence. "And do take a seat." After a moment's hesitation George slumped down into the chair opposite her.

"That would be wonderful, white no sugar for me please," smiled Victoria. She preferred coffee or herbal tea but now did not seem to be the right time to be picky.

"Coming right up!" Sam gave her a warm smile, and this time it was Victoria's turn to think 'Hmmm'.

"So, Mr Ansome…"

"Call me George, too many Ansomes round abouts, gets confusing."

"Right, thank you George." She busied herself with her pen and notepad as she wondered how best to tackle this prickly character. Albert had said he was a softy underneath the crusty exterior. Giving her best 'interested and intelligent' expression, Victoria leaned forward and said, "Well, George, could you start off by telling me some background on Ansome Violets?"

"Well, I don't rightly know where to begin. Aren't you just going to ask me a load of questions?" he said, scowling.

"That's fine," said Victoria and thought through the research she had done before setting out. "So, from what I've read, I gather this is a family business, handed down through several generations and now to you and Sam?"

"Pah!" George said. "Sam's about as much use to this business as a posh hat in a hurricane. I do all the real work around here and the business belongs to me."

"Well of course I don't really do anything connected with the business except all the invoicing, accounts, debt collection, phone work, admin and general office work. Complete waste of space me, eh George?" Sam said, placing a mug of tea in front of Victoria.

It didn't take a genius to work out that the two brothers were not on the best of terms and Victoria wondered just how to navigate the hostile waters. She sipped her tea, playing for time (and remembered why she usually chose coffee).

"Well, for a start, perhaps you could show me some of the greenhouses, explain to me about the types of violets and pansies that you grow and fill me in on the history as we go? Then perhaps I could talk to you, Sam, about some of the less practical details of the business, split the interview between the indoor and outdoor angles?" She felt pleased with herself at this suggestion and hoped they would go for it.

"Greenhouses pah! Those were the days, days when people sold equipment at decent prices rather than the inflated sums they charge today. You'll find no glass here at Ansomes, we make do with polytunnels I'm afraid." George sat back in his chair and folded his arms.

"George, for heaven's sake! Victoria will get quite the wrong idea of our business. You chose the polytunnels as they take less upkeep than glasshouses and we said only the other day we'd saved a pretty penny over the years. It also doesn't compromise the quality of the violets, so stop sounding like the voice of doom."

Victoria smiled at Sam in what she hoped was an understanding way. "So George, shall we go outside so you can give me a guided tour?"

"Go on George, take her out, I'll stay here and start on the invoices, all the menial stuff, don't you worry yourself." Sam winked at Victoria over George's head as he walked back into the kitchen.

"Well I can't spare long, work to be done you know." George pulled himself up out of the armchair and marched through the front door. Victoria followed, almost having to trot to keep up with his long stride. Seeing him marching along in the sunshine with a hint of a smile on his craggy his face she thought, for the first time, she could see a family likeness. But George was obviously a lot older than his brother and seemed to carry a greater burden.

They turned left towards a cluster of run-down-looking polytunnels, which surprised her as she'd expected the plants to be grown in pristine conditions. Then, as they got closer, she realised there were no plants in the tunnels, just people. A group of young men and an older woman were packing tray after tray of small viola and pansy plants carefully into boxes and filling them with straw and extra packaging, then labelling and piling them up along one edge of the moth-eaten structure.

"Despatch" said George, waving a large hand as they approached. Victoria smiled at the crowd of packers and wondered if George would let her speak to them as their 'hands on' side of the story would add colour.

Sam came running down the path, waving to attract their attention. "George, George! RHS on the phone, suggesting changes to the Chelsea stand!" George went quite red in the face before stomping off, muttering, "Upstarts! Bloody idiots, think they can organise a show!"

Sam turned to her and gave her a wan smile. "I'm sorry, but Chelsea Flower Show is a very special thing for George and if they want to move his stand by even a foot he may just blow a gasket, so I thought it best to play safe and get him to deal with it. Maybe we could have our chat now instead?"

"Well actually I would welcome the chance to talk to some of the staff involved in despatch if that's OK? Then I can chat to you later?"

Sam gave her his winning smile. "That's fine with me Victoria, I'm ready and waiting!"

Victoria felt he had slightly overdone the flirting, but he was certainly easier to deal with than his brother. Wandering over to the polytunnel she introduced herself, and explained about the article. All the young men nodded but seemed more interested in getting on with their work than talking to her. The older woman, however, wiped her hands on her apron and gesticulated towards a garden bench.

"Come over here my lover, take the weight off. Your young legs may be happy but mine need a rest now and again!" She was a very well-upholstered woman and Victoria could imagine how hard a standing job must be on her feet. "Have you been working here many years?" asked Victoria, getting out her pad and pen.

"My heavens dear, I'm sorry I didn't say, June Truscott." June held out a still-grimy hand, despite wiping it on her apron first, and Victoria shook it. "I'm one of the Ansome sisters, me and May – we come in between the two of them. Younger than old Georgie boy and way older than that scallywag Sam."

"Now you mention it, I can see the family resemblance. So there are four of you?"

"Indeed there are," smiled June.

"So, do you all own and manage the business between you? Doesn't that get complicated?"

June laughed and slapped her mountainous thigh. "Lord no!

Eldest sons get the lot! It's the way it is in farming families. George was the heir to the violet world and got treated very different to the rest of us." June fell silent and seemed to be lost in thought.

"So although you all work for the family business, it's really all George's?" Victoria scribbled more on her pad. "That doesn't seem fair."

"Well now, as a youngster and an incomer, you might well think that," said June, "but it's what we've always been brought up to know, so it's just accepted. As the eldest and the one who would take over, George was worked to within an inch of his life and Dad never let him have a moment's peace or play. Always the violets, he had to learn everything about them, all the old ways, every part of the business. It were a tough life for a young lad and no mistake."

"Goodness, that's a rather sad story," said Victoria

June laughed. "Not all sad my lover. George inherited the lot when Dad went, so he's worth a pretty penny, and never let him kid you otherwise. He's just mean with it, which is no surprise as our Dad dinned it into his head day in day out that frugal was best. No wonder he never got a wife, too tight to pay for a night out I reckon!"

June returned to her reverie and Victoria could see that despite her kind words about how hard George had fared as a boy, there was resentment there regarding the money. She sighed – wasn't it always the case? Money was so often the root of all problems.

June chatted on about how they despatched the young plants – the violets when in season and the violas the rest of the year – and how many different labels she'd had to learn and print out, and Victoria took notes. Hearing a noise up towards the house Victoria looked up to see Sam and George gesticulating wildly and shouting at each other.

"Oh there they go again," said June, grimacing. "They spends more time yelling than they do working, would save a lot of effort if they just declared a truce. Mind you, there's plenty others in the family would just take over on the yelling if Sam stopped." She shook her head sadly and shrugged at Victoria as if she might guess what she had been referring to. "Come on lass, we've been yapping and I need to get a few more parcels packed before postie comes and then get off to the house to get their tea sorted."

"You cook for them too?" Victoria asked.

"Of course, you know how useless men are in the kitchen! Actually Sam does cook a bit, but George won't eat it. So I does most of the cooking and then little May comes in and does the house for them. Little angel she is, despite being a martyr to her knees – and she has her own to do too even though her kids have left!"

Victoria marvelled at the power of the brothers to get their sisters to run round and look after them, despite having families of their own to look after. She hovered between thinking how nice it was to see old traditional values and thinking 'you wouldn't catch me doing that sort of thing'.

George came striding down the path, flushed and puffing, and June made herself scarce, Victoria wondered for a second if June was scared of George, but then decided she was probably just well practised at avoiding trouble.

"Right maid, come on, quick look round the tunnels, I've got work to do, bloody admin lot think they can move things about without so much as a by-your-leave. Whole stand will have to be replanned!" He rubbed his hands together and, despite his agitation, Victoria felt he was relishing the chance to work on it all over again.

George charged off towards a cluster of very new and grand-looking tunnels with open stable-type doors, for ventilation she assumed. Inside the tunnels were beautifully laid-out beds with a mass of plants neatly and carefully planted in varieties. She was only a novice gardener but it was immediately obvious they were strong, healthy, good-quality plants with vivid green foliage.

"This bed here," George pointed at a group on the left, "are special for next year, old variety my Granddad raised that I'm working on bringing back to good numbers and this one here," pointing again, "is another rare one, has a brilliant scent, great little plant."

So George continued throughout the tunnel and on to the next, talking away to Victoria in an animated manner, stopping and bending over individual plants and pointing out their particular merits. This was his passion – not money, or women, or beer – but these exquisite little blooms that he had spent his entire life nurturing. When immersed in his plants he was a different person; he spoke more softly, his big farmer's hands touched leaf and stem with great delicacy, his eyes alight with pleasure. Victoria came to the conclusion that the rough, bluff exterior was a hard shell that he had developed to hide his shyness and lack of social skills.

"So, the violets are your absolute passion?" He nodded and brushed some earth off the edge of a pot. "But their season is early spring isn't it? So, do I take it the pansies and violas are your bread and butter for the rest of the year?"

He puffed out his cheeks. "Yes, you could say that. They're pretty enough in their own way and we sell a stack of them, that's for sure, but they're not special, they're two-a-penny. Not like violets." He shook his head. "There's nothing like my violets for sheer delicacy, colour and fragrance. You'll have to come back next spring and I'll let you have a tray. Course, we sell them on the point of flowering, so they're at their best when they get to the retailer, but you take some home, put them in your garden, nurture them and they'll reward you for years to come. Nothing like spotting the first violets when they appear every spring – magic." He smiled, a faraway look in his eyes.

George turned and walked on up the polytunnel, stepping slowly, his hands clasped behind his back, telling her more about how he propagated the violets, spelling out Latin names and even letting slip a few tricks of the trade. Victoria followed in his wake, scribbling furiously, and making encouraging noises whenever he seemed to flag.

They reached the end of the tunnel and George turned to her – almost as though he had forgotten she was there – and gave a contented-sounding sigh, instantly looking ten years younger. "So, this enough for you, or did you not get it all?"

"That was fascinating, thank you so much," she smiled at him and was pleased to see a small, shy smile, in return. "I've written pages and pages of notes but I am bound to have missed some bits, so maybe I could come again to check some details with you once I have roughed out the article?" He grunted acknowledgement and shoved his hands in his pockets and regarded his wellington boots. A bit like an embarrassed schoolboy, thought Victoria.

"That's fine, lass. Nice to find someone so interested. You just give me a ring if you needs to know anything else."

"Thank you. I could do with talking to Sam now too as he handles the paperwork and advertising side of things?"

In an instant, the old George returned and he scowled. "Fat lot he'll tell you of any use, but yes help yourself, he'll be up at the house with his feet up no doubt!" With that George marched off towards another tunnel and Victoria, feeling she had been dismissed, found her own way back to the house.

"Hey Victoria!" A voice hailed her from a short distance away but she couldn't see anyone. "Here, behind the beans!"

She peered round some very vigorous runner beans that were running riot over a massive bamboo frame. There on his knees was Sam, pulling weeds from the area behind the canes. "I didn't see you there – goodness, those beans are going crazy!"

He laughed. "Maybe I do have a touch of the family green fingers after all! It's just that George doesn't acknowledge it."

"I think you must if this is your vegetable plot – I wish mine looked half as wonderful. Those tomatoes look amazing – are they striped?"

"Yes indeed, I like messing around with unusual varieties of veg. Purple potatoes, yellow tomatoes, green cauliflower, I grow the lot."

"I'd appreciate some tips on how to grow better veggies, but right now I was hoping we could discuss Ansome Violets, and perhaps you could give me details on some of the areas George didn't cover?"

"Any excuse to sit and chat with you is fine with me." He gave her another winning smile and seemed about to place his hand on her waist to guide her towards the house, then realised how muddy his hands were and laughed. "I'll just wash up a bit and get this mud off and make us a brew and then we can have a nice chat."

Victoria loved his smile but then thought of Albert and dismissed any feelings of attraction. "You go on ahead and I'll just plan where I want to take photos on my way back to the house. Should I head to the front door?"

"Nah, come round the back to the kitchen, no-one ever uses the front door! There's a small garden there where we could sit in the sun." Sam walked off towards the house and Victoria grinned to herself. Much as she didn't want or need another admirer at her age it was still gratifying when someone showed an interest.

Victoria knocked on the back door and peered into the big

farmhouse kitchen with an Aga and a massive table and chairs that could surely seat at least ten. The room was so large there was space for a sofa and chairs at one end which looked very snug and perfect for cold winter days when you'd been stuck in a freezing polytunnel for hours. As there was no response to her knock she wandered in and stood by the sofa to wait for Sam. On the small table was a pile of magazines including a copy of Your Chickens which she pounced on enthusiastically.

"Sorry to keep you waiting." Sam appeared through the door, drying his hands on a towel. "You into chickens then?"

"Yes, I have three and really don't know much about keeping them yet. As it was on the table I thought I'd have a look."

"Feel free, take it with you if you like. It's a good magazine, I've learned a lot."

"Do you keep chickens then? I didn't spot any."

"No, not yet, I was just checking out what we'd need. Love the idea of chickens but George is tight when it comes to new ideas and investments. I keep telling him we could rescue old layers and feed them scraps but he's always so resistant to new ideas."

"I'm sure you could manage, I was given mine by some friends and the eggs are just out of this world. There's a massive difference between supermarket eggs and ones you have just that minute gathered from your own hens."

"I bet there is. I'd love to come and talk more about your hens sometime, perhaps see how you house them and things?" Victoria tried hard not to giggle as she thought of her 'unusual' chicken house – more of a bijou cottage than a coop – thanks to her London friends Gray and Sebastian, and wondered what Sam might make of it.

"You'd be welcome any time, but I am still a complete novice when it comes to chicken husbandry," she smiled, then caught sight of the kitchen clock and realised she had been there far longer than planned and still hadn't really got all the information she needed. "Actually, I've just seen the time and I really need to get back, so could we postpone the tea? Perhaps I could come over again, to talk to you and to George and get the rest of the detail I need for my article?"

Looking a little crestfallen, Sam said "Indeed you can, beautiful women are welcome here anytime!"

Victoria winced inwardly at the over-egged compliment but merely smiled warmly and said, "Thank you so much for all the help and please thank George too. Sorry I haven't quite gathered enough details yet, but I can make a good start now and I'll be in touch to make another appointment and to take photos."

"Anytime Victoria, anytime." Sam bowed slightly as he walked her to her car. "Very nice," he said, eyeing the little sports car. Victoria smiled, ignoring his double meaning, and slid into the driver's seat.

As was often the case, her journey back to Swaddlecombe went without mishap. It seemed to Victoria that she was on the end of a very long piece of elastic attached to her home; it would let her muddle her way to her destination and then pull her back quickly as soon as it could. She found it was a sensation she rather liked. The weather was so glorious that she put the MGB's roof down. She drove slowly, enjoying the breeze in her hair, the birdsong and the smell of the wildflowers around her. To say it was a change from her London commute would be an understatement: she could never, ever go back to the noise and the fumes and the dirt of the city.

She pulled into the kerb and parked outside the village shop, the eccentric emporium presided over by the Drewe sisters, grey-haired triplets of a certain age. The shop and its owners held a terrible fascination for Victoria and she was a regular shopper.

She often called in just for the entertainment and bought some unnecessary random food item; anyone inspecting her larder at home would think her very odd indeed.

She paused to look at Lavender Drewe's 'Special Offers' basket outside the door. A few seashells, all slightly damaged, had pride of place and there were a pair of flip-flops, one with a broken strap, and many small bits of rope. Victoria felt there might be some sort of seaside theme, but the inclusion of a worn garden trowel and a range of mismatched crockery made her doubt her earlier assumption.

The shop bell rang as she entered. "Miss West!' trilled Dahlia, the tallest sister. "How grand to see you and on such a fine day!"

"Isn't it just?" agreed Victoria, smiling at Iris, the middle-sized sister, and looking around for Lavender.

"She's off on one of her bargain-hunting trips," said Iris. "She's at the car boot in Westerley."

"Oh yes, she told me she got much of her inspiration there," said Victoria.

"Inspiration? Oh, I don't think Lavender has any of that dear!" said Iris as she and Dahlia both laughed, but not unkindly.

"Is she working on a sort of marine, or nautical theme at the moment?" Victoria ventured.

Iris frowned. "How do you mean dear?"

"In her special offers basket, I thought…" but Victoria could see the two sisters looked completely flummoxed and got the distinct impression she was the one coming across as 'not quite right', rather than their completely batty sister.

Victoria remembered her father advising that it was always best to put down the spade and stop digging once you found yourself in a hole, so she did just that. "Oh right, well actually, I need some milk and cheese please."

"Now you like that mature Cheddar, don't you?" said Dahlia.

"Yes please, half a pound would be lovely."

"We haven't got any dear."

"Right, no problem, what about the Double Gloucester you had last week?"

"That's all gone too dear. We've had a bit of a run on cheese, haven't we Iris?"

"That we have," agreed Iris.

"So, what cheese have you got?"

"We've got some Scottish Cheddar, but I don't know if you fancy that, it being foreign?"

Victoria put on a contemplative face and tried hard not to smile, then said, "I think that will be fine, thank you." She moved over to the counter where vegetables were displayed. "Have you any beetroot?"

"Beetroot? Well, that's a new one for you, haven't known you want that before. Having some with your salad?" asked Dahlia.

"No I...," but Victoria stopped herself just in time; if she gave away Albert's cake recipe he might get really upset. "I mean yes, I am, I might even pickle it!' she said wildly, having no idea how to do such a thing.

"Right you are then," Dahlia picked up a bunch of very muddy-looking lumps attached to dark green leaves and put them in a bag. Victoria wanted to query if they were actually beetroot, but decided to just buy the stuff and then check with Albert. "And do you sell dark chocolate, you know, the plain stuff?"

"Would that be for cooking, or eating as a naughty treat?" laughed Dahlia.

"Oh, naughty treat!" lied Victoria, and both sisters tittered and added the bar of chocolate to her purchases.

She left the shop clutching her bag of shopping, smiling to

herself – how she loved the place! – but her smile faded as she spotted the tail of a flapping mackintosh and a small white dog disappearing round the corner into a side road. She was sure it was that awful Percy Shooter again. Had he been following her, or was she being paranoid?

Victoria took a deep breath and raised her face to the sun. Stupid little man, he wasn't going to get her down. She turned round quickly and bumped straight into Bunty Beacham-Brown.

"Oh! I'm so sorry, I wasn't looking where I was going," cried Victoria.

"No harm done! I was just coming up to tap you on the shoulder and say 'See you and little Moss later.'"

"Yes, of course, we are both looking forward to it," said Victoria, fibbing again.

"Super!" beamed Bunty. "I do love the start of a new puppy class. Just like the first day at infant school, don't you think? No, I suppose not, silly me, it's your first time, so how could you?" She puffed out her cheeks and put her hands on her broad hips. "Hope it will have cooled down a bit by this evening, this damned weather is no good for dogs, makes 'em dopey. Never mind! I expect there will be lots of excitement tonight, the odd fracas and a puddle here and there – and that's only the owners – ha!" She barked with laughter and Victoria almost jumped out of her skin.

But figures like Bunty reassured her, and she felt England would never fall while good old girls like her were still around. She noticed, for the first time in their acquaintance, that the dog trainer was not encased in tweed. This was a clear indication that it really was a 'bit of a scorcher', as Bunty would say. Instead she was wearing a long denim button-through skirt, lightly spattered with mud, presumably the result of a passing spaniel as it shook itself dry, and huge old loafers that looked like canoes. Victoria actually wondered if they were Bunty's or if she had accidentally stepped into her husband Kenneth's shoes, as they seemed far too large.

"Is Moss coming along alright? Are you using the puppy crate, as recommended?"

"Yes I am, and thank you so much for suggesting it. Moss seems quite happy in it, although the little blighter has still managed to chew quite a few things, despite my best efforts."

Bunty shook her head and her jowls wobbled slightly. "Ah dear, dear, we are making life hard for ourselves, aren't we? Puppy must respect boundaries so you must instil discipline! Consistency, consistency, consistency!" She smacked an ample thigh to emphasise each word. "That's what puppy needs, then he knows where he is and harmony will prevail. A badly behaved dog does not make for a happy household, I can assure you of that my dear! The sooner you get the upper hand the better. Remember, you are top dog! You are leader of the pack!"

Victoria found it hard to think of herself as the leader of anything, let alone a pack –and it was so hard to discipline such an adorable scrap.

"Well, one can't stand here putting the world to rights all day Victoria, as much as one might like to. I need to go home and gather my wits – what's left of 'em – ha!" She squeezed her eyes shut when she laughed and looked quite oriental, thought Victoria.

"Righty ho, I look forward to seeing you and your little man in the Parish Hall at six-thirty – sharp!" boomed Bunty and she sailed off down the road to her battered maroon Volvo. As she opened the car door a frenzy of barking rent the air and she yelled "BE QUIET ANGUS! FERGUS! WILLIE!", slammed it shut and drove off, and peace was restored.

Victoria smiled to herself and climbed into the little MGB. Glancing at her watch, she realised time was getting on and she needed to stop dawdling and get on.

Moss was wagging excitedly when she got home. "Come on then young Moss, let's go and say hello to the chickens." Victoria was anxious that he should get accustomed to the birds and not chase them. The chickens seemed untroubled by his presence and only paid him any attention if he did one of his high-pitched puppy barks which seemed to burst out of him on odd occasions just from sheer exuberance.

Victoria went into the chicken run and scattered some old lettuce and cabbage leaves and watched the birds squabble over them enthusiastically. Edwin Ruminant, the local vicar and hen fancier, had said that greenery, whether grass or bits of veg, helped give the yolks such a rich deep yellow colour.

She had grown to love her hens after they arrived as a surprise gift from her friends Gray and Sebastian, complete with a fancy hen house painted in shades of Farrow & Ball. The birds had settled in nicely and were now quite placid and would let her pick them up and stroke them, emitting contented 'pock, pock' noises as she did so. Victoria would often take a break from her computer and sit in a deckchair next to their run, drinking a cup of tea and listening to their chatter; it was immensely soothing, and watching their antics was endlessly amusing. Animals had never really figured in her London life and were yet another wonderful discovery in this new rural world.

Victoria opened the nest box and was delighted to find three nut-brown eggs resting in the straw. "You clever, clever girls!" she cooed and the hens seemed to 'pock pock' even more, acknowledging their genius.

She gathered the eggs and shooed Moss back into the house. She thought that jeans and trainers were probably OK for the puppy class. Goodness, she hoped Moss didn't disgrace himself! She found his new lead, red to match his collar, picked up his special dog towel, red with black-printed paw prints, her phone and her notepad and went back to the car. Moss travelled in a cardboard box in the footwell but the puppy's arrival was yet another reason why she had to buy her own car soon and stop relying on Gloria, as Albert called the MGB. She'd have to get a sensible hatchback, an estate, or something. She put up the roof and, together, she and Moss set off for the village.

Albert was leaning nonchalantly against the Range Rover when she drove into the yard almost two hours later. He smiled at her, "Well maid, you took your time!"

"Oh God!" Victoria climbed out of the MGB and leant heavily on the bonnet of the Range Rover. "I thought it would never end! It was purgatory!"

"That good, eh?" laughed Albert and patted her shoulder gently.

"The puppies were OK, it was the people – hopeless, it was chaos! I am shattered!"

"And the little chap?"

"Sleeping happily in his box, can't you see his halo? He was absolutely wonderful, but he's exhausted too."

Albert was grinning hugely and obviously highly amused by her state. "Come on then, get yourself sorted, shall I put Moss in his crate? Let's get some dinner and you'll feel better then. A stiff drink and one of Trudy's meals and you'll be right as rain."

As they sat in the Swaddle Arms, their food ordered, a pint of beer in front of Albert and a large glass of Pinot Grigio in front of Victoria, she gave a huge sigh. "Ah, now I can relax!"

Albert lifted his glass. "Cheers then." Victoria clinked her glass against his and smiled at him over the top as she took a good swig. "Mm, that's better."

"Want to tell me all about it then?" asked Albert.

"Oh Lord, not really, I don't think you want to know, do you?"

He chuckled. "I reckon I can guess most of it…"

"Well, the dogs behaved as you'd expect, en masse, but the owners were utterly hopeless! No one listened and everyone kept doing their own thing, and then a couple of dogs would have a scrap and their owners would start bickering, poor Bunty! Actually, she seems a very good trainer – of dogs – it's the people who ruin it. People speaking in silly little voices or not saying the right commands, I don't know how she keeps her temper! Anyway, I think Moss and I did OK, he was very calm and well behaved. He'd often just sit and watch the others with a sort of patient expression on his face. And whenever he did something right and Bunty praised him, he wagged like mad!"

Albert smiled and shook his head. "Bleddy carry on, I ask you!"

Their food arrived and they tucked in greedily, Victoria was having a ploughman's and Albert, unfazed by the hot weather, was tucking into a roast lamb dinner. "Talking of bleddy carry ons," said Albert through a mouthful of roast potato. "You see that lot over there?" A table of ten or so people were crammed into one corner of the bar. "That's the Swaddlecombe Show committee."

"Really?" said Victoria, her interest piqued. She recognised several people seated around the table – Tufty from the garage was there, as was the large farmer Albert had introduced her to but whose name she had forgotten, and the Reverend Ruminant seemed to be in the thick of it and trying, and failing, to bring the table to order.

"'Tis always like that, chaos!' grinned Albert.

Victoria tuned in and heard that they were discussing publicity and posters, or indeed the lack of. "I could help with that," she said to Albert.

He nearly choked on his beer. "I'd keep me head down if I was you! You show any interest and they'll haul you in as easy as winky."

"But, I'd quite like to help," she said, trying to catch Edwin Ruminant's eye, as he attempted to calm down one small very red-faced man who was banging the table with his fist and saying "No, no, no – I'm not 'aving it!"

Having demolished his dinner, Albert sat back and folded his arms: "Well, on your head be it Victoria, but I'd think carefully before I volunteered."

"Oh, don't be silly! I want to get involved in village life and anyway, it could be useful material for my blog on the magazine's website." As she said this Edwin spotted her and raised a hand in acknowledgement, and she waved back.

Chapter 3

She peered at Albert's typed recipe, and wiped a smear of butter off the corner. He had made notes, added things and crossed bits out so it wasn't easy to follow. She also felt rather sulky (ridiculous really) about having to try and bake this beetroot cake. Cookery really wasn't her 'thing' and carrying off this grand pretence that she had baked the cake simply to save his manly pride at the village show was irritating her this morning.

Victoria had cooked and peeled the beetroot and was now feeling like an actor in a second-rate murder film. She looked at her bright red hands and wondered if the colour would ever fade or if she was stuck like it forever. Albert had insisted it had to be fresh beetroot and NOT the pre-cooked and peeled chunks she had spied in the supermarket during her last visit. Just washing it seemed a pain: all that mud and mess once she got it home from the shop! So, she'd done as he'd asked and had now got beetroot stains all over her hands, under her nails, on her top, and ruined a tea towel into the bargain – thank you Albert.

Victoria sighed and read the recipe again. 'Grease the tin with butter and line the base with baking parchment.' That was the roll of tracing-paper-type stuff Albert had delivered yesterday and she'd fought with for ten minutes to get a circle the right size. The recipe declared preparation time was less than thirty minutes – well, the recipe lied!

She ploughed on through the instructions, separating the eggs (a minor triumph: it had never worked successfully before). 'Fold the sugar and egg whites' – drat – what was folding again? She checked her notebook. Albert had walked her through the recipe several times now. Surely she could do this?

Eventually it was there, the chocolate cake mix – with the ghastly beetroot – poured into the tin. She had stuck to her guns and insisted on using the neat new electric oven, the Rayburn being one step too far, despite Albert's grumbling. This summer was such a scorcher that heating the house wasn't on her 'to do' list for now. No doubt it would loom large when the colder weather arrived in the autumn and she would have to let Albert fire the thing into life.

Using the ruined beetroot-coloured tea towel she carefully manhandled the cake tin into the oven. Yes, she had even remembered to preheat it, she hadn't missed a trick! As if on cue her phone rang and she picked it up smugly, thinking how organised and laid-back she was: cake in the oven, and all well with the world.

"Sweet pea – is that you?"

Victoria smiled at the sound of Gray's voice.

"Gray darling, hi!"

"I just had to catch up, with you emigrating to deepest Devon we're missing all the gossip. Come on, 'fess up – how's your divine male model farming neighbour and how go my beauteous chickens?"

"Gray," she laughed, enjoying her friend's irreverent humour; just occasionally she did miss elements of her old life. "Albert is wonderful, he's turning into a great friend and I think he's rather attractive, but I'm not sure he could ever be classed as a male model. You'd have a fit if you saw his clothes – he's very much a working farmer, nothing fashionable about him."

"Well so long as all is well with you," said Gray. "We miss

you like crazy up here of course, but life goes on. Did you know Sebastian has decided it's time he gave something back? Don't laugh sweetie, he's applied to become a magistrate – I'm rather hoping it will involve a uniform or something, you know how I just love men in uniforms, but it seems to be keeping him happy."

"No uniform I fear, just some interesting extra work and good on him for being community spirited," Victoria laughed. "And what about you? Community service, looking after young babies or sick animals in the near future?"

There was a loud splutter from the other end of the phone which Victoria deduced was a 'no', perhaps involving a cup of coffee.

"Oh look what you've made me do, this top is ruined and it was one of my best – this season's Ted Baker, no less. Shame on you, I had to fight like crazy to snatch this in their spring sale."

She sat at the kitchen table as they chatted and laughed; it was as though they had only seen each other yesterday. The one thing she had always been able to rely on was Gray and Sebastian's ability to make her laugh and feel good. They had a wonderful way of sharing their determination to enjoy life, no matter how hard the issues they had faced over the years. They had been hugely supportive of her when she'd fought and won her battle with breast cancer, and now the three of them had a bond that she hoped would never break.

"Now look I really have to go, I've just put a cake in the oven, yes a cake, and I must keep an eye on it or Albert will be furious." As she said that she turned to face the cooker and saw what appeared to be smoke seeping out of the oven door. "Oh no! My cake, smoke! We can't have been talking that long, surely?"

A wicked chuckle came from the other end of the phone line. "No, not long no, maybe an hour, definitely no longer... bye sweetie! Talk soon."

Victoria hurried over to the oven, grabbed the tea towel and opened the door to a blast of hot air, smoke and a distinctly unpleasant burnt cake smell. Presumably lured by the aroma of 'better than nothing, even if it is burnt cake', Moss came trotting into the kitchen. He nuzzled behind Victoria's knee and she pushed him out of the way.

"Yes I love you to bits Moss, but not now." Juggling the hot cake tin, she turned to place it on the kitchen table. The back of her knee felt sticky and, without thinking, she wiped at it and her hand came away looking distinctly odd. She looked down at Moss and his nose and most of his face was covered with white slimy liquid. There, in his mouth, was her extra-large tube of fabulously expensive shampoo that she'd been using frugally, trying to save for times when she wanted a treat.

She gave a gasp – what effect would soap have on Moss's insides? Then she picked up an aroma that answered her question: the smell of her wonderful shampoo and vomit in equal proportions.

"Give me the tube Moss, NOW! Give me the tube." She wrestled with the plastic and Moss decided this was a good new game and was thrilled that she liked it too. Finally Victoria wrested the remains of what had once been a large tube from his mouth. The question was: had he eaten the rest of the plastic, or was it in the bathroom, or...?

On searching the house she found pieces of plastic, chewed and spat out in various spots. She also discovered several patches where he had been sick and others where he had chewed particularly hard on the tube and the shampoo had been squirted onto the carpet and even the walls. Oh joy! Heading back to the kitchen for a bucket and lots of hot water she foresaw a great day ahead.

Having had a bad start, Victoria was determined to make the rest of the day count and not get depressed about how hard puppies can be to train or cakes to bake. Of course, it was her own fault for getting so immersed in her phone call that she'd missed both timing the cake and keeping her eye on the pup. So as she set off for her second appointment at Ansome Violets she rapidly went through all the additional questions and details in her mind that she hoped George could clarify.

Parking on the rough, unmade land near the polytunnels, she locked the door of the MG securely. She always felt aware that it was Albert's and took more care than she would have done of her own car. Looking to her left she saw one of those big muscle-bound 4x4 trucks, black with lots of gleaming chrome. It was the style of vehicle you usually saw littering the streets of Chelsea but were pretty rare down here in Devon, the very place where their four-wheel drive capability might have a practical purpose.

Should she go to the front door, over to a polytunnel or... she hesitated and then spotted George away in the distance. She set off towards the straw-hatted figure.

"Hello! George." Victoria called and waved but there was no response. As she got closer she called again. "Hello? Hello George?"

George looked up from the tray of seedlings he was watering with a small milk jug. "What do you want?"

"We had an appointment George, we spoke on the phone?" Victoria sighed, hoping her journey hadn't been in vain.

"Maybe. I'm a busy man, can't be remembering every little thing." George continued to add water to the roots of the new little plants with the utmost care.

Oh dear, we seem to be back to square one, she thought. "Well I'm sorry to disturb you but I need to take some photos and I hoped you could help with a few details that are still a bit hazy for me?"

George transferred his small seedling tray to a bench nearby and then started to water the ground around it with a fine sprinkling from a watering can.

"Why do you water the ground?" asked Victoria.

"Seems to deter the red spider mites," said George. "Little buggers, their sole aim in life is ruining my violets, years of battle I've had with them. "

"Fascinating," replied Victoria, scribbling in her notebook. "Can I ask you just a couple of historical questions about Devon violets?"

"Ask away, not saying I'll answer right, but I'll try, not enough appreciation for these flowers out there."

"So your family has grown violets for – how many generations was it?"

"Don't rightly know," replied George, "Certainly four, mebbe five, my Dad was never clear on that one. But there's more history around if that would help, wasn't thinking last time you came, should have found the papers. We were going to do a little pamphlet but nothing came of it, too expensive, more important to buy shuttering for the tunnels really."

Victoria wondered whether June's opinion that he was worth a pretty penny was true, or if things were indeed tight, as George frequently suggested.

"Seems a shame, the world would love to know more about such lovely plants. I remember Aunt Edith loving Devon Violet soaps and bath cubes."

"Ah Edith, she were a fine girl." George paused and looked into the distance. "She was good friends with Clary, I remember. Clary and I helped out down the orphans' home most Saturday mornings, only time Dad let me off working." He paused again and his expression seemed melancholy. "Made you realise that some kids were worse off than what we were, they had a rotten life, not that ours was much better. I wanted to take Clary to the Violet Ball that year, but you know how it is, no money when you're a young lad and my Dad never thought it was right."

"Violet Ball?" asked Victoria.

"Oh yes there was a right smart do every year, crowning the Violet Queen and Clary got to be one of her attendants that year, so proud she was. But I never got to take her out, reckon she got tired of waiting and she found another chap."

He stopped. His face seemed to close up, and he changed the subject. "Talking of money being tight, typical example right now. This hot weather, killing us all it is, as well as the plants. The water bill is through the roof, how this government thinks honest hardworking men are meant to survive I'll never know. Hosepipe ban, then flooding, then straight into a drought, can never make their mind up. But there'll be a storm soon, you mark my words and that'll be the end of us all."

"But I thought a storm and plenty of rain would be good news?"

"That's where you're wrong my girl," he straightened up and squinted into the sun. "Weather this hot for this long, ground is rock hard, no rain will sink in, it'll run off and the drains won't cope, all the outside stock'll be flattened, and we'll be ruined you see!"

Victoria had a sneaking suspicion that he wouldn't be ruined if the rumours of his wealth were correct, but the weather did seem to be a vital part of country life. When she'd been in the city, rain was just an annoyance if you had to walk to the tube station. Now she could see that sun and rain and the seasons were what farmers lived by.

Getting out her camera, Victoria asked, "George, why are you using such a small jug to water those seedlings?"

"Why? Because water is precious for starters and it needs to go to the right place, can't be splashing it about carefree and, secondly, these plants need handling with care." She crouched down and, zooming in, took some close-up shots of George gazing at his beloved plants, speaking softly as if he might disturb them. "These are the future of the nursery – the children – if you like, of the enterprise. It's important to get water and feed to every root, every seedling and get it right, every seedling wasted is a sin in God's eyes, that was what my father said and no doubt his before him."

"I see," said Victoria, not really knowing how to respond to that.

"See this one here." He was crouched low over a tray of small plants. "This is a lovely variety coming on for next year. A bit taller than normal and more refined looking. I was trying to think of a name for it."

"I can see that coming up with something both original and appropriate must be difficult," said Victoria, peering closely at the plant.

George gave a small, shy grin and said, "Well, I thought I might name this one 'Miss West' – what do you think to that?"

Victoria straightened up, temporarily lost for words. "Goodness, well, that would be wonderful – for Aunt Edith, of course."

George gave a small shrug. "Well for Edith, and for you, I reckon."

Victoria put her hand to her mouth. "George, that's wonderful, I feel really touched, thank you."

He removed his hat, scratched his head and looked embarrassed. "Yes, well, just a name really."

"Well, thank you, it's lovely."

"Are well, I'd better get on." He began straightening trays. Victoria took this as her cue to leave him to it. "Maybe I could go and talk to the packers again before I take a few more final photos?"

The gruffness returned as George replied, "Do as you please, but no holding them up from their work mind; time is money, and I'm not sure anything good will come of this newspaper thing."

Victoria sighed inwardly, and decided this was a good time to make a quick getaway. Explaining that it was a glossy magazine wasn't going to help. She walked over to the packing polytunnel and again marvelled at the difference between the beautiful new tunnels for the plants and the tattered old ones in which the humans worked. She snapped a few photos of the team at work and the parcels waiting to go out and then saw June, so waved at her and smiled.

"Hello my lover, you back again – hope old George hasn't put you off too much, we're right excited to be in a magazine!"

"Hello June, yes last visit this time I think. I just wanted a few more details and more importantly a couple more photographs, nearly done now."

At that point an attractive – if in a very obvious way – young woman appeared. She was probably in her early thirties, thought Victoria. The amount of make-up she wore seemed at odds with the job of being a packer in a draughty polytunnel and Victoria marvelled at the length of her nails, complete with nail art.

"So you going to introduce me then Mum?" she said in a very bold manner, chewing gum rapidly as her eyes flicked from June to Victoria.

"Of course dear! Victoria – this is my daughter Madeleine."

"How lovely to be able to work with your family," replied Victoria. "Must be nice to have your daughter here with you."

Madeleine seemed put out by this comment. "Christ no, I don't work here, I'm just helping out as they have a rush, Mum insisted even though she knows I have more work than I can handle."

"Really?" replied Victoria, "What do you do?"

"Trading mainly, buying selling, specialist markets." Madeleine nodded and chewed and Victoria realised that was the only explanation she was going to get. Did she mean money trading as in banking, international trading? Victoria smiled. "That sounds interesting, can I include you in a group shot of the parcels and packers or would you rather stay out of sight?"

"I thought that's why you wanted to be up here today, Madeleine?" said June.

Madeleine quickly smiled at Victoria. "Do make sure they spell my name right, won't you?" Victoria was about to say it would probably just have a general heading like 'Plants packed up and about to leave the nursery' and then decided to keep quiet.

"Could you gather round everyone, Victoria wants a picture of us all with the parcels. Come on Joe, look lively, we haven't got all day."

"Certainly bloody haven't," said a grumpy voice behind them. George was standing there watching.

"Could I possibly ask a huge favour and have you in the middle of the photo, George? After all you are the centre of this business and such an important figure and if you remember you didn't have time for me to take any photos on my last visit…" Victoria held her breath and hoped.

"Just one, it's time I went up to the far end," replied George and took his place centre front of the group, thereby obscuring two of the smaller lads but they soon moved around and Victoria got her shot. George stood, centre stage, arms folded, scowling, with smiling packers ranged around him – this would surely be the main shot for the article.

Feeling satisfied with her work, she packed away her camera and was pleased when George walked with her towards the car.

"Thank you so much for your help George. I think between you all I have managed to get a really lovely picture of a rural business that is doing so well."

"Pah, you try paying the bills then young lady. Nothing but endless hard work pays the bills here," he said, nodding firmly, as if repeating an oft-mentioned fact.

As they reached her car, Victoria caught a flash of white at the end of the driveway and heard a definite sharp yap. They looked up and she was sure it was the tail end of Percy and his Westie disappearing.

"Was that Percy?" she said to George.

"Bloody little toad, I'll have his guts for garters one day, you mark my words. Damn little weasel always poking his nose into other people's business."

There were more yaps and she could see they had walked past the entrance again; if she didn't know better she'd assume he was spying on her. George was outraged and, red in the face, charged down the drive yelling threats at the man and his dog.

When he returned Victoria asked, "Are you OK George? You seemed very angry with him."

"Little blighter's been reporting me to the council for getting mud on the roads when I go in and out of me own drive in the general course of business. Damn man has too much time on his hands." George growled and stormed off towards the house without even saying goodbye. Victoria decided on balance she wouldn't go after him just to say thank you again.

She turned to unlock the car and saw the black brooding 4x4 from a different angle and spotted the number plate 'MAD 4 1T', including illegal spaces casually dropped in and immediately guessed that must be Madeleine's car. Obviously a very successful trader. It seemed impressive that June's daughter was able to earn so much money out here in the sticks.

Chapter 3

As Victoria seated herself in the MGB, once again enjoying the freedom of the open top in the glorious sunshine, she heard her name being called and looked around. Sam was strolling towards her, waving casually. She smiled and waved back.

"Hi again! Thought I'd missed you!" he said as he leaned on the door and smiled down at her.

"Hi Sam, yes – just had a final chat with George, got some more photos and I'm pretty much done and dusted."

"Ah, that's a shame, you're like a breath of fresh air around here!" He stood back to admire the car. Running his hand along the bonnet he murmured "Lovely lines", and Victoria felt herself blushing as his double-edged meaning was perfectly plain.

"Sadly, not my car," she said, annoyed to hear a girlish giggle in her voice. "Belongs to a friend of mine."

"Good friend," said Sam, walking round the front of the car and studying the radiator grill, "to lend you this little beauty."

"Yes, yes he is," she added. Victoria felt ridiculously guilty. She wasn't doing anything wrong, yet she felt she was (and she could almost feel its owner's outrage seeping out of the little car's upholstery).

"Mind if I…?" Sam had his hand on the passenger door handle.

Victoria just stopped herself from crying "No you mustn't!" like a nervous child, but instead managed to squeak "No, of course not, hop in."

Sam settled himself beside her and made much of studying the dashboard and its wonderfully old-fashioned dials. "A proper car! All chrome and leather, lovely, it smells like a car should. I actually owned one similar to this when I was at college."

"Really? Where did you study?"

"I was up in London, art school," he waved his hand vaguely. "But it wasn't really my scene, too formal, so I dropped out and went to see the world. Very different back then though, world was a nicer place."

"Do you really think that? Or is that just nostalgia talking?" Victoria was interested and turned towards him.

"Yeah, I do, but then, as you say, maybe it's a case of looking at the past through rose-tinted spectacles." He held her gaze and smiled again. "And what about you, Victoria West? Where have you been all my life?"

Victoria's stomach did a strange flip and she felt a cloud of butterflies take flight and start fluttering around her insides. What on earth was it about these Westcountry men? They were all such flirts and so non-PC! She thought of herself as a liberated modern woman and yet they managed to make her feel like a gauche teenager at the drop of a hat. She was in her early forties, for heaven's sake!

Victoria smiled in a casual way and, leaning back, propped her elbow on the door, trying to look cool. The metal had grown very hot in the sunshine, but she felt she needed to maintain the nonchalant pose, painful or not.

Sam leaned forward and put his hand on her arm – the one that wasn't in the process of being scalded – and said, "Look, I can't hold you up like this, you being a busy journalist, I just wondered if you'd like to stop by one of these lovely summer evenings and come and see a bird hide that I've made on the far side of the farm? You'll see some great birdlife and quite possibly the odd fox and badger. Perhaps we could take a picnic with us too?"

Damn, thought Victoria: he was an attractive man! His face was expectant and his eyes, an annoyingly lovely sea green, were twinkling at her. No, she thought, say no, think of Albert... But instead she heard herself saying "Well, I need to get the article all signed off and submitted first, but perhaps I could give you a call after that?"

He smiled again. He had very attractive laughter lines around his eyes and, she had noticed, very fine hands, artist's hands. "That would be great, I look forward to it." He gave her a final rather-too-intimate look and then climbed languidly out of the car.

She started the engine and selected reverse. "Drive carefully," he said and patted the boot of the car which, to Victoria's fevered mind, was almost like having her own behind patted.

She drove home badly, stalling the engine and even crashing the gears at one point. "I'm sorry Gloria," she said earnestly. "Really I am, I'm just not concentrating. You don't know what it's like!" The two walkers she was overtaking at that point exchanged puzzled expressions as the solo woman driver crawled past them in the narrow lane talking animatedly to herself.

Victoria arrived home feeling ashamed. She parked the car and slunk into the cottage, hoping against hope that she wouldn't bump into Albert. Dear kind Albert. She was turning into a strumpet, as her mother would have said.

She stood in the kitchen and lamented, yet again, the lack of a decent shower. She was hot and sticky and fed up and a quick powerful cooling shower would have been a real pick-me-up.

As if on cue, she heard a strong knock at the door and Moss instantly started barking from inside his crate. "Hang on, young man!" Victoria bent down to open the catch on the cage and watched a wonderful example of wheel spin as Moss tried to gain purchase on the smooth floor, paws a blur as he stayed pretty much in the same place before eventually managing to bound forward. You couldn't stay fed up in the company of a puppy for long, and Victoria was laughing at his antics as she opened the door to find Kev beaming at her and brandishing a sheaf of colourful brochures.

"Hi there!"

"Hi Kev, do come in. Cup of tea, or something cold?"

"Lovely! I reckon a pint of cold water would be just the job – know what I mean?"

Victoria filled the largest glass she had, and handed it to him. He downed it in one. "Cool – thanks. I bet you wish you'd got your power showing going in this weather, doncha?"

"Exactly what I was thinking barely two minutes ago. It's so hot and sticky, a cooling shower would be wonderful," she sighed.

"You have a shufty through these brochures then give me a call in a day or two and we can get this show on the road, know what I mean? Or I can come in and discuss the options, if that's easier."

Victoria was already leafing through the brochures. "Ooh, that's nice." She stroked a page illustrating a particularly palatial bathroom with freestanding bath and huge walk-in shower.

"Yeah, right, also the most expensive option here – you got good taste!"

"Hmmm, typical. I'll go through them all Kev and draw up a short list and then maybe we can have a quick meeting and then get started. How does that sound?"

"Ideal!" He looked down "Oi, you little beggar!" Moss had been busily eating one of Kev's trainer laces.

"Oh Lord. I am so sorry! I think he's teething, or something. He chews absolutely everything."

"Nah, he's alright. Right, hear from you in a few days then Victoria." Kev loped off into the yard and his waiting van.

Victoria poured herself a glass of elderflower cordial and watched Moss as he charged around the garden. "I'll take you out for a walk later, it's too hot just now." She started up her laptop and typed up her notes from the visit to Ansome Nursery. Next, she set about her weekly blog, but her mind kept wandering. Why had she not politely declined Sam's approach? She rested her chin on her hand and was wondering if she might go and sit in the sun for ten minutes when there was a gentle rap on the open door.

"I hope I am not disturbing your afternoon reverie, Victoria?"

She turned and smiled warmly at the pink-cheeked vicar as he entered the kitchen, removing a battered sunhat from his wispy hair.

"Of course not, it's always a pleasure to see you Edwin! I was just contemplating sneaking outside to sit in the sun for ten, or even twenty minutes. Shall I make you a glass of elderflower cordial to take outside?"

"Sounds marvellous!"

The vicar was wearing huge shorts that came down past his knees, with large pockets stuffed full of goodness knows what, and a proper pair of 'Jesus' sandals (as well he might) over a pair of grey socks. This ensemble was topped off by a short-sleeved black shirt and dog collar, and a white sun hat, much frayed.

They strolled outside with Moss bouncing around them and made their way to the two deckchairs near the chicken run. A slightly rickety parasol stood nearby giving a little much-needed shade.

They sat side by side and the Reverend Ruminant sighed. "Cheers! This is the life!" Sitting in companionable silence they watched the hens. "A good spot for them there I think Victoria, they get the best of all worlds, sun, shade, shelter and plenty of greenery."

One hen was taking a very elaborate dust bath, squirming down into a shallow depression in the dry earth and flicking dirt extravagantly over her back, then lying very still as another hen came over and pecked invisible mites from her feathers.

"A hen's idea of heaven, I suspect," said Edwin, smiling indulgently.

"Not a lot to get excited about though, is it?" said Victoria

"Getting covered in muck and then painfully pecked by one of your friends?"

"To the hen, it is paradise. Each to their own, dear lady, each to their own." And Victoria thought of her bathroom dreams and realised that perhaps she could see where the hens were coming from.

"Well now," began Edwin. "You very kindly rang and offered some help and I was wondering if I could press you to take more than a passing interest in the Swaddlecombe Show committee?"

"I'd like to know a bit more about what's involved before I commit," she replied cautiously.

"Of course, of course. The thing is though, time and tide wait for no man and I regret that the show is less than a month away and I'm afraid I have, er, got rather behind with things." He took out an enormous spotted handkerchief and mopped his brow. "You see, your dear aunt was a much valued member of the committee. No one has stepped in to fill her very capable shoes and I, foolishly, thought that I could take on her roles as well as my own." He took his hat off and fanned himself. "And now, quite frankly, I have to confess to being in a bit of a pickle."

Victoria suppressed a smile and instead leaned down to stroke Moss, who was gnawing the leg of the deckchair with great concentration. "I see. Well, tell me the worst."

"Your Aunt Edith used to handle the publicity – you know, producing the posters and contacting the press, all that sort of thing. Now, for a capable and cosmopolitan lady such as yourself I would think this would be, as they say, 'a doddle'!" He turned a beaming face to her, and she couldn't help but smile back.

"It certainly does sound the sort of thing I should be able to take on – it's pretty much my line of work, after all."

"Do you know, I was hoping you'd say that! I have a folder of all your aunt's contacts and old press releases in Gertrude's glovebox, I'll go and get it shortly. Obviously, your aunt never dallied with the black arts of email, so I'm sure you'll have it all streamlined and organised in no time on your Apple Mac!"

"Yes, that should be fine. Posters too, they'll be easy for me to lay out and design, so I'm happy to do those too." She felt rather pleased with herself; she seemed to be stepping into her aunt's shoes rather neatly and had visions of her efforts being warmly applauded by all and sundry.

"And then there's the role of secretary…" Edwin threw in casually.

"Oh, do you mean taking minutes and…"

"Yes, yes, terribly easy for you I'm sure with your journalist's shorthand and touch typing and all that!" He waved his hand casually as if it was all too trivial to mention, but Victoria sat up like a startled rabbit.

"I'm not so sure about that Edwin. I don't do shorthand, people don't these days, and I'm not sure I know how to produce minutes properly and…"

"You are too modest and, again, I took the liberty of bringing your aunt's excellent efforts with me so you can see how she used to produce them. With your word-processing package and writing skills, I'm sure it can all be sorted in a trice!"

Victoria felt the startled rabbit was now trapped by the headlights and couldn't seem to get out of the way of the oncoming juggernaut that was the Show Committee. "Well, I suppose I could have a go," she said rather lamely.

"Excellent! How marvellous. I cannot tell you what a relief it will be to have you on my team, I do find it a bit of a battle."

"You do?"

Realising what he had said, the vicar gave his high-pitched

little giggle and said hurriedly, "Oh, just my joke! Your aunt and I used to have fun working together and it was always so lovely when it all went off so smoothly on the day. The after-show party is a riot, I can promise you!"

Victoria smiled, but was not entirely convinced.

"Well, it's been lovely. I think I'd better toddle on back to Gertrude, hand over your aunt's files and drive back to the vicarage." He struggled to his feet. Exiting a deckchair is never an easy manoeuvre and for someone of the Reverend's build it was particularly hazardous, but eventually he broke free of its clutches and stood swaying, triumphant, on the lawn. Victoria picked up Moss and followed him towards Gertrude, his immaculate Morris Traveller.

"There's just one other thing," he said handing her the folders, "we have a meeting tonight. Is there any way you could come along and meet everyone and make a start? It's at 8pm in the Arms, and I don't expect it will go on for too long." He beamed at her expectantly as she juggled puppy and folders, eventually putting the dog down and meeting Edwin's benevolent gaze.

"Yes, I expect I could, I don't have anything else planned," she said, thinking it would also keep her mind occupied and stop her feeling so guilty about Sam (even though she really had nothing to feel guilty about).

She waved the vicar goodbye as he drove sedately out of Albert's farmyard. "Come on then Moss, let's go for a walk, shall we?" The puppy sprang up and started bounding in circles, a sure sign that a walk was needed.

Walking around the farm was lovely and easy with the puppy as she didn't have to worry about traffic, but it did mean that getting Moss to walk on the lead was not really progressing very fast. But she wasn't in the mood for disciplining him and just wanted to stroll around the edge of the fields, picking at wild grasses and admiring the peacefully grazing cows from afar.

Just as she turned to come home, she spotted a dust cloud moving towards her across an adjacent field and realised it was Albert's tractor. She stopped and felt a surge of happiness as she saw him wave at her from the cab. Moss started yapping excitedly, and she realised that she wouldn't be phoning Sam Ansome any time soon, if ever. What had she been thinking? Perhaps she'd got a touch of sunstroke?

Albert stopped the tractor at the gate and walked over to her, the dust cloud subsiding as the engine died. "Well, how are you today Miss West?" he smiled, blue eyes twinkling in his very tanned face.

"All the better for seeing you," she said, with rather more feeling than she'd planned.

He smiled. "You alright? You look a bit, I dunno, disturbed?"

Goodness, how perceptive he was. "Oh I think I'm OK, a bit too hot perhaps and..." she paused for effect, "I think I have just made a terrible commitment to the Reverend Ruminant."

Albert sighed. "You've gone and volunteered for that committee haven't you?" She nodded. "Daft beggar, I did warn you!"

"I know, but well, he's awfully persuasive and I felt sorry for him..."

Albert laughed. "Oh, you and Edith came out of the same pod you did! He used to be just as persuasive with her and she used to cuss and swear about it and every year she'd say she'd never do it again!"

"Did she?"

"Oh yes! And every year, he'd talk her round again."

Victoria looked deflated. "Oh dear. And I have to go to a meeting tonight."

"And there I was about to suggest a cosy little evening at my place…"

Victoria felt she might cry at any moment. Albert put his free arm around her shoulders and gave her a squeeze. "Daft beggar! If you could see your face! Don't you worry, I'll drive you to the pub and then come and pick you up at closing time."

"Oh there's no need for that, Edwin said it wouldn't take long, and I won't be drinking anyway and…"

Albert gave a shout of laughter. "You won't be home before 11pm and believe me, you'll be wanting a drink, or several, as the time goes on!"

Chapter 4

"You must have heard the kettle boil."

"Always did have the best timing," Albert smiled.

"Come and sit down, I must tell you more about last night's show meeting – why didn't you warn me that everyone on the committee was quite impossible to work with? Well except for the Reverend, of course," said Victoria, smiling back at him.

"Excuse me, but I think you'll find that I did warn you against the flaming lot of 'em. Daft bunch they are – price of a raffle ticket can take hours of debate!"

"Albert! Were you there listening?" Victoria laughed. "I couldn't believe how difficult some of them were – I'm surprised Swaddlecombe ever has a show at all given the arguments that were going on. How much for this, so many pence for that. Can't have a lucky dip for 50p, it's always been 30p – no matter that today prizes can't be bought for either amount. Honestly!"

Albert sat at the table and seemed very grateful for the large mug of tea.

"Are you alright? You do look tired."

"Oh I'll be fine once I have this and, um, maybe a piece of cake?" He looked meaningfully at her cake tin. "I've been up for hours, we've got the vet coming as it's TB testing time and I'm a bit worried about some of 'em. But nothing unusual about that – just me getting older and not enjoying getting up at 5am. Used to be a time when I took it all in my stride, but just seems to have got to me today. Now where's that cake?"

Victoria wished her disaster with the chocolate beetroot cake hadn't been quite so complete and that she had been able to salvage some of it. "Sorry, I'm afraid the cake-baking episode went very wrong yesterday. I thought I'd got it right but then there was a phone call and…" she tailed off and saw Albert smile and shake his head.

"You, miss, are never going to make a baker at this rate!"

"No. I despair of me, but there's worse. While I was chatting on the phone not only did I burn the cake but Moss decided to eat my expensive shampoo and was sick in lots of places around the house, so things really didn't go too well."

"Never mind, another day eh? I've tweaked the recipe just a bit anyway so you can have another go." Victoria groaned inwardly. "We've gotta crack this one, can't risk losing my crown – so to speak!"

"You really are pretty competitive aren't you? Not really the laid-back farmer." She smiled at him and promised herself she would try harder with the cake this time – and if the phone rang, she'd ignore it.

While they were talking the puppy had been racing around the kitchen fetching toys, bringing them to Albert and then chasing after them as he threw them down the hallway. At the end of one particularly manic run Moss slid across the floor and crashed against one of the kitchen cupboards. The door flew open and several cake tins, timers and general junk slid onto the floor.

"Oh Moss!" shouted Victoria and scooped him up into his bed. She gave him a fierce look and said, "Stay in your BED!" Moss sank down and put on his deeply wounded face which was always impossible not to love. Victoria put her head in her hands and sighed. "What am I to do with you? Oh – seeing all that junk reminds me, I wanted to talk to you about eBay!"

"What do you mean? You're not putting that there pup up for sale are you?" Albert smiled at her.

"Oh get on, you know I don't mean that. No I heard from Kev, of bathroom fame, that you sell lots on eBay and I wondered if you could help me with some of Aunt Edith's old junk?"

"Now, now, none of that 'junk' talk, 'tis kitchenalia!" Albert laughed and she felt her insides go gooey. He had such a lovely smile.

"Kev said his wife Kelly sells similar stuff to you on eBay. It really surprised me, I would never have taken you for an eBay type."

"I'm not rightly sure if that is a good thing or bad, but yes Kelly and I chat by email about one lot or another, compare notes about things. You want me to help you sell some bits then?"

"Well I can't believe there's much of a market for it, but there are so many old gadgets of Edith's that I just don't have room for on top of my own bits and pieces and I'd probably never use them anyway. Would you help?"

"Happy to – and as for any market for it, you'll be really surprised how much old kitchen stuff fetches. There are loads of collectors, with luck you'll make enough to help towards some of the bits that need doing round the house."

"Wow," Victoria was amazed. "Just goes to show one man's meat is another man's poison so to speak. It would be wonderful if you could show me what to do. I can take the photos and clean things up but if you could do the putting on the site that would be wonderful."

"No problem maid. Now talking of money, how's this article of yours going, did you go back up to Ansomes'?"

"I did indeed. George took a while to come round but he was

fine by the end. Actually, he even talked about naming a plant after me and Aunt Edith which was really sweet. I think I have most of the bits I need now. Some nice pictures and some colour, thanks to the packing team I chatted with. Sam was welcome light relief too, he seems very friendly."

Albert scowled. "As well he might, weaselly chap, wouldn't trust him with me granny, never mind a fine young thing like you." He looked grim and Victoria smiled at his obvious dislike. "Now George, he may seem a bit of a crusty old beggar but he's good at heart. He had a rough time when his Dad was alive and I reckon it's hard to recover when you've been kicked for a lifetime."

"Yes, I can understand that. George was quite hard work but, as you say, kind at heart. But then Sam has made the visits there a lot more bearable."

Albert snorted then smiled and said: "Ah well, I must be getting on, thanks for the nice cake." He laughed and Victoria felt rather flustered.

"I'm sorry, I will try harder when I make it again, promise!" She picked up the recipe that Albert had left on the table and pinned it to the noticeboard on the wall. "There, pride of place to remind me to get more ingredients tomorrow!"

Albert gave her a quick peck on the cheek. "You just do what you can, I know you've got work to do. Now I'll be back at 7pm sharp – quiz night tonight down at the pub."

"Oh right, OK – I'll need a bed down there at this rate!" Victoria smiled and reflected on how her life had changed, and watched Albert as he strode off across the farmyard.

Picking up her laptop, Victoria sat back down at the kitchen table intent on finishing the article. After a couple of hours, she paused and gazed out of the window, and frowned; goodness! How dark it was looking for the time of day. She got up to stretch her legs and make another coffee. She stuck her head outside the kitchen door and looked up – clouds were gathering and the sky was brooding and purple, looking angry and bruised. Obviously the storm George had complained about was gathering. She'd better take a coat with her tonight.

Prompt as always Albert arrived at seven and was wearing one of his waxed jackets, an unusual sight after all the incredibly hot weather they had enjoyed this summer.

"C'mon let's crack on maid, best get to the pub before the rain, eh?"

"OK I'm coming, just need my bag – should I bring an umbrella?"

"Don't be such a townie!" replied Albert. "You're only walking half a dozen paces into the pub, get on with you."

"Yes sir!" smiled Victoria. "On your head be it if I get soaked – took me ages to get my hair straight earlier on."

"Well I likes it straight or curly, doesn't matter which, so you're on to a winner there."

"Hmmm – you sweet talker, Albert Moreton!"

"And I'd chuck your wellies in as well if I were you, just in case we have to walk home."

"Walk home, but…"

Albert grabbed her wellingtons and threw them in the back alongside his own.

"I hope this quiz isn't going to be too hard, I shall feel a right idiot if I can't get any answers right."

"Oh I wouldn't worry – we've got a red hot team. Old Tufty and Jean Burnicombe."

"What – Jean that cleans here, that Jean?"

"Now then don't you get all uppity on me madam. I'll have you know that Jean is my secret weapon when it comes to the pub quiz.

Frightening, the information held in that woman's brain. Stuff I've never heard of and, mixed with the Tuft, who knows more about sport than all the encyclopaedias in the world, I tell you we're a killer team. Hence the name."

"Oh no, don't say we have a name?"

"Of course, we are the Hot Potatoes," said Albert.

"Tell me you're not being serious!" said Victoria, staring at him in horror.

"Completely, Tufty and I came up with it and your aunt and Jean never seemed to object." Victoria felt her aunt must have had an opinion but obviously felt it was best to keep it to herself on this occasion. One of Aunt Edith's pieces of advice to her had always been 'pick your battles'.

They drew up outside the pub and, with perfect timing, rain began to splash against the windscreen, and within seconds a proper downpour was drumming on the roof of the Range Rover.

"Oh no, my hair!" wailed Victoria, feeling this must surely be an omen of a grim evening ahead. "Could you just back up and drop me by the door instead of us parking in the car park?"

"Don't be such a fusspot," replied Albert, peering through the rain as he manoeuvred into a space at the back of the pub.

"Well thank you very much, my hair matters to me, it's OK for you men." Victoria felt quite miffed.

"Oh for goodness sake woman! Here, this'll keep a few drops off your head." Albert reached over to the back seat and pulled up a plastic feed sack.

Despite her annoyance Victoria couldn't help laughing. "Gee thanks, you know how to spoil a girl!" Grabbing the proffered sack she held it above her head and made a dash for the pub door.

Once inside she shook rather like Moss would have done and took a deep breath. There were a few people already seated, although she had expected it to be chock-a-block on a special event night like this. Albert came in and seemed a lot wetter than she was. Maybe he didn't have a second feed sack!

Albert waved at Jean who was already sitting at a table for four, a large cardboard sign in the centre declaring 'Hot Potatoes' in black and red felt pen. Jean waved back and pointed at the bar where Tufty was ordering drinks.

"Ho Tufty – get us a couple in too, will you?"

Victoria wondered if Tufty knew what she drank or whether it would be a mystery round. Whatever it was, she was determined to just enjoy it. Tufty came back to the table with a heavy tray and four pint glasses of what Victoria guessed was cider. Well, she'd never drunk a pint of cider before but maybe it was time to live dangerously – this was Devon after all!

"Thanks Tufty, my round next time," said Albert. Victoria wasn't sure after a pint that there would be a next round for her but she'd give it a go. The stories she'd heard about the local cider were slightly alarming.

"No trouble mate, 'tis only fizzy stuff out the pump, not the real stuff out the barrel. I thought we better concentrate tonight what with the quiz and everything." Victoria found it tasted really rather good. Maybe the pint wouldn't be so hard to get through.

"Lovely to see you both," said Victoria. "I hope I don't let the side down. I love puzzles and quizzes but I'm not too sure what the questions are like, but I'll do my best."

Victoria turned to Jean and was asking after her sister when she spotted a pretty middle-aged woman waving and "Coo-eeing", looking at Albert. Albert noticed the woman and smiled back. He started talking to Tufty again but the agitated waving went on and the woman beckoned him over to her table. Albert got up and went over and the woman stood up and flung her arms around him and they hugged for a moment, chatting animatedly – well, the woman was doing the chatting. Albert had his back to her so she couldn't see what he was doing. As they hugged again, all Victoria could see were the woman's arms curled around Albert and her face very close to his... goodness, had he given her a kiss too?

"Jean, who is that lady Albert's chatting to?"

Jean smiled at her. "Oh, that's Carol, she's the friendly type. She and Albert were a couple for a time, but then she met her husband Neville and poor old Albert was out on his ear!"

If Victoria had felt anything sisterly towards Carol before hearing that she certainly didn't now. "Oh poor Albert," she said.

"Ha! Not so much of the 'poor Albert', kept her hanging on for years he did, not knowing if he were going to make an honest woman of her. Nope he 'ad it coming and he were a bit of a lad at the Harvest Supper that year. He definitely 'ad it coming." Having made her opinion clear, Jean took a long swig of her drink and wiped her mouth with the back of her hand. Victoria tried not to smile.

The landlord, Roger Mudge, stood up. "Right, is everyone here that's coming then? Best get cracking before this weather gets any worse. I'm sure we can have a bit of a laugh even if we have got a smaller crowd than usual." He had a small table set up in the corner of the bar on which was a suitably important box file labelled 'Questions' and a small gavel.

Albert, having extracted himself from Carol's arms, sat down next to Victoria and she raised her eyebrows at him. He gave an apologetic little shrug and whispered in her ear. "'Tis the one I named the tractor after." Victoria grinned and felt happy that she and Albert had developed such a strong friendship. It had been a long time since she'd found a man she could trust.

Jean was fussing, checking everyone had pens and paper then

smiled at them all and made an exaggerated 'thumbs-up' sign.

"First question ladies and gentlemen, what tourist attraction in London is called Big Ben?"

"Well c'mon maid, you're the Londoner, you'll know this one for sure," said Tufty to Victoria.

"Well actually I do," replied Victoria. "It's..."

"Keep your voice down!" hissed Jean, eyes darting conspiratorially to see if any other teams were listening in, "and it's obvious innit, it's the big clock tower near the Houses of Parliament, don't need to be a Londoner to know that!"

"Actually..." Victoria paused and the other members of the team all looked at her. In an exaggerated whisper she said, "Big Ben is technically the name for the large bell that tolls inside the clock tower rather than the clock itself."

"Ah well," said Jean. "Good job we got a townie on the team to know the right answer." She seemed torn between being pleased they had the right answer and annoyed at being wrong.

"Well done mate," said Tufty.

"So everyone got an answer?" asked Roger. There was a murmur of assent. "Next question. Who scored a hat trick in the 1966 England versus Germany World Cup final?"

Victoria smiled to herself. She couldn't begin to answer this one, but she had a feeling Tufty would.

Tufty perked up, reminding Victoria of Moss when he sensed a walk was due. "No brainer eh? It was Geoff Hurst! Bobby Moore picked him out with a long pass – unmarked he was. At the time, the England team was known as the 'wingless wonders', on account of their then-unconventional narrow attacking formation..."

Victoria tuned out as he burbled on in great detail. The quiz continued and she felt she wasn't performing too badly. She was hopelessly out of her depth on sport and all local knowledge, but did well on anything arty or literary. As Albert had predicted, they made a pretty good team, complementing each other's areas of knowledge.

"Right, now we've got a music round…" began Roger but he was interrupted by the sound of the church bell, tolling over and over. The whole pub went silent and everyone looked around. Usually church bells were so joyful, but this constant sonorous tolling was a distinctly eerie sound.

"Is that normal?" asked Victoria looking at Albert. He was frowning.

"No maid, it's not."

Roger pushed past their table to the door, with Albert close behind him, and flung it open. "Bloody hell!" exclaimed Albert. "It's a river out here! The whole main road's under water."

Victoria peered past Albert and could see the pub lights reflecting in fast-flowing water, just a few inches below the front steps of the building.

"Oh my Lord! How will I get home?" Jean looked frightened, her hand to her mouth.

"Don't you be worrying Jean my duck," said Albert. "They'll get the fire brigade out soon enough, and you're warm and safe in here anyway, so I'd have another cider and sit tight."

Jean looked a little mollified but still unconvinced.

"What do you reckon?" Albert turned to Roger.

"I reckon the Reverend must have a problem," he said. The bell continued to toll and Victoria felt her unease growing.

"Wonder if there's something wrong at the church?" said Bill Bramley, seated at the next table.

"Maybe flooded?" suggested Albert.

"Could be," replied Bramley. "We'd better go and see. I tell you what, I've got me tractor out the back with the hay trailer hitched up. Anyone want to hop on and we'll drive over to the church? Reckon as it won't be too deep."

"You be careful Bill Bramley, no need for heroics!" said Trudy, overhearing the conversation as she emerged from the kitchen wiping her hands on a frilly pinny, the like of which Victoria had only ever seen in 1960s sitcoms.

"I'm up for it," said Albert. "I'm thinking the Reverend wouldn't make all that racket without good reason."

"But is it safe?" said Victoria, aware that she sounded a complete wimp.

Bramley snorted. "Don't know, but us'll find out soon enough! Come on then…" Victoria hesitated, unsure whether to stay warm and dry or join in on what could be a bit of an adventure.

Bramley strode towards the back door, followed by Roger, Tufty and three sturdy-looking men from other quiz teams. Albert, pulling on his coat, turned to Victoria with a questioning look, she gave him a confident smile and they followed the others.

"Roger!" cried Trudy, "What are you doing?"

Roger stopped in front of her and jutted out his chin. "Sometimes Trudy, a man's gotta do what a man's gotta do."

"Oh!" she gasped, clasping her hands together in classic melodrama fashion. Victoria was slightly disappointed she didn't hear her say "My hero!" as they went out through the back door.

The rain was still steady but less intense than it had been, but in seconds they all looked like drowned rats – so much for worrying about frizzy hair! Bramley heaved himself up into his blue tractor and it roared into life. Victoria saw Albert grab their boots from the Range Rover. Tufty hopped nimbly onto the trailer and reached down to haul Victoria up, while Albert assisted her from below, finishing the manoeuvre with a small smack on her behind. He, Roger and the other men then clambered up as well. Albert banged on the tractor cab window. "All aboard Bill!"

"Now you hold on to the bars Victoria," he advised and she saw his eyes sweep over her hair. "D'you know, I think I prefer it curly," he said with a grin a mile wide. Victoria slapped him playfully and then hung on for dear life as the tractor lurched forward.

Bill Bramley drove down the incline at the side of the pub to meet the main road. "I reckon the water's dropped a bit," he shouted over his shoulder as he eased the tractor into the black flowing water. Victoria gaped, half frightened, half fascinated by the power of nature as she watched the water all around them like a sinuous, shining, living creature. The tractor turned down towards the church where the bell could still be heard tolling.

Everyone in the trailer was quiet, watching the water as it slapped and gurgled at the edge of the trailer. The tractor chugged powerfully on, leaving a wake like a boat behind them. "As long as it stays below the air intake, we'll be alright," stated Tufty, pointing to somewhere below the tractor's engine. Victoria nodded, not having a clue what he meant.

"Alright?" asked Albert as they cruised past the houses in the main street. Most of the houses, like the pub, were a couple of feet above the road and reached by steps. Some people waved from upstairs windows, seemingly quite cheerful about the whole thing. In the distance, Victoria could see blue flashing lights. "That'll be the fire brigade, pumping out the cottages at the end there," explained Albert. "'Tis lower there and I expect they're flooded out." They all seem so calm, thought Victoria, hoping her terror wasn't too obvious; why wasn't there more noise and fuss?

"What about the shop? Poor Iris and the others!"

"Oh, they'll be alright, they're up along and won't get their feet wet I reckon," said Albert.

The pitch of the tractor's engine changed as Bill Bramley turned slowly left and drove past the lych-gate. "He's going to the higher side," said Albert, as the tractor pulled its way out of the water and then drew to a halt by the churchyard.

"Everybody out!" cried Bill and lumbered out of the cab. "That wasn't too bad now, was it?" he said, beaming at Victoria as he helped her down.

"Well, no." She felt her legs were shaky so she made a pretence of jogging on the spot to look like she was warming herself up.

"Here, slip these on." Albert handed over her wellingtons. She noticed all the other men were already wearing them, such was the rural dress code.

"Not quite three feet of water on the road," added Bill, matter-of-factly. "I've seen worse though, admittedly, not come up so fast or..." he squinted as he looked back at the flooded road "...seen it go down quite so quick neither."

"True meaning of the word 'flash flood', I reckon," added Albert. "Right – let's go and see what the Reverend is making all this fuss about."

The men fought to push open the main door of the church and were confronted by a scene that was eerily beautiful. The whole of the church was awash; hymn books and hassocks floated sedately past and the whole scene was softly lit by candles. The tolling bell ceased.

"At last!" cried a familiar voice and there, processing like a galleon down the nave, was the Reverend Ruminant, his cassock gathered about him like windless sails. "I do apologise for all the noise! The electricity went off so I looked out of the vestry window to see if it was just the church or the village as a whole that had lost power and there, coming through the churchyard, was what appeared to be a tidal wave!" He mopped his brow with the end of his cassock, frowned at it and then wrung out the soaking wet cloth.

"No divine intervention today then vicar?" laughed Bill Bramley.

"Sadly, no," replied the Reverend. "Now, if you wouldn't mind all gathering up the hymn books and other floating relics…" Everyone began grabbing bits and pieces of flotsam and stacking them on the window ledges and pews. "Some financial intervention, rather than divine, a few years ago may have prevented this current predicament," Edwin Ruminant went on. "The roof and gutters are in a state of shameful disrepair, hence all the water. It was quite impressive at the height of the storm; as well as the tidal wave water was gushing in from everywhere. I felt as if I was in the midst of the Trevi Fountain!" He gave his high-pitched giggle and Victoria wondered at his stoicism. She was sure she'd be in tears and no use to anyone if her home or office were in this state.

"After the electricity went off, I thought I'd best light some candles."

"Very romantic!" quipped one of the other helpers.

"Thank you Jim, I thought you'd appreciate it," said Edwin, as they waded around the pews picking up the debris.

"You're going to have a hell of a mess – excuse me vicar – to clean up tomorrow," said Tufty. "Mud and all sorts I shouldn't wonder,"

Bill Bramley had stuck his head out of the door. "'Tis almost stopped raining altogether now. Damned weird weather."

"Got any brooms Reverend?" Albert asked. "We could start sweeping the water out through the porch and hopefully some of the muck too."

"Good idea!" Edwin trotted off towards the vestry.

"You alright? You look a bit pale maid." Albert peered at her in the soft light. He touched her cheek gently.

"Yes, yes, I'm fine, just a bit… you know."

He grinned. "All this country living's a bit too exciting for you, isn't it?" She smiled back, and knew that if Albert wasn't with her she'd be feeling a lot more frightened.

"Here we are!" Edwin was back, clutching several brooms and mops and buckets.

All the men started sweeping and mopping, chatting and laughing as they worked, and Victoria felt distinctly superfluous. "Can I do anything useful? As there's no electricity I suppose I can't even make tea."

"Sadly not," said Edwin as he spread out some sodden hymn books on the radiators. "At least when the boiler comes back on the paper might dry out." Victoria helped him with the remaining books. She secretly thought the hymn books were beyond saving, and as for the hassocks – surely they'd smell dreadful after this immersion? She looked at the one she held in her hands. The embroidery was exquisite and, although much of the design was barely legible, she could see a date: 1886. What a shame if such lovely old things were ruined.

"Well, I think that's the best we can do tonight – we really need daylight to see what we are doing," said Edwin after ten minutes or so of determined effort.

Victoria had gone outside to check the weather and came back in, looking stunned. "It's amazing! There's no rain, all the water has gone from the road, the sky is clear and there's a full moon!"

"'Tis that global warming," said the man called Jim. The others muttered their agreement.

"Well, I reckon that's enough excitement for one night," said Albert. "I think Victoria and I will walk back to the Arms to get the Range Rover. You coming Mudge, or going back on the tractor?"

"You go on, I'm just catching up with the Reverend, then we'll be down."

"See you all tomorrow I expect, for the grand clean up!" said Albert, and they all called their farewells.

He opened the heavy door for Victoria and they stepped out into a soft moonlit summer night. There was the sound of water trickling softly from the eaves and dripping off foliage and, in the distance, voices and the hum of the fire engine could be heard.

"Well, that's the subject for your next blog sorted out maid," said Albert.

"Absolutely," she agreed, feeling incredibly tired. All the adrenalin she had felt earlier had now left her system and she felt she could fall asleep on her feet.

"Let's just do a quick circuit of the church, I've got me torch here." He switched it on. "See if we can spot any obvious damage. Poor old Edwin, he's going to have his hands full sorting all this out. Bit of a bugger really, I reckon we were doing pretty well in that quiz too."

Victoria held onto his arm as they walked slowly around the side of the church. Albert's torch beam picked out rivulets of water still streaming down the ancient stonework. "There's something come off there I reckon," He pointed the beam on the edge of the roof where several chunks of masonry seemed to be missing.

"Oh yes!" Victoria stepped back to see more clearly and gave a cry as she toppled backwards.

"You alright?" Albert swung round, trying to see her among the gravestones.

"Yes, yes, I think so, but I tripped on something."

"Gravestone I bet, you daft beggar."

"No, it was something soft..." As Albert's torch swept towards her over the grass Victoria let out a piercing scream.

"Don't look!" Albert twitched the light away. "Dear God..." he said under his breath. He strode towards her and pulled her to her feet and she stumbled. "Come on, walk over here."

"I saw, I saw…" She was shaking and felt terribly sick, and tried to turn back.

"Don't look!" he almost shouted at her, propelling her back towards the porch.

"What's happened?" The others were suddenly in front of them on the path. "We heard a scream. Was that you, Victoria?" asked Roger.

"There's been an accident. Edwin, can you take Victoria inside, she's had a shock." He thrust her towards the Reverend's open embrace and he and the men set off back around the side of the church.

"My dear girl, come in and sit down." He led her into the vestry. She was shaking quite violently now and had a horrible feeling that she might faint. As if detecting this, Edwin made her sit and put her head between her knees, while he pulled various garments from a cupboard and draped them over her to warm her.

The lights came back on. "Ah, divine intervention after all," he said quietly and quickly filled the kettle and switched it on and busied himself with mugs and teapot.

"Can you tell me what happened?" He sat down opposite her, holding one of her hands, while she tried to hold a cup of tea in the other, but it was jiggling about so much that he set it on a table, and held both her hands instead.

"Albert was checking to see if we could see any damage to the ch-church," she swallowed, "we saw this big g-gap on the roof, the – the parapet thing with the gargoyles." He handed her the tea and she sipped it gratefully; her mouth was so dry. "I stepped back to get a better view and I tripped…" she closed her eyes, "…over something soft, but inert. When Albert shone the torch to see what it was, that's when I saw it. The body."

81

Edwin rubbed her hands and nodded as if encouraging her to go on. "The head... well, there was just..." Victoria couldn't find the word "...pulp, just a mess, the head had been crushed by the falling stones." Edwin gazed at her. "I only saw it for a moment, Albert moved the beam away, but it was awful. Awful."

"My dear, how ghastly for you." He was patting her hands now.

Victoria closed her eyes and took a few deep breaths. "But I know who it is, was."

He gaped at her. "How could you...?"

"I recognised his cap and his mackintosh. It was Percy Shooter."

The Reverend Ruminant's mouth formed a perfect 'O'.

Chapter 5

"Albert, you seen Jack?" A fireman put his head round the church door and barked at Albert.

Albert looked up a little startled and shook his head. "No mate, why? Is he missing?"

"Don't be daft, Jack's the first responder. We need him to deal with the body." The fireman closed the door with a heavy thud.

"Oh right," replied Albert. Victoria looked questioningly at him

"Guess Jack is the one with the training," said Albert gently, "the one to pronounce him dead and contact the hospital. Can't be easy for a local crew to deal with an emergency like this, not as though it happens every day."

"Be thankful for that I suppose," said Victoria. She felt a little calmer now. She had seen accidents before, but never anything as shocking as this.

The door opened again and a chilly gust of wind wrapped around her legs, making her shiver. Looking up she saw a policeman, notebook in hand. "I gather it was you Miss that made the discovery?"

"Yes it was." Victoria felt wobbly again.

"Detective Sergeant Jackson, Miss. If you have a few minutes I just need to ask you some questions?"

"Yes, yes of course." Victoria felt her stomach clench with

nerves as she realised she was going to have to describe what had happened. She spoke carefully, doing her best to be accurate and confirmed the time, why they were at the church and how she had identified Percy.

Albert leant over once she had finished. "If it's OK with you sergeant, I'd like to get Miss West to the pub, medicinal brandy called for I think."

The police officer frowned and then nodded. "Very well, but I will need contact numbers for you both and would like you to remain available for further questioning should we need it."

Crikey, it was all sounding rather like a TV detective show, thought Victoria, but she simply nodded. "Yes officer.".

They walked slowly back to the pub, avoiding the area where the body lay. The pub seemed a warm and welcoming refuge after the terrible weather and awful events that had unfolded in the past couple of hours. There were quite a few people sitting around the bar, talking quietly. They turned as one to stare as Victoria and Albert came through the door.

"Come on in my love," said Trudy bustling towards them, arms outstretched. "Sit yourself down and let me get you something strong. You must be in shock!" She brought over two glasses of brandy and settled herself down at the same table. "Nasty business for you both, what with you knowing the victim and everything." She spoke in theatrically hushed tones and leant forward across the table as if wanting to form a conspiratorial huddle. "Mind you, can't say there will be many in the village as will miss him, not that I want to speak ill of the dead, obviously."

Trudy produced a powder compact and lipstick from her pocket and proceeded to touch up her make-up. "Presumably the police will be coming here shortly to find out more information and local background, that sort of thing?" She looked questioningly at Victoria.

Victoria stifled a smile and replied, "Yes I'm sure they will, Trudy. There was a police sergeant up at the church who we spoke to."

"Oh just a sergeant? Well, I expect there will be some of those forensic people too, they'll no doubt need feeding. Roger, Roger, can you watch the bar? I must get an extra lasagne in the oven just in case," and hurried off towards the kitchen.

Victoria looked round and spotted Jean sitting at the end of the bar, propping herself up on one elbow. Clearly she had remained in the pub throughout the drama and was now more than a little squiffy.

"Do you think we should help Jean get home?" she said to Albert quietly.

"Jean? You don't mean she's still here, good God!" Albert spotted her. "Yes, of course, we can take her on our way, easy. How you holding up, you feeling a bit better now?" Victoria nodded in reply just as several of the people sitting at the bar came over to their table.

"So they reckon someone done 'im in then?" said one man.

"Nah. Knowing Percy he upset the Almighty so much he decided to do 'im in 'isself!" laughed another. Victoria had disliked Percy, but it seemed heartless to be quite so callous about his death.

"Well I can think of a fair few that might volunteer to bash him on the head," said Roger from the other side of the bar.

"I'd've bashed 'im with me handbag if I'd got close enough I would!" slurred Jean.

"Now come on!" said Albert. "This isn't a decent way to talk about Percy's accident. And accident it surely was with that great big stone missing from the parapet, the Reverend said so himself, although he did add that it might have been divine intervention! But somehow I reckon he were joking!"

"You sure?" said someone in the far corner, and Albert turned and frowned.

"No more talk of murder, good Lord! This village beats 'em all for wild stories. No it were a gargoyle broken off the edge of the roof that hit him – freak accident. Rain probably got into the stonework and the gargoyle worked loose, great heavy thing, bigger than a football it was, smashed on the ground next to him."

"Well if you say so," said Trudy, back from the kitchen.

"We do," said Albert, "and now, if you don't mind, I want to get this young lady home and into bed, she's had a nasty shock."

There was much joshing and nudging from the onlookers and Albert looked even crosser. "You can cut that out you lot, she's had a rough time."

Victoria felt torn between grinning because it felt lovely having a man to look after her and being fed up with the constant references to Albert being a ladies' man – he was so gentle and trustworthy. Poor chap, it was only because he was so good looking that all these ribald comments kept getting made.

"Now come along then Jean, I think we'd best give you a lift home." Albert took Jean's arm and held her as she swayed away from the support of the bar.

"That would be most kind, most kind. I am feeling just a little bit tiddly widdly," she said, grinning broadly. As Albert tried to propel her away from the bar, she reached back for a final swig of her drink, said, "Cheers everyone!" and downed it in one. "My, I haven't had so much fun since…" she swayed, "well, I reckon not since Prince William was born and I come and wetted 'is 'ead good and proper!"

"That's more than thirty years ago woman!" shouted one of the wags in the corner.

"I know, disgraceful, innit?" Jean giggled and said "Oh my!"

as Albert steered her purposefully out of the back door of the pub. They processed slowly across the uneven ground, with Jean saying "Whoopsie!" and "Oh my!" every so often.

As they passed Bramley's tractor trailer, Albert reminded Victoria to retrieve their shoes, which were rather damp. It took him a few moments to bundle Jean into the back of the Range Rover and twice she slipped back down, giggling excessively. "Ooh, mind where you're putting your hands!" she squawked and Albert sighed and gave her a final firm shove and she was in. Victoria was glad of the distraction – it brought a feeling of normality to the night's proceedings. She and Albert climbed in and, for once, the Range Rover started first time and Victoria heaved a sigh of relief.

"Right then Jean, we'll have you home in two ticks," said Albert loudly as they made their way out of the car park and down the main street.

"I live at number 3 The Butts!" Jean enunciated slowly.

"I know you do, you daft besom, you've lived there as long as I've known you."

In a moment, they were outside her neat former council house, one of a row on the rise out of the village. Albert opened the back door and just about caught her as she slithered off the seat.

"Bit bleddy high this ve-hicle," she muttered, as Albert stood her up straight.

"Good night Jean," Victoria called from the front.

She waved vaguely at Victoria as Albert helped her up the front path. Her key was eventually located and he managed to steer her into the front hall, and sat her down on the stairs. "You be alright now then Jean?"

"Oh yes, don't you fuss young Albert!" she said smiling broadly, her ample teeth shining in the porch light. He patted her shoulder, shut the front door and climbed in next to Victoria. "Blimey," he said, "daft old maid, I've never seen her so sozzled."

"You did suggest she stayed in the pub! Well, I hope she doesn't feel too awful tomorrow." Victoria sighed as Albert turned the Range Rover around and went back down the main street. "I don't want to live through another evening like that, poor Percy."

"Well, I don't suppose there'll be many that miss him. He worked hard to be a snoop and as unpleasant as could be. Don't suppose he had many friends or family to mourn him."

"Oh I know who will miss him – little Mitzi, his Westie. Poor little thing – she may be locked in the house! We have to check Albert, we just have to, I couldn't sleep worrying about the little thing if we didn't check, she's such a sweetie."

Albert gave a long-suffering sigh. "OK, we'll go and see if a neighbour has a key or if we can hear barking."

They drove out of the village towards Percy's bungalow. The lawn was immaculate; even though they had been short of rain he had obviously watered it daily. They knocked on the front door, but there was no answering bark. They could see very little through the windows as net curtains hung at every one, but there was no sign of a small white Westie.

"There aren't really any neighbours that close by are there?" said Victoria, looking around for inspiration. Albert looked carefully at the front porch and then lifted the doormat to look for a key.

Victoria laughed, "Don't be daft – Mr Neighbourhood Watch is surely not going to keep a key under the mat. I'm surprised we haven't been blinded by security lights already, and I bet he has a burglar alarm that alerts the local police station!"

Albert said nothing but frowned with concentration.

"What is it?" said Victoria.

"I'm trying to think just what Percy would do about security on his house if he couldn't afford much." Albert scanned the garden and then pointed to a pretty rockery nearby with a small stone squirrel perched near the summit.

"Surely, not the squirrel?" said Victoria.

"Nah," replied Albert. "'Tis too dark to see proper, but..." he took three steps over to the rockery, picked up a rock and smiled triumphantly.

"No – don't smash a window Albert, for goodness sake!" cried Victoria.

"Daft woman, as if I would!" Albert snorted. "This wouldn't break a window even if I threw it." He tapped the stone. "Plastic. You hide a key in a fake rock, haven't you seen them?"

"I don't understand," Victoria looked confused.

"Saw them advertised in a newspaper and on that shopping channel thing on the telly. You have a fake plastic rock in the garden and there's a sliding bit on the base with a space inside to hide your spare key!" As he said this, Albert produced a couple of keys and looked smug.

"Mitzi! Mitzi? Where are you girl, you there little one?" Victoria called and looked around as they went through the front door. Everywhere was so sparsely furnished it was positively Spartan. This was no comfy home for a pensioner in retirement. Percy must have been hard up, she thought.

"You check the bedrooms, I'll check the kitchen," said Albert.

Victoria peered into what she assumed must be the spare bedroom and was taken aback to see pictures and newspaper cuttings pinned all round the walls and across an old-fashioned dressing table. Some pictures were tucked into the triple mirror, and lots were stuck on the wall with tape.

She switched on the dressing-table lamp so she could see the display more clearly. There were pictures of lots of village people that she recognised. Some were in rather compromising situations;

others seemed to be arguing, or looking furtive as they left a shop or a house.

She saw Jean waving her finger at another woman outside the village shop and there were multiple pictures of cars parked on double yellow lines, including Kev's van. There was another section that seemed to have a dog-poo theme with pictures of various dogs and their owners walking away from large piles of mess, and even some dogs caught in the act. Poor old Percy really did have a bee in his bonnet about people not clearing up after their animals. Mind you, Victoria thought, he did have a point, but this was a rather extreme way to monitor it.

She looked at the pictures tucked into the mirror. She gasped in surprise, and then looked again. Here were pictures of her and Albert. Two were taken through her kitchen window and one showed Albert with his arms around her and she was looking up lovingly at him. That one photo shocked her – it said in a single shot far more than she had accepted in her heart. There was another of them holding hands outside the village shop. She smiled as she remembered that day. The newspaper placard outside the shop had a headline saying 'Urgent shipyard job's talk's' and she remembered making a fuss as she hated apostrophes in the wrong place. Despite asking Dahlia about it she had been met with a shrug as, apparently, it was impossible to alter. It had been a lovely day – they'd been talking about having a nice meal in the pub later and – she stopped as her brain registered the other images of Albert.

In the next little group of shots were pictures of Albert, some with a young woman with a baby and others with the blonde woman who had been at the pub quiz. What was her name, Carol? And they weren't just discussing the weather either! There was a shot of them sitting in Albert's car 'canoodling', and another of the two of them leaving a house, his hair looking distinctly ruffled and unbrushed. She tried to quell the feelings of jealousy stirring inside her. Heavens! He had said she was an old girlfriend, so there was nothing here that she didn't know already. She sighed and looked at the last picture and her heart lurched: Carol and Albert were blatantly kissing each other outside the village shop. But worse still, the newspaper placard was the same as in the other picture. The apostrophe mistakes, the same angle as the shot of her and Albert... she could only assume that they were taken within hours of each other.

She reached into her coat pocket and touched her phone. She swallowed, hesitated and then made up her mind. She took out her phone and quickly took general photographs of all the pictures tucked in the dressing-table mirror and those on the walls too. She felt as though she was in slow motion; her mind felt clouded and she could hear her own breathing. You've done it again, you stupid woman, she chided herself; yet again you've got fond of someone and let yourself get hurt. Stupid, so stupid.

"No sign of the dog then?" said Albert as he popped his head round the door. "Time we were making a move. Thinking about it you know, that little thing followed him everywhere so stands to reason if Percy was out and about so was Mitzi. I'll talk to the fire station or police when we get back."

"Yes," said Victoria pulling back her shoulders as she turned to face him. "Good idea."

After a silent journey home, along lanes streaked with mud and gateways full of leaves and debris from the flash flood, Albert turned off the engine. "Would you like me to kip in the spare room tonight? I s'pect you're still feeling a bit wobbly."

Victoria pushed her hair back from her face. "Thank you, but no. I feel so shattered, I just want to have a quick bath and then get into bed. I don't think I'll have any trouble sleeping."

He walked her to the front door and gave her a hug. "Well maid, I'm sorry you had to see such a thing, really I am. I hope tomorrow you feel a bit better and..." he tailed off and gave her a wan smile.

Victoria didn't want to meet his eyes, so blue and frank. "Thanks, right... I'll just turn in then."

"Right, well, you give me a call if you want anything." She touched his arm and turned and unlocked the door, closing it gently behind her.

Once inside, she let Moss out of his crate and sat cuddling the puppy for some minutes. His warm silken body and affectionate snuffles and licks made her feel even more sorry for herself, and her tears fell onto his fur and disappeared.

"Oh Moss, Moss..." she mumbled into his neck as she ruffled his ears. She opened her laptop, downloaded the photos off her phone then flicked through them again. What did it all mean? Was she jumping to conclusions? She had a pounding headache and felt lower than she had done for a long time. She put the pup outside briefly before tucking him back in his crate and slowly climbed the stairs, too tired to have a bath. She pulled off her damp clothes and fell into bed.

Victoria woke to the sound of her phone ringing. "Hello?" she mumbled and, glancing at her watch, saw it was past 9am.

"My dear!" boomed Bunty. "I do hope I didn't wake you, but I thought you'd be anxious to know! Mitzi is here with me."

Victoria's mind seemed to be full of cotton wool, or was it treacle? Perhaps it was a gooey mess of both. Who on earth was Mitzi?

"I heard you and Albert had been to that rotter Percy's house looking for the dog last night – well don't worry my dear. One of the firemen found the poor little thing cowering behind one of family vaults in the graveyard and had the sense to bring her to me. Poor dog still had the lead attached. Lucky she wasn't killed with her master, or washed away," she paused to draw breath and Victoria attempted to gather some words of her own, but wasn't quick enough. "So, all's well that ends well – well, for the dog at least! Mitzi will fit in fine with us – we are, as you know, a bit of a doggy household."

"That is good news Bunty, I'm glad," Victoria managed. "But how one earth did you know we'd been out to Percy's?"

There was a bark of laughter. "Goodness, you still have a lot to learn about this part of the world Victoria! The village grapevine doesn't miss a thing. You were spotted my dear, peering through the man's windows and calling for the dog. Very good of you to worry about her after such a difficult time. Anyway, as I said, all's well that ends well!" and with that she hung up.

Victoria sat up and took a deep breath. She needed to be firm with herself; she knew she had a tendency to wallow in self-pity if she wasn't careful, and moping and worrying would get her nowhere. "Get up and get on!" she said aloud and went downstairs.

In ten minutes she had taken a turn around the garden with Moss – who greeted every new day as the most exciting thing he had ever, ever seen – fed the hens and made coffee. The animals gave her a focus she was glad of.

The day was warm, but cloudy with a breeze, so Victoria kept the kitchen door shut, pretending it was because of the weather and not because she wanted to avoid Albert.

Her article on Ansome Violets was almost finished, so she made that her first priority. Once completed, she sorted the photos and then emailed everything up to the magazine. She sat back, willing herself not to open the file of last night's photos. Just as her finger hovered over the mouse, the phone rang.

"Hi, it's Sam. How are you? I hear you had a bit of a nasty time of it last night and I just wondered if you were OK?"

Victoria felt tears spring to her eyes. He sounded so concerned and she had to swallow hard to stop a sob escaping.

"Sam, how kind of you to call. I am fine, really," she said, determined to keep her voice steady.

"Are you sure?"

"Well," she swallowed again, "it wasn't very pleasant, actually, and I'm feeling a bit ropey today. I suppose it's delayed shock, or something."

"Oh, you poor thing. Look, I was thinking you might like a bit of distraction. The weather is meant to improve tomorrow and I wondered if you'd like to come over and have a look at the bird hide I've built?"

Victoria hesitated. She didn't particularly feel like going anywhere, but she also didn't want to just sit and mope. Some quiet time focussing on birds might be a welcome relief and she was quite keen to get into birdwatching.

Into the silence, Sam said in his most persuasive voice, "Say yes, I think it would do you good."

"OK, thank you. I'd like that. What time would suit you?"

"I'm easy. Say around noon?"

"That's fine, I'll see you at the nursery tomorrow," then added, "I won't be able to stay too long as my puppy is still quite young and I need to let him out."

"That's no problem. I look forward to it."

Victoria stood and contemplated. His voice was as attractive as he was, slightly husky and somehow intimate. Should she be doing this? She felt uncomfortable, but wasn't sure why. No, that was stupid, of course she knew why. She felt as if she was betraying Albert.

Victoria picked up her phone to call Sam back and cancel, but stopped. She had no formal 'arrangement' with Albert. She was a free spirit, as was Sam – and so, clearly, was Albert. She'd heard lots of comments about him being 'a bit of a lad', but she hadn't really taken them in, assuming it was a joke. Perhaps he was just charming to all the women he met and spread his affections freely? And then she remembered how Albert had said that Sam was a bit dubious. Well! Victoria put the phone down again and went to make herself presentable.

As usual, her food stocks were non-existent, so she decided to pop down to the village shop for a few essential items. As she parked Gloria she glanced at the newspaper placard. 'Man killed in flash flood' it proclaimed. Victoria felt slightly sick as she remembered the photos of Albert and Carol taken outside the shop, and the lasting image of the man who'd taken them lying dead in the churchyard.

Without even noticing the latest display in Lavender's bargain bucket, she walked into the shop. As the doorbell pinged and announced her arrival every face turned towards her and the conversation died. Victoria suddenly wished she had not chosen that moment to go shopping. Of course, everyone would be gossiping about the events of the previous night.

Then people smiled at her and the chatter resumed. Victoria busied herself in investigating the contents of the chiller cabinet and even rummaging in the freezer.

"Well, t'was a right drama of course!" a woman in a headscarf said loudly. "My lounge carpet is ruined and I don't reckon our budgie will ever be the same again!"

"My Arthur says he's never seen so much water and he's eighty-two," said another matriarch, her chins wobbling with excitement.

"And that Percy Shooter – well!" said another. "Struck down by the hand of God!"

"Or just dodgy building work!" chortled a very round woman with a savage perm that made her look as if her whole head had shrunk. "He were a nasty piece of work that Percy, and that's a fact!"

"I heard Albert Moreton was in the thick of it!" said the headscarf lady. "T'was his lady friend what fell over Percy." Victoria stiffened. Someone else made a shushing noise. "Mind you, which lady that was I don't know, 'tis hard to keep up. Was it that Carol, or the new one from up-country?" Someone nudged her in the ribs and she said "What?" and cupped her hand to her ear under the headscarf. Victoria made a lunge for a loaf of bread and moved to the far side of the shop, apparently in pursuit of cereal.

"Oh, right!" said headscarf woman and glanced at Victoria. "I'm sorry I'm sure! Well, I'll have a jar of gherkins then Dahlia, and I'll be on my way."

The chatter continued but at a more subdued level. The ladies of the village paid for their goods and gradually sidled off, several of them smiling at Victoria kindly. The one with the perm even patted her arm.

"Miss West, how are you?" said Iris, her brow furrowed with concern.

"I'm fine, thank you. As ever, poor planning so absolutely nothing in the house to eat!" said Victoria over-brightly. "Could I have some tomatoes and some of the nice Cheddar?"

"Of course dear, no beetroot today then?" She looked at Victoria enquiringly over her glasses.

Victoria frowned. Beetroot – why on earth would she want beetroot? And then she remembered Albert's cake and felt a physical stab of pain somewhere close to her heart. "No, not today, thanks." She handed over the bread and other bits and pieces for Dahlia to wrap and put in a bag while she paid Iris. "Is Lavender alright?" she asked, suddenly realising one triplet was missing.

"Oh Lord yes, she's in fine form. She's thinking of producing a special display all about the flood, a sort of 'celebration' or some such," said Iris with a sigh. "She is a one!"

The shop's doorbell sounded and Jean came in, wearing a pair of sunglasses.

"Morning Jean! And how are you this morning?" trilled Iris.

"I don't rightly know at the moment," Jean said, leaning against the freezer cabinet for support. "I reckon that Trudy half-poisoned me with her beef pie last night."

Iris and Dahlia made clucking noises. "Nothing to do with all the excitement and a bit too much cider then, dear?"

"Well, I don't know about that, but I reckon you might be right. I don't usually have any more than two halves and I rather think I had more like six, but I can't be sure."

There were more clucking and shrieking noises and much shaking of heads and Victoria was reminded yet again how closely the village women resembled a flock of elderly hens.

"Victoria, I'm glad I've seen you," said Jean, turning carefully towards her. "Would you mind awful-like if I didn't come and clean this week? I promised the Reverend that I'd help him get the church back in order as it is a fearful mess at present."

"Of course I don't mind Jean. It was in a real state last night – we were there when it was still swimming in water. Poor Edwin, I think he was pretty devastated."

"Poor man," agreed Dahlia.

"And such a lovely man," added Iris, her head cocked to one side. "Such a wonderful vicar."

Just then, the door at the rear of the shop opened and Lavender loomed into view. She was dressed in her usual eclectic mix of clothes, all of them in a muddy hue. "Ah Lavender dear, there you are! Miss West was asking after you, and I said you were working on your celebration of the flood."

Lavender nodded solemnly. "I am."

"She's always so full of ideas, always got her finger on the pulse!" said Dahlia with great enthusiasm.

"You don't think it was divine intervention, do you dear?" said Iris, adding for Victoria's benefit, "She's more in favour of the global-warming angle at the moment."

"There was too much rain all at once," explained Lavender in her unexpectedly deep voice. "I might go and get a bit of that gargoyle that struck down that Percy Shooter. It was symbolic." She nodded emphatically.

"Was it dear?" asked Iris, looking round from where she was dusting the row of old-fashioned sweetie jars. "Would you like a quarter of lemon sherbets Miss West? I know they're your favourites?"

"Call me Victoria, please, and yes, now you come to mention it, I would."

"I didn't like that Percy Shooter," stated Lavender. "He was a busybody and he spied on people."

"Now now," chided Dahlia, "we shouldn't really speak ill of the dead, should we Lavender."

Her sister regarded her steadily. "Why not?"

"Well…" began Dahlia starting to look flustered.

"That's eighty pence please, Miss… er, Victoria," said Iris.

"Well, it's not polite," Dahlia ploughed on, beginning to turn slightly pink.

"He's dead so he doesn't know. And anyway, he wasn't polite when he was alive." Victoria secretly admired Lavender's way of not mincing her words; she always got straight to the point and, rather like a child, said exactly what she meant. If only the rest of us were more like that, she thought, life would be much easier.

Dahlia was patting her bun distractedly, always a sure sign that she was embarrassed, and Lavender was gazing into the middle distance with a contemplative air.

"Well, I must get on," said Victoria. "Thank you for..." she almost said "the entertainment", but managed to stop herself "...for everything. I'll see you in a couple of weeks then Jean," she added, making for the door. Jean was still trying to compose an answer as the door closed behind her.

After a lunch of bread and cheese, Victoria walked Moss around the farm and was relieved, but at the same time sorry, to see no sign of Albert. That woman in the shop had obviously seen him with Carol, so she was definitely on the scene. Victoria sighed and picked up the flagging puppy. "At least you love me, don't you Moss?" He snuggled into his mistress's arms and gave her several warm licks on her hand to prove his devotion.

Victoria spent the afternoon sorting out the bits of kitchenalia she wanted to get rid of. Perhaps she could ask Kev's wife Kelly to sell them for her on eBay for some commission? She didn't think it would be right to ask Albert to do her such a big favour. Then she turned her attention to the bathroom brochures and made her final selections. She phoned Kev and told him her choices and was delighted to find that he could start work in a couple of days.

"Summer time, innit? No one wants the builders in while they're on their holidays," said Kev, explaining his availability.

"Really? I would have thought it was an ideal time, but I'm not going away, so the sooner you can start the better as far as I'm concerned," said Victoria.

"Yeah, who'd want to go on holiday when they live somewhere like this? Must be mad – know what I mean?" And for once, Victoria was pleased to say she did know what he meant.

"It is a glorious part of the world, and I haven't even begun exploring the coast yet," she said.

"Aintcha? Come on Victoria – get out there! All round the south coast is stunning – Bigbury, Bantham, Slapton – and towns like Dartmouth and Salcombe – well! You can't beat 'em."

"I'll get you to make me a list next time I see you," she laughed.

"Well, I'd just ask Albert – you've got a ready-made travel guide on your doorstep love," added Kev, and Victoria bit her lip.

"Yes, I suppose so. Anyway, see you in a day or two," she said and finished the call.

She sat down to work on her next blog. She wasn't sure if it would be acceptable to write about the flood as someone had died, so she decided to opt for the peculiarities of the Swaddlecombe Show committee, heavily disguised of course.

A little later there was a tentative knock at the kitchen door and she looked up to see Albert. Moss launched himself full pelt and she watched as the two of them greeted each other joyfully. She felt an immense sadness.

"Well then Victoria, how are you feeling now?" He leaned nonchalantly against the doorpost looking all blue-eyed and tanned and slightly dishevelled in a terribly attractive way. Damn, thought Victoria. Damn relationships, damn men and damn everything!

"I'm OK, thanks Albert, had a busy day finishing off bits of work, and things…" she trailed off.

"Well, I've had a right awful day bouncing around in a dusty, hot old tractor, so I reckon we could both do with a trip to the pub, a drink and a nice meal. What do you say?"

Victoria looked down, avoiding his smiling eyes. "I seem to be spending rather too much time in the pub lately, so if you don't mind, I'll give it a miss. I just want a quiet night in and a bath and then early to bed."

"Damn, you're a clean-living woman! You had a bath last night too."

"Actually, I didn't, I was too tired and just fell into bed." Well, it was almost true, she thought.

"Well," he puffed out his cheeks. "That's a shame, but if you don't feel like it, I'll pop down on my own and have a bite of Trudy's pie. You sure you're alright?" Victoria swallowed. She was feeling sad and guilty and about to cry – why didn't he just go?

"Yes, just tired thanks," she managed to say.

Albert sighed. "OK maid, well, maybe I'll see you tomorrow." And he turned and left.

Victoria felt tears trickling down her cheeks and wiped them away crossly.

Chapter 6

Victoria drove slowly along the narrow lane towards Ansome Violets and wondered for the hundredth time whether she should be going to see the bird hide with Sam. She really didn't want to think about Albert. She'd got too fond of him too soon and felt she'd made rather a fool of herself. It appeared that he wasn't as fond of her as she'd thought and now, well, wounded pride and all that. She sighed as the road ahead became blurry through welling tears, but took a deep breath and blinked them away.

Pulling up in the yard she patted the leather steering-wheel cover. She did enjoy driving Gloria, but she ought really to look for a vehicle of her own so that she was not in Albert's debt. She was about to climb out of the car when she heard angry voices in the distance.

"You're just being a bugger for the sake of it!" shouted one voice she didn't recognise.

"'Tis my land, I'll sell to whoever I bleddy like," replied a voice she easily recognised as George.

"Well I think you're a fool to make an enemy out of me – damn years we've known each other and you turn on me now George Ansome. You'll be sorry, you can be sure of that!"

A tall man, red in the face, fists clenched, strode past her; she could almost feel his anger from where she was sitting. George appeared round the corner, determined to see the other man off his land, and waved his fist at him in a victorious gesture. She tried to sink down in her seat so he wouldn't see her, but with the roof down it was a pretty feeble attempt and George was now approaching the car.

She got out and smiled at him.

"Hello maid, you back for more?" asked George, sounding quite his normal self.

"Well no actually, Sam invited me to come and see his bird hide on the far side of the nursery land."

George snorted and shook his head. "Bloody scamp, wouldn't know a decent day's work if it hit him in the face." Victoria thought there was almost a disappointed look in his eyes as he spoke. "Well, you get going then, I expect he's in the kitchen sitting on his backside as usual." With shoulders slumped, George stomped off towards his beloved polytunnels.

Victoria peered around the kitchen door and there, as predicted, was Sam, sitting with a mug of tea in his hand and feet up on a second kitchen chair.

"Hi there, George said you would be in here."

"And he was right! I'm sure he took great delight in telling you I am always sitting here with my feet up, the old rogue! No one would ever get a tea break if he had his way. You like a cup?"

"Well yes, now you mention it I just fancy a cup of tea – have you got any Earl Grey?"

"Of course, one of the few little luxuries that I seem to be allowed by the master!"

"Oh surely George isn't that bad?" said Victoria. "Isn't he just a bit grumpy on the exterior?"

"Exterior and interior," said Sam. "Mean old swine wouldn't give me a penny of the family money if he could get away with it. I'm not surprised old Weston was mad at him."

Victoria looked at Sam and frowned. Did he need to be quite so damning of his own brother? Surely George wasn't all bad? But then she hadn't played second fiddle to him all her life. "So why were they arguing, assuming that was Mr Weston he was with out in the yard?"

"Yeah, it was old Charlie Weston, his nemesis really. He and Charlie were at school together and, to give George his due, Charlie was a bully back then. Charlie would often get all the other lads in the class to give George a hard time. Our Dad was really mean about new shoes, new school trousers, that kind of stuff, said it was all a waste of good money as we'd just grow out of them."

"So the others were mean to George and teased him?" said Victoria.

"'Teased' would be a rather genteel way of describing the times he had his face pushed in the mud or his satchel chucked in the river – they even broke his arm once when they tripped him up on the way home from school. Charlie Weston was more than a little nasty to him."

"Oh that's awful, poor George. I hate hearing about children having unhappy childhoods, it's so unfair. Bad enough to be bullied, but for your father to be so tough too, that's sad." Victoria got the impression Sam hadn't been given such a hard time. "So it didn't leave you feeling hard done by?"

"Well the girls and I didn't suffer so much – George took the brunt really and I came along much later anyway… Dad seemed to single him out, said he had to toughen up if he was going to make a go of running the nursery. That's all Dad cared about – the damn business."

"So," said Victoria, "if I'm not been too nosy asking, what was George arguing with Weston about?"

"Oh – a parcel of land at the back of the nursery. Weston wants to buy it as an entrance to a plot he has planning permission to build on. With that small piece he'd have direct access to the main road so it would add hugely to the value of his land. We'd all have sold to Weston like a shot. Len, that's June's other half, he was the one trying to organise it, but George wasn't having any of it, his final chance for revenge on Charlie Weston I guess."

"Well, to be honest, I think I rather agree with him," said Victoria with a smile.

"It's all well and good falling for the 'poor George' routine," said Sam, looking rather petulant, "but I had plans for developing the barns on the south side of the nursery into eco-friendly holiday cottages. It would have finally given me a bit of independence if I could make a few bob off them. The money from old Weston would have come in very handy for that."

"Would you be able to do all the renovation and building work yourself then?" asked Victoria, thinking she already knew the answer to that.

"Me? No, not something I have the skills for, but there are plenty of blokes in the village would welcome a job for a few months." Sam flashed a not-very-successful smile at her and Victoria guessed physical labour wasn't really Sam's thing. "I'd sort of project manage it all," he added, waving a teaspoon vaguely in the direction of the barns.

"So George isn't really keen on the barn development idea?"

"George isn't really keen on any of the ideas I've had. We could have made a fortune several times over if he just listened to me a bit more and focussed less on his damn plants. Trouble is he hasn't got any faith in me. Come to that, my sisters are as bad. They'd never put me before George and that's a fact." He sighed in a resigned way and made Victoria's tea.

Victoria felt a little uneasy; some of Sam's appeal was being diluted by this rather unattractive outburst of indignation. But, she told herself, she didn't know all the ins and outs of the situation so she would give him the benefit of the doubt. But still, she didn't feel entirely happy. "Shall we go and look at the bird hide then? It's not something I've ever seen before. My uncle was something of a birdwatcher, but I'm not really clued up on the subject."

"Oh far better than that, I've packed up a picnic and thought we'd head over to the coast – enjoy this good weather while we can. I love the beach – just lying there watching the sea, maybe even a refreshing swim!"

"Well there won't be any refreshing swimming for me," retorted Victoria. "I didn't bring a swimming costume as I was expecting to be birdwatching!" She felt guilty at the thought of a day by the coast with him. It was too much like a date, and she still felt some ridiculous loyalty to Albert. Then she remembered the photos... "But then, if you've gone to the trouble of packing a picnic, it would be nice. And I haven't seen much of the coast yet. Where would we be going?"

"There are a few nice spots I know down in the South Hams, leave it to me! We'll go on a magical mystery tour. Mind you, the price they charge for parking down there – can't believe everyone just pays up."

"Oh I'm sure I could pay for the car park if you like, seems only fair!" said Victoria, thinking how Albert would never have made a remark like that; he was such a generous soul.

"No, couldn't hear of it, I know a few places where you can park on the road and walk – the basket won't be too heavy with two of us carrying. I'll just get a few more bits packed – could you perhaps go and tell George we're just off? He'll be out in the far polytunnel." With that he turned to the fridge and began extracting bottles and jars and putting them on the table.

"OK – I'll go out to George and meet you by the car. Shall we go in yours or mine?"

"Oh I think yours would be so much more suitable for a lovely day like this. I won't be long, just want to get a couple of nice glasses and a bottle!"

Victoria headed out of the kitchen and over to the polytunnel she had visited last time she came to the nursery. Sure enough, there was George tending his seedlings, bent over and working among them with infinite care. He nurtured them more carefully than one might a baby, she thought.

"George!" She waved enthusiastically in the hope he might meet her at the doorway to the tunnel, but no such luck. He just looked up and stared at her as if he'd never seen her before.

Victoria walked down the length of the tunnel. "George, there's been a change of plan and Sam's taking me to see some of the beaches round here. Apparently he has a picnic all packed, so it should be fun. He asked me to let you know he was going out." If she didn't know better she might have thought George looked like a sulky child, but it was probably just her imagination.

"Nice for those that has the time to skive off all day. That lad never did a decent day's work in his life, bleddy beaches, waste of time." Still muttering he turned back to his plants and Victoria sighed. He hardly seemed the same man who had so bashfully offered to name a plant after her.

Walking back towards the house she bumped into a woman who must surely be related to Sam, eyes and nose being identical. She had a bucket and mop and was walking towards the house. Victoria smiled and said hello.

"Hello, I'm May, Sam's sister," she said returning Victoria's smile. "I heard about you from June, you're doing the article on us. Bet it's exciting being a journalist, eh?"

"Well it is fun sometimes, other times just hard work. But yes, I've enjoyed writing about the history of the violet trade and how this nursery got started. It's a shame you weren't in the photo as well as June."

"Oh that's alright dear, I'm not so fussed about having me picture taken. You got the important one – young Madeleine – she was front of the picture, wasn't she? Very excited she was to get some press attention." Victoria wondered why Madeleine would find 'press attention', as her aunt called it, in a country lifestyle magazine particularly interesting, but perhaps it was just the novelty of appearing in print.

"You must be very proud of your niece, she seemed a nice girl."

"Oh I am, if only I'd had her chances as a girl. Such a successful businesswoman she is, very clever. Never guessed she would inherit her granddad's genes rather than June's, she can't add up to save her life!"

"What exactly does Madeleine do then?" asked Victoria

"If I'm honest, love, I don't rightly know. She always says she's done such and such a good deal and I don't like to ask about business really. I know June says she's forever on that computer and sending really important messages. Whatever it is she seems to be right busy so that's all good isn't it? Although I hope she'll find herself a good man before too long. Money and work isn't going to keep her warm on a cold night now is it?"

Victoria smiled, despite finding May's old-fashioned views rather irritating. "Well, it must be nice for June to have a daughter who's successful enough to keep her in her old age though," she laughed.

"Oh goodness me that's a way off!" replied May. "No, at the moment she is needing, what does she call it, 'seed capital', all the time. Sounds like old-fashioned loans to me, but there you are."

Victoria wondered where this was leading but kept quiet, hoping the woman would continue.

"What a family! The lot of 'em as mean as can be. George would have me on my knees scrubbing till I have no knees left I reckon. Happily sits back and lets me clear up their mess and do the washing and ironing and doesn't even pay me a proper wage. Not sure he realises just how hard that house is to keep clean, especially with their galumphing great muddy boots everywhere."

Victoria's smile was becoming rather strained, so she tried a concerned look instead. "Well, I'm sure George must be proud of his niece being such a success?"

May gave a snort of indignation. "Pah. Stuff and nonsense, never takes a blind bit of notice and he's turned her down flat when she's suggested he might like to invest in her business. He'll be the one that's sorry in the end when she makes a million and won't let him have a penny of it – you see! "

At this point Sam came out of the house and Victoria felt relieved. "Sam, here!" Victoria waved at him and then saw he couldn't wave back as he was carrying a large wicker basket – more of a laundry basket than a hamper – and she suddenly felt hungry.

Between them, they just managed to wedge the basket in Gloria's tiny boot and Victoria wondered just what kind of a feast he had prepared. "Right," she said, starting the engine, "where to?"

They meandered along the narrow lanes, high-banked and billowing with wildflowers. The heat of a long summer was giving everything a slightly tired look now, but the sheer lushness and profusion of everything still amazed Victoria and she loved smelling the different scents as the little car brushed its way past. The weather had been so good she had sometimes, when the roof was down and the windows all open, trailed her hand lazily through the wildflowers as she drove slowly along. It reminded her of trailing her hand over the side of a rowing boat into the cool waters of the Thames as a romantic teenager all those years ago. She came back to reality with a jolt as she braked hard and stopped face to face with an elderly lady, who could barely see over the steering wheel of her small red car.

"Oh dear," said Sam, "usual hazard! A lady driver!" and laughed uproariously. Victoria resisted the urge to make a smart reply, and hoped that her faultless reversing into a gateway impressed him and showed that not all lady drivers were hopeless. This was the first of many encounters. It seemed that most people were either incapable or unwilling to reverse and Victoria was getting pretty fed up with it, feeling she was taking two steps forward and one back all the time.

Sam was chuckling again. "This is what happens when you live somewhere as wonderful as Devon! Full of tourists this time of year and they haven't a clue where they are or how to reverse."

"Perhaps now wasn't the ideal time to go to the coast then," snapped Victoria, as she selected reverse for what seemed like the hundredth time, but Sam seemed oblivious to her criticism and waved merrily to the red-faced people who had just squeezed past.

"Oh don't worry Victoria, you'll get used to it."

They came to a T-junction, turned left and then immediately right and snaked their way uphill. "I always used to love roads like this when I was a child," Victoria said, trying to lighten the mood, although she felt sure that Sam was oblivious to her frustration. He appeared perfectly happy lolling back in the passenger seat, hands behind his head, sunglasses on, while she sweated and toiled with the gears and the heavy steering, designed before the days of power-assistance.

She heard herself wittering on. "I always used to say to my mother 'Is it a sea view road?' and I'd cross my fingers and hope and hope that when we got to the top of the hill, the sea would be on the other side of it." She changed gear. "Of course, it rarely was – oh!" she exclaimed and pulled into a gateway. She gazed down at a view of utter loveliness. "Oh!" she said again. "Isn't that gorgeous."

The sea was Mediterranean blue, the sand pale gold – and were those really palm trees? Sam turned to admire the view too and she felt his hand slide across the top of her shoulders as he adjusted his position.

"Impressed?"

"Absolutely! I didn't realise it could look so tropical here. I've been to the coast, well more to estuaries I suppose, a couple of times near home, and once I walked on the beach near Teignmouth, but it was blowing a gale. This is wonderful! Where are we?"

"We're on the south coast, not far from Dartmouth. But it's all a bit too popular on this stretch, so we'll go a little further south to a nice secluded cove that I know, where we can eat our picnic in peace, I hope." He brushed her neck slowly as he removed his arm. A little shudder of excitement ran down Victoria's spine, and she felt instantly guilty.

"Well OK, but I really can't leave the puppy for too long," she said, pulling back onto the road.

"Oh I'm sure it will be fine," said Sam waving one hand vaguely in the direction of home.

After ten minutes, Sam pointed out a small pull-in on the verge that was a tight fit even for a small car like Gloria. Victoria parked up and, having struggled to remove the hamper, started to put the roof up. Sam suggested it would be fine to leave it down, but Victoria wouldn't hear of it. She wasn't even sure about leaving the car parked in such an out-of-the-way place. What if someone broke in or, worse, slashed the fabric roof? Poor Albert would be heartbroken and she'd feel awful.

They set off down a narrow path, the heavy picnic hamper between them banging painfully against their legs. Victoria felt sure she had gone unattractively red in the face and that her hair was sticking to her forehead and turning frizzier with every step. Eventually, they arrived at a small crescent-shaped cove with pale golden sand and edged with low cliffs. The waves were small on the turquoise sea and the whole effect was very pretty.

"Oh," said Sam, sounding disappointed, "we haven't got the place to ourselves, what a nuisance." Victoria followed his gaze and saw about a dozen people dotted about the cove, all well spaced out and mostly sitting with their backs to the cliffs. Well, it was quieter than any other beach she'd ever been on! It was a perfect suntrap and the only sound came from the waves and a few gulls wheeling above.

"Well, it's not exactly busy, is it?" said Victoria briskly, relieved to find that she wasn't going to be entirely on her own with this man. "Let's find a spot, shall we?"

They settled into a small alcove in the rocks and set about their picnic. It was a pretty good spread but, Victoria was somewhat aggrieved to notice, the immense basket was not so much packed with goodies but stuffed full of bottles and jars which could have easily been decanted into plastic containers or left out altogether. No wonder it had been so heavy – and with a sinking heart she realised they'd be lugging most of it back to the car again.

She decided to make the best of a bad job. Smiling broadly, she said "Cheers" and sipped her glass of warm white wine, at the same time thinking what a shame that all the paraphernalia had not included a bag of ice.

They sat and chatted for an hour and Victoria relaxed a little and enjoyed the sun on her skin. She'd had the foresight to put suntan cream on her arms and legs, but felt her face was possibly getting burned – or was that the wine? They did a little beachcombing after lunch and Sam found several extremely pretty shells and presented them to her with great ceremony. He was sweet, but clearly more one of life's dreamers than doers.

Their walk back to the car was almost as tortuous as the one down to the beach. Back on the road, Victoria was delighted to see an ice-cream van parked up. "Ah! Just what we need!" said Sam. "You sit here," he patted the top of the hamper, "and I'll fetch us both an ice cream. You're looking a bit hot and bothered, Victoria." He rummaged on his pockets and frowned. "That's odd, I'm sure I had a five pound note in my pocket." He began patting himself all over, and looking more and more pathetic.

Victoria sighed and reached into a pocket. "Here," she said, handing him a fiver.

"Oh great, thanks!" He strolled over to the van, and returned with two huge cones of rich yellow ice cream.

"Thank you," Victoria said, with just a hint of irony, and waited for him to give her the change. There wasn't any. But perhaps £2.50 was about right for each cone? She wasn't sure, but… oh well, she'd have to give him the benefit of the doubt – again.

She really preferred things like choc ices and hadn't had an old-fashioned cone like this since she was a child, quite possibly on holiday with Aunt Edith and quite probably just a dozen or so miles from where she was now. But she was hot and the cold creamy mounds looked very inviting and were already starting to melt, so she gave in and had a good lick. "Mmmmm!" she said, and licked some more. "Wow, that's good!"

"Of course! It's made with good Devon clotted cream," Sam said proudly, as if he'd made it himself.

"Gosh, it's delicious. Rich and smooth and much tastier than I remember from my childhood. Is this locally made then?"

Sam nodded, licking his lips and twirling the cone round in front of him as if to admire it from every angle. "Yep, it's made just down the road, a place called Church Farm Dairy."

"Hmmm," said Victoria as she savoured another mouthful. "I wonder if I could have just found the subject for my next local business article?"

"Good idea! I know the owner's daughter," added Sam. "Lovely girl. Nice family. I can give you their contact details if you like?" Victoria smiled; why was she not surprised he knew the daughter?

Having finished the cone, she stood up. "Right! I'm afraid I really must get back! Not only will poor Moss have his legs crossed, but I need to start sorting out the adverts for the show programme. I don't suppose…?"

Sam laughed. "No don't ask! You know what George's answer will be. NO! He never spends money on advertising."

"Not even supporting the local community?"

"No," he said, lifting one end of the hamper while Victoria took the other.

Thankfully their return journey went without mishap. After dropping Sam back at the nursery, and being rewarded with a peck on the cheek, she finally got back home and was glad to enter the relative cool of the kitchen.

Victoria sat at her laptop and sorted out her notes for those wanting to advertise in the programme. There seemed to be a healthy list of some forty or so businesses signed up and she glanced through the previous year's programme to see what size adverts they had taken last time. She realised this was her aunt's handy work, and smiled. The programme was effective, but a little rough and ready and had obviously been typed and cut out and stuck in place before copying. It would be a doddle for her to design it using the layout program on her computer. She'd have it sorted in no time.

She made a cup of tea, settled herself and picked up her phone to dial the number for the first name on the list, a gentleman who erected stables and sheds. "Hello, Mr Bird? It's Victoria West here, I wanted to ask you for the copy for your advert for the Swaddlecombe Show programme."

"Who?" came a gruff voice.

"Victoria West, Edith West's niece, I was…"

"Yes, yes, but whadya want?"

Slightly taken aback Victoria explained. "I am organising the Swaddlecombe Show programme and I need your copy for your advert…"

"Copy? Whadya mean copy? Who's copied it?"

"No, no," she laughed. "I want the words – it's called copy – that you want in your advert."

"Who says I wants an advert?"

She consulted her list. "The Reverend Ruminant has given me a list of advertisers and…"

"He has, has he?" There was a snorting sound. "I 'aven't confirmed nothin'. So 'ow much is it then?"

Victoria was flummoxed. "Erm, oh dear, I thought the space had all been booked and paid for already…"

"What space? And paid for? You must be joking maid! You'm a lot more la-di-dah than your aunt used to be, young woman. She used to come straight to the point!"

"Well!" said Victoria, starting to get rather riled. "I am only working from what I've been given and I assumed…"

"Ah well, that's dangerous. You shouldn't never do that."

"What?"

"Assume. Now see here. I'll have the same as what I had last year, but I'm not paying no more for it." Victoria could envisage

Mr Bird on the end of the phone folding his arms across his barrel chest and looking smug.

"Right, well, er, I expect that's OK. Of course I'll need to check with the Reverend…"

"No, no, that's all I'm prepared to do, there's nothing to check. And that's my final word on it."

"Oh. Well I'll put you down for a quarter page then. Do you want the measurements?"

"Measurements? What d'you mean maid?" He sounded indignant and Victoria felt she was about to get into a major misunderstanding if she wasn't careful.

"For the advert, measurements for the advert, Mr Bird. Or are you not supplying finished artwork?" There was a stunned silence and Victoria sighed. "Mr Bird, could you perhaps just email me your logo and then I'll design the advert for you?"

"Nope. You've lost me. No idea what you're talking about. You just need to make me an advert like last year's. Just 'copy' the damned thing – that's what you said, wasn't it? Just copy it, stick it in the programme and then post the bill to me, A. Bird Esquire, The Old Barn, Uppacott and I'll pay it after thirty days at the earliest. Alright? And none of the VAT nonsense neither."

And with that, he hung up. Victoria sat back and stared at her phone as if it was personally responsible for the man's impossible nature. "That went well," she said to Moss, lying full stretch on the cool stone floor, and made a note next to Mr Bird's name. Who was next? James Bridger, who apparently sold various sorts of animal feed. She must try and be more precise and keep things simple; she was obviously dealing with people who rarely handled things like adverts and artwork.

"Hello, Mr Bridger? My name is Victoria West, I wanted to ask you about your advert for the Swaddlecombe Show programme."

"Yep?" said a much younger voice.

"Will you want to take the same advert as last year?"

"Nope."

Victoria frowned. "No? Oh dear, why not?"

"Gone bust."

"Oh, I'm so sorry, I didn't realise. You were on the list and…" but she realised she was talking to dead air. "Moss, this is not going to plan. I wonder where Edwin got this list from? It seems very approximate." She crossed out Mr Bridger and looked down the list, making a pact with herself to get through at least half of the names before the end of the day.

After her fifteenth call, Victoria felt like opening a bottle of wine and drowning her sorrows – or possibly herself. Almost every call was as difficult as the dreaded A. Bird Esquire and she realised she was going to be writing, designing and laying out the whole programme. Would she ever stop being so naïve? Why did she take things on without thinking them through? Of course she would have to produce the whole thing, it was obvious, and she was sure her aunt had probably been just as frustrated by the task every year as she was.

And while she was in this rich vein of self-criticism, she may as well ask herself why was she so naïve about everything? She was forever blundering into things and emerging bruised. It was the same in all areas of her life. Look at Albert, for goodness sake! She knew little about him, not in detail anyway, and she had trusted him totally, believed he was a faithful and charming friend and was hoping he'd soon become something more – and look what she'd found – those photos. For a moment, her hand hovered over the mouse, poised to click on the folder of incriminating photos. She put her head in her hands instead and sighed loudly. Moss got up and came over and leant against her leg. "I know Moss, you're my faithful friend, aren't you?"

Then she sat up straight and clicked on the folder. "Right," she said out loud. She scrolled through the photos again, even though she knew every detail off by heart. Why was she torturing herself like this? He could do what he liked! Albert was a free spirit – very free apparently – as was she. She had no claim over him.

Was she misreading the images? Was it all innocent? Maybe she should just ask him? No, that would be awful! She had no right to confront him outright; it was none of her business. She gazed at the photo of the two of them together in her kitchen. It seemed like another age, when life was less complicated and definitely happier. She thought of Sam. She was relieved that she'd found his character less appealing than his looks and realised she felt rather sorry for him. He was obviously a weak man and was dominated by George. Or perhaps he was just too lazy to make a go of things himself. And then she realised she was actually looking at a photo of Sam.

She peered closer at the screen. He was jabbing his finger into his older brother's chest and George was jabbing back. Both men were snarling, their lips drawn back like two fighting dogs framing up to each other. Victoria was shocked; they looked so angry. She scrolled on and found another photo of George looking furious, this time with Charlie Weston, the red-faced farmer she had seen the other day. And there was another one of George, arms folded, legs planted firmly apart, his stance stating very firmly 'No'. Annoyingly, Percy's prying lens had not got a clear view of George's opponent – the edge of a door or wall had obscured part of the shot – but Victoria thought it was probably a woman; there were gesticulating arms and a glimpse of blonde hair. Goodness, George did like a good row!

Victoria scrolled back through the photos, past the ones of Albert with the woman and baby, and with Carol. Her eyes caught a movement and she looked up and gave a small squeak of surprise as she saw the real Albert smiling at her through the window. He waved and came in the open door. She slammed the laptop shut and was aware of the blood rushing to her face, almost as if she'd been caught cheating in an exam.

"My word Victoria. Where have you been? You've got a right good bit of colour in your chops!"

"Have I?" she touched her flaming cheeks and then realised that as well as her blush, her skin felt tight and hot with sunburn. She probably looked like a beetroot. Beetroot! Oh Lord! She'd forgotten all about the damned cake!

"You alright?" He said, concern creasing the edges of his very blue eyes.

"Yes, fine, thanks. I'm just a bit hot and bothered. I've been trying to get this show programme sorted out and, well, it's like you said, a bit of a disaster really." She folded her arms and frowned at Moss, who was trying to climb up Albert's leg. "Moss! Stop that!"

"He's alright, aren't you young'un?" He hoisted the pup into his arms and was rewarded with licks. He slung the puppy on its back and patted its pink belly. Moss lay perfectly still, as if in a trance, gazing up at Albert. I bet he has that effect on all the women he meets too, thought Victoria.

"Well now. I wondered if you were free this evening and would care to accompany me to the Swaddle Arms?" He was being playfully gallant and executed a little bow, putting the pup down as he did so.

Victoria felt slightly sick. She so wanted to go, but at the same time knew she must not. She must maintain her dignity and her independence and try and harden her heart against this charming man. "I'm sorry Albert." She opened her laptop again and clicked busily about the screen. "I've been out to lunch already today so I couldn't possibly eat another meal out."

"Really? Well never mind, come and have a half of cider and a bag of crisps then!"

If he didn't go in a minute, she was going to cry. "No, really. I've made such slow progress with these advertisers that I still have lots of work to do." She shuffled her notepad and pen. "Besides, as I look like a beetroot, I really don't think I should show my face in the pub, it might not do your reputation any good." Oh well done Victoria! A pathetic attempt at sarcasm and you've just made yourself look really, really stupid, she cursed herself inwardly.

Albert puffed out his cheeks and frowned, clearly bemused. "Well, I don't quite know what to say to that maid." He scratched his head, began to say something, then stopped. Victoria pretended to read her list of advertisers with great concentration. "Right, well, I'll be off then. I'll maybe pop by in a day or two." He turned slowly and walked out of the door.

As soon as he was out of sight, Victoria put her head in her hands and wept. Moss gently licked away the tears that trickled down to her elbows.

Chapter 7

Moss raced on ahead as Victoria wandered back towards the cottage, carrying her daily collection of eggs. Despite doing the same thing every day for the past few months she still marvelled at the whole concept of living in the countryside, keeping hens and the million other things that were so new to her.

She smiled as Moss yapped at the back door. It obviously didn't occur to him that no one was inside to answer his call. Victoria had been amazed to find that nobody locally really bothered about locking doors. The nearest thing to organised crime in Swaddlecombe was the family of foxes that regularly knocked over and vandalised the wheelie bins when they were standing by the roadside for collection.

Pushing open the back door – which was still sticking a little after the epic downpour – she put the basket of eggs on the dresser and looked across to the kitchen table. In the centre sat a magnificent chocolate cake. Swirls of chocolate ganache covered the whole creation and balanced daintily on top was a small group of delicately sugared violets. Her heart lurched; Albert had obviously popped in and left this vision of deliciousness for her to find. She felt so guilty. She knew she was being unreasonable not explaining why she felt she had to cool their relationship. Maybe she should have been strong and explained why his behaviour simply wasn't acceptable and that they would have to remain just friends.

She plugged in the kettle and sighed loudly. Albert had been, she had thought, the answer to all her prayers. He seemed kind and caring and they'd laughed and cried together. They shared interests and she really had dared to dream that there might be something special developing. Not once had it crossed her mind that he could be that casual with her affections, two-timing her without batting an eyelid.

Mechanically, she prepared the pup's breakfast and set it on floor. He pounced on it as if he hadn't eaten for a week. She sighed again. Chocolate cake seemed a good answer to heartache, so she cut a good-sized slice and smiled as she saw how perfect it was and – not for the first time – marvelled at her inability to make anything even resembling a cake. Just at that moment there was a screech of tyres as a vehicle came to a sudden halt in the yard.

A cacophony of sound – singing and whistling – came from the vehicle and Victoria looked out of the kitchen window to see Kev and a younger lad, laughing and joking as they climbed out of the van. Great – this was one step closer to having her longed-for power shower in the bathroom!

The cheery sounds grew louder when she opened the back door.

"Morning Kev."

"Morning Miss Victoria, and may I present my mate Andy, otherwise known as Shortie!"

Andy seemed immune to the nickname. No doubt he had suffered with digs about his height – or lack of it – for years, so he merely rolled his eyes, gave a small nod but said nothing.

Victoria smiled. "Welcome Andy! Won't you both come in – do you need to bring any tools or equipment inside?"

"Nah it's fine," replied Kev. "Shortie can lug it all up once we've had a cuppa, if you know what I mean."

Victoria certainly did know what he meant. "Right, I'll get the kettle on then. Would you both like tea?"

"Does the pope wear a funny 'at?" Kev laughed. "If there was a tea river out there I reckon we'd 'ave drunk it dry! Two teas, five sugars, many thanks."

A quiet voice muttered something that Victoria couldn't quite catch, and she looked towards Andy. "Sorry Miss, but um, could I have coffee, no sugar." Andy looked down and away from Kev.

"Do what? Blimey, your girlfriend's getting to you mate, next thing you know you'll be drinking that herbal tea stuff!" Kev feigned shock and nudged his shy friend.

"Not a problem," said Victoria trying to make the lad feel more at home. "I'll have coffee too and I don't have sugar either so that's two of us."

Kev looked longingly over at the chocolate cake. "I don't suppose there'd be any of that going spare would there?"

"You two go on upstairs and I'll bring up a tray with the drinks and some cake for you." Smiling to herself Victoria thought how childlike men can be when cake is involved.

The two men marched through the kitchen and, with Kev still ribbing his workmate, made their way upstairs. The whistling started again and Victoria hoped it might stop for a while as they downed cake and tea. She could always turn on the radio to drown them out.

Both Victoria and the pup jumped as there was an almighty crash and then Andy appeared and scooted through the kitchen, mumbling "Tools, s'cuse me." He reappeared loaded higher than a packhorse with various tools and gadgets and staggered back upstairs.

The banging and crashing started almost immediately and Victoria wondered how long the really noisy part would take.

Between thumps and bangs she heard a mobile ring and realised it must be theirs, not hers. Silence reigned, and she couldn't help overhearing Kev's conversation.

"No, you don't say, he never? Struth!"

There was a pause and then a clatter of feet down the stairs. A shocked-looking Kev appeared in the kitchen. "You'll never believe this. My wife Kelly just rang, her mate works up at Ansomes packing plants and stuff. I don't rightly know how to say this..." He paused and frowned.

Victoria looked up, worried by the strange expression on his face.

"I asked her twice to make sure she had it right, seems old George Ansome is dead and her mate seemed right cut up about it."

"Oh no!" gasped Victoria, thinking of poor George: so full of bluff and bluster on the surface but, she was sure, a softie underneath. And now she would never have the chance to get to know him better. Victoria didn't know how old he was but it was sad for someone to be cut off before their time. He'd seemed physically quite fit – she wondered if he'd had a heart attack or a stroke.

"Thanks for telling me. Goodness – what a shock. I think I might give Sam a ring, he's bound to be pretty upset."

Kev gave her a long look, started to say something, then muttered, "Right you are" and took off back upstairs where the banging and crashing started up again.

Victoria realised she hadn't made their drinks, so she boiled the kettle again and cut two slices of cake. At least that might keep them focussed on her project. They might not flit off on another job if she could keep them regularly fed and watered.

She laid a tray with the mugs and cake, all the time wondering whether to ring Sam with her condolences. Often people avoided you when you'd lost someone close, just because they were unsure what to say. She remembered the embarrassed silences after her parents had died when people found it hard to express their pity for her. Mind you, the way Sam and George argued, maybe Sam would be happy his brother was dead. Perhaps now he could get on with his grand building plans.

She laid the tray down on the floor as the bathroom door was closed. "Hey guys – drinks and cake out here on the landing!"

As if by magic the noise stopped and the door was thrown open. Both men plonked themselves down on the floor and started to devour the cake. Worse than feeding puppies, thought Victoria, smiling as she made her way back to the kitchen.

She opened her laptop and stared at the blank screen. She realised she was never going to get any work done until she'd rung Sam, so she might as well call sooner rather than later. She checked the number on her phone and pressed the button.

"Hello?" came a quiet but recognisable voice.

"Sam, is that you?"

"Yes this is Sam, who's speaking?"

"It's Victoria, Sam. I just wanted to say how sorry I was to hear about George. I'm sure everyone is terribly shocked. I don't know if I can be of any help at all, but would you like me to come over?"

There was a long pause, and then, "Um, well I really don't think that's such a good idea Victoria."

She was taken aback; he sounded so unlike his normal carefree self. "Of course, I'm sorry. I was just worried that you might need some moral support, but I'm sure you have May and June there, so..." she trailed off, feeling foolish and wishing she hadn't rung.

"I'm sorry Victoria, but I've got the police to deal with, June sobbing in one room and May wailing in another – I really don't think there's anything you could do to help. I threw up my entire stomach contents when I had to identify the body, and right now I just need a bit of time to think."

A long drawn-out pause filled the air and Victoria swallowed hard. He sounded so cold. "Sam, I'm sorry, I obviously wasn't told all the circumstances – I assumed he had died of a heart attack or something. So why did you need to identify the body?"

Sam sighed heavily, "George was shot, not a nice natural, tidy death. He was shot. Shot in his beloved polytunnel at almost point-blank range so the resulting mess was horrible. I recognised what he was wearing this morning so that helped make the identification easier, but of his face there was close to nothing left. They'll have to follow through with dental records or whatever it is they do."

"Oh my God, I don't know what to say. I mean, did he kill himself?" As soon as she'd said it she wished she hadn't.

"I would think it's pretty near impossible to shoot yourself in the face with a shotgun and then have time to dispose of the weapon before you die," he said savagely.

"But Sam – that means he was murdered! Oh no, who would..." Victoria faltered and, again, wished she had said nothing. The thoughts furiously charging through her mind raced from possible suspects to reasons – to Sam. He would have so much to gain with George dead – but never enough for murder, surely? She started to pace around the room, her head spinning.

"I am going to have to go Victoria, the police will need to interview me again in a moment I'm sure. Jesus, Victoria, you should have seen the mess in the polytunnel... it's not a sight I will ever forget – his face was blown away, pieces of flesh scattered across the plants, his..."

Victoria cut in hurriedly. "Yes I can imagine it would be horrendous." It was weird – he sounded almost excited, and not as upset as she'd expected – it was probably shock kicking in. She certainly hoped he'd be calmer with the police or he could find himself under suspicion. "Look, I'm really sorry Sam. Please just let me know absolutely anything I can do to help, anything for your sisters too – this must be such a difficult time for you all."

"Sorry but I've got to go, seems the police need to talk to me right now – hang on." The sound was muffled as he put his hand over the mouthpiece and Victoria could hear voices before he continued. "Look, thanks for ringing Victoria, I know you meant well. I'll get back to you once things are quieter here."

The line went dead. Victoria put down her phone and stood stock-still. She had been shocked when she'd heard George had died, but to think that he'd been murdered was horrendous. No one deserved such a violent death and George had become quite kind and friendly towards the end of her interviews for the article. She had been so flattered when he'd chosen to name a violet after her.

In a trance, she walked towards the kitchen table and flopped down into a chair. Her coffee was stone cold but she drank it without thinking, trying to process the new information. She blinked hard but was unable to stop a few tears. Poor George: hadn't he suffered enough in his life from his father's abuse and the lack of love and friendship? And then to lose his life in such an awful way; it all seemed so unfair.

There was a quiet knock on the open back door and she turned to see who it was, hurriedly wiping her eyes. Albert saw her tearstained face and rushed over to her. "Victoria! What's wrong, what's happened?"

Moss shot out of his bed and began dancing around Albert's legs just as Victoria allowed herself to be enfolded in his arms and, not for the first time, felt as though she had come home. Her tears increased for a moment to sobs and then, comforted by his presence, she took a deep breath and pulled herself together.

"Down pup," said Albert as he sat Victoria gently back down in her chair, at the same time stroking the little dog's head. "In your bed now, give your mother a break." Moss seemed to understand she was unhappy and walked slowly back to his bed and curled up.

"It's so sad, George Ansome has been shot, point-blank range Sam said, in one of their prized polytunnels, and it's just shaken me a bit." Victoria sniffed, then smiled gratefully as Albert offered her his huge white handkerchief.

"Well – t'would shake anyone I'd have thought. Murder's not an everyday occurrence, is it?" He patted her arm as if he felt his hug might have over-stepped the mark. Let's get that kettle on."

At that point there was an immense thump and a flurry of bangs and crashes from upstairs that made Albert look up.

"Just Kev and his sidekick working on the bathroom," said Victoria. "I'd made them tea and cake and then Kev had a call from his wife to say George had died. I just assumed that he'd had a heart attack or an accident or something."

She blew her nose. "So I rang Sam to say how sorry I was and ask if I could help and he sounded really odd, not his usual self. I couldn't understand it – and that's when he said that George had been shot and that he had found the body."

"Did he indeed," said Albert looking thoughtful. He walked over to the kettle and proceeded to make her a cup of Earl Grey, some ordinary tea for himself and found two plates for the cake. "Did he indeed."

They drank their tea and ate the cake in silence for a few moments, then – surprisingly, thought Victoria – Albert asked, "So what do you think of the cake?"

Victoria dragged her mind back from the gory scenarios at the nursery and thought about the cake. "It's lovely. I mean, all your cakes are lovely, but this is extra lovely, it's so chocolatey and yet it's so light... but Albert – if feels really odd discussing cake when we were just talking about George being murdered. Don't you think?" She looked at him quizzically.

"Hmmm," he said, still eating. "True. But do you think this cake is as good as it could be?"

Victoria took another forkful and pondered on the question. "Yes. Yes, I think it is."

Albert pursed his lips and nodded. "I reckon you're right. I'll type out the recipe for you again and you can have another go. Maybe I'll stand over you this time."

How important was this blasted cake? Wasn't Albert being a bit too single-minded? It wasn't exactly a matter of life and death and there was poor George... but before Victoria could work up any more indignation Albert broke into her thoughts. "Poor old George. He didn't deserve that, and that's a fact. But 'who done it'? I suppose that's what you're fretting about?"

Victoria felt her cheeks start to colour. "Well, I don't know about fretting, but yes I am concerned. I mean, surely Sam wouldn't do a thing like that! And then to be the one who found the body – seems a bit obvious, doesn't it?"

Albert shrugged. "Might be, might not. I've never thought Sam was the sharpest knife in the box. Good at making himself seem all deep and meaningful, when it was obvious George always had all the family's brains, but none of its charm."

"Oh," said Victoria, rather taken aback by this blunt summary but, at the same time, knowing it was quite correct.

"Why are you so sure it's murder anyway?" he asked, cutting himself yet another slice of cake – where did the man put it all?

"Well, Sam was quite sharp with me about that – he said of course George hadn't shot himself – how could he have managed to dispose of the gun after half his..." she hesitated and then finished

"…his face was shot off?"

"Ah," said Albert and nodded slowly. "Sounds like a shotgun job then if it was as messy as all that."

"Yes, Sam did say it was a terrible mess. Ugh! I don't really want to think about it!"

"It's not impossible to shoot yourself with a 12-bore, but takes a lot of rigging up with a chair and string and…"

"No! Don't tell me any more!" Victoria squeaked, and put her hands over her ears.

"You're the one wanting to discuss whether it's murder or not. Anyway, not only do I not think George was the type to shoot himself, he damned well wouldn't do it in one of his polytunnels. Should think it's shredded, and would make a right mess of his beloved plants too!'

"Albert!"

"Sorry maid. Anyway, I reckon you must be right and someone has finished the poor old bugger off." He glanced at his watch.

"Meeting someone?" Victoria asked sharply and, as ever, wished she had thought before speaking.

"Yes. Feed rep coming in quarter of an hour, so I'll have to push off before too long.

Victoria drank the rest of her tea and avoided looking at him. Why was she being so stupid? Of course it was a feed rep – why did she automatically think it was Carol or some other floozy?

There was a tense silence. "Course, George was a one for picking fights. His brother-in-law, Len, he made his life hell."

"Really? Is that May or June's husband?"

"June's, May's is called Bill."

"So what was the problem between Len and George then?"

"Well George never feels – sorry felt – he owed anyone a living. Len's a bit of a whinger I suppose. A couple of times he asked George for a favour – he wanted to convert one of the farm outbuildings into a workshop. He mends things does Len, quite a clever old boy really. It wouldn't've hurt George, and Len would have done all the conversion work but no, George wouldn't have it." He peered into his empty mug, which Victoria took as a signal and got up to switch the kettle on. "And he asked a lot of June, ordering her about and not appreciating her I reckon, and Len resented that as well."

"Oh dear, George didn't win many prizes for generosity, did he?" She handed Albert his second cup of tea. "Thanks, I'd better not have another slice of cake, two's my limit. You got any biscuits?"

She smiled. "Sorry, no. I think I'll have to get some in to keep Kev and Andy happy, although I know they'd far rather have your cake!"

Albert snorted indignantly. "I bet they would! You get 'em some biscuits, that's more than generous enough!"

"Careful, you're starting to sound like George." She watched, amazed, as Albert proceeded to cut another, smaller, slice.

"Will just have to be cake again then," he said, winking at her. Trying not to be distracted, Victoria turned her thoughts to something else relating to the incident at the nursery. "Oh, I know! What about that farmer chap, Weston?"

Albert frowned. "You mean Charlie Weston? Has the farm next door to Ansomes?"

"Yes, he and George were rowing last time I was there. Sam said it was something to do with access to some land."

He nodded, and sipped his tea. "Yes, heard about that. Mind you, I think I'd've held out against Charlie Weston. He's rolling in it and could afford to pay a lot for the access."

"Yes, but as I understood it George didn't hold out for more money, he sold it to someone else for quite a sensible price just to spite Charlie!"

Albert grinned. "Well, he were a bit of a bully at school was Charlie, I reckon George might've been getting his own back!"

Victoria sighed. "Goodness. But, you don't think Charlie Weston might have…?"

"Murdered George? Nah!" Albert laughed. "He was far too sensible for that! Charlie wouldn't risk everything just to put George in his place. He'll find his way around the problem, like as not. He's as much a businessman as a farmer."

A distant hooting made Albert jump up. "Blast! That'll be Cyril from the feed place and I haven't got the paperwork to hand! Right, I'd best be off." He hesitated. "Will you be alright? I've not an NFU meeting later. I could pop in, but it will be a bit late."

She looked at his anxious face. "I'll be fine, thanks Albert."

"See you tomorrow then?" She nodded as he smiled and hurried out of the door.

Without asking, Victoria made the two workmen more drinks and took them upstairs, removing the used plates and mugs. She called to them through the door. She didn't fancy seeing the state her bathroom must be in at present.

She sat at the kitchen table and switched on her laptop. The mouse hovered over the folder of photos she'd taken at Percy's, but she veered away from them and opened the Swaddlecombe Show programme instead. She really had to get on with this and right now she needed to keep her mind occupied. The distant banging and whistling which would normally have driven her mad was a useful distraction at present.

Victoria had planned the content for each page and was still chasing in logos and text and then designing the adverts as she went along. She was quite enjoying it really and knew that the end result would look a lot more professional than it had before. Who knows? Next year she might even get some more advertisers or manage to get people to pay a little more. She stopped – next year? What was she thinking!

She realised there needed to be an introduction from the chairman, which was the Reverend Ruminant. She'd give him a call about that, but before then she wanted to read through the programme of events. It all seemed terribly organised and formal. The list of judges was extensive and covered vegetables, flowers, floral art, photography, handicrafts, preserves, cookery (here Victoria gave a little yelp) – that must be where Albert's great subterfuge would be entered – and, last but not least, the children's classes.

These sounded adorable and included prizes for three funny-face cupcakes, the tallest weed – in flower – and, rather excitingly, 'animal (max dimension 24 inches) made with vegetables and fruit'!

There was a dazzling array of cups – twenty in all – awarded for everything from best exhibit in the cookery class – surely Albert's goal – to 'best-kept children's pet'.

The rules and guidelines were precise and extensive and Victoria imagined local families, young and old, pouring over the details before the great day arrived, measuring vegetables, grooming pets and baking cakes. It was so lovely and 'homely' and terribly English; she'd had no idea such things still went on.

She perked up when she saw that there were two classes for hens' eggs: 'six hens eggs, all brown', or 'six hens' eggs of any other colour'. Maybe she could have a go at that? She'd be so chuffed it she could win anything. Realistically, though, she thought her best chance might be in the 'tallest flowering weed' class although that, sadly, seemed to be reserved for the children.

The list of events in the main ring was pretty impressive with lots of classes for dogs: 'waggiest tail', the one that could eat the most dog biscuits in one minute and the 'dog looking most like owner'. Victoria glanced at Moss: waggiest tail, maybe, but she couldn't see any resemblance between the two of them. There was also terrier racing, sheep shearing, sheaf tossing, welly wanging and clay pigeon shooting. She wasn't entirely sure what all of these things were, but they all sounded nice and rural. She must make the most of the show in her blog – she was sure most of her readers would think it either highly amusing or very weird!

There were also all the usual stalls, things she remembered from her childhood: candy floss, Punch and Judy, coconut shy, pin-the-tail-on-the-donkey, cream tea tent and, according to the site plan, two huge marquees for the flowers and produce. Goodness, there was so much going on! She was starting to get quite excited and nervous at the same time, not entirely sure how much of this she was supposed to get involved with.

Just then Kev and Andy appeared carrying bits of her bathroom out to their van. She watched, bemused, as her toilet was carried out and then the old wash basin. Various bits of pipe followed, as did Albert's wobbly shelf unit. After that, the disgusting lino was wrestled down the stairs, rolled up like an enormous grubby sausage and finally, the bath itself. This caused much huffing and puffing and Victoria wasn't sure if she was more worried about the men's backs or the state of her walls. Oh well – she'd need to repaint anyway, especially after Kev said "Oops, sorry love!" when a corner of the bath caught on the kitchen doorframe, removing a lump of paint in the process.

Kev stuck his head around the door. "Right then, that's the place cleared! That's all we can do for today. We'll go off, get rid of all your stuff at the council tip and then collect the new bits and pieces, know what I mean?"

"Oh, right." This seemed to be rather a short day but she guessed that now everything was cleared the real work could only start when they began plumbing in the new stuff. "So will I see you tomorrow?"

"Hope so! All things being equal, know what I mean. We might have to buzz around a bit collecting everything, but you should see us at some point tomorrow. You be in all day?"

"Erm, I don't know, I hadn't thought. Best to give me a ring. I can always leave a key somewhere, or Albert might be around."

"Right you are then! See ya!" and with a wink, he was gone. The van lurched out of the yard and all was still.

Victoria sighed. Lord, she felt tired suddenly. She poured herself some orange juice and, calling Moss, went and sat next to the hens for ten minutes. The day was warm, but hazy. The weather hadn't returned to its former glory since the great flash flood, but the forecast said it would in a day or two. She sat back and closed her eyes.

She jumped as she heard a male voice calling "Coo-ee, Victoria?" and for a terrible moment she thought it was Percy Shooter back from the dead, but as Moss bounded across the lawn she saw Edwin Ruminant waving at her. "Edwin, how lovely to see you, I'd just sat down for an orange juice and a few minutes with the hens. Will you join me?"

"Well, I am in a bit of a rush, but I've certainly got ten minutes. Orange juice would be lovely."

They settled themselves in the deckchairs and Victoria felt very comforted by his presence. Perhaps this was what made him such a popular vicar; there was something about him that soothed the nerves. "I was going to call you this afternoon to ask if you'd written your introduction to this year's show programme?" Victoria had a feeling she already knew the answer, but looked at him enquiringly anyway.

"Oh dear me, no. Well, to be quite candid with you, it's the same message every year. I just change the dates and slip in a topical remark or two. Rather like rewriting the pantomime scripts to bring them up to date. Or my sermons, come to that!" He gave his funny little high-pitched giggle, and Victoria laughed too.

"Do you think you could have a go at it for me? I'm sure it will be fine, just edit it a bit and let me read it through, would you be a dear?"

"Yes of course, that's not a problem."

"Oh my word, I've just thought of something!" He put his hand to his mouth. "We'll need a new flower judge. My dear – have you heard?"

Victoria's mind was spooling back through her perusal of the programme; she didn't remember the names of the judges.

"Poor Mr Ansome has died," said Edwin quietly. "I do hope that hasn't come as too much of a shock – I believe you knew him a little through your work?"

"No, it's alright, I had heard earlier. Of course I was shocked, especially as it seems, well, as if he has been killed." Victoria didn't really want to be viewed as a gossip, but then again...

The vicar sat bolt upright and the old deckchair creaked ominously. "Really?"

"Well, I was speaking to his brother, Sam, and he said he'd been shot, but there was no weapon, so one assumes..."

Edwin nodded slowly. "Well yes, one would, wouldn't one. Oh dear. Oh dear, oh dear!" He shook his head. "And what with poor Percy Shooter the other week, Mr Groves, the gravedigger won't know what's hit him!"

"Mr Groves, the gravedigger?" repeated Victoria, trying to keep a straight face.

"I know, unfortunate, isn't it. Many times I have called the poor man Mr Graves the grovedigger." He sighed and shook his head.

"Lamentable. But then, being called Ruminant, I have no right to comment."

He slapped his chubby knees and began the laborious process of extracting himself from the deckchair. "Well my dear, I regret I have to get to Westerley on some church business, so I must make a move. Are you getting on alright with the programme in general?"

"Yes and I'm doing some work on it this afternoon. I seem to be writing and designing most of the adverts myself! I hope this will go down alright with everyone?"

"I am sure it will be capital and a great improvement. We will need to get posters out PDQ, as they say, but I'm sure you have that and the press releases all in hand! Our meeting is next Tuesday in the Arms. Can you make it?"

Victoria had not the faintest idea, but smiled and said she was sure she would.

The vicar went over to the chicken netting and peered at the hens. "They are looking well! Are they laying?"

"Oh yes, very well, the eggs are wonderful."

"Excellent, just make sure Mr Fox doesn't get to them and all will be well. And young Moss, you're growing fast, aren't you? Oh dear – there's not much of that chair leg left." They regarded the chewed deckchair and the reclining puppy next to it, a look of innocence on his face.

"I think these deckchairs have had their day, so I'm not going to worry about it."

"Well, I must go, thank you for the juice… George Ansome, killed, well I never." He shook his head and headed back towards his trusty Morris Traveller, still shaking his head as he went.

Victoria carried Moss inside and put him in his crate for a rest. She looked at her mobile phone. No messages. She picked it up, then put it down, then picked it up and dialled the Ansome

Nursery number. After quite a number of rings a woman answered, cautiously. "Hello?"

"Oh, hello, is Sam there please?"

"Who wants to know?"

"It's Victoria, Victoria West. Is that June?"

"Yes it is. I'm sorry to sound so strange dear but, well, we've had all sorts of calls and I was a bit worried who it might be."

"I'm sorry to trouble you, but I wondered how Sam was? I spoke to him earlier and, well, he sounded rather odd and I have been worried about him." She sat down. "Is he there? Could I have a word with him?"

There was a pause, and then: "I'm sorry, no, you can't. They found the gun, see. The police have found the gun, chucked in a ditch along the lane from the farm entrance."

"Oh I see. Isn't that good news?" asked Victoria.

June dropped her voice and spoke conspiratorially. "Well, you might think so but no, no it's not. It's Sam's you see."

Victoria was confused. "What is?"

"It was Sam's gun dear, they found it in the ditch and it'd been recently fired and they think it's the murder weapon. So they've arrested him."

"Arrested Sam?" Victoria was glad she was sitting down. She found her heart was racing.

"Yes, they put handcuffs on him and all. It were terrible. He went as white as a sheet, poor lamb."

"Oh my goodness."

"Well, it doesn't look good, does it? I mean, those two always arguing and that."

Victoria was stunned. "But June – you can't possibly think Sam did it?"

"Well not really, no. But you never know what people will do when they're riled, do you? And it was his gun. I said to the police, you never know someone 100% do you? Even your own brother."

Victoria couldn't believe her ears.

"Oh now, there's a policeman making a face at me – I think he wants to ask me something, so I'd better hang up now Victoria," and before Victoria could say anything else, the line went dead. She stared at her phone for a moment and then tucked it in her pocket. "Come on Moss, I need a walk to clear my head."

Victoria walked Moss around the farm, but her mind was elsewhere and she was oblivious to the glorious birdsong and the clearing western sky, worrying instead about what had happened at the nursery. Who would shoot George? She was sure Charlie Weston had looked angry enough. Or was it Sam? Had he finally snapped? She really didn't think he had it in him. And what was June thinking, saying things like that? It was almost as if she was wanting her to think it was Sam. Victoria stopped and chewed her lip. Was that it? Was someone – his own family? – trying to frame Sam?

Moss yapped impatiently. "Sorry," she said. "I was just having some rather ridiculous thoughts Moss. On you go." She put the chickens to bed and then made herself a cheese sandwich. Really, she must do something about her diet; she was getting worse, not better.

To keep her mind occupied she rummaged about in some cupboards in the lounge, a room she never seemed to spend any time in. It was more of a winter room with its large inglenook and dark, panelled walls. For the summer, she was enjoying the light and airy kitchen with its door out into the garden. She poked around in the cupboard, which was built into the old stone wall and quite damp. She found some old newspapers, mouldy and unreadable, an ancient lampshade, equally ruined... and an old-fashioned china potty! She smiled and held it up to the bare light bulb hanging in the middle of the room. The chamber pot seemed to be in perfect condition. Perhaps it was worth something? It was quite ornate and she thought it might look quite nice in her new bathroom with a potted palm sitting in it. But no, she reminded herself, she always managed to kill houseplants. Perhaps she'd just use it as an ornament and put some bath and shower products in it.

As she passed the grandfather clock in the hall, she realised it was ten o'clock. Might as well head off to bed, she sighed. Not for the first time she was aware of missing Albert's company, his cheerful smile and just his very presence.

She trudged upstairs, opened the bathroom door and stopped dead. Stripped of bath, toilet and other bits and pieces, the room looked quite large. Victoria stared dumbly at the pipes sticking up out of the floorboards. She sighed and rested her head on the doorjamb. "Victoria West, you are an idiot!" she said aloud and plodded back downstairs to wash in the kitchen sink and make use of her newly discovered chamber pot.

Chapter 8

Victoria tiptoed out of the back door, her eyes scrunched up against the early morning sunlight. It had no right to be so bright so early. She pulled her dressing gown tighter around her, her wash bag dangling from her wrist, swearing under her breath as she stumbled on a stone. This early-morning excursion across the farmyard was not her idea of a good time and she could cheerfully throttle Kev if he bounced around the corner now – but actually she had to take some of the blame. It never crossed her mind that she might be left overnight with no bathroom and, even worse, no toilet. What had he been thinking? What had she been thinking not discussing it with him!

She was embarrassed having to ask Albert if she could use his bathroom but it seemed preferable to squatting behind a shrub in the garden. She knocked on his back door and hoped he wouldn't take too long to answer. Despite the sun, it was still quite chilly.

The door opened and Albert, looking irritatingly bright and breezy, grinned at her.

"Victoria – well, there's a thing! Bit early for you isn't it? And…" he waved at her clothing and tried to suppress a smile, "you seem to have forgotten to get dressed!"

"Ummm, well, it's a bit embarrassing really." She was finding his cheery grin less than endearing this morning. "The thing is, I really need to borrow your bathroom if that's possible. Kev has left me with no facilities at all and I, well I do really..." She tailed off and hoped he got the drift.

Albert's smile spread and he opened the door wide. "A real damsel in distress. You'd better come in then maid!" The smile got wider and wider and broke into a laugh as Victoria pulled her dressing gown tighter around her in an attempt to maintain her dignity. "It's really not funny Albert. I feel very embarrassed and more than a little angry with Kev."

"Yes obviously," said Albert, the grin not leaving his face. "You women are all hopeless with toilets and the like. There's a perfectly good field out there, you know!"

"Albert! Stop teasing me – it's not funny!"

Albert cleared his throat. "OK, you get yourself into the kitchen and I'll put the kettle on."

"Er, no Albert, I really do need the bathroom first."

He laughed, but turned it into a cough as she shot him a look. "Sorry, of course, well you know where it is, upstairs first on the right. You've got your toiletries and whatnot by the look of it – so why don't you have a nice long relaxing bath and I'll get some breakfast underway. I'll also go and sort that scoundrel Kev Wilks out when he gets here."

Victoria swallowed her pride and walked past him with her head held high, then rushed up the stairs to the bathroom.

She ran a hot bath and lay there with her eyes closed. She almost snoozed for a few minutes until the water began to cool, then added a bit more hot. It was chilly in the bathroom despite the warm weather; these older houses stayed cool even in hot weather, she supposed. Then she realised that the window was wide open and the net curtains were gently swaying in the breeze. She supposed Albert was a fresh air fiend, leading such an outdoor life. She contemplated climbing out to close the window, but instead sank further down into the fragrant water.

She heard a loud slamming of car doors and, listening to the voices, guessed Kev and Andy had appeared.

"Now then young Wilks, I want a word with you!" That was definitely Albert.

"Morning Albert, another nice one then."

"Well not so nice if you're Miss Victoria West. What do you mean by leaving the maid no toilet or anything?"

"Aw come on mate, she just stayed at yours, surely? I know your reputation with the ladies, know what I mean? She never said nothing about needing a temporary set-up."

There was a pause and Victoria sat up suddenly, clutching her sponge and straining her ears to hear Albert's reply. "Well, that's just where you'd be wrong, so I suggest..." and their voices faded away and disappeared as they went into her cottage.

She sighed. Albert's reputation with the ladies seemed to keep smacking her in the face. She sighed again and climbed carefully out of the bath onto a rather slippery lino floor, then towelled herself dry with far more vigour than was strictly necessary. In the distance, she heard the front door bang as Albert returned from sorting out Kev.

As she walked down the stairs the wonderful smells of freshly brewed coffee and toast wafted up to meet her. "Ah right, there you are then," said Albert, looking up as she came in. "All better? You look all pink and newly scrubbed!"

"Thank you for the loan of your bath, I do appreciate it. I do feel much better now."

"Well that's all good then." He looked down at the pan he was stirring carefully. Mmmm – scrambled eggs, she thought. He walked over to a new shiny looking French coffee jug with plunger and tentatively pressed the top.

"Can I help?" asked Victoria, hoping she wasn't being too bossy. He did look as if he wasn't sure how it worked.

"Nope. All fine here thanks, it may be new but it can't be too difficult. It's the same plunger thing you have so I'm sure it's not beyond me."

"Well, I think I'd try adding the hot water as well as the coffee before you press down the plunger..." Victoria tried to stifle a smile, but it crept out anyway.

"Yes right bleddy funny, as if I ... oh!" He stared at the empty pot. "Damn, you're right, that'll need water. I was just about to do that when that Wilks character bowled into the yard and distracted me." Albert boiled the kettle again and casually filled the pot.

"That looks lovely – I can't wait for a cup!" Victoria tried to get the right balance of excited-happy-coffee-enthusiast and annoying-neighbour-who-had-been-proved-right.

"Well, you'll have to wait a bit as I s'pect this stuff needs to stew, or brew, or whatever it does. I done the pup by the way – ran him round the field and back, so don't listen if he tells you he's a poor neglected soul. And I fed him too!"

"Thank you, that's very kind." Victoria was feeling somewhat 'managed'; all she'd needed was to borrow his bathroom facilities for a wash, but now this seemed to be turning into a full-blown rescue operation.

"Right, sit down right there, scrambled eggs on toast coming up – a decent breakfast for a change, bet you rarely feed yourself right."

Victoria's initial reaction was to make some comment about being perfectly able to look after herself but, frankly, she was rubbish at it and it was wonderful to have somebody taking care of her – and the breakfast he was putting in front of her really did look delicious.

Albert joined her at the table with a matching plate. They both ate in silence for a while, partly because conversation seemed difficult but also because they were both really enjoying her hens' beautiful eggs and Albert's expert scrambling.

Once he had finished his plateful, Albert mopped his mouth with a napkin and scraped his chair back from the table. He put the coffee pot, milk and two mugs on the table, folded his arms, and sat back. "Right then, I think it's time we had a bit of a chat."

Victoria felt distinctly uncomfortable, and wondered where this was heading. "I'm sorry?"

"Look Victoria, we need to sort this out. Why are you being so distant? I've obviously done something wrong, but you haven't told me what. Now seems to be the ideal time so, please – will you talk to me?"

"Well…" She paused, partly because she wasn't sure what to say and partly because she still had several forkfuls of egg left. "Well, it's difficult." He watched her intently as she finished off her scrambled eggs. "I'm not sure where to start really…" Albert sighed. Gaining confidence, she looked up at him sharply and said, "I found some pictures, that evening when we went to Percy's."

"Pictures? What do you mean, pictures?"

"Look, I'd need my laptop to show you, so maybe we could discuss this another time." She felt cornered and uneasy.

"No, not another time, maid, now. I want to know what's going on."

Victoria looked at his stern face and realised there was no way of avoiding this confrontation. She took a deep breath. "OK, but I do need to go and fetch my laptop."

Albert jumped up. "No, you stay right where you are. You finish that toast and pour the coffee and I'll be right back. Just tell me where it is."

Victoria felt her heartbeat racing. She really didn't want an argument with Albert, especially since he'd just been so kind, but she could see there was no stopping him. "It's on the kitchen table. Careful of the charging lead – it's plugged in."

Albert shot out of the kitchen like a sprinter out of the starting blocks and she was left feeling very unsure about the conversation that was sure to follow. Would he apologise? Would he deny everything? She began chewing her lip in anguish.

Albert was back before she'd even finished pouring their coffee, triumphantly placing the laptop in front of her. "Well, here we are then." Victoria opened it, let it start up, typed in her password and clicked on the folder with all the pictures from Percy's house.

Albert leant forward, peering at the screen intently as she clicked through the pictures of him with Carol, him and Victoria with the identical newspaper poster, yet more of him with Carol and some with yet another woman with a small baby. His face remained impassive. They moved onto pictures of George, Sam and then some more of himself.

Once they had clicked through them all, he sat down at the table and stared at her steadily.

"All those photos were in that room at Percy's?" Victoria nodded and chewed her lip. "What a devious little bloody snitch he was," he said and shook his head. "Spying on me, and you, and everyone like that. He must have been off his head!"

Victoria was frowning; this wasn't the response she'd expected at all. "Well, yes, maybe..."

"So what's all this about then?"

Victoria was starting to feel her anger rise. "Well for heaven's sake, it's obvious, isn't it? There you are with Carol, then with me, then with Carol, then with some other woman and her baby as well. And in some pretty compromising positions too! I mean – what's going on here? I thought we had something special, I…I mean, we were at the start of, perhaps, possibly…" she petered out as Albert's expression got blacker and blacker.

There was a long and very uncomfortable silence. Then he said quietly, "I can't rightly say, Victoria, when I have been more angry and hurt at the same time." He clammed up and Victoria wondered if she should say something or do something.

"But, I mean, can't you see how it looks? To me, I mean? I thought we had something special and then I discover that you seem to think it's quite OK to have several girlfriends on the go at once."

Albert's face grew stony. "Why on earth did you put such an interpretation on those photos? Why do you think that I'm that kind of person? Why couldn't you talk and ask and question like a normal person would? You've been thinking badly of me all this time for absolutely no reason at all."

"But… but it's all there! How can you deny it? The photos of us together outside the shop when everything was so happy and then a matter of hours, for all I know minutes, later – there you are kissing Carol, who I know used to be a girlfriend… so I very much assume she still is!"

Victoria could hear her voice getting shrill, and hated herself. "And who is this other woman here – I assume with Percy's nasty snooping skills that he has unearthed another old flame and – and whose is this child? I mean… and then, everywhere I go everyone talks about what a ladies' man you are and…"

"Now hang on!" Albert banged the table and their coffee mugs jumped. "This is all nonsense and now you've even sunk to bringing in local gossip as evidence!"

"Well, it's all out there – I've heard it time and again!"

"Look, do I get no right to answer here? I'm just found wanting with no chance to defend – no, not even defend – explain myself? That man Percy has a hell of a lot to answer for, only of course he can't. Seems people were right when he said he got what he deserved." He sat back and looked away from her, his eyes blazing.

Tiny niggles of doubt and discomfort were beginning to form in Victoria's mind. Could she have been wrong? "But Albert, the newspaper headline…" she proffered awkwardly, "…they say the camera never lies."

"Well we all know that's not true with today's technology anyway, but with a malicious mind like Percy's and someone as disbelieving as you… it seems anything can happen. There's nothing wrong about those photos, nothing wrong at all." He looked down into his mug and studied the bottom of it, then refilled it from the cafetiere.Having taken a long swig of coffee, he looked straight at her. She felt distinctly uncomfortable and lowered her eyes.

"Let me just tick these things off one at a time, Victoria. The young lady with the baby – far from being anything I should be ashamed of – is my brother Oggy's youngest, Miriam, with her first baby. I don't believe you've had the pleasure of meeting my brother or his family yet, have you? I bumped into Miriam outside the shop and it was lovely to see her and the baby – I'd not seen him as he'd been in the hospital a few weeks before they'd let him come home. He was premature."

Victoria felt as though she was sinking slowly into a quagmire of guilt mixed with a large side order of stupidity. Why had she just taken the photos on face value and not asked him outright?

"Oh. I am so sorry…"

"No!" He held up his hand. "Please don't interrupt – let me just get through them all so you don't have any other crazy ideas about me. I know you've got a problem with Carol, but believe me, you shouldn't have! She's a poor maid – first she lost her husband, which certainly did not turn her into any kind of a merry widow – she was beside herself with grief. Then, not ten days after the funeral, she was diagnosed with breast cancer." At this point he looked up at her and she felt as if she would die of shame.

"I expect that's something you'd know a bit about Victoria, awful nasty thing to go through. The day that picture was taken, I bumped into her outside the shop just as you'd left to come home and she told me she'd had her latest results back and they were all clear. She was so relieved and happy, and I gave her a hug – that's all. Carol has been a friend for nigh on twenty years now and I was as happy as she was to hear she was in the clear."

He swilled the dregs of his coffee in his mug. "I can't tell you how furious I am at the late Percy Shooter. But somehow, it's almost harder to accept that you really thought I could be that kind of person."

Victoria could feel a tear running down her cheek. She felt so ashamed that she had let everything get so out of hand. "Albert, I'm sorry. I have no excuses, I should have spoken out, but I didn't, I couldn't. I'm not good at confronting things. All I can say in my defence, and it's pretty useless, is that I have met so many men that were like that, and who treated me badly, that I just assumed..."

"Well don't bleddy assume with me."

"No, I realise now that I was wrong and that the local tittle-tattle is also totally unfair."

"They're just old maids with nothing better to do. They enjoy talking about people and blackening their characters, surely you realise that? Listen to Jean! There's not a decent soul in Swaddlecombe if you believe her."

Victoria nodded and wiped her eyes. "I'm sorry Albert, I have been a fool. I let a previous experience affect my judgement and I'm really sorry."

"I see," said Albert quietly. "D'you want to tell me about it? It might just help me to understand?"

Victoria took a deep breath. "I don't like talking about it, but I think you are right, I probably should tell you what happened. It was when I had breast cancer. I was seeing a chap – no let's be honest, I was about to move in with someone I loved and who I thought really loved me. His name was Nigel and I'd know him for several years." She blew her nose. "Sorry. Well, it's pretty devastating to be told you have cancer, it can be a really lonely place. My parents, as you know, were both dead and Edith being down here... well, I didn't think it was fair to burden her with it all, but I had Nigel, he was my rock, or so I thought."

"Anyway, he wasn't quite as supportive as I'd expected him to be when I first told him, but he was OK about it. Some men aren't good with illness or weakness and I suppose I just thought he was a bit scared about what it would all involve. He suggested we postpone moving in together to give me more space while I was having treatment, and I could see his point." Albert snorted and folded his arms.

"Luckily for me I had some other very good friends up in London, in particular Gray and Sebastian,who I'd met at an art exhibition a few years before." She smiled as she thought of their first meeting and the hilarious times they had shared since then. "They proved to be true friends and were hugely supportive of me throughout my treatment and surgery."

"So what about matey then? This Nigel character?" asked Albert, looking cross.

"He didn't exactly cover himself in glory. The excuses for not seeing me got more and more frequent and obscure. Although I was off work, the hospital trips and my general tiredness meant I wasn't on the ball and it took me ages to realise he was no longer around that much. I can't say I was very good company at the time, but still, I thought he would have tried to be decent about it." She sipped at her almost cold coffee.

"Anyway, the upshot was, Nigel had started playing the field the moment I told him about my illness – he couldn't cope with it, in fact he was repulsed by it. By the time I'd realised what was happening, he had actually married someone else. And, just to really hammer it home, he had married Lucy, who'd been one of my best friends." There was a silence.

"What he did was bad, but I think what made it worse for me in the end was the lying and deceit. It seemed quite a few friends – if you can call them that – had known and it was all kept from me – the wedding preparations and everything, as they didn't want to 'upset me'. Gray and Sebastian took me away for a wonderful two-week holiday in Antigua, and when I got back I decided to make a fresh start. I cut off all my old contacts, except Gray and Sebastian, and got on with my life. Then, when Edith died, it gave me the chance to start again here, in this wonderful place – and to meet you. It's just so sad that it's Edith's death that made it possible."

Albert sighed and rubbed his face. "Well maid, that's a sad tale if ever I heard one and you are well shot of that nasty piece of work. But look, you daft besom, I care a lot about you and I would have thought I'd made that plain enough. I don't hold with romancing two ladies at the same time, it's not my way of carrying on. But that's not to say I'm not a big fan of pretty women, because I am – but right now the pretty woman I am quite a big fan of is you, Victoria West, despite you being a complete imbecile quite a lot of the time."

Victoria nodded. "Thank you Albert, that's quite the nicest thing you've said to me all day."

He smiled at her and extended his hand across the table.

"I'm sorry maid, sorry for what you've been through, but we're all different and some of us are better than others. So, are we friends again?"

She nodded again and took his hand. "Absolutely, although I don't think I deserve your forgiveness quite so easily."

"Who said it was easy? You will bake that chocolate and beetroot cake, and you will get it right. And what's more, you come out to dinner with me this evening or there will be trouble."

Grinning like a fool, her insides feeling all gooey again, she said, "Oh alright then!", then giggled like a teenager as he put her hand to his lips and kissed it.

They both jumped at a sharp knock on the kitchen door. "Oi! Sorry to break up your cosy little tête-à-tête, but your puppy seems to have eaten one of your slippers, Victoria, then been sick on the mat!" Kev was leaning around the door beaming. "Thought you might wanna come and sort it out! And a cup of tea wouldn't go amiss either! That's assuming you can tear yourself away!" Laughing, he moseyed back across the yard in the direction of Victoria's cottage.

"Well bugger!" said Albert. "I forgot to shut that little devil in his crate. Teeth like needles has that puppy!"

"Oh never mind, I can buy some more slippers," said Victoria, getting to her feet.

"Come here." Albert pulled her to him and gave her a hug. She was very conscious of still being in her nightclothes. Her phobia about her breast surgery still made her terribly self-conscious, even though she knew it was hardly noticeable.

"I'm so sorry, I've been such a fool," she mumbled into his shoulder.

"Yes, but I forgive you. Now, you go and get some clothes on – or the gossips will be having something to say about your reputation, never mind mine. And go and make that irritating bleddy builder some tea. I'll bring your laptop over in a minute." He patted her bottom as she went.

After returning her laptop, Albert went off to check on one of his cows that had something wrong with its foot, and to decide whether he needed to call the vet or not. Now dressed, and the builders furnished with tea and biscuits, Victoria set about clearing up and assessing the remains of her slipper. It was beyond saving, having been scragged to within an inch of its life by a very naughty pup. Moss, now lying quietly in his puppy crate, looked suitably contrite.

"You are a very, very wicked dog," said Victoria sternly and held the ruined slipper in front of his face. The puppy's eyes, large, brown and soulful, slid away from her, unable to face the shameful tattered object. "Oh Moss." She picked him up and cuddled him, burying her face in his warm soft fur. She knew it was completely the wrong thing to do, but she felt so happy now that she and Albert were friends again.

"Come on, let's sneak off and see the hens for ten minutes." She put the dog down and he trotted after her, the whistling and banging of the builders receding as they crossed the garden to the chicken run.

Sitting in a deckchair with the pup on her lap, Victoria went over and over the morning's events in her mind. She felt both relief and intense guilt; she'd been such a fool. She also knew, deep down, that part of her foolishness had been due to having her head turned by Sam. She was old enough to know better – how shallow could you be? She watched the hens go about their daily business, pecking, preening and scratching about in the grass. Why was life so complicated? Maybe she'd come back as a chicken next time... surely that was easier?

But Sam wasn't all bad – a bit of an idealist, a bit of an idler, maybe – but a murderer? No, she was sure not. She'd been stunned by his sister's attitude and wondered if anyone was fighting the poor man's corner? It would be truly awful to be locked up for something you hadn't done. Victoria let her mind wander over those dreaded photographs taken by the horrible snooping Percy. She ought to have another look – there were plenty of other people in them and George and Sam featured in a number. Perhaps there was some clue there?

When Albert reappeared, just in time for afternoon tea, he was surprised to see Victoria looking at Percy's photos again.

"It's not what you think!" she said hurriedly. "Come and sit down, I need to talk to you."

Furnished with tea and a few digestives – "Sorry Albert, but that's the best I can do" – he scowled at the laptop. "Well maid?"

"I don't think I've told you yet about Sam."

Albert paused, his mug of tea halfway to his lips. "What about him?"

"He's been arrested for George's murder."

He put down his mug. "Really?"

"They found a shotgun thrown in a ditch up the lane, and it's Sam's, so they arrested him. I don't understand about these things, but I assume they will know the gun's been fired recently and then they'll do tests and things to see if it was the weapon that killed George and… well, it doesn't look at all good for him."

Albert made a face. "Well, I don't rightly know what to say."

"You don't think he did it, do you?"

"Me? I don't see that it matters what I think, if the evidence points…"

"Yes, yes," said Victoria impatiently, "but what if he's been set up – I mean, we both said he's a terribly weak character and that he wouldn't have the gumption to shoot his brother."

"As far as we know, yes I'd agree with that, but…"

"Well, when I found out he'd been arrested, it was June that told me and she was speaking as if it was a foregone conclusion. No sympathy for her brother; she seemed perfectly happy to accept that he'd done it. And that seems odd to me."

Albert munched on a biscuit. Victoria had often noticed how intense thought on Albert's part seemed to require lots of fuel in the form of calories. "I'd agree with that statement," he said, nodding. "But they're a funny bleddy family the Ansomes really, lots of jealousies and in-fighting. Mind you, I reckon most families are a bit like it."

Sipping her own tea, Victoria turned the laptop towards Albert. "I was looking at these photos that snoopy Percy took." She didn't add that she had deleted all the ones of the two of them. "And there are lots with Sam and George and other people, all shouting and rowing, so Percy knew there was lots of conflict going on."

"Well, they were pretty public about it," said Albert. "I mean, we've all seen poor old George raging at one person or another. I think he used to enjoy it, the old dog! Bit like a terrier, always a bit fightable was George."

Victoria scrolled through the photos. "There's Charlie Weston, all red in the face. There's George and Sam going at it hammer and tongs."

Albert studied the shots. "So who's that then?" He waved a piece of biscuit at the screen.

"I was hoping you'd know that," said Victoria, looking at the person partly obscured in the photo with George. "It looks like it might be a woman to me," she added.

"I reckon you're right. I reckon that might be Madeleine, his niece."

"Oh yes, I met her. Wonder what they were rowing about?"

"Money, I s'pect. The whole family seemed to think that George owed them a living."

"But I thought Madeleine was doing really well. She drives round in that big flashy 4x4."

Albert snorted. "That doesn't mean anything! Her's got a lot of talk and a lot of front that one. She's only buying and selling on eBay, she's nothing special."

Victoria looked confused. "Buying and selling on eBay? She told me she was into buying and selling in specialist markets."

"She would, lot of front, like I said. She's always bidding for stuff, but her problem is she doesn't set herself limits, she gets carried away and bids over the odds for stuff."

"Hang on, how do you know all this?"

Albert tapped his nose. "Uz bayn't be as daft as uz looks maid," he said in his broadest comic Devonshire accent. "If you follow auctions on eBay and you look up sellers' and buyers' track records, you get to know these things. Me and Kev's wife Kelly, we keep our eyes open and we discuss who's looking at what, and what's trending and so on."

"Trending?" said Victoria, looking even more confused.

"Don't you worry your pretty little head about it!" said Albert and waited for her to slap his hand, as she duly did. "Anyway, never mind about Madeleine and her adventures on eBay – didn't you want me to sort out some of Edith's old junk to sell on there for you?"

"Yes, I do but… well, I didn't like to ask before," she said, sheepishly.

"Don't be daft. That's all behind us now, I am very pleased to say."

"It's all jumbled up in these cupboards here, and it's chaos," said Victoria, opening one of the doors. There was a loud crash as whisks and scales and spoons clattered onto the floor.

"Blimey," said Albert. "That's a right Aladdin's Cave. I reckon we can do well with this lot."

"Really? It just looks like bits of old junk to me."

"Well, that just shows how much you know, young lady." They emptied everything out and Victoria found one of the big sturdy cardboard boxes she'd used when she'd moved in. Albert filled it up with all the bits and pieces from the cupboard.

"Right, you can leave that with me. I'll sort through it, photograph it and get it listed."

"Isn't that a lot of work?"

"Not really, I'm used to doing it; got a little studio set up in one of the bedrooms with a light box and stuff to photograph things in. It won't take me too long."

"You never cease to amaze me!" she said, and laughed.

"Let's hope that's how it remains then maid – there's nothing worse than getting boring and predictable."

As if on cue, there was a clatter of feet on the stairs and Kev and Andy appeared. "Right then, that's us done for today. We've installed a loo for you as a temporary measure and we'll be back tomorrow with some of the new items and the flooring."

"Goodness, is it that time already?" Victoria glanced at the clock and saw it was five o'clock.

"Yep and I'm off home to get the barbie out and open a few cans!" said Kev, rubbing his hands together. Andy looked bashful as usual and gave a small wave as they left.

After they'd gone, Albert took her hand. "Let's leave all that kitchen stuff until tomorrow. It's a lovely evening – what do you say we walk the pup around the farm together and then head off for a bite to eat?"

Victoria smiled. "That sounds a lovely idea. I'll just get Moss."

Showing no ill effects from eating half a slipper or from his telling off, Moss bounced along beside them with puppyish enthusiasm. Albert took her hand and they strolled along the farm track between the fields.

"This is the romantically named 'Eight Acres," he said, opening the gate, and Victoria laughed. "Oh," she said, hesitating, "there are cows in here, is it safe?"

"It's fine. Safe as you can ever be around half tonne animals anyway. They're a docile lot. They'll give the pup a glare or two if he gets too boisterous, but he needs to learn not to overstep the mark – and the sooner the better if he's going to be a farm dog."

Albert pulled her forward. "Come on maid, don't be daft." They walked up to a particularly placid-looking beast, stolidly chewing its cud and gazing at the horizon. Albert smacked her rump and began vigorously scratching her back. The cow's eyes half closed and she pushed against his hand, then her tongue began lolling.

"Well! That cow has got the hots for you!" Victoria said, laughing. "What a funny animal! She's completely soppy!" The cow was now swaying slightly.

"Told you they were. Having their backs scratched is pretty much heaven for a cow, bit like a woman having… well, anyway…!" he said and grinned at her. Predictably, Victoria felt herself begin to go pink.

Albert slapped the cow's flank and then moved up to scratch her ears. "Come on now Mary, pull yourself together!"

"She's called Mary?"

"All my cows have names and no – before you even think it – they are not named after my previous lady friends! It's whatever comes to mind. That one there," he pointed to a handsome black-and-white cow, "is called Gin, and that brown one there is Brandy.

Depends on my mood."

Victoria smiled to herself; he was such a funny man. They strolled on. A couple of the cows waggled their heads at Moss as he yapped and lunged, but you could tell they were not really concerned and seemed to know he was playing. "They'll get a bit more feisty with him as he grows bigger. We need to teach him not to chase or nip at them – Collies tend to do that, in their nature to round up things."

"What – even cows?"

"Oh yes," said Albert. "Although he's not pure Collie, I s'pect he's got the instinct, little beggars they can be sometimes. Mind you, a cow will soon put him in his place, especially if she's got a calf."

"Really?"

"Always be careful when you're out walking with a dog if you see cows and calves, probably far more risky than a bull. Mother will always want to protect her young. Same with any animal." He patted a brindle cow as he passed and she continued chewing, untroubled by their presence.

"They smell all warm and grassy, it's rather lovely," said Victoria. "I thought they'd just smell – well sort of cow pooey really."

Albert smiled. "The smell of hay or silage or newly mown grass, you can't beat any of 'em. That and a cow's sweet breath on a summer's morning – lovely! Better than any man-made smell if you ask me."

Victoria felt happier, and lighter than she had for days; it was lovely to be back on good terms with Albert. How idyllic it all was… and there was poor Sam sitting in a police cell, perhaps even a prison cell for all she knew. What did the future hold for him? She really ought to try and see if she could do something to help.

Albert decided to celebrate their renewed friendship by taking his daffodil-yellow Jaguar XJS out to the pub. "Oh, I love this car Albert!" cooed Victoria as she slid into the seductive, low-slung leather seat.

"Not more than Gloria, surely?"

"No, not more, but in a different way." She stretched out her legs and listened to the big engine burble as they pulled away. "Why ever do you have so many cars?"

"Dunno really. I've always had lots of vehicles – tractors, motorbikes and such like –and as I've got the space to store them I just sort of, well, collect them." He shrugged. "None of them is worth a fortune, Gloria's probably the best one. As you know the reason I don't take the Jag out much is thanks to the hole in the fuel tank – so local trips only." He patted the steering wheel. "Never mind, good for trips to the pub."

"And talking of Gloria, I absolutely must get myself a small estate car. I've taken advantage of your generosity for long enough," Victoria stated with conviction.

"Well, I don't mind, and you look rather good in Gloria," he said, grinning.

"Thank you! But I need an estate for Moss and to cart my photography stuff round in really. Perhaps you can keep your eyes open for something for me?"

"Will do. But you're always welcome to take Gloria out for a spin – she enjoys being driven. She's too pretty a girl to spend her life cooped up in my barn."

The Swaddle Arms was busy but on arrival Victoria realised Albert must have booked a table in advance and they had a nice cosy corner spot. The landlord Roger bustled over with menus and a bottle of white wine in an ice bucket. "Goodness!" said Victoria. "This looks smart."

"I reckoned we deserved a bit of a treat." Albert poured them both a glass and they clinked glasses. "To us," he said, blue eyes atwinkle. Victoria smiled. "To us."

The bar was quite noisy with early evening drinkers enjoying a few pints after a hot day's work. Victoria still revelled in the local community atmosphere and was pleased to see she recognised several faces. She was starting to belong.

In a flurry of floral print and frilly apron, Roger's wife Trudy was suddenly in front of them, clutching her notepad. "Well now you two, you look very cosy, you celebrating something?"

Albert gave an enigmatic smile. "I am just enjoying the company of a beautiful woman and that's enough celebration for me."

Trudy's mouth formed a conspiratorial 'Oh' and she moved closer. "Right you are then! Well, you chosen what to eat yet?"

"Nope, give us a few minutes Trudy and we'll be right with you," said Albert raising his glass to her, but she didn't take the hint and moved in closer.

"Course, you know about all the drama at the nursery?" Her eyes were wide now and she was jerking her head in the direction of the bar.

"Yes, we had heard about poor George," said Victoria quietly. She never ceased to be disappointed by Trudy's obvious love of the ghoulish.

Trudy was looking increasing like someone with a severe tic as she kept jerking her head towards the bar. "Got Len Trusscott, June's husband in at the moment, he's had a few, over there, at the bar," she said in theatrically hushed tones. "Not got a good word to say 'bout George and reckons he pushed Sam too far and that's why he done it!"

"Done what?" said Albert, being deliberately obtuse.

"Why, murdered his brother of course! Blood and brains

everywhere there was! And Sam's gun found in the ditch." She folded her arms. "Seems pretty cut and dried to me! Len says he did everyone a favour."

"I think we should wait and see what the police discover, the actual evidence, rather than the gossip," said Albert, making a point of studying the menu. Victoria followed suit, but Trudy was not to be deflected.

"What more evidence do you want? I mean, stands to reason it must've been him! They were always rowing, we all know that, and then t'was his gun!"

"What's your dish of the day then Trudy?" asked Albert, fixing her with a beady eye. Trudy looked bemused and then managed to focus her brain back on the menu. "Oh, right, it's steak and kidney pudding today."

Victoria closed the menu. "Bit too heavy for me on a day like this. I'll have the seafood salad, thanks."

"Good choice," said Trudy as she scribbled on her pad, "fresh in from Dartmouth this morning. Same for you Albert?"

Albert closed the menu shut with a loud snap and glared at her. "You lost your mind Trudy Mudge? Me, order a seafood salad?"

Trudy's hand flew to her mouth. "Oh my, I'm sorry Albert! I don't know what I was thinking."

"You want to worry less about the local gossip and more about the local customers. A beef farmer ordering fish indeed! I'll have a sirloin steak, medium rare with vegetables and chips. And none of your fancy sauces mind."

Trudy scribbled furiously on her pad and then meekly collected their menus and scuttled off.

Victoria giggled. "You rotter, I think you frightened her a bit."

"Frighten Trudy? Take more than me winding her up to do that! Daft maid. Mind you, she's good at what she does, so we ought to forgive her the odd slip, I suppose."

In the background they could hear one man's voice above the general hubbub. "Hmmm, that's Len, seems to be getting himself well stewed," said Albert, sipping his wine.

Victoria tried to ignore the man's voice, but she couldn't help overhearing, as he was getting louder and more slurred by the minute. "He had it coming to him! Silly old bugger! I said to him, I said 'George, you're delib – er – deliberately difficult! You've always been obstrop – obstruc – obstructive to me!'" Other voices chimed in, trying to placate him. "No, no! S'true! He were a mean man. He made enemies and I needs to support my family. We shan't miss him and I told him I'd get my workshop one way or another!" Then there was lots of laughter.

"Oh dear," said Victoria, sipping her wine.

"One of the down sides of close communities I suppose," said Albert and squeezed her hand. "Hope it's not going to put you off?"

"No, of course not. I love it here."

"I said to June, I said, that George will push someone too far one of these days! And look what's happened, aye? Sam's gone and lost it. I was right see. Pushed my family too far." In the general chatter voices could be heard saying "maybe you've had enough", "time to go home, Len", and then "Get his car keys Mike, he can't drive home like this. Someone call June, or Madeleine, or someone."

"Well, not everyone's daft with drink anyway," remarked Albert.

"Do you think it was Len? He seems to be getting in a real state."

"No, surely not. If you'd shot someone you wouldn't go down the pub and shout about it, would you?"

Victoria sighed. "Lord, I don't know, but I'm sure it wasn't Sam."

"I'm inclined to agree with you there maid, but I don't see what we can do about it."

There was a commotion at the bar as Len, now incoherent, stumbled as he was helped to the door. "Bye all!" he slurred and waved, as two burly men helped him outside.

"I'm just worried there's going to be a major miscarriage of justice here as everyone seems happy for it to be Sam to save a lot of bother and that's just not right!"

"But the police have got to do all their forensic stuff, and whatnot yet. They're not complete idiots." Albert paused. "Mind you, they do have their moments, but I reckon we should leave it to the professionals."

Just then, Trudy barrelled into view carrying two large plates that she plonked down on the table. "There you go my lovers! A lovely big juicy steak for you, Albert, and a delicious platter of seafood for you, Victoria! Now that loudmouth Len Trusscott's gone, maybe we can all have a pleasant evening! Any condiments for you?"

"Ketchup and vinegar for me," said Albert, rubbing his hands together in eager anticipation.

"Mayonnaise for me, please," said Victoria, eyeing the glistening prawns, cockles and smoked salmon.

As Trudy bustled off, Albert peered at her plate and pulled a face. "Ugh! How can you eat that stuff?"

"Easy!" she said and, grinning, popped a prawn into her mouth.

Chapter 9

"Left a bit mate."

"I'm trying… I'm trying…"

"Gawd's sake! I know you're small but try having another Weetabix for breakfast. Put it down for a bit." Kev huffed and puffed as he lowered his end of a very long, unwieldy roll of wood-effect vinyl flooring destined for Victoria's bathroom.

So far they had only reached the front door. Victoria watched from the window and wondered whether she should laugh at their almost Laurel-and-Hardyesque progress from the van to the door, or panic as they had yet to navigate her old and rather narrow staircase.

She went through to the kitchen and switched on the kettle. The least she could offer would be a cup of tea or coffee once they'd reached the bathroom. There was an ominous sound of swearing followed by a thump. Moss, ears flat to his head, gave a feeble whine and slunk under the table; he didn't like the look of how the lino was progressing either. Victoria decided, on balance, that it would be less nerve-racking to keep clear until it was all over.

The previous day had tested everyone's patience with new boarding being laid over the old uneven and tatty floorboards, resulting in a great deal of hammering, whistling and swearing. Moss had been as unimpressed as Victoria and they had both slunk off for a long walk in the middle of the day to avoid the chaos.

The pile of junk accumulating outside the back door was also something Victoria hadn't thought about; she had just assumed Kev would magic it away. Now, it seemed, a skip was needed.

She made herself a coffee and sat down to enjoy the brief silence which, she felt sure, was just the lull before the storm. After a while, she roused herself from her reverie and wondered if it had been quiet for long enough and whether now was a good time to offer them some refreshment. Slowly she peered round the kitchen door, but there was no sign of either man or the offending roll of flooring. She crept to the bottom of the stairs; still no sign. Tentatively she called out, "Hello? Kev, Andy? Would you like a cuppa?"

"Well it's your flamin' fault, you said hard left!"

"Yeah, but, not THAT hard left – what use is a roll of lino in a spare bedroom? And how the hell do we get it out of here now?"

Victoria sighed and went quietly up the stairs. She found the two men sitting on the floor of the small spare bedroom, hot and very bothered, squashed in with the long roll of lino between them.

"Hi, sorry to interrupt, either of you fancy tea or coffee?"

Two sets of grateful eyes looked up at her and both men nodded.

"He said hard left," said Andy defensively.

"But why back into the spare room at a hundred miles an hour so I couldn't stop you and had to follow?"

"Well I was going backwards and I couldn't see and…"

"I'll go and make those drinks," said Victoria quickly. "I'm sure you'll get it sorted."

She crept away and made their drinks and put a full sugar bowl and an entire packet of biscuits on the tray in the hope that some extra energy might help solve their problems.

Once they were fed and watered – and sounding more positive, with a plan to poke the lino out of the window as part of their exit strategy – Victoria sat at the kitchen table and contemplated her own problems. She was still confused by everyone's attitude to George's death; nobody seemed to be mourning his loss. In the short time she'd known him she had glimpsed the kindness and slight shyness that lurked beneath the bluster and grumpiness. Maybe more questions were in order? She just couldn't put the idea of Sam being innocent out of her mind – the whole thing just didn't ring true. But on the other hand she had been wrong before, and she knew she wasn't the best judge of character.

She dialled the number. "Good morning, Ansome Nurseries, June speaking, how may I help you?"

"Oh hello June." Victoria was somewhat taken aback by the professionalism of the phone answering. "It's Victoria here, Victoria West. I just wondered how you were all getting on and whether there was any news of Sam?"

"Oh everything is running just fine here, thank you Victoria," replied June. "It's magic being able to do all the stuff George always refused to let us do. New packing benches and new storage for all the paperwork ordered and arriving next week and, of course, Len is like a dog with two tails working on his workshop over in the barn. So lovely to see everyone getting on and doing what they'd always wanted without all that negativity and argument. I tell you the place is transformed!"

Victoria stared at the phone and frowned; it all seemed so wrong. "Oh well – that's all good then, I suppose. What news of Sam? I am so worried about him."

"Oh I expect he's fine. I am sure they are looking after him alright dear, don't you worry."

"That's not really what I meant June, I meant…"

"Well, I know, being in prison can't be fun, but surely you can't get away with murdering your brother, can you now? I know it's all worked out for the best as far as we're concerned, but it's not right, is it, and he has to pay."

Victoria wondered if she was hearing the woman correctly. She took a deep breath and mustered her thoughts. It was important to try and find out if he was really guilty; and if she didn't it was clear nobody else was even going to try.

"Can I just ask, was Sam always really careful with keeping his gun locked away? I just wondered, as he didn't seem the meticulous sort?"

"Heavens no," replied June. "Bit late now but Madeleine was always telling him to keep it locked up in the gun cabinet. Of course, she knows a lot about guns, does Madeleine, she and Len done lots of clay pigeon competitions. Shame she gave up on it when she started doing those teenage things, boys and dances and what have you!"

"So Sam didn't always lock his gun away like he's meant to?" That sounded ominous to Victoria, who found the whole concept of guns terrifying.

"No, I remember he had it propped up in the kitchen for ages, even George told him to get the damned thing put away."

"Oh dear, well I expect you told the police that..."

"They never asked. Not my place to tell them more than they ask, sooner that lot left the better, muddy feet everywhere messing up the house. Now what was it you wanted dear, as I am very busy? Did you want to order some nice violas for your hanging baskets?"

"Oh, I err... just wanted to ask someone to send a message to Sam to say I'm thinking about him, that's all."

"Well I'm sure if anybody sees him they'll pass that on. Now I must get on, bye for now."

Victoria sat down at the table and drank the rest of her now cold coffee. How unfeeling could a sister be... did June really hate

Sam that much? Suddenly there was a loud thud, then a volley of grunts and minor swear words out in the hall. She rushed to see what the commotion was. There stood Kev and Andy with a long rectangular package that she could only guess might be her shower cubicle. "Everything OK out here?".

"Yeah fine, just fine, Shortie didn't need his feet anyways. Daft beggar dropped the end of the shower, hurt a bit I expect, that's why we wears steel-toe-capped boots. Come on then mate, put your back into it."

A very pale-looking Andy picked up the end of the large package and they manoeuvred their way up the stairs with much mutual huffing and puffing.

"Hulloo, anyone home?" came Albert's voice from the back door.

Victoria returned to the kitchen and smiled. "Hello you! Will you come in and have a cup of tea?"

Albert smiled back. "Bet you haven't got a piece of cake to your name – doesn't encourage a bloke much! Poor do when he 'as to bring his own cake." He produced a tin from behind his back that no doubt contained something cakey and delicious.

Victoria switched on the coffee machine and the kettle, while Albert grabbed a plate and put out some totally irresistible chocolate brownies. "Wow, you certainly know the way to my heart," she grinned at him. "Would it be OK to take one up to the boys upstairs? They're having a pretty tough day of it."

"Well just the one, cut in half, only seems right and proper."

"Could you just take it up to them while I get our drinks sorted? I've not long done drinks for them so they're fine on that front, but cake always helps with lugging things about."

Albert opened the kitchen door and quickly stepped back as Kev, Andy and a hand basin marched past and up the stairs. Albert looked back at her. "I see what you mean."

Once the brownies had been delivered he sat at the table sipping his tea, and said between mouthfuls, "So what's new with you today?"

"Hmmm, mainly bathroom-related traumas for the lads, but I just rang Ansomes – really just to see if there was any news about Sam."

Albert's face clouded over. "And?" he said, taking another mouthful of brownie.

"Well it was strange, and I have to say not very pleasant. June answered and was bright and breezy, full of how good everything was and how wonderfully they were reorganising everything."

"What about Sam?" said Albert, looking intently at her.

"Well that was the worst of it – she just didn't seem to care! I got talking about Sam's gun with her, just an idea I had. Anyway, seems it was rarely locked up properly, so surely anyone could have grabbed it. Did you know Madeleine was an experienced shot?"

"Yes, course, the whole family is pretty good. June was a real hotshot in her day, won prizes left, right and centre."

"June? Ha! She never mentioned that, she just said that Madeleine and her dad used to shoot a lot, never mentioned that she did."

"Not being rude maid, but frankly pretty much everyone round here knows how to use a shotgun. It's just a way of life, goes with the territory – shooting vermin, magpies, those damned foxes when they go after nice townie ladies' hens!" He raised his eyebrows at her.

Victoria felt very townie indeed at that point. She was really nervous around guns and the thought of using one scared the life out of her. It was a weird concept to her that whole families would shoot together: her family had preferred playing Monopoly or Scrabble.

"Oh, so I didn't really uncover much of a clue when she said his gun was often lying around – it could have been anyone that used it." Victoria frowned and felt deflated, just when she'd thought it might have been a lead. "It feels as though the family has just walked away from Sam. He just seems too convenient, a scapegoat, and I wish I could do more to investigate."

Albert didn't seem overly impressed. "There's no doubt plenty going on at the police station about all this and I wouldn't be so sure Sam isn't guilty. Very convenient that not many people were around and his gun was just lying there – and you know how badly those two argued – maybe Sam just lost it," he shook his head, "but I must say I didn't think he had it in 'im."

"But the rest of the family just seem content to accept the fact that George was murdered and are happy to leave Sam rotting in jail while they enjoy all their new-found freedom. What about if it was one of them who killed him?"

"Doesn't seem that likely to me. Shooting isn't usually a woman's crime and they were frustrated by George, yes – but shooting him? I think you're just reading too much into everything. Leave it to the police, they know what they're doing."

"But..."she started.

"Now look," Albert butted in, "we've got better things to do than play detectives today, I brought round some beetroot." He indicated the back-door step where sat a bunch of small muddy balls with tattered leaves. "But I'll be betting you haven't got the other 'gredients in stock to make that chocolate and beetroot cake?"

"Well no, predictably I haven't," smiled Victoria, "but I could nip down to the shop and stock up."

"Done deal. I haven't had a trip out in Gloria for a while, would be nice to get a bit of wind in my hair!"

"Well I need to leave a note for Jean. She's just coming to clean downstairs today. Kev and Andy scared her away last time, making more mess than she cleaned up in the first place, so she said 'no more upstairs cleaning until they're done finished'!"

Victoria scribbled a note explaining they wouldn't be long, in case Jean arrived while she was out. She shouted up the stairs to Kev and grabbed her purse.

Automatically she walked towards the driver's door but the hangdog expression on Albert's face was easily interpreted and instead she handed him the keys. Albert smiled and started folding down the roof as Victoria slid into the passenger seat, thinking how lucky she was: a lovely man, a pretty car to drive (or rather be driven in) and the sun making everything look so beautiful. She gazed across at the pansies she had bought out at Ansomes – it seemed ages ago now – and admired their bright and prolific flowers. She thought that poor old George had probably nurtured them himself and marvelled at how nature just kept on growing and evolving, never pausing, and how human life, in contrast, was so fleeting.

They zoomed down the lanes, Albert as always assuming that nobody else would be coming towards him, when a Land Rover did just that. It was black, but so covered in dried mud and dust it looked sandy brown, and the passenger seat seemed to be filled with a large roll of wire netting. The driver, she realised after a moment or two, was Charlie Weston.

Albert backed up a little to a spot where the lane was just wide enough for two cars to pass and, as he drew level, Charlie wound down his window. "Nice for some eh? Flashy sports car in the sunshine and a beautiful woman, not a lot more a man needs, eh?"

Victoria smiled stiffly and decided she really didn't like this man.

"Ah, but there are some other things a man needs," smiled Albert in response. "We're off to the shop for supplies for some cake baking, can't beat a good home-made cake. Victoria here wants to practise for the village show."

"Coo, you lucky bugger, some men get it all!"

Albert glanced at Victoria and gave her a reassuring wink. He clearly recognised that Charlie was not her cup of tea.

"So, rum news about old George, eh?" said Albert carelessly.

"Dunno about rum," replied Charlie, "more like champagne in my case. Good riddance to the old bugger and full speed ahead for my building plans, I say. The family'll be a pushover if I ups the offer a bit, deal done, land sold!"

"Ah yes, of course, you need that access to your land," said Albert, as if he'd only just realised it. "Bit of a shock to hear Sam is in the nick though, you think he dunnit?"

"Who bloody cares, I say," replied Charlie, leering at Victoria and giving her a very pronounced wink of his own (one with completely different meaning to the one she'd just received from Albert). "S' long as I am on my way to a bundle of money that's all that makes Charlie Weston 'appy."

Victoria shivered with distaste and glared at Albert trying to send a 'hurry up' message, but he seemed oblivious. "Tough on the family though, losing two brothers so to speak. Old George was OK underneath, just a bit of a grumpy old sod on the surface – but then he'd suffered a lot when he was younger, as you'd know."

Charlie hesitated and looked quite aggrieved for a moment, then seemed to rethink what he'd been about to say. "Nothing he didn't deserve as a youngster, and he'd more than taken his pound of flesh off me once he could. Nah, good riddance I say, good riddance to 'im and Sam!"

With that he waved, gave a toot and squeezed past Gloria, getting very close to the wing mirror, which Albert hastily pulled in.

"What a horrible man!" Victoria burst out as the Land Rover's dust wafted over Gloria's lovely bonnet. "I'll bet it was him! He had means, motive and, oh damn, what's the other thing?"

"Opportunity," said Albert selecting first gear and roaring off down the lane in typical 'local' fashion.

After a rather exciting dash through the lanes, Albert brought Gloria to a rapid halt outside the village shop. "Phew!" said Victoria. "If I'd been wearing a hat, I'd've been holding onto it!"

Albert laughed. "Well maid, no point hanging about." He lowered his voice. "Now, you know what you gotta buy, I don't want to have to prompt you, it'll look odd."

She sighed. "Oh really, this is so silly! Yes, I do know…" She rummaged in her bag and recited: "'Dark chocolate, cocoa powder, plain flour, baking powder, caster sugar' – the beetroot and three large eggs we already have."

Albert strode up to the front of the shop. He peered at Lavender's bargain basket and shook his head. "'Tis a sad state of affairs that is."

"Oh, I don't know, I sometimes see quite interesting metaphors and artistic leanings," said Victoria, eyeing the basket from different angles.

Albert scowled. "You are having me on, aren't you?"

She broke into a broad grin. "Perhaps!" He snorted and opened the door for her with such a flourish that it sounded as if the bell would jump right off the doorframe.

"Oh my!" said Iris Drew, patting her chest as if in shock. "Mr Moreton – you did make us jump!" Albert came to an abrupt halt as he saw a cluster of elderly women's faces all turned towards him with startled expressions on their pale and wrinkled countenances.

"I'm sorry ladies, I was a trifle over-manful with the door there."

There was a general tittering and fluttering and Victoria heard "Manful!" repeated several times, somewhat breathlessly, from the gaggle occupying the body of the shop. At least six ladies of senior years were all clutching baskets and bags and clearly having a really good gossip with the Drewe sisters who stood ranged behind the counter.

"Well," said Albert, rubbing his hands together. "I reckon 'tis a bit crowded in here, so I'll leave you ladies to it. I'll let you get your shopping sorted out Victoria, and I'll wait in the car," and he shot out of the door like a frightened rabbit.

Victoria hid her smile as she delved in her bag for her purse and shopping list, while the ladies continued their musings. She picked up a lettuce and some tomatoes, not wanting to be seen just buying the cake ingredients. Two of the elderly ladies were paying and this seemed to take an eternity as purses were mislaid, found, then dropped, and change was sorted and counted. Eventually, they left.

Daphne smiled at Victoria expectantly. "Well dear, what can I help you with?" The remaining elderly ladies were now in a huddle apparently discussing knitting patterns, but Victoria wasn't entirely sure. She handed over the tomatoes for weighing and asked if they sold cocoa. "Of course, here you are." Iris brandished a popular make at Victoria, who nodded her approval, and it was dropped into a carrier bag along with the tomatoes and lettuce.

"Do you have any of that nice nutty brown bread left?"

"We do!" said Iris, lunging for a loaf in the bakery cabinet. She seemed to be the one doing the fetching and carrying today, while Daphne held centre stage at the till.

"I also need some more of that fine dark chocolate, a bag of flour, baking powder and sugar," recited Victoria.

"Baking a cake are we? That'll be nice!" grinned Iris.

"Erm, yes, possibly," said Victoria realising she wasn't managing to deceive anyone with her decoy shopping items. "And some butter," she finished rather lamely.

"That's nice. Your aunt used to bake some lovely cakes, didn't she Lavender?" said Iris.

Lavender nodded slowly. "She always used to win prizes at the show," she said in her deep, rather husky voice. "One year, I remember I'd been poorly, and she made me a lemon drizzle cake. I preferred her Victoria sponge, but it was still nice."

"Oh, I see," said Victoria, making a mental note to ask Albert about this apparent act of kindness.

"Anything else dear?" asked Daphne, her fingers poised over the till.

"Cheese, Cheddar please, that nice strong one." This was found and a slab weighed and added to the bag. Victoria handed over a £20 note and waited for her change.

"Terrible about George Ansome. Isn't it?" said Iris, as she returned the remainder of the Cheddar to the cheese cabinet.

"Yes, absolutely," said Victoria, trying to disentangle her mind from cheese, sugar and chocolate and think of some searching questions. "I'd got to know him a little, such a shame."

"And such a terrible way to go too – murdered!" Iris went on.

Hushed mutterings of "Terrible!" and "Murdered!" rose from the quartet of old ladies who switched from dropped stitches to death in an instant.

Victoria said casually, "I understand they have arrested Sam."

"Yes, what a surprise! I always thought him such a gentle soul. But I suppose, if someone pushes you hard enough…" said Daphne, looking just a little pointedly at Lavender. "And with families, well, you never know what goes on, do you?"

"Well, I know they've confirmed his gun was the murder

weapon, but I'm not entirely sure why everyone is so keen to pin it on Sam. Surely any number of people could have shot George?" Victoria said, looking innocently at Daphne as she took her change and her bag of groceries.

"Do you know, I thought that," said Iris, aligning a piece of Stilton and giving it a friendly pat. "I mean to say, June's wasted no time in taking everything over, so she's not exactly bereft, is she?"

One of the old ladies muttered, "Her was always pushy that one." "George was a decent fellow when he was younger," said another. "I think he just found life a bit of a trial as time went on," said a third. "And of course, he never married," she added and they all shook their heads and sighed as if, given the chance, any one of them would have taken George on. But then perhaps they had tried and been spurned, thought Victoria. She never ceased to be amazed by how everyone knew everyone or was related to everyone in this part of the world.

"That big black car, that was there," said Lavender suddenly. Everyone turned to look at her.

"What dear?" asked Iris.

"Thursday week. I saw it. Parked up it was, in the lane."

Daphne looked at Victoria and rolled her eyes. "Ignore her dear, gone off on one of her fancies."

But Victoria was intrigued. "Where do you mean, Lavender?"

"I was out on one of my nature rambles, looking for ideas for my next shop display," she said gravely.

"Of course you were Lavender," said Iris and sighed.

"Where was it parked?"

"It were about seven in the morning and it were parked up past the nursery, almost half in the ditch it was."

"The day George was shot?" Lavender nodded.

Daphne clapped her hands. "Well now there's a thing! How on

earth are you supposed to remember it's the day poor Mr Ansome was gunned down, young lady, when you don't even know what day of the week it is normally? Tell me that?"

Lavender turned towards her sister and said slowly. "I know it was that day, because I heard the shot."

A great twittering and squawking burst from the old ladies and Victoria tried to ignore them and concentrate on what Lavender was saying. "What sort of car was it?" she asked, trying to sound casual.

"Black. It was black, and it was big."

"Right," Victoria nodded, feeling progress wasn't being made quite as fast as she'd hoped. Blast Albert – why had he slunk off back to the car? He was far better at winkling things out of people than she was. "Did you see anyone nearby?"

But before Lavender could reply Daphne said, "I think someone's imagination might be running away with her," and she looked at Lavender over the top of her glasses just as Victoria's old headmistress used to do.

Lavender gave a huge shrug. "Only saying what I saw," and wandered into the back of the shop.

"Now Victoria, don't go reading too much into what she says, you know by now that she's a bit of a one for muddling fact and fiction," advised Daphne, and began realigning the jars of sweets rather forcefully.

But Iris Drewe was looking thoughtful. "You've set me thinking now. I reckon you're right to doubt it was Sam. He was so gentle as a little boy. I remember him bringing me an injured rabbit once, crying his eyes out he was. Come in the shop with it. Most little boys are spiteful and would probably have bashed the poor thing on the head, but not him. He wanted to make it well. I don't think he's got it in 'im to kill anything, let alone his brother."

Victoria felt vindicated – so she wasn't the only one on Sam's side! "Well, I'm going to keep my ears open and see if there's any other clues – perhaps you'll do the same, Iris?

"That I will."

At the door, she turned back and asked. "By the way, what happened to the rabbit?"

"Died."

She climbed into Gloria and Albert raised his eyebrows. "I thought you were never coming back – and that looks like a lot of ingredients for one cake!"

"That's because I was trying to do some 'decoy' shopping to put them off the scent, but it didn't work. Anyway, I needed some basic foodstuffs as my fridge is always so empty."

"That's true. Were they old maids all a-gossiping?" he said as he put Gloria in gear and roared off.

"Yes they were, and Lavender said something very interesting."

"What, loopy Lavender?"

"Albert! Don't be so rotten! It seems to me she quite often talks more sense than most of the people in this village. She has no pretentions or ulterior motives, she just says what she thinks."

"That's as maybe."

Victoria grabbed the door handle as they shot around a bend. "Look, could you slow down a bit? The tin of cocoa has just fallen out of the bag and rolled under the seat. Anyway, Lavender said she was on an early morning walk past the nursery and she heard the shot that killed George."

Now Albert did slow down, and glanced at her. "Really?"

"Yes, and even more interesting than that, she saw a big black car parked up, right near where they found the gun."

"Well there's a thing," he said, frowning.

"And who did we meet in a big black Land Rover earlier on?"

Albert nodded. "Charlie Weston." They drove on in silence. Albert swung the little car into the drive and skilfully avoided the many potholes. He parked Gloria in the barn, and Victoria groped under the seat for the tin of cocoa. "The thing is," she said, as she retrieved it, "Madeleine drives a big black car too."

"So she does." Albert climbed out, took the shopping from Victoria and opened the door for her. "And guess what June drives?"

"Don't tell me," sighed Victoria. "Something black?"

He nodded, "A big old black Volvo estate."

"Damn."

They walked into the kitchen, where the air was cooler and the sound of an enthusiastic puppy's tail could be heard clanging against the bars of the crate. Albert released Moss and he charged around the kitchen, skidding on the floor.

"Don't tell me Len drives something black as well?"

"Nope, his work van is white, but 'course, he might drive June's Volvo, so I don't reckon you're any the wiser."

"Tea, or a cold drink?" she asked.

"Do you know, a nice glass of orange wouldn't go amiss."

They downed their cooling drinks and then Albert said, "Right then maid, prepare yourself." Victoria looked startled. "Get your rubber gloves on!"

"Oh, I see," she said, slightly crestfallen. "The dratted beetroot!"

Albert spotted a note on the kitchen table. "It says 'Finished for the day – electrician will be in tomorrow to wire up power shower, he's called Mike – see ya! Kev xx' – what's with this 'kiss kiss' business?" he asked.

"Oh they all do it these days, text speak and all that nonsense, it doesn't mean anything," she replied, pulling on the rubber gloves and washing the beetroot. "It is such messy stuff, why can't we just buy it cooked?"

"Because it tastes better when it's freshly done."

Albert turned on the oven then got out the cake tin and began greasing it lightly. He switched on the kettle and when Victoria had finished the beetroot (with much complaining) he put them in a pan and added the boiling water. "Be done in half an hour," he said. "Right, on you go then, there's the recipe." He sat down at the table, picked up Moss and began stroking the pup.

"Oh, right…" Victoria looked nonplussed, but set about finding bowls and spoons, melting the chocolate, sifting flour and separating eggs. Albert was patient, letting her muddle through and only making and comment when it meant averting disaster. "No hang on! Fold that in gently, gently… Now use a figure-of-eight movement, that's it, remember, folding not stirring." He whipped the beetroot off the hob, as Victoria had completely forgotten them, and – donning rubber gloves – ran them under cold water, deftly slipping off the skins and cutting off the roots before chopping and crushing them.

"Thank you – that's not my favourite job!"

When she had finally shut the oven door she sank down at the table, hot and flustered. "It's so much work! Good god, why can't I just go and buy a chocolate cake and enter that?"

"Don't be daft maid, it's only because you're not used to it. I reckon this will come out just fine. I've set the timer, forty minutes. Let's walk the pup and get back in time to take the cake out of the oven, and leave it to cool."

"Oh honestly, the day is whizzing past and I was supposed to go to Church Farm Dairy, the ice-cream place, and see about interviewing them for my next article." She pushed her hair away from her face. Albert grinned. "What is it?"

"You're pretty much the colour of beetroot yourself at the moment!"

She swatted him with the tea towel. "Let me make a phone call to Church Farm, and then we'll walk the dog."

"Tell you what, why don't we go out there tomorrow and see the set up? Have a little day trip? What do you say?"

Victoria hesitated, remembering her last little 'day trip' with Sam when she'd discovered the delicious ice cream. "Erm, yes OK, we could do that tomorrow or the day after? I'll suggest it to the company when I ring up." She didn't add that she had been hoping to find out if she could visit Sam tomorrow. She wasn't sure if Albert would think it a good idea.

On picking up her phone she saw she had a message, so pressed play and heard Jean, speaking slowly and clearly as if addressing an idiot. "Hello Victoria. Jean here. I hope you don't mind, but I'm going to help the Reverend at the church today. It's still a right old mess, bit like your place really, what with those builders and all. So I'll not come in until next week now, when I hope they might have finished. I hope that's alright. Bye bye."

After she'd rung the dairy and arranged to visit in two days' time, they strolled around the farm in a leisurely fashion and were back just before the kitchen timer told them the cake was cooked. Albert removed it from the oven, tested it very carefully with a toothpick pushed into the moist centre and professed it was "Done to a 'T'. Now, we leave it to cool and then take it out of the tin."

"I have a Show Committee meeting tonight," said Victoria, as she put down the pup's food and watched him chomp his way through it, tail whisking with pleasure.

"Ah yes, shall I play taxi?"

"If you don't mind, that would be great. I've got some paperwork to sort out before I go and then I suppose we'd better have some supper."

"Not eating in the pub tonight?" he asked.

"No! Honestly Albert, you must have shares in the place! I am just going to have a light cheese salad."

He looked crestfallen. "Is that it?"

"Well, I got a nice brown loaf from the shop too."

"Tell you what, I've got to go and check on that cow that's been off colour and then I need to make some calls of my own. Then I'll go and raid the pantry. I've got some of my special picked onions and some cold ham, with some of my chutney of course. I'll come back around six o'clock and we can have a bite before I drop you at The Arms."

"Sounds great!" How spoilt am I, she thought as he disappeared across the yard to raid his own fridge, and how lovely it was to be so spoilt. She thought of Sam again, sitting in some windowless cell, probably eating ghastly food and wondering if he'd ever have his freedom again. It was an awful prospect.

Albert dropped her off at the pub and she made her way to the bar. It wasn't quite so busy, being only seven o'clock on a weekday evening. She ordered a half of cider and sat down at the long table, next to the Reverend Ruminant.

"My dear! How are you? You're looking very fresh faced and well, country air obviously agreeing with you!"

Victoria smiled bashfully and feared that she was still rather pink from the baking episode. "How's the church coming on? I understand Jean has been lending you her considerable cleaning skills."

"She has indeed; an absolute brick that woman. The church will soon be back in service, I've no doubt. Meanwhile we are camped out in the Parish Hall which gives everything a rather carefree holiday atmosphere and attendance has improved no end!"

After ten minutes the committee was assembled and the Reverend got the business underway. Victoria's programme layout was well received, as were her posters, but there was consternation about the layout of the map and competition details. The debate (or argument as Victoria saw it) raged for some time and, although she kept saying if they would only explain HOW they wanted it she would change it, no one seemed to take any notice.

In the end, she banged her empty glass down and said, "PLEASE! Could one of you just explain what you want me to change and I will do it." There was a moment of stunned silence before everyone began talking at once again, pointing at the pages and taking out pens and drawing on her design. Eventually, Edwin clapped his hands. "Now now, come along. Jim, you discuss this with Victoria, you know how it needs to be arranged. You've got the full list of events – which we didn't give Victoria before, so she couldn't include them all! We need to move on now…"

Everyone sat back and shuffled papers, and Victoria felt as if she'd been run over by a flock of sheep. Why had she ever got involved?

"Len Trusscott, did you pick up that fencing last week?" A man called Everett suddenly barked at Len. Victoria had been trying to keep an eye on Len all evening to see if he was acting normally, but she'd been so buffeted about the programme that she hadn't heard him say a word.

"Eh?' Len looked startled. "What fencing?"

"God's sake man. You was supposed to collect the netting and posts from Hannafords last week."

"Oh, er, yes, clean forgot, what with this n' that happening." Several people murmured comments about 'family tragedies', but Everett seemed oblivious. "They had it all ready for you last Thursday."

"Ah, well I've 'ad a problem with me van," said Len. "So I been driving June's old Volvo and I don't reckon it'd all fit in that."

"Heaven sake!" said Everett, testily. "You leave it to me. I'll get me trailer hitched and do it tomorrow. 'Tis the fencing for the clay pigeon competition. Bleddy loads of it to sort out and get put up, posts bomped in, the lot. You know what they're like on 'ealth and safety. If we don't get that done, there won't be a competition. Ironic as you're bound to be one of the beggers taking part!" He sat back and folded his arms, scowling at Len, who seemed unperturbed.

"That's a fact, I'll be having a turn at the clays," he said, nodding. Victoria wondered if he was either a bit tiddled or on some form of anti-depressant; he seemed not quite with them.

"Right, jolly good," said Edwin, eager to move on to the next point on the seemingly endless agenda.

It was almost eleven o'clock when the meeting broke up and Victoria sighed as she climbed into Albert's Range Rover. "Oh Lord..." She closed her eyes as he started the engine.

"Brace up maid! It'll all be worth it on the day!" He swung out of the car park. "And just you wait and see how your cake has turned out – that'll cheer you up a bit!"

Chapter 10

As Victoria sipped her morning coffee, she became aware of a car revving loudly nearby and then a cheery 'Pip pip' of a horn. She finished her drink and walked out into the sunshine to see what all the commotion was about.

"C'mon maid – look lively – or we'll be late for your appointment!"

Albert was leaning across the front seats of a bright red Mercedes SLK and grinning broadly at her. A new car? The engine was still revving very loudly.

"I'm coming, just give me a minute!" She hurried into the cottage, checked Moss was comfy in his crate, grabbed her notebook and camera and made her way back outside. Opening the passenger door she frowned. "Have I missed something Albert – I don't seem to have seen this car before?"

"Nah, 'tis new, you're right. Put it down to a mid-life crisis. I felt I needed a red car! Main problem seems to be starting and stopping though – she doesn't like it, so I just keeps her going as much as I can."

Victoria wondered whether to mention that being able to stop and restart a car all seemed fairly fundamental to her, but decided she'd keep quiet.

She stroked the fine cream leather seats and had to agree it was a lovely car, but she hadn't yet got to grips with what drove Albert to want – or, as he said, 'need' – so many slightly dodgy vehicles. She realised he was smirking. "What?" she asked, grinning back.

"You are fondling my upholstery!"

She slapped his arm. "Well, it's certainly a beautiful car. Let's just hope you can solve the problem of getting it to start and stop."

"Ah 'spect so, I've got a mate that works at a classic car place up in Exeter, he said he'd give me a hand, knows these girls through and through." He patted the car's dashboard.

Victoria looked out of the window at the vivid blue sky and the burgeoning hedgerows gliding by and wondered why it was that cars were always female. "So is it far, Church Farm Dairy? I forget how long you told me it would take to get there."

"Oh, not too long. I just want to stop at the shop, grab a sausage roll or something, I had to go and check on a cow and missed breakfast."

"I'm so sorry, you should have said, we could have delayed the trip a little..."

"Nope, it's fine, one of Iris's rolls will do me. I'd never admit it to her face, but they're better than mine – she always wins at the show, resident sausage roll star!"

"I didn't know, maybe I'll try one too even though I did have breakfast."

They slowed as they reached the main part of the village and came to a halt just before the shop. The newspaper placard sat outside in its usual place, and with horror Victoria read: 'Violet death: man remanded in Exeter prison'.

"Oh no – that couldn't be Sam, could it?" There was a catch in her voice and Albert glanced at her sharply.

"Couldn't say, but they'll have a paper inside – but you can guarantee the triplets will tell you anyway. We can grab a paper with the rolls." He switched off the engine, and silence reigned.

"Damn," he muttered. "I didn't mean to do that, now she might not start again." He climbed out of the car and sauntered into the shop.

Victoria got out of the car very gracefully – knees together, swivel to the side – her mother would be proud. It was the kind of vehicle that made you feel elegant, but then she spoilt everything by almost tripping over a small fox terrier that, oblivious of the rest of the world, was charging towards the shop.

"Roxy, bad dog, wait!" came a fierce voice that should have been obeyed. But Roxy didn't seem to share Victoria's view of Bunty's commanding tones and completely ignored her and began sniffing enthusiastically at Lavender's bargain basket.

"So sorry m'dear, new recruit. Rescue dog that has obviously never had a moment's decent training in her life. And it's a terrier, always wilful little blighters."

Roxy had clearly had second thoughts about ignoring the 'voice' and was now quietly waiting, looking anxiously at the two humans. "Sit!" boomed Bunty – and Roxy did.

"Well there, you're obviously progressing Bunty."

"And how is young Moss getting along – not got him with you I see?"

"No, well, actually, we're just off to do an interview for my work and it didn't seem right to bring him." Bunty somehow made Victoria feel guilty that Moss wasn't with her twenty-four hours a day.

"Well I'm sure you don't plan to leave him for long – and are you all set for puppy's class tomorrow night?"

"Yes, oh of course, we look forward to it," said Victoria, who had completely forgotten about it. She did like the classes but had lost track of the days, something she would never have done in her London life.

"What about the show – you have entered him into the relevant classes I hope?"

"Erm…" Victoria looked pensive. Goodness, she liked Bunty hugely, but she could be so intimidating – Victoria felt about six! "Well perhaps we'll try him in the dog with the waggiest tail, or prettiest puppy class."

"I think we could do better than that you know, he's a fine little chap! We can discuss it tomorrow. I have all the entry forms. Now I must be off, Roxy! Roxy here, now!" But the little fox terrier ignored her and bustled on towards the shop. Just then, Albert came out and, before he had a chance to close the door, Roxy had trotted straight past him and inside.

"Roxy!" bellowed Bunty and strode after her, the shop doorbell clanging wildly as she barrelled her way inside.

Albert looked perplexed and shook his head.

"Time to go, I think!" laughed Victoria, and got back into the car.

"Fine by me! That woman gives me the jitters. Always feel I should sit, stay, roll over or go and wee in the corner," he said, climbing into the driver's seat. "Here you are then, a sausage roll each, and a copy of the paper. And you're right – it is Sam in the headlines."

Grabbing the paper from him she cried, "Oh no, poor Sam, not in prison! Why isn't he out on bail, or whatever they arrange? Oh, this is awful. I should go and see him; someone needs to stand up for him. Oh, maybe I'm not allowed to visit? I do hope he's OK."

"Slow down now, keep calm woman!" Albert patted her arm. "Look, I'm sure if you feel you need to help we can arrange something. Meanwhile, eat your sausage roll while it's warm."

Victoria took a deep breath and tried to calm herself with the thought that just at this minute there really was nothing she could do. Albert passed her a sausage roll wrapped in a Happy Christmas napkin, obviously old stock. She carefully took a bite, not wanting too much of the flaky pastry to fall all over her clothes. Albert was right: it was delicious. She looked over to him and nodded with her mouth full.

"Mmm – s'nice."

Albert didn't attempt to talk at all and just nodded back. He was just starting his second roll. He patted his stomach as he wiped the last crumbs from his mouth.

"Best rolls this side of the river."

"That's not much of a compliment. I'd have said it was the best I've ever had."

"No, Beryl who's up the Teign Valley – she makes a cracking sausage roll, many of hers I've…" Albert trailed off and looked thoughtful. Victoria couldn't decide whether he was stopping himself from mentioning yet another old flame or dreaming about her sausage-roll prowess.

"OK, looking on the map you're going to head through Torquay are you?"

"Well, t'will be a bit hectic, but it's the most direct route," said Albert, and tried to start the car. Sadly she was living up to her reputation and spluttered and then failed. He muttered something darkly and sat for a moment, then tried again. This time there was no delay and she burst into life with a roar.

Albert negotiated the route with apparently no need of her navigational skills which, on balance, was probably a good thing. While the Mercedes glided effortlessly down the lanes and the bypass, getting them to the farm well in time for their appointment, Victoria read the newspaper article and worried about Sam.

Although this was only a first reconnoitring visit to the long-established Church Farm Dairy, she was sure it would be a great topic for her next article. They had been making very special ice cream there for decades and sent it all over the country and even abroad. It was also the choice of some very famous people. Legend had it that a helicopter had landed in one of the fields, much to the surprise of the resident cows, and a famous rock star's PA had hurriedly collected several tubs and stored them in a mini freezer in the helicopter, before taking off again to get to a rock festival up near London. She thought this would make a fun introduction to the piece, especially if she could get them to name the celebrity.

Today, all she wanted were some basic pictures as aides-mémoires and to chat to the team that ran the business to identify the angle of the article.

All of this was achieved in double-quick time as the couple running the dairy were rushed off their feet with a special order for a London store. Victoria smiled and fantasised that it might be one of the stores with a Royal Warrant and that HRH The Queen ate nothing but Church Farm ice cream... then came back down to earth with a bump when she realised they were looking at her rather pointedly and waiting for her to wind up the interview and go. She had more than enough to make a start and planned another visit, when they assured her she would be able take her time and have some free samples as well.

Back in the car she smiled over at Albert. "Right – all sorted – and they've promised that next time they will be quieter and there will be free samples... maybe you'd like to come along for that visit too!"

"Sounds good to me," grinned Albert.

Back home and sidling yet again past the latest debris from the bathroom –,a tangle of old piping – she felt it was time Kev gave her a timescale for finishing this Herculean task. It just seemed to be going on and on.

"Thanks so much for driving me, I did enjoy the journey. I

haven't asked what the car's name is – I assume she's going to have one?"

"Well funny you should say that, I were just pondering that as you went round the ice-cream place. What do you reckon to calling her Edith? Think your aunt would smile at that idea?"

"I am sure Aunt Edith would have been suitably flattered," laughed Victoria. "Now I must get on; I have show posters, programmes and goodness knows what to get sorted."

"Well why don't you come over to mine tonight and I'll cook us a nice dinner and you can avail yourself of the facilities, so to speak, and have a long bath?"

"That sounds wonderful, thanks," she sighed. "I was just wondering how I could kick Kev up the backside to get this job finished. He couldn't do more than two hours this morning as they are working on another job, but I really can't face being bathroom-less for much longer."

"Right oh, you go and tackle the show paraphernalia and you leave Kev to me. I'll ring his missus and see if I can't crack the whip a bit!" Albert grinned as he said this, and Victoria didn't doubt for a moment that he would work miracles.

Moss yapped and bounced as she let herself in. Once freed from his puppy crate he raced round and round in excited circles and headed towards the back door to go out into the garden. A combination of Albert and the dear little dog gave Victoria such happiness and contentment she sometimes wondered if it was all too good to be true.

Switching on the kettle she thought about Sam, and that brought her back down to earth with a thud. There had been nothing new in the newspaper report. Someone ought to be questioning whether he was guilty or not, but the police just seemed happy to get a quick result. She just hated the idea that he might be innocent and nobody was fighting for him.

She opened her laptop and searched for the visiting details for Exeter prison before she lost her nerve, fished her phone out of her handbag and rang the contact number. The visit was organised in a surprisingly short time; the officer on the other end was both polite and helpful, and she felt annoyed at herself for assuming it would be a horrible ordeal. A visit was fixed for the following afternoon and she was reminded to bring photo ID with her. Putting down the phone she sighed and tried to persuade herself that visiting a prison was an everyday occurrence and that she didn't feel even remotely nervous.

Time to get on with all the show stuff. Although jt was starting to feel quite overwhelming she knew that once she got down to it she would not only feel better but also it would probably take far less time than she'd thought.

She clicked on the show programme. Actually, it was very nearly there; just that advert from the greengrocer in Teignmouth to add and a thorough proof read and it was complete. The posters were all fine, she'd double-, triple-checked those. After a solid hour of concentrated proof reading, she stretched her back and loaded all the artwork onto a memory stick, grabbed Gloria's keys and set off for the printer's.

On her return she parked Gloria neatly in the barn, feeling rather smug at how much she had achieved that day. When she'd agreed to join the Show Committee, she'd had no idea how much work would be involved – she should have heeded Albert's warnings. If there was any way she could escape it before next year she certainly would, but the dear Reverend was very persuasive.

Now she had a wonderful evening ahead – a relaxing bath and then being cooked for! She was a little anxious about telling Albert she had arranged to visit Sam in prison, since he still seemed unconvinced as to the latter's innocence. She knew that his view was probably partly down to her getting pally with Sam while she and Albert were 'estranged', so to speak. She'd wait for a suitable moment and then casually drop the visit into the conversation.

In a flash of inspiration she delved in a cupboard and brought out a bottle of bubbly and put it in the fridge to chill. It wasn't particularly special champagne, but champagne it was and it might just help her to alter Albert's view of the situation.

Albert was indeed suitably impressed and insisted that she take a glass up to drink in the bath while she was relaxing. "You look like you could do with it!" he said and patted her cheek, rather like her mother had used to do. She smiled and enjoyed the comfortable feeling of being with him; he was so caring, and she felt so lucky to have him in her life.

Despite the relaxing bath, thinking of telling Albert about visiting Sam sat like a lead weight in her stomach.

Albert had excelled himself and produced a delicious meal of beef (one of his cows, she wondered?) in red wine, fresh, local vegetables and a chocolate and brandy pudding that had more than a dash of brandy in it. He had lit a candle in the centre of the table and had obviously taken great pains to create a relaxed atmosphere.

Looking over at him she said, "That was wonderful. I loved every mouthful, thank you. You really are an amazing cook!"

"Thank you kindly maid, glad it was to your liking." He took her hand, adding "For someone that's just had such an amazing meal, it hasn't taken that worried little frown off your face."

Victoria realised she had to get it over with. "Well, I am just a bit weighed down with something, something I feel I must do for a friend..." she trailed off and saw Albert looking at her with raised eyebrows.

"And might that involve visiting a certain person in prison?"

"I er, I well ... yes, how on earth did you guess?"

"Well as you've had a face like a wet weekend since you read that newspaper, I did think it had something to do with that."

She sighed and leant forward, studying her empty bowl. "I rang Exeter prison earlier as that's where the newspaper article said he had been taken. Seems I am allowed to visit and they could arrange it for tomorrow afternoon, so I booked in." She looked at Albert, hoping he would understand.

"Well of course you did. Apart from some useful sleuthing it would be good to go and support a friend. I understand that, but there is one condition." Albert tried to look stern, and then smiled.

"One condition?" asked Victoria.

"Yes, you're not going on your own – I'll come with you, even if I have to wait in the car park. I don't imagine prison visiting is something you've made a habit of. Unless of course there's a whole part of your life you haven't told me about?"

"Oh thank you Albert, that's such a relief!" She sat back in her chair. "I would love you to drive up with me. I think it's too late to book you in as a visitor too but yes, I would love your company. I felt confident when I booked it and then, ever since, I've been getting more and more worried about it."

"Done," said Albert. "Now can I interest you in more champagne, coffee, more pudding?"

"Oh goodness – I couldn't manage another mouthful!. That was a wonderful meal. I would like to have an early night if that's OK. It's been a pretty busy day and, to be honest, I'd just like to sleep."

Albert's looked crestfallen, "Oh, I was hoping you might stay over, I could cook you breakfast in the morning?" he said in a last-ditch effort to get her to stay.

Victoria felt mean, but she was also barely able to keep her eyes open. "I'm sorry. I am so tired… but can I come over for breakfast anyway?"

"You can indeed," Albert smiled and, taking her hand, walked her over to her house.

The electrician, a pleasant and business-like chap, arrived at 8am the following morning, throwing Victoria into great confusion. With very little noise and fuss he got on with the wiring for the power shower and some extra lighting Victoria had chosen. She was amazed to see he had brought his own sandwiches, and a flask.

After lunch, they set off for the half-hour trip into Exeter. They drew up to the prison and followed the signs to visitor parking. No amount of reassuring handholding on Albert's part could stop the butterflies in Victoria's stomach. The building itself was intimidating and she just wanted the whole visit over. Albert reassured her that he would be waiting in the car park.

Being searched was really no different to what happened when you went through airport security. The drug-detecting dog was very sweet; however – as warned by a rather severe warden – she didn't start petting him and cooing over him, much as she was tempted. Victoria had gone overboard with identification and brought her current driving licence, her passport and anything else she could think of to prove who she was. She had at least had the presence of mind to realise that they would search her handbag so had removed the dog chews, hair bands and fluff-covered lemon sherbets from its depths so that part of the search was uneventful.

She was shown into a square, very drab room with multiple tables and cafeteria-style hard chairs. She sat at a table and waited for them to fetch Sam. Her heart was beating furiously and she felt quite sick.

A man walked towards her and it took her a moment to recognise him. Sam had aged about ten years; he looked ill-kempt, unshaven and his eyes, once his most attractive feature, now looked haunted, dull and scared.

Sam sat down and looked at her. "Victoria, it's really good of you to come."

She smiled and tried to look reassuring. "That's OK, I was worried about…" He interrupted her, his voice low and urgent. "No one has been near me, no one from the family. There wasn't one of them in court – can you believe that? They've just abandoned me!'

Victoria realised he was on the verge of hysteria. On impulse she took his hand and gripped it tightly. "It's OK Sam. I'm here now and if I can do anything to help, I will." Other people's fear or pain always seemed to bring out the best in her. Recognising her compassionate nature, her mother had suggested she might like to nurse. Unfortunately, Victoria tended to faint at the first sight of blood so it would not have been the perfect career choice.

"I don't know what to do! I haven't got any money, I can't get bail. I can't believe this, I am in prison – me! Sam Ansome!"

"Sam, calm down." He was starting to shake. She knew he was what her aunt would have called 'highly strung', but she was never going to get anywhere if she couldn't get any sense out of him. He leant forward and grabbed her other hand. "I didn't do it, you do believe that, don't you?" He stared into her eyes.

"Yes Sam, I do," she said quietly, not adding that she thought he was far too much of a coward to do anything so violent.

He let out a huge sigh, almost a sob, and slumped back in his chair, releasing her hands. "Thank God," he said. "You have no idea how good that is to hear."

"I don't know what I can do, but I'm certainly going to try and help you. I am shocked at how your family have abandoned you," she said, and took her notebook and pen out of her bag.

Sam rubbed his face as if trying to wake up and she could hear the rasp of the stubble on his chin. He took a deep breath and sat forward again, his hands clasped. "Right," he said.

Lord, thought Victoria. Now that she was sitting here with an accused man in front of her, what on earth was she going to ask him? She thought of some of her favourite fictional detectives and decided to try and be methodical and get to the facts. Yes, she thought, use those little grey cells, interview him as if she was going to write an article, that might work. "OK Sam, if you don't mind, could you tell me what happened that morning, you know, when George... I mean, right from the beginning. When did you wake up? Did you hear anything?"

He closed his eyes, recalling the events. "I was in bed, dozing when I heard a shot. I think it was about 7am. I didn't take any notice, I just thought it was someone out rabbiting in the woods."

Victoria nodded and wrote rapidly. "So, when did you get up?"

"Oh, about 8am it was. I went down to the kitchen, and there was May, frying breakfast as usual."

Victoria kept her head down to hide her surprise. "She hadn't heard anything?"

"Seems not, she has Radio 2 on and I reckon that must have drowned out the sound of the shot."

Victoria made a mental note that if the shot had been fired at 7am, or a minute or two after, it would have been during the news bulletin, which wasn't usually very noisy at all, just spoken word and no music. But she realised this stroke of genius was probably useless unless Sam could be precise about the time.

"Hang on – when you heard the shot, did you look at a clock to check the time?"

He frowned. "Yeah, I think I opened one eye and saw 7.01 on the digital display."

Victoria nodded, feeling rather pleased with herself. "And is the clock accurate?"

"Erm, I think so, yeah." He nodded and looked at her intently. "Why?"

"Oh, it might be nothing, I just wanted to check," she smiled. "And what happened next?"

"Well, I stood there and thought, that's a bit odd, where's George? He's never one to be late for his breakfast. May said she hadn't seen him. So I thought what's the silly old bugger done now..." He stopped and Victoria realised he was quite upset. "He was a silly old bugger. A really irritating man most of the time." He paused. "But he was my brother and... and I would never have harmed him," he finished quietly.

"It's OK Sam. Go on, what did you do next?"

He took a deep breath. "I went marching outside, all indignant, expecting a row to get the day off to its usual start and I saw the polythene flapping in the breeze. I looked at it and I thought, what the hell is that? I couldn't make it out for a minute. So I went over to the polytunnel and as I got closer I could see it was all ripped, and ruined and..." He stopped and looked down at his hands. "There he was."

"It's OK, take your time." Victoria read back over her notes. She became aware of him looking at her, and she raised her eyes to his.

"Why are you doing this?" he asked.

"What do you mean?"

"What do you care what happens to me?"

She felt herself start to go a little pink. "I don't know Sam, to be honest. I just, well, during the time I got to know you, I felt..." What had she felt? "I don't like injustice and I don't believe you are the sort of person to shoot his brother," she finished in a rush.

He nodded and his eyes filled with tears. "Thank you."

Victoria looked away, embarrassed. Sam blinked back the tears and cleared his throat. "I didn't need to go any closer, I could see George was definitely dead, so I ran back to the house and called the police." He gave a snort of indignation. "Much good that did me!"

Victoria chewed the end of her pen. Now what? "Your gun, tell me about that? Did you keep it locked up?"

Sam scratched his chin and looked away. "Well, I was always fairly relaxed about that, wasn't I? More fool me!"

"So...?"

"So no, it wasn't locked up like it should have been. I think it had been propped up in the kitchen, by the Rayburn. But I'm not one hundred per cent sure."

"OK. Look, I know nothing about guns, so I'm sorry if I ask anything stupid, but what about the bullets?"

"Not bullets, cartridges, shotgun cartridges."

"Oh, those orange cylindrical things with metal ends? I've seen used ones lying about on the farm."

"Yep, that's it. I keep a box of them on the dresser."

"The dresser?" she squeaked, and realised she was starting to sound like a character in a farce.

"Hmmm, I know, but it's what people do. You see a rabbit out the window, you grab a couple of cartridges and boom, boom!" He shrugged. "By the time you've gone to the gun cabinet, unlocked it, got the gun out, got the cartridges from the place where you keep them locked up and loaded the gun... bunnykins has eaten all your lettuce and scarpered."

Victoria pondered for a moment. "Were your prints on the gun?"

"Well they must have been, it's my gun!"

"I suppose what I mean is were there anyone else's prints on there?"

He shrugged. "Dunno, could well have been. I mean, anyone, May or June, could have picked it up and moved it at any time."

"Yes, but that's not the same as holding it and firing it, is it?"

He nodded. "True. The police said there were no 'significant' prints on it, so I suppose they mean no one else but me had fired it." Victoria stared at him. "No! That's not what I mean! I mean whoever did do it must have worn gloves – for Christ's sake Victoria!"

She nodded. "It's OK, I do see what you mean. So they must have been prepared. Would you need to know how to handle a gun to shoot someone?" Sam hesitated and she pressed on. "I mean, could I shoot someone with a shotgun?"

"Possibly. The recoil kick would probably knock you off your feet, but if you were close enough, and you'd loaded the cartridges properly and had taken the safety catch off, then yes. It's hard to miss with a shotgun, that's the point of them," he finished quietly.

Victoria sighed and sat back. "OK Sam, I think that's all I can think of, and that warder is looking at me so I guess my time must be up. There's just one other thing…" He looked at her expectantly. "Do you have any suspicions who might have done it?" She watched his eyes slide away from her face and he shook his head. She felt sure he was lying. There was a silence, but he didn't speak, so Victoria gathered her things and got slowly to her feet.

"Thank you," he said and made as if to shake her hand, but hesitated and instead put both hands in his pockets.

"I know it's a trite thing to say, but try and keep your spirits up and, if you think of anything, write it down for next time as I'll come and see you again."

"Really?"

"Yes," she said, and gave him her warmest smile.

She made her way back to the car park. Albert jumped out of the car and came round to open the door for her. He gave her a quick hug. "Alright?" he asked, holding her away from him to look at her expression.

She nodded. "Yes, strangely, it was OK. I sort of took charge. He seemed so helpless, like a stray dog that someone's been kicking and so obviously needing help."

Albert smiled. "Just like your aunt! Always back the underdog."

They drove back to Swaddlecombe, both wrapped up in their own thoughts. At a crossroads on the edge of the village, Albert paused. "Nursery, or home?" he asked.

Victoria shot him a glance; how well he knew her. "Nursery I think, don't you?"

They parked by the gate next to Madeleine's monstrous black truck and June's old black Volvo and other staff cars. The place looked as if someone had done a TV makeover. There were hanging baskets, tubs full of pansies, and a signwriter was in the process of hanging a new sign, proudly proclaiming 'Ansome Nursery for 'ansome plants!' Victoria winced. Oh dear – she'd always thought such a slogan was lurking and gave herself a mental pat on the back for resisting it for her own article.

"Blimey," said Albert. "They don't hang about, do they?"

As they walked towards the house, June appeared. "Hello there Victoria – oh – and Albert Moreton too! How are you?"

"We're fine thanks you. How are you all doing?"

June smiled and opened her arms expansively. "Well, see for yourself!"

Victoria nodded. "Well yes, interesting. I went to visit Sam this morning in Exeter prison."

June's face fell. "Oh. Why did you do that?"

"I thought he possibly needed some support."

Albert moved closer to her and glared at June. "I thought blood was meant to be thicker than water, but it doesn't seem so in your case."

June's face flushed red. "I don't know what you mean by that! The police think they've got their man, they found his gun. It's all sorted and we are moving on with our lives."

"But anyone could have shot George! Sam left his gun lying about, why do you all automatically assume he's guilty? You didn't even go to his court appearance." Victoria felt herself grow quite steely. "I just don't understand why you've abandoned him like this, your own baby brother."

June's mouth was opening and closing like a stranded fish. "I, well... we..." She swallowed and looked down at her hands. "They was always rowing, it was terrible, and when George was shot, and then the gun in the ditch... we just assumed... you know."

"Sam says he was in bed when the shot was fired – he's not exactly an early riser, is he? And May saw him come downstairs and into the kitchen an hour later. How's he supposed to have shot George, crept back in past May and then come down again an hour later? I'd be asking lots of questions if it was my brother, or even just a friend, who was in this awful situation."

A range of emotions flashed across June's face, from fear to shame and finally anger. "What's it to you? Coming round here, sticking your townie nose in. This is family business and not your concern."

Albert made an exasperated sound and touched Victoria's arm. "Come on maid, you'll get no sense out of this lot. Best we get going." June looked as if she was going to speak and then just shook her head and stalked off towards the polytunnels, where discarded police incident tape could still be seen flapping in the breeze.

A skinny young man in a grubby checked shirt sidled up to them on the pretext of sweeping up some old dry leaves. "You working for Sam?" he asked quietly, still sweeping in a lackadaisical way.

"No, not exactly," said Albert, "But we don't think he's getting a fair crack at the whip and we're trying to establish some facts here."

The young man nodded. "I feels bad I do. I told the police about the row I heard him and George having the day before, but it was just how they was. Once I told 'em that, they sort of packed up and went." He pushed the broom about some more. "I reckon I shouldda kept me mouth shut. I don't reckon Sam'd do a thing like that," he shook his head. "Soon as I spoke, I knew I done wrong and Madeleine and June, they all piled in as well, he didn't have a chance."

"What's your name?" asked Victoria.

"Shane, but I don't wanna get in no trouble, I can't afford to lose my job." He looked terrified and scuttled off, still sweeping.

Victoria and Albert got back into the car. "I smell a rat," said Albert.

Back at her cottage, the electrician was just tidying away his tools. Victoria was slightly alarmed by all the bits of wire sticking out in the bathroom, but he explained that all was now ready for Kev to come and finish everything off. He would invoice Kev direct and that was it.

Tea was made and Victoria's chocolate and beetroot cake was consumed. Swallowing the last mouthful, Albert said, "See, I said you could bake a cake."

"I must say, I have surprised myself," Victoria replied, dabbing up crumbs with her finger. "Mmmm, great recipe! I wonder if we will win?"

"You wonder if you will win – it's nothing to do with me, remember! By the way, the bids are coming in well for your kitchenalia."

"Really? Gosh, I'd forgotten all about that!"

"Yep as I thought, people are keen for the old traditional stuff.

Quite a few bids from that Madeleine too," he added.

"Oh dear, I don't really understand much about eBay. You can see all those details can you?"

"Yes, and she's really keen on some of the items and there's a bidding war going on." He frowned and sipped his tea.

"Funny family if you ask me," said Victoria. "Oh Lord, I need to get ready for Moss's puppy class – maybe we can talk about the Sam situation later?"

Albert stretched and got up. "Sounds like a plan to me. Can I entice you into my lair again this evening, or are you going to have another crisis of conscience, or something?"

Victoria smiled. "Hmmm, well, we'll just have to see Mr Moreton… but I think I could possibly be persuaded to stay over."

Albert beamed. "Right you are then! I'll see you around eight then?"

Chapter 11

The weather the following week was set fair, perfect for the preparations for the Swaddlecombe Show. The terrible flash flood had been so short-lived the water had barely penetrated the ground, instead running off in a powerful torrent. The field on the edge of the village was dry and the big lorries had trundled into place and teams of people were off-loading poles and acres of tentage… it was quite a sight! Victoria manoeuvred Gloria into a small gap between a couple of Land Rovers and switched off the engine. She watched the workers enthusiastically tackling their jobs like a nest of busy ants and she felt a thrill of excitement – a show, and she was part of it! Well, in a small way, admittedly – but she was still involved.

"Hello there Victoria, you come to watch?" smiled a small redheaded man with definite squirrel-like features.

"Tufty! How are you?" She got out of Albert's car and went to talk to him. "I have been meaning to pop in and ask, would you know of a good second-hand car for me? I'm looking for something sensible, a small estate or hatchback and, if possible, low mileage?"

Tufty looked confused. "So you not keen on Gloria then?"

"Oh I love her, but of course she isn't mine, and I ought to give her back to Albert as it's just a temporary loan."

Tufty smiled in an irritatingly knowing manner. "Oh I'm sure Albert's not too fussed about that – I should enjoy her while you can. Lovely little runner – there's many a Saturday evening Albert and I have spent underneath Gloria!

Victoria's mind was still a little flustered after the previous night and she failed to stifle a giggle. "Well if you would keep a look out for me anyway, it would be great. I've got a puppy now and it wouldn't be right to start carting him around in such a lovely thing as Gloria on a regular basis."

"You have a point. Yep, I'll keep an eye out then," said Tufty. "Now I have to get going, the missus wants to choose outfits for the dance on Friday night and I shall be for it if I'm not there to help her out."

"Oh, right," replied Victoria, not quite knowing how to reply. Helping the wife choose a dress seemed above and beyond the call of duty for most men, especially someone as unsophisticated as Tufty who seemed to spend his entire life in oily blue overalls. "I haven't really thought about the dance on Friday. I know it makes good use of the marquee while we are paying for it anyway, but it's not really my sort of thing."

"Oh you can't miss that," smiled Tufty. "Source of gossip for the whole of the rest of the year, important part of village life! Anyway I must get moving, nice to see you." With that he scuttled off, visions of squirrels creeping back into Victoria's mind.

She spent half an hour watching the proceedings, trying to match up the plan she had drawn in the programme with what looked like organised chaos in the field. But somehow, everyone seemed to know what they were doing and she guessed the same things went pretty much in the same place every year. Victoria wandered out to where Len and some other men were banging in posts and roping off an area away from the main marquees and showrings. Len afforded her a curt nod. "Is this where the clay pigeon shooting will be?" she asked a young, rather good-looking lad with black curly hair.

He grinned at her. "Yeah, you taking part?"

"Me? Oh dear no, don't know one end of a gun from the other! I think entering my puppy into a class will be about my limit."

The handsome lad and his friend laughed and carried on with their work.

When she arrived home, she checked her phone and saw she had a message. The vagaries of the mobile signal in the area meant she often missed calls, especially if she was travelling in the car.

She pressed the button and listened to a hesitant voice. "Victoria this is Sam. If you could possibly see your way to coming and visiting me again, I er, I realised I had missed an important point that I should have told you about. Could you come and see me again? Please?"

Victoria felt a lead weight in her chest. It made her feel so sad to hear the laid-back and rather spoilt man that Sam had appeared to be reduced to this pathetic soul who had nobody but her to help. She grabbed her notebook and found the number for the prison. As before, the office was helpful and upbeat and she booked a visit for the following afternoon, wondering just what Albert would say. She would approach the subject when he came over for lunch. It always seemed to be easier to bring up difficult topics when there was food to distract him!

Albert arrived with what would technically be described as a packed lunch rather than a picnic hamper. It was more of a box than a basket and the contents looked amazing. He unpacked a pie, sausage rolls, coleslaw and slices of ham, cakes and what looked suspiciously like home-made bread too. Victoria didn't know whether to smile with pleasure or feel guilty about her lack of ability in the kitchen.

"I've got a nice selection of things to drink," she said, slightly too enthusiastically. It didn't seem much, but at least she was

211

contributing to this feast. She thought back to the snatched sandwich from a nearby coffee shop that would have been her lunch in the old days, and decided this was a definite step up.

"I've got apple juice and orange juice, mineral water and oh... how about some of the locally brewed beer they sell in the village shop... 'Wily Old Vixen' I think it was, or perhaps 'Rancid Old Goat' or something similar." She peered at the label.

"Well you have done us proud. I'll have a beer, whatever it's called, if you've got some. Not more than one mind, as I have to work this afternoon."

Victoria poured Albert's beer and some apple juice for herself. Hurray for local producers! This apple juice was a world away from the supermarket brand she was used to.

"So what you been doing this morning then maid?" said Albert, demolishing his second sausage roll.

Victoria hesitated and then came straight out with it. "Actually I had a message from Sam. He asked if I could go and visit again as he had forgotten to tell me something..." she trailed off and looked up at Albert.

Albert was smiling. "So what time you made the appointment for then?"

Victoria felt a bit embarrassed. "Oh, well I..."

"Well of course you rang straight away, wouldn't expect anything else! So when we going?"

"Tomorrow, three-thirty. Is that OK?"

"It's a date. I'll be here to make sure you get safely there and back again."

"Thank you so much Albert, it would make it all so much easier."

"Well that's it then. So on to more interesting things. I have some money for you from all they kitchenalia bits, with more to come. Old Madeleine's being a bit tardy on her PayPal bits which worried me slightly – checked her feedback on eBay and looking quickly there's some pretty nasty negative comments on her account, but I can't believe she would let down a local – too close to play silly blighters with us I'd have thought."

"I'm sure you're right," replied Victoria. "I can't see it being a problem; the negative comments were probably just someone being awkward – you must get all sorts on there."

"Generally people are pretty good and, as I say, I've got some money already for you." With that Albert drew out a cheque from his breast pocket and passed it over to her.

"£203! My goodness – I had no idea all the junk I gave you was worth that!"

"Oh there's easy another £80 or so still to come and I know you've plenty more stashed away, so get sorting girl – this could be your aunt leaving you a secret fortune!" Albert smiled and reached over for yet another sausage roll. "Nice these rolls, eh?"

"We are heading down to the pub later for dinner, aren't we? Maybe I should put them away for another time…" said Victoria, wondering just how many Albert could down before he was full.

"Not a problem, you pack away maid. I'm off to the top field. I gotta make sure Daisy-May's getting on OK, she had twins and that's a worry, always causes more trouble than singles. See you here at what – seven-thirty-ish?"

"That would be lovely, thank you."

At the appointed time (how Victoria liked men that were punctual), Albert knocked on the back door and, as happened so often, she was just sending an email so wasn't quite ready. As she rushed round the kitchen shutting Moss in his crate, grabbing her bag and pulling on a cardigan, she made a mental note to try harder herself to be ready on time.

They walked inside the pub and were surprised at how busy it was for a weekday evening. A large gaggle of men was clustered around the bar with much carousing and ruddy cheeks, and a group of far quieter women sat in the far end, having pushed several tables together.

"Evening you two, usual table?" said Trudy.

Victoria hadn't realised they had a 'usual table' but it was nice to be welcomed, so she smiled and followed Trudy's bustling figure. "That'll be just fine," replied Albert.

"Whoa! Not so fast you pair, come over here and have one on me," came a rather slurred voice from the bar, accompanied by spirited cheering.

Albert peered over the crowd and then turned to Victoria conspiratorially. "Charlie Weston... bottles of champagne and lots of glasses."

They moved along the bar until they joined up with the loud and excitable group and Charlie beckoned them closer. "Come on you two lovebirds, don't be stand-offish, have a glass of Mudge's best champagne!"

Victoria looked up at Albert, feeling very puzzled. "What's the celebration?" she whispered.

"'Ello Charlie, so what's you been betting on to be ordering champagne then?" Albert called across to Charlie whose cheeks were shining like red apples, his whole face glistening.

"Got me land didn't I? I got me land! The bank manager won't know what hit 'im when I get down there in the morning. He always said there wasn't a way. He didn't reckon on old Charlie then did 'e!" Charlie half slurred this bit of news. He had obviously been in the pub for quite some time.

Albert moved closer again. "What – the deal that needed access through Ansomes? I thought that was a no go." He paused and continued, "So things have changed, 'ave they?"

"They have indeed Albert, they have indeed… and I'll be in the money!"

"But how's that changed then… not sure I'm following?"

"Been down the nursery, June and May… in the bag!" He clapped his hands together. "Happy as Larry they are to sell."

Victoria butted in here, unable to stay silent. "But surely there's probate and police enquiries and Sam and…" She trailed off, not knowing how to finish her sentence.

"Pah, good as a done deal." He waved his hand at her dismissively. "I know there's all that legal stuff still to do but that's all just a formally – a formallily – a, well, hell! It's as good as done! So I thought a little celebrating was in order!"

"But what about Sam agreeing?" asked Victoria.

"Sam? Oh that boy was keen from day one – he and I had an agreement weeks ago, we just had to come up with a way to persuade George and that's been done for certain."

Victoria felt a flush of anger, followed by a knot of unease in her stomach.

"Come on lads, another bottle here! Albert, Victoria – come and grab a glass."

"Sorry to be a party pooper but I'm not sure either of us is the champagne type, Charlie, if you don't mind. We're just having a quick bite over in the corner, but you enjoy yourselves." Albert smiled broadly at the drunken farmer and waved cheerily, before taking Victoria very firmly by the hand and dragging her over to a table in the corner furthest away from Charlie's group.

"Well!" said Victoria indignantly. "Thank goodness you got us out of that. I would have felt really uncomfortable joining them."

"Hmmm, that was pretty plain. I can't say I was all that keen myself."

"So, Sam knew all about the deal and George had said no?"

"That's what it sounds like. Doesn't sit well with me the idea that George's murder should benefit someone so quickly and easily. All feels downright uncomfortable."

Trudy came over to their table. "So what can I get you two tonight? I've got a much-praised lasagne in the oven. That food critic for the local paper called it 'inspired'. Or I have a very nice chicken and leek pie, if I do say it myself." She leaned forward and, in her best conspiratorial voice, said, "And then, Victoria, I want to hear all about your time inside that prison, it all sounds very exciting!"

Victoria looked taken aback. "Oh, how do you know about that?"

Trudy winked at her. "Everyone knows everything round here my dear! I thought you were right brave. Ooh," she shivered theatrically, "I don't think I could go into somewhere like that – all that testosterone in one place! All those bars and chains and…"

"Really Trudy, it was nothing like that. I think you've been watching too many American films," said Victoria rather tartly. Albert nudged her foot under the table as Trudy started to look rather affronted. "What I mean is, I just sat in a visitors' room, with tables and chairs. It was all very boring and quite civilised."

Trudy looked crestfallen. "Oh, was that it?"

"Yes."

Then she leant forward again. "But how was he? Sam, how's he bearing up under the strain? I mean, was he in handcuffs, or did he have those chain things on his legs?"

Victoria opened her mouth to deliver what she hoped would be a withering put-down, but before she could utter a word Albert placed the menu very firmly into Trudy's hands and said, "We would like two rump steaks. Mine medium with all the trimmings.

Victoria's rare with just a green salad. And, as you pass the bar, I'll have a pint of my usual and Victoria will have a glass of the house red. OK?" He fixed Trudy with his piercing blue eyes and she nodded mutely. "Thank you Trudy." He turned very pointedly to Victoria. "Now then, tell me what you've been working on today."

Trudy scuttled off with her tail between her legs. "Oh Albert," said Victoria, holding his gaze and raising one eyebrow suggestively. "I do so love it when you're all masterful!"

He ruined the effect by sniggering and they both started giggling, and then laughing. The rather subdued-looking group of women at the far end of the bar started giving them dirty looks.

"Whoops, better keep the noise down!" said Albert, wiping his eyes. "Oh my, that Trudy, she is a one!" he said, shaking his head.

"I know she's very nice really, but she can be such a dreadful gossip," agreed Victoria, rooting in her handbag for a tissue, as she was sure her mascara had run after such intense silliness.

A moment later Trudy appeared with their drinks, smiled primly and put them down, then sidled back to the kitchen. "I think she got the message," said Albert, raising his glass. "Cheers!"

The following morning Victoria sat at her laptop, sighing in frustration and trying to concentrate on her next article about the ice cream company. The words would not come and she kept deleting and starting again. Her mind kept wandering off, either reliving the previous evening's rather nice moments with Albert, or anxiously wondering what the visit to the prison would bring later on in the day.

Coffee – that would undoubtedly help focus her mind. She got up and switched on the kettle. Coffee made and sat down again she nearly fell off her chair as Moss suddenly shot across the floor from his favoured position under the kitchen table, barking madly.

"Hello little fellow!" said a familiar voice. "Victoria, it is I. May I come in?"

She turned to see the Reverend Ruminant in the doorway, cradling a wriggling puppy that was busily licking his ear and then his glasses.

"Oh Moss, for goodness sake! I am sorry Edwin – let me get a tissue so you can wipe your glasses and do come in, it's lovely to see you." She took Moss from the grinning vicar as he wiped his spectacles clean. "You've timed it well – I've just made coffee."

"Ah excellent – I thought I could smell it from the end of the drive!" He sat down, and accepted the mug of coffee placed before him. "Well, how goes it at April Cottage?"

"It all goes well, I think," said Victoria, sipping her coffee and pushing the cake tin towards the vicar.

He hesitated momentarily and then prised off the lid. He sighed. "Oh dear. I really shouldn't eat any more cake; I fear I am getting increasingly spherical. But it is such good cake! You really do seem to take after your aunt in so many ways, Victoria."

She smiled benignly, knowing, for once, that her conscience was clear and that this was a chocolate cake she had actually baked herself. "What do you think?" she asked, trying to sound casual.

The Reverend's eyes rolled and he made a sort of whimper, before licking his lips and sighing. "I'm not sure I can find the words. Delicious, rich, velvety, chocolatey and…" he frowned, "there's something else – now what is it?"

Victoria beamed. "Aha! I'm not saying what the special ingredient is! It's our – I mean, my – well, Moss's and my entry for the show." Oh dear, she was such a hopeless liar – but the Reverend did not seem to have noticed.

"Well my dear, I am sure it will do well, utterly delicious!" He clapped his hands. "I am so glad you've embraced village life and the show and everything! So, what will you be wearing to the dance?"

"I'm sorry?"

"The show dance. I know Albert has got tickets, I'm keen to know what your get-up will be!"

Victoria made a face. "Oh, we won't be doing that, I don't do dressing up. Actually, I didn't know Albert had even got tickets. Dressing up's really not my thing..." she trailed off as she saw the vicar's look of astonishment. "What is it?"

"Not dressing up? But, but, well, my dear... it's simply not done! There's tradition, you see. Everyone on the Show Committee has to go to the dance, and everyone dresses up!"

Victoria looked nonplussed. "Oh, I'm sorry, I had no idea." She paused. "You mean my aunt used to dress up every year?"

"Oh yes, yes indeed!"

Victoria frowned as she envisaged her no-nonsense aunt in her tweed skirt or sensible slacks, headscarf firmly tied under her chin.

"I just can't imagine it! What ever did she dress up as?"

The vicar sighed. "Well, to be completely truthful, she did used to cheat a bit. Edith always went in the same costume, year in, year out."

"Really? Do tell!"

He paused. "She always went as the abbess from the 'Sound of Music.'"

Victoria began laughing. "You mean she went as a nun? What, in the full habit and everything?"

Edwin nodded, chuckling. "Yes, she was a scoundrel! I know for a fact that she was wearing her wellies underneath and that she probably hadn't taken her headscarf off either."

They both laughed then, and Victoria suddenly recalled her aunt's rather wonderful deep contralto voice. "You're not going to tell me she used to sing 'Climb Every Mountain' as well, are you?"

Edwin's high-pitched giggle escaped him and he nodded. "I'm afraid so, usually after a bottle of red wine and just after the raffle had been drawn."

They both collapsed with laughter and, not for the first time, Victoria reflected on how much she had laughed, really laughed, since she'd moved to this charming part of the world. "Oh goodness!" she gasped, wiping her eyes. "Fancy dress! I don't think I've done that since I was about ten and went as a fairy to a friend's birthday party."

"Well, you'll have to get your skates on, the dance is this Friday."

"I suppose it is. Well, can you recommend a fancy-dress-hire place and I'll go and see what I can find?"

Edwin shook his head. "There's nothing around here, I'm afraid. Not even in Westerley as far as I know. I think you'd need to go to Exeter or Plymouth."

"Oh Lord, I don't really have time for that and I still don't know my way around. I'll try Googling and see if there's anything I can find online."

"To be quite frank my dear, everyone else makes their costumes."

Victoria looked shocked. "Really?"

"Yes, put it down to long dark winter nights and everything being too distant, but people around here do tend to enter into the spirit of the thing and keep up the old traditions. You'll find everyone gets involved."

"Will you be dressed up?"

Now it was Edwin's turn to look shocked. "Of course! I think I'd be lynched, or at the very least defrocked if I didn't!" Then he started giggling again. "Oh dear, defrocked! Perhaps that could be my theme for this year!" Victoria joined in his laughter, but just then there was a knock at the back door and Moss shot out from under the table again and began a frantic dance of greeting. They both turned to see Kev in the doorway.

"Aye aye!" he said. "What's all this then? Lot of laughing going on for this time of the day!"

"Kev, we were just discussing the show dance and all this ridiculous dressing up business," said Victoria, getting up to switch the kettle on. "Please tell me you don't get involved in all this nonsense too?"

"Nonsense? What does she mean, Vicar?" Kev stood, hands on hips. "I'll have you know me and Kelly, the wife, we have won the Best Couple Costume award more than once, haven't we Vicar?"

"Absolutely my dear chap, your wife is a whizz with fake fur fabric!" Kev beamed, obviously proud of Kelly's creative skills.

"Good Lord, well… I don't quite know what to say," said Victoria, handing Kev a mug of coffee. "Erm, well, I'd better start rootling around and see what I can find."

"You'll be wanting to deck Albert out too, no doubt," added Kev with a twinkle in his eye.

"Don't tell me he gets involved as well?" Now Victoria was really shocked.

Kev and the Reverend laughed and exchanged knowing looks. "Oh yes, likes a bit of dressing up does Albert, if you know what I mean, surprised he hasn't discussed this year's effort with you already."

"Well, you have thrown me into a quandary – I'd better start rummaging in some cupboards and hope inspiration strikes."

"My Kelly always swears by a trip to that bargain barn on the edge of Westerley – you know, that big place 'Bargains-R-Us' or summat, with all those signs along the road. Says she gets all sorts of bits of material and kiddies' accessories and stuff that gives her ideas for costumes."

"She sounds a lot more imaginative than me!" wailed Victoria. "Right OK, gauntlet thrown down, challenge accepted," she said, then glanced at her watch.

Edwin took the hint. "Well my dear, I must be going. You've done a sterling job with the posters, very colourful and effective, and the programmes I know are at the printers, being delivered in tomorrow I believe?"

"Yes, that's right. They're coming to you at the Vicarage, as agreed."

"Marvellous! Well, I think we are pretty much 'all set'! Just your costume to sort out by the sound of it."

"Hmmm," said Victoria, "you'd better leave that one with me."

Edwin bade his farewells and Victoria turned to Kev, suddenly feeling rather empowered. "Right then. When am I going to have a working bathroom?"

He gulped a mouthful of coffee and his eyebrows almost disappeared into his highlighted fringe. "Well, any day really. We've got all the electrics for the shower in now and all the plumbing, know what I mean."

"When is that very irritating roll of lino going to be removed from the spare room? If I've fallen over it once, I've fallen over it a hundred times!"

Ken rubbed his chin. "That'll be going down any day now, and then we can fit the shower and the loo and all that. And then we can do the tiling."

"So, I can be enjoying my first power shower – when?"

Kev rubbed his chin again and looked thoughtful. "About middle of next week, I reckon."

Victoria sighed. All this 'hassling people' business was hard work. "OK. Let's agree on you finishing here end of next Tuesday – is that possible?"

He tried the contemplative chin rub again, but Victoria narrowed her eyes and sighed, so he stopped. "Yeah, I reckon."

"Only I am getting a bit fed-up with the chaos – if you know what I mean!" she said with a grin.

Later, as Albert drove them towards the prison, Victoria thought it might be a good time to lighten the rather serious mood in the car and ask him about the fancy dress dance.

"Albert, I have it on very good authority that you are given to a bit of dressing up?"

"Eh?" He glanced at her quickly as he negotiated a tight corner.

"I am told that you quite enjoy it."

"What you on about maid?"

"The fancy dress dance – you didn't mention it to me at all and now it seems I not only have to go, as I am on the Show Committee, but that I have to dress up too!"

"Course," he said and drew up at a crossroads. After looking both ways, he added, "'Tis a fancy dress dance, so everyone dresses up. It's tradition. As you did the programme and all the posters, I assumed you'd realise it was all part of the show and that everyone would take part. Why wouldn't they?"

Victoria sat back, bemused by this quite logical, yet infuriating, response and simply said, "Oh."

After a few moments, Albert glanced across at her again, grinning. "Here, are you sulking? Don't you townies do dressing up?"

Victoria bridled at his jibe even though it was true. He had an unerring habit of pinpointing little absurdities and teasing her about them. "Well, no, we didn't actually. We were a bit more sophisticated that than." She realised as soon as she'd said it how pompous it sounded and, as Albert pulled faces and made 'Yah yah' posh noises, she ended up grinning. "Oh shut up!" she said, and smacked his arm.

They parked at the prison and she took a deep breath. "Right, here we go then."

Albert opened the passenger door for her. Giving her a quick hug, he said. "You'll be alright. Got your notepad?"

"Yes, all set."

"See you in a bit then."

Victoria was subjected to the same procedures as before, the staff helpful and polite and seemingly well aware of how uncomfortable she, and probably most visitors, felt in such alien surroundings.

Sam entered the room looking more haunted than ever. He looks like Moss when I've told him off, she thought, and half rose to greet him as he reached the table.

"Thank you," he said with great sincerity. "Thank you so much for coming. It really matters to me Victoria."

She nodded, "That's OK, I said I would visit you again. I've been asking around a bit, but I can't say I've discovered anything much... well, maybe one thing that I didn't know."

"Oh, what's that?"

She hadn't planned to come out with it so early on, but she was useless at intrigue or subterfuge. Her mother always said she'd have made a lousy poker player. "Charlie Weston told us – well, everyone in the Swaddle Arms actually – that he's 'done a deal' with May and June and that you'd already agreed to it. He said the only obstacle had been George and now, of course, he's gone."

She looked at Sam, and watched as his eyes slid guiltily away. He really wasn't helping himself. "Is that true?"

Sam shrugged bony shoulders. "Yeah, I guess so. I mean, I always said I thought we should strike a deal with Charlie. He had the money, we needed it..."

"YOU needed it," she interjected.

Sam looked up at her. "Yes OK, if you like, I needed it. I wanted to get the eco-building idea off the ground. Selling that bit of land to Charlie made no difference to the nursery's business, it was just George being bloody-minded." He sighed. "So yes, I'd said 'fine' in principle, but that didn't matter one jot if George didn't agree. It wasn't a secret, other people knew about my plans."

Victoria had to agree that, put like that, she couldn't really see that Sam had said or done anything very wrong. "OK, so what was it that you forgot to tell me?" She asked, getting her notepad and pen out of her bag.

Sam brushed his fringe back from his face. His skin looked grey and clammy whereas he'd always looked so well and sun-kissed before. Victoria marvelled at how quickly such a ghastly environment could have an impact on someone. "Well, I was thinking about the morning it happened, and I realise that I heard a vehicle at about the time of the shot."

"What do you mean?"

"The lane runs quite close to the house, my bedroom window was ajar and I heard this vehicle go past just a bit after I heard the shot."

Victoria had picked up her pen. Now she put it down again. "So... did you recognise the vehicle or something?"

He nodded and picked at some skin round his thumbnail. "Yes I did."

She picked up her pen again. This was like drawing teeth. "So, whose was it?"

"I reckon it was Charlie Weston's Land Rover."

Victoria wrote this down and tried to process what that might or might not mean. A black vehicle had been seen in the lane, and Charlie's Land Rover was, indeed, black.

"It's got a hole in the exhaust, he's too mean to get it fixed, and it pinks a bit, so I'm 99% sure it was him."

Victoria had no idea what pinking was, but let this pass, (Albert would know, she was sure.) She wrote it down as a reminder to ask him. Without looking up, she said, "I thought you said you were asleep?"

Sam rearranged himself on the hard chair. "Well, I was sort of drowsy, but I reckon I heard the engine a minute or so after the shot."

"And now Charlie reckons he's got a deal on your land." She held his gaze for a moment and felt a bit sick. It was all starting to look rather damning for a certain party. She gathered her wits. "And this was at 7am?"

Sam scratched his cheek. "Well, I think so. But I didn't get up until 8am, I know that, but I can't be sure it was 7am, not absolutely." He shrugged, and Victoria thought how utterly hopeless he was.

She scribbled a few other thoughts down to try and make it look as if she was brimming with ideas whereas, in reality, she was feeling quite anxious. "Was there anything else you wanted to tell me?"

Sam gazed at her and reached out for her hand. "No, nothing. I just wanted to see you again. It means so much to me, to have someone rooting for me."

She smiled, aware that her face felt tight and the smile false. "No problem. But I don't know that I am much help."

"Oh you are, believe me. You're keeping my spirits up."

She withdrew her hand and stood up. "Right then, I'd better get going. I'll see whether I can make anything of this new information. Albert and I did call in at the nursery after we left you last time, but I don't think we got anywhere."

"Is Albert with you then?"

"Yes, he's waiting outside now. He's been very supportive. This is all a bit, you know, daunting for me."

"Bit daunting for me too," added Sam quietly.

"Yes, yes, I'm sure." Victoria was feeling increasingly

uncomfortable. "Look Sam, if it's any consolation, neither Albert nor I believe you did this."

He sat up taller. "Really? Albert thinks that too?"

"Yes, he does."

"Wow! I never thought he had any time for me. That's really gratifying to know. Say 'thank you' to him, will you?" How sad that just one other person's belief in him seemed to give Sam such a lift. She felt desperately sorry for him again.

"Yes I will," she smiled and touched his arm. "I'd better go as Albert's waiting."

"Will you come and see me again?"

She nodded. "Yes, but let's hope that I won't need to and that you'll soon be out."

He smiled weakly and she saw tears well in his eyes again. She quickly turned and left.

"Alright?" said Albert, as she slid into the passenger seat.

She sat back and put her head against the headrest. "What's pinking?"

"Eh?"

"What does it sound like?"

Albert looked thoroughly confused. "Pinking? Well, it sounds a bit like ball bearings being rattled in a jar. It's to do with the engine's timing being too advanced and – why on earth do you want to know that?"

"Because Sam says he heard a vehicle with a noisy exhaust and a pinking engine just after he heard the shot."

Albert looked at her. "Sounds like Charlie boy's Land Rover to me."

"That's what Sam thought."

Albert tapped his index fingers on the steering wheel, then started the engine. "Hmmm," he said, "That's a bit of a bugger!"

Chapter 12

Victoria filled the enamel bread bin with some smaller items, plus two ladles, a potato masher and a couple of rolling pins. She gazed at the selection of copper jelly moulds and wondered if it was really daft to put one on as a temporary hat just to get as much as possible across the courtyard in one go? She shrugged and crammed most of the moulds into the bread bin, placed the largest one squarely on her head, hefted the bread bin by one of the handles, tucked the black kitchen scales under her arm and set off.

She staggered out of the back door of the cottage and narrowly avoided tripping over Moss. As she nudged Albert's door open, she could hear a strange muffled noise that gradually became louder as she entered the room. It reached a crescendo when she spotted Albert laughing so hard that he was wiping tears from his cheeks.

"I'll thank you not to laugh at me!" she said in mock anger. Still wearing her copper headgear she continued, "You said bring over more of Edith's kitchenalia and here you have it. These are the contents of the cupboard next to the sink – I still have the walk-in pantry and two more drawers to clear, so judging by the money you've raised already we might even get enough to pay for most of the bathroom!"

Albert was trying to straighten his face. "So maid, you planning to take the jelly mould off your head or is it a posh London fashion that's not made it down to the wilds of Devon yet?"

Victoria smiled and removed the offending jelly mould – at least everything had made it over in one piece and she was chuffed about how much things were fetching on eBay. She looked over at the big farmhouse kitchen table spread with papers, photos, a digital camera and Albert's laptop computer.

"Wow, this is all looking very complicated! Is this all for eBay or is it the farm accounts or something?"

"No, all eBay – but it's not as complex as it looks. I'm just in a mess at the moment as I've run out of files and folders; I ordered some more online yesterday so hopefully they'll turn up today. Then I can get the latest bits organised."

Victoria went over to the laptop and looked at him with an excited smile. "So have we sold any more of my bits or has any more money come in?"

Albert paused and said; "Hmmm, let's check again. I sent another reminder email to Madeleine. I'm pretty ticked off at her. You'd think you'd pay friends or people you know a darn sight quicker than strangers, but it seems not."

They sat down together at the table and Albert opened up the laptop. He clicked and tweaked the mouse a few times and up came his eBay seller page. He peered at all the figures and then frowned, clicked on another page and sighed. "Bleddy woman – she's paid for a few small things but not the main set of the blue-and-white-striped Cornishware china. Hang on – there's an email."

He clicked on his email programme and opened one from Vintage Cookie. Victoria raised one eyebrow. "Vintage Cookie, really?"

"Guess it's as good as any for an eBay seller's name – there's some pretty bleddy daft ones out there."

The email read: Albert sorry meant to get some 'Buy It Now' items listed to up the cash but forgot. Should have the money to you v. soon. Mad

Albert sighed and clicked over to his 'My eBay' pages. He clicked on the item Vintage Cookie (aka Madeleine) hadn't paid for and Victoria gasped. "£178 for Edith's old breakfast set – and some of it was cracked, wasn't it?"

"Well, she and some other person got into a battle for it. Seems to me they lose track of what's sense and what isn't and the bids just go flying up sometimes."

Albert clicked again on the number beside Vintage Cookie's name. "What does that number mean then?" asked Victoria.

"Oh that's feedback, references if you like, from happy customers and happy sellers."

Victoria frowned as she read the screen. "Oh, not looking so hot for Madeleine then."

"True. I haven't had time to look too hard, just thought as we know the lass best just to be patient."

They read a few very depressing sentences that all indicated Madeleine was neither a fast payer as a customer nor a fast deliverer when she sold items. "Pah, that's enough, this is depressing, I'm sure the girl will pay up before long. Now then, we must sort this cake."

"But I'm really amazed," replied Victoria. "Madeleine always made it sound as though she was a city trader in stocks and bonds and things, not an eBay trader!"

"Don't knock it till you've tried it," replied Albert. "Just look at the money you're making at the moment."

"Yes, but I have a load of free stuff to sell thanks to Aunt Edith. You can't make a business out of that."

"Well technically you can; buying second-hand or antique or vintage or whatever you like to call it and selling it on can be a very lucrative business. Nothing that antique fairs and antique shops haven't been doing for years."

"But eBay... surely?"

Albert looked at her fiercely. "Now don't you go being all snobby about eBay – there's many on there makes a tidy living off the proceeds. Twenty-first century entrepreneurs some of them are. I wish farming paid as well as the little sidelines I have on eBay, so you just hang fire before you talk it down!"

"Oh sorry, didn't realise I was touching a nerve. Right, I will respect eBay a touch more in future. But there are a lot of scams on there too, surely?"

Albert rolled his eyes. "I s'pect so, just like in any marketplace, yes there are bad rogues, but you have to take the rough with the smooth and keep your wits about you. Now then – cake."

"OK." Victoria sensed that he'd had more than enough of eBay as a topic and she should move on.

They both read through the recipe Albert had written out by hand. "Is this the 'final-revised-definitely-not-changing-it-again' recipe then?" she asked, smiling up at him.

"Maybe," he replied and gave her a very superior look. "I might make some last-minute tweaks, who knows, depends how I feel."

Victoria sighed with exasperation. "But how do I know what to buy then?"

"Oh it'll probably only be tiny amounts, not the main ingredients – if you just get what's on that list then that'll be fine. You happy to buzz down to the shop and get it all? Wouldn't do for me to be seen buying any of it!"

"Fine, I'll go, though really this whole charade is a bit daft. I mean, in this day and age, lots of men cook! What's to be embarrassed about?"

"It's tradition maid, jus' tradition. And it's a tradition your aunt and I built up over many years. Brought us a lot of smiles and didn't do nobody any harm so I like to carry on for Edith."

Victoria wondered if it was all as open and honest as that and more likely he was still afraid he would get teased for making cakes – never mind winning a prize at the show – but he was right; Aunt Edith loved the tradition, so she should continue it.

"Right village shop here I come, let's hope they have all the bits you need."

"Oh no, I'm not leaving anything to chance. I've got all the 'gredients here already. 'Tis just a show so the sisters think you bought the stuff for the cake at the shop. I bought different bits at different times, just in case there's any espionage going on and people try and guess my recipe!"

Victoria laughed and shook her head. "You are something else Albert, you really are – talk about taking things seriously. Right – I, the decoy, will go the shop and buy the wrong ingredients like…" she glanced at the list, "vanilla and candied orange peel to put them off the scent, right?"

"Yep," said Albert staring at the screen with a quizzical look on his face. "See you later."

Victoria smiled to herself as she walked across the yard to collect her handbag, and changed her shoes for good measure. Gloria always made her feel she should be wearing proper driving shoes and possibly even driving gloves if it was cold enough.

As she reversed out of the barn, she could hear Moss whining indoors and, feeling soft this particular morning, stopped the car and fetched the pup in his harness. She strapped him into the front seat, with a blanket underneath him to protect the leather, and was sure she could see him smiling. There was a distinctly happy look on his face, ears pricked, eyes shining as he looked around keenly.

The grin on his face increased to a full-blown panting, lollopy-tongue look as the car picked up speed and his ears flew back in the wind. He was obviously a dog meant for speed and was loving every moment. He barked at cheeky hedges whose leaves came too close to 'his' car and the sight of a squirrel running up the road ahead made him yell with excitement and quiver with anticipation. When the squirrel bounded off the road into the bank he managed a nearly 360-degree head swivel as he tried to follow its progress.

Two riders on horses approached and Victoria worried that he might bark and upset them. She pulled over tight to the bank and stopped, giving them plenty of room, and glanced to her left at her silent companion. Moss was averting his eyes from the very large horses that strolled past so close that the riders' boots were almost in Victoria's face. Riders and driver exchanged thanks, but the little dog continued to examine the footwell carpet with great concentration.

"Well you softie, Moss!" said Victoria, laughing at his obvious discomfort as the two huge animals moved on past. She couldn't help giggling again when he bounced back into happy puppy 'look at me' behaviour the minute they were safely out of the way.

Victoria parked outside the village shop, in a position where she hoped she might be able to keep an eye on it (and Moss). Moss seemed happy to watch the world go by and didn't whine or complain as she shut her door and left him in guard dog position, looking out over the bonnet. She felt so lucky to have a convertible car, but she really ought to get something more sensible. Moss was behaving beautifully today but a very wet and muddy Moss after he had been swimming in the sea would do Gloria's upholstery permanent damage.

She glanced at the newspaper placard. She actively avoided it most of the time as it made her cringe, reminding her of its role in her misjudgement of Albert and Carol. Today, the headline caught her eye: 'Flood victim inquest adjourned', it proclaimed. Victoria frowned. It must be referring to Percy Shooter, and she wondered why it had been adjourned – surely it was a simple enough verdict? It wasn't very likely he'd dropped a gargoyle on his own head. Still frowning, she pushed open the shop door and was deafened by the bell as usual.

There was quite a crowd gathered inside, the triplets holding court and everyone apparently very keen to express their opinions. Victoria couldn't easily make out what they were talking about. Random words like 'shame' and 'credit' and 'consequences' seemed to be flying about, and she couldn't decide whether to listen or just keep her head down and choose the products she 'needed' for Albert's cake.

Then she caught the word 'Sam' and then the phrase 'had it coming' and she decided to ignore her conscience and eavesdrop.

"All I ever heard was that George barely paid him a penny and he must have worked as hard as any of the others up at Ansomes, isn't that right?" Dahlia looked across at Iris as if to confirm her statement.

"Well it's not a fortune to be sure, but it's still unpleasant to think we're owed over £40 by a man currently in prison, poor fellow, and that's all I'll say on the subject." Iris pursed her lips and folded her arms to enforce her point to her audience.

"Maybe his sisters will pay up if you ask," suggested a thin elderly woman Victoria hadn't seen before. "They'll come into a tidy fortune I would imagine, some folks get all the luck!"

Victoria pondered quite what luck meant in this context.

"Well George was always a mean old skinflint even back in our younger days, never would pay his share on a date I heard!" said Dahlia

"Oooh you never did date him, did you?" asked another lady Victoria couldn't name. "Fancy dating a man that's bin murdered, there's a thing."

"Well maybe I did, or maybe I just heard from a friend, what's the difference?" said Dahlia, obviously quite embarrassed by the reply to her last comment.

Lavender heading for her display outside, stepped past the ladies then turned back. "Maybe if George hadn't been so mean, he might not have been killed." Silence greeted her blunt statement and Victoria realised, yet again, that despite her strangeness Lavender often got to the heart of the matter a lot quicker than everyone else.

"Well we must be getting on," said Dahlia in a rather brisk tone as though they had umpteen deadlines looming, and began to busily rearrange the cheeses.

Victoria decided to get her question in quickly in case the chatting started up again. "Dahlia, Iris, would you have any vanilla pods at the moment?"

"Vanilla now, is it? Albert fancying a change from chocolate, is he?" Everyone in the shop stared at Victoria and she felt the blush spreading up her neck.

"Oh no, it's for me, I really like vanilla. Very healthy." She didn't think she sounded at all convincing.

"He sent you in with a list did he?" smiled Iris.

"What... he? Albert? No I, it's my list, I mean just a few bits I need." She waved the list about as if reinforcing her ownership. Victoria felt very uncomfortable; her ability to fib was not improving and the whole cake subterfuge seemed so ridiculous. "Just gathering bits for supper."

"That's fine dear, we wouldn't say a word." Dahlia looked furtively round the shop as though she were passing secrets to a Russian spy. The other ladies in the shop were all silently inspecting packets or the contents of their purses, their ears obviously burning. "What we know we know, what we say is a very different matter. Here you are dear: two vanilla pods, they're a bit pricey mind."

"You baking at all at the moment then?" asked Dahlia. "Will you be making something for the show?" She flashed a conspiratorial smile at her sister.

"Well yes, now you come to mention it. I will be having a go at a cake," said Victoria nonchalantly, hoping to bring the conversation to an end as she fished out her purse. "I haven't quite decided what type yet."

Lavender came back into the shop holding a wet wellington boot and two large branches of leaves.

"It didn't work really using the boot as a vase, I tried but it kept falling over. Maybe these branches are too long." She turned round and noticed that Victoria was still standing there. "So what are you and Albert wearing for the dance? How is your costume looking? Good job mine doesn't need wellingtons, I'm thinking!"

Victoria realised that trying to forget the fancy dress dance had neither helped her get ready for it nor made it go away. What was Albert planning – what would they go as? Oh dear, it was too awful to contemplate! Maybe she could plead a migraine or something… She looked at the triplets, all eyeing her keenly. "So, erm, do you all wear costumes to the dance too then?"

Lavender gave a slow ho, ho, ho laugh and said, "Of course we do! And do you know, we have a really good costume this year! I thought it all up myself!" Then she stopped and put her fingers to her lips and looked warily at her sisters. "But it's a secret and you won't hear it from me!" She gave Victoria an exaggerated wink and carried her boots and branches off into the back of the shop.

The other two sisters smiled in an almost parental way at her and then turned to Victoria.

"So yes, what are you and Albert going as?" said Iris.

"Oh all a big secret for us too! Well, we'll all find out later on, won't we!" With that Victoria took the change that Iris proffered and left the shop as fast as she could without seeming undignified. She was aware of the hum of village gossip starting up again as she scuttled out of the door.

She returned to the car to find Moss dozing and very happy in the sunshine. He bounced up in his seat as she got in and they zoomed back to the cottage with Moss's ears flapping and his little face 'grinning' for all it was worth.

She let the puppy have a mad five minutes out in the garden and then decided to take him with her over to Albert's; he couldn't do much harm, surely, and the farmer's own working dogs would be safely in their kennels.

Albert was singing loudly and fairly tunefully – at the same time beating cake ingredients together in a bowl – as they made their way in through the back door. He continued the semi-operatic rendition of 'Just One Cornetto' that he had started, complete with large theatrical tenor gestures, until Moss started to whine quietly.

Albert stopped and looked at Moss. "I feel quite offended young man, many have admired my singing."

"Just not dogs though…" mused Victoria, "but perhaps cats?"

"How rude!" Albert grinned over at her and continued to beat the mixture with huge enthusiasm.

"Did you know the inquest into Percy's death had been adjourned?" asked Victoria, as she unloaded the shopping into the fridge and the larder.

"I had heard something about it."

"Well, don't you think that's a bit odd?"

"I've no idea maid. I'm no expert on how these things work. Maybe it was some technical wotsit, or medical query," Albert paused in his beating. "Hmmm, dunno what it means…"

"Can I help with anything?"

"Oh no 'tis fine, better that I concentrate and do the thing myself I reckon."

He whisked and whipped and grated. He seemed to beat everything with great energy and Victoria felt quite exhausted just watching. The final mixture was then dolloped into two cake tins and ceremoniously put in the oven. "You could help with the clearing up," suggested Albert.

"Thanks, I rather thought that might be the case."

As Albert carefully set the alarm on his mobile – the bake had to be timed to perfection – Victoria rolled up her sleeves and filled the sink with hot soapy water. "Albert…" she began.

"Yes my beauty?"

"About tonight…"

He sidled up behind her and put his arms around her waist. "What are you proposin'?"

"Oh! Cheeky." She held her soapy hands out of the water and giggled as he nuzzled her neck. "Stop that, or I'll put my soapy paws on you! I was referring to this ridiculous fancy dress dance. Surely we don't have to…"

"Now then!" He spun her round to face him. "Let's have no more of this 'ridiculous' business, 'tis tradition and everyone will be there and everyone will be dressed up. You'll look a complete twit if you're the only one not." She bit her lip and he frowned. "Victoria – you have got something arranged, haven't you?"

She shook her head. "Um, I sort of ignored it and hoped it would go away. It's really not my 'thing', you know."

Albert sighed. "You are hopeless sometimes, you know that? You townies, I dunno!"

"Look, you go, and just tell everyone I had a migraine or something. Really – I don't mind missing it at all. I haven't got anything to wear, so it's too late now really."

Albert scratched his head. "Well, 'tis no good, you're going to have to go, so either I'll have to have a rummage and see what's stashed away here, or you could have a look and see if Edith's costume is still serviceable."

"Edith's? But – well, I don't know that that would be right." The thought of appearing in public dressed as a nun did not fill Victoria with wild enthusiasm – but then again, she'd look very sensible, so no one could laugh at her. (Well not much, anyway. She certainly wasn't going to break into a rendition of 'Climb Every Mountain'.)

"There's a cupboard in the eaves in the back bedroom. I reckon she used to keep all that sort of stuff in there in an old brown leather suitcase." He picked up his mobile and checked the timer. "Well look here maid, I've gotta go and check the cows so I'll leave you to it," he said. "Just about time before the cake's ready in thirty-seven minutes!"

"Oh, OK." Victoria looked perplexed. "I thought you might help me look. So what are you going as, then?"

"Ah well, you'll just have to wait and see later!" and with that he strode out of the door.

Victoria washed up as fast as she could – the cake mixture seemed to get everywhere and stick to everything – and then trotted back to the cottage.

She went into the back bedroom. It didn't get much sun and she had barely spent any time in it other than to pile up books and some bedding on top of the old bedstead. The eaves cupboard door was quite large, coming up to about waist height, and ill fitting so that she had to tug hard to open it. She sniffed, detecting either damp or mice, or possibly both. She wasn't yet all that comfortable with the small furry people that seemed to share odd corners of her home with her, or the insects, or even, if she could bear to even think it, the fungi. Peering into the dark space, she thought something moved and leaped back with a squeal.

This was no time for feebleness, Victoria told herself sternly and fetched a torch from downstairs. She braced herself and leaned into the oddly shaped space. A leather suitcase was within reach; behind it she could see two cardboard boxes, what looked like a tin trunk and a hatbox.

She pulled out the suitcase and noticed a hole in one corner. She flipped open the old-fashioned latches and was confronted with a wodge of neatly folded black material. Victoria smiled. Good old Aunt Edith: of course she would wash and iron and then neatly pack away her fancy dress costume! Sadly, her niece had not inherited her tidy ways and would have stuffed it into a carrier bag and forgotten about it until the next year.

Victoria shook out the garment and heard a gentle thud as she did so. Puzzled, she looked around and then gave a small cry as she spotted what looked like a mummified mouse lying by the skirting board. She prodded it with the toe of her shoe just to be sure it was thoroughly dead. Victoria shuddered and then lifted up the habit – was that the right word? – to inspect it and smiled as she thought of her aunt singing her head off in it.

But her smile faded as she peered more closely. The desiccated mouse had clearly been very busy shortly before death and had chewed its way resolutely through the folded garment. When the neatly folded cloth was shaken out Victoria was reminded of those folded paper chains you made as a child, where you fold carefully and then cut through all the layers at once and ended up with a pretty pattern. The habit was spectacularly holed repeatedly at about knee height. The amount of chewing of a bone-dry habit had obviously done for the poor mouse. It had also done for Victoria's fancy dress outfit. She sat down on the bed and sighed loudly.

Moss padded up the stairs and came in to see why his owner sounded so fed up. Before she could stop him he had hopped into the cupboard. "No Moss!" she cried and lunged after him. Victoria had visions of the puppy slipping between cavities and becoming trapped behind wainscoting, howling plaintively as she and Albert ripped down plaster walls to get to him. But she managed to grab his back leg and in no time had hauled him out and was being rewarded with liberal kisses and much wagging. In the ensuing mêlée the hatbox was dragged out, as was one of the cardboard boxes.

"Naughty boy!" said Victoria, slightly shocked by how close they had been to disaster. "Sit, and lie down!" she said very sternly. The little dog did as he was told and rested his chin on his paws, his eyes watching her every move.

Victoria unstrapped the hatbox and found a magnificent wide-brimmed straw hat inside, decorated with all sorts of imitation flowers and the odd bit of wax fruit. It should have been ghastly, but was really very pretty and looked as if it was a few years old, perhaps from the 1950s. Somehow, the mouse and other beings had not found their way inside the hatbox. Victoria instantly tried on the hat and admired herself in the old blemished wardrobe mirror. She felt it rather suited her. Perhaps she should wear it to the show tomorrow?

As she went to replace the hat, she realised that there was something underneath. She drew out the starched white fabric – the wimple to complete her nun's costume. This was undamaged and Victoria breathed a sigh of relief. She re-examined the habit and knew the only possibly option was to cut off the chewed fabric. She laid the two items to one side and opened the cardboard box that also looked undamaged. Why on earth had the mouse gone for the leather suitcase and not touched anything else?

Inside the box were several pairs of gloves, one long black pair, a long white pair and what looked like soft kid gloves in a pale yellow. She stroked them, their softness reminding her of Moss's ears. Underneath the gloves was a large wooden crucifix on a leather thong. Her aunt had not been a religious person, so Victoria assumed this was part of the abbess's costume and added it to the pile of clothes.

At the bottom of the box were a collection of letters and some photos. Victoria hesitated. She knew if she started reading them she'd be lost. The day would fly past and she really would miss the dance. She sighed and placed everything but the crucifix back into the box, and put it on the bed. She went back to the cupboard and lugged out the tin trunk – a whole other treasure trove just waiting to be opened! She pushed it into the corner of the room near the door to remind her to look in it later. Then she firmly closed the eaves cupboard door and gave Moss a meaningful look. He responded with a "Me? What have I ever done face?" and she laughed.

"Come on, you little tyke, let's go and find a pair of scissors and let's see if we can make something out of this wreck!"

Later, just as Victoria finally put down the scissors and just before she was about to burst into tears, Albert strode into the room looking immensely pleased with himself. "Well my beauty, it looks fantastic!"

"Do you really think so? I think it's a complete disaster!" She held up what remained of the habit. "I can't possibly wear that – it's indecent!"

"Eh?" Albert peered at her. "What you on about? I'm talking about our cake! What are you talking about?"

"This!" She flapped the black fabric in front of his face.

"Oh my. Is that Edith's abbess thing? Whatever have you done to it maid?" He started laughing. "Well, you'll certainly get some admiring glances in that!"

Victoria flailed the habit at him several times until he backed away, still laughing. "It's not funny Albert! I've got nothing else to wear! A mouse had got into the suitcase and chewed through the habit about halfway up, so I had to cut it off. And now it looks like some awful joke shop sexy nun outfit!"

Albert was trying to stop laughing and making a poor job of it. "Well, I reckon, a pair of black stockings, some high heels and a bit of lipstick and you could win a prize!" He burst out laughing again and Victoria couldn't help joining in.

"You are rotten, really you are," she said as she put the habit onto a hanger and hooked it on the end of the dresser. "Honestly, whatever will people think?"

"That you're a good sport and that you've paid tribute to Edith and brought her costume up to date!"

"Really? Oh well, I haven't got a lot of choice, have I. I'll have to go and see if I've got any stockings – correction – tights, I don't want to get arrested, and somewhere I think I have got some black high heels."

"Oh good," said Albert, with a bit of twinkle in his eye.

"Men! You are all so predictable."

"Yes, I know we are, simple souls. But some of us are rather better than others and I reckon I have just baked the winning cake!" He gave his smuggest smile.

"You're also getting rather insufferable!" she said and slapped his arm.

"You want to come and see it?" Their eyes met and they both dissolved into laughter again.

"Oh really, this is just so childish! Come on, let's see the cake, then I must walk Moss before we get ready to go out." She sighed. "I cannot believe I am going to a fancy dress dance, or worse, that I am going as a nun. Thank God none of my old friends can see me."

"There's always Facebook," said Albert, casually.

She snorted. "If you think I'm going to put a photo on that…"

At seven o'clock Victoria heard the sound of a familiar engine revving away in the barn, Gloria had been started up. Interesting – that must mean Albert was driving them to the dance in the MG. She went back to peering in the mirror, still trying to get used to seeing herself without any hair, all hidden by the wimple. When she'd had her treatment for breast cancer she had been fortunate and not lost her hair, which she had dreaded. Of course this was completely different and, looking at herself in the wimple, she found the effect quite flattering. The white starched wings seemed to reflect light and, rather than making her look drawn as she'd feared, she found she felt quite glamorous and somehow illuminated – if not from within, then from all sides! How odd. She checked her eye make-up and then carefully applied the strongest lipstick she owned. It wasn't bright red, but it certainly made an impact.

Victoria stood back and inspected herself in the full-length mirror. "Oh dear God," she muttered. "I look like a kissagram!" She knew her legs were one of her best features but, really, at her age, she felt a mid-thigh-length skirt was pushing it a bit.

"Hello? Mother Superior?" called a voice from the kitchen.

"On my way!" She tottered carefully down the stairs. She hadn't worn a pair of high heels since she'd moved to Devon and she felt distinctly wobbly.

An ear-piercing wolf whistle greeted her as she descended into view. "Well, I say Miss West! That's a fine pair of pins you've got there!" said Albert, hands on hips.

Victoria stopped on the last step and gawped at him.

"Crikey!"

"Like it?"

"Very dashing."

Albert was swaggering about the kitchen in flying goggles, sheepskin flying jacket, white silk scarf, huge leather gauntlets that he was thwacking against his thigh and some very snug breeches and knee-length leather boots.

"I think we can safely say you are cutting a dash in that outfit!" She stroked his silk scarf. "Hmmm… perhaps you could wear this the next time we go down the pub?"

"OK, if you'll wear your naughty nun's outfit."

"Absolutely not!" she said, instinctively trying to pull the hem of the habit a little lower.

"You look great, stop fussing! Let's get going or we'll miss half the fun. Cheerio little pup, we'll see you later." Moss's tail thumped several times before he settled down to sleep in his crate.

Getting into the low-slung MG was a challenge and took Victoria several goes. "Just don't look Albert, it's just too embarrassing!" She ended up almost falling in backwards yet managed to keep her knees firmly together.

"Well, that was different, if nothing else," grinned Albert as he closed the door for her. "Don't worry – I'll give you a hand out when we get there. We don't want strong men fainting. Did I detect a flash of lace there, Miss West?"

Victoria blushed. "Oh dear, did you see much? I'm so paranoid about how short this is I've put a pair of silk camiknickers over the top of my tights to try and ensure complete modesty. Trouble is, they're red."

Albert smirked. "So I saw!"

They set off in the old car with Albert looking quite the part, the earflaps of his flying helmet batting gently in the breeze. Victoria found it really odd not to feel her hair blowing around. Wearing the wimple was rather like having her head in a bucket, or encased in one of those collars you put around a dog's neck to stop it chewing itself.

Victoria hung on as they zoomed around a tight corner. "Don't go too fast Albert, it will look awful if I arrive with get dead gnats and flies spattered all over my wimple…" This reduced them to helpless giggles and they had to pull into a gateway to regain their composure.

The show ground was a picture of traditional English village life, with people milling about, laughing and joking, the marquee aglow in the evening light and bunting everywhere fluttering in the gentle breeze. The sound of a fiddle and accordion filled the air and Victoria suddenly felt excited and nervous at the same time, like a child going to a birthday party.

Albert drove Gloria slowly into the field – she was not a car designed for rough ground – and found a nice flat area near the main track.

"Right, come on then maid, best foot forward and all that!" He opened the car door and Victoria swung her legs neatly around, knees together, and he pulled her quickly to her feet. "There we are, very elegant. Hardly saw a thing!" he whispered. He beamed at her and she could feel the start of a blush; he looked so dashing. And then she remembered she was dressed as an abbess in a mini skirt in the middle of a field and the romance of it all started to fade.

"Albert, let me take your arm, walking across grass in these heels will not be easy." Together they made stately progress towards the marquee. As they went, they passed various people they knew, or rather Albert said they knew, as she didn't seem to recognise any of them. Batman was apparently the man from the paper shop while a beautifully dressed Little Bo Peep, complete with live lamb on a halter, was the girl who sometimes waited at table in the Swaddle Arms. A small bustling fox, with huge brush tail, whiskers and tophat was identified as Tufty from the garage. Victoria stared at him in disbelief. She resisted saying she'd always thought of him as more of a squirrel and marvelled at his costume lovingly made from fake fur, complete with paws and even fur stuck on his face. She'd expected a few masks and some dodgy costumes, not these amazing creations.

Just as they reached the entrance to the marquee the devil himself strode towards them coloured red from head to foot, eyes flashing, hair on end as if electrified and forked tail waving from side to side.

"My dears! How wonderful to see you!" boomed the devil, breaking into a broad grin. "Why Victoria, you look as shocked as a good Mother Superior would be on being confronted by Lucifer himself!"

Albert and the Reverend roared with laughter and Victoria found herself gaping, then quickly shut her mouth and tried to regain her composure. "Well Edwin, I don't think I would have recognised you unless you'd spoken! What an amazing outfit!"

"I like to have a good go at it – such fun! And one rarely gets the opportunity to dress up these days. Well, I suppose I do more than most," he giggled. "Every Sunday, and all that!"

"So do you create a different costume every year, or is it more of a recurring theme, as favoured by my late aunt?"

The devil smiled. "I like to ring the changes. I was Lady Gaga last year, great fun!" He eyed Victoria. "Your dear aunt's costume seems to have undergone something of a 'makeover' this year – jolly good show Victoria, that's the spirit!"

"Oh don't," Victoria tugged at the edge of the habit. "I feel terribly self conscious. It's all the fault of a mouse."

Edwin looked puzzled. ""Really? Well you can tell me all about it later – we are seated on the same table. Meanwhile, I need to go and press some flesh, as the bishop would say." He swanned off towards a group that seemed to consist almost entirely of aliens.

Victoria wasn't sure if they were from Dr Who or some other popular TV show; sci-fi wasn't her strong point.

Albert took her arm. "Come on maid, let's get right into the fray and find our seats."

Victoria was puzzled – there was a seating plan? Surely everyone just sat about on hay bales, drank cider and did a bit of country dancing (or, heaven help her, line dancing)?

Once inside the marquee Victoria felt rather as if she had stepped into Dr Who's Tardis and, once again, found herself gaping in amazement. The huge tent was beautifully decorated with strings of pretty lights draped everywhere, while swags of filmy fabric had been cleverly arranged to disguise supporting poles. A band with fiddles, an accordion, drums and a guitar or two were playing a pleasant tune on the small stage area. In front of the stage was a big wooden dance floor taking up about a third of the marquee, while long tables and chairs banquet-style were neatly arranged in another third. Behind this was a bar and lounge area, with comfy sofas, more subdued lighting and large potted plants in tasteful clusters.

Victoria realised Albert was peering at her. "You alright maid? You've gone awful quiet. Were you expecting straw bales and a hoedown, or summat?"

"Oh no," lied Victoria, grinning broadly. "No, not at all, I just wasn't expecting anything quite so… so grand! It's amazing!"

"A lot of people put a lot of work into it every year. It's our main event really. Well, there's the Christmas panto too, and the crowning of the May Queen and the beating of the bounds and…"

"Beating the what?"

He laughed. "You Google it later! It's all traditional community stuff that we poor old country dwellers do to stop ourselves going mad from boredom stuck out here in the sticks."

Victoria looked at him. "I don't think anyone would ever think of you as a 'poor old country dweller' Albert!"

"Right, let's follow the Reverend's example and go and press some flesh!"

He steered her towards a throng gathered in front of the bar. "Albert! Victoria! Coo-ee!" cried a familiar voice and Victoria saw a fish waving at her from behind the bar. Next to the fish was a tall figure encased in a long thin yellowish costume that appeared to be made of foam, with arms, legs and face protruding. Victoria waved back as she'd realised the fish was Trudy, more from her voice than any physical signs – but what was the other one supposed to be? She pondered this as they approached the bar.

"What can I get you, Mother Superior?" asked Roger Mudge, deadpan. Seeing her expression, he sighed. "I'm a chip. Get it? Trudy's a fish, I'm a chip. I reckon I'll get a sign made and stick it to me forehead so I don't have to keep explaining to everyone."

Victoria laughed. "It's very good Roger and, you really do look like a chip!"

"Yeah, I know," he nodded. "White wine? I've got some bottles of prosecco if you want something a bit more partyish. People generally buy bottles, then they don't have to keep coming back to the bar all night."

"Sounds a great idea! I love bubbles! Albert, what about you?"

"Well, I'm the driver, so I reckon I'll have a pint of cider, Mudger, and then we'll see."

"Right you are," said Roger, and turned awkwardly in his chip costume to get their drinks.

"I hope you'll help me out a bit with the fizzy, I can't drink a whole bottle."

Albert grinned. "Oh I don't know, I reckon you could have a good go at it."

The band suddenly struck up a lively jig and Albert picked up his pint and Victoria's bottle. "Come on maid! Grab your glass and let's get stuck in!"

The marquee was filling up fast and they made their way towards where the Reverend, aka the devil, was now holding court, "Stake your claim!" he said, brandishing his devil's pitchfork at them. Tuft was also on the table with a mousy lady – literally – that Victoria assumed must be his wife. Just as they sat down, two leopards slunk by.

"Where on earth do people get all these amazing costumes from?" marvelled Victoria. "They must spend hours – or a lot of money."

"The former. It's all a bit of fun and, let's face it, in the modern world there's not much chance to have some harmless fun is there?" said Albert, raising his glass. "Cheers, Mother Abbess!" and they clinked glasses.

A loud chorus of greetings made them both look round. Two furry dog-like figures, both with floppy ears and blackened noses, were taking seats at the table. One was distinctly dog-eared and shaggy, while the other was sleek and wore a jewelled collar. "Oh good grief," muttered Albert. "It's that dog woman and her long-suffering husband. I reckon she's got him as well trained as her dogs!"

Victoria was chuckling to herself as she waved to Bunty Beacham-Brown, and her husband Kenneth, who were doing excellent impersonations of Lady and the Tramp.

"You up for a dance in a bit?" asked Albert, leaning across to make himself heard. The noise level was climbing as everyone came and took their seats.

"I don't think I can manage anything energetic in these shoes, but I am sure I could totter round for a slow dance later," she said into his ear. He smiled at her and she detected a distinct twinkle in his eye.

In the background Trudy was rushing about organising her waiting staff with huge dishes of food. As she was still dressed as a fish – Victoria presumed she was a cod, or perhaps a haddock – it was really completely surreal.

"What do you keep grinning at?" said Albert, close to her ear.

Victoria took a swig of her wine and waved her glass expansively. "This! I mean, look at it!"

"What about it?"

"Well, it's bonkers! I mean, where else would you sit down with leopards, a dogs, Batman and – what on earth is that person meant to be?"

Albert followed her pointing finger. "Oh, that's Bill Bramley. Don't you recognise him?"

"No, of course not! What on earth is he meant to be?"

"An apple tree – seems obvious to me."

"Why?"

Albert gave her one of his old-fashioned looks. "You townies – I thought you were meant to be smart! Bill Bramley – as in Bramley apple, clue in the name! Every year he comes along in that tree-bark costume with all they leaves and branches worn as a headdress. Pretty good I reckon." Albert took a gulp of beer and gestured towards the nodding foliage that could be seen making its way to the bar. "You watch him – as the night goes on, he starts handing out apples to all the ladies he fancies, sort of rustic chat-up technique," and they both started laughing.

Before Victoria could gather her wits, huge dishes of food were being hefted onto the tables and everyone started tucking in. She picked up a printed programme, one of several scattered on the table. This stated the meal was 'Lasagne, chicken pie or a veggie option – on request – salad and jacket potatoes'. Beneath this was printed the running order for the evening. After the meal, there'd be ten minutes for everything to be cleared away, then the fancy dress would be judged with prizes for best topical entry, best animal entry and best traditional entry. Victoria wasn't too sure which categories some of these costumes would fall into, but she guessed not everyone entered; they just liked an excuse to dress up. After the fancy dress, the disco would start and then the raffle would be drawn at 11pm, with more dancing until midnight.

Helping herself to lasagne and salad, Victoria asked, "Does Trudy do all this?"

Albert nodded, spooning out a huge portion of pie. "Pretty much, it's her and a team of local women, they're like a catering corps for the show. They use her recipes and she oversees it all and they make a couple of big dishes each, that way there's plenty for everyone."

"Mmm, it's as tasty as her usual lasagne, what a great way to spread the workload." Once they'd finished Victoria said, "But there's something else I don't understand."

"What's that?"

"Well, how on earth is the show going to be in here tomorrow morning when this doesn't end until midnight?"

"Ah well, this marquee is where they have the beer tent, so they just expand the bar a bit, and also the cream teas, so they rearrange the tables and chairs and there's a bit of a tea dance, so they use the dance floor for that. All the produce and arts and crafts and stuff are in the other marquee, and that's pretty much all set up and ready to go. That's where we have to deliver the cake at eight o'clock tomorrow morning for judging."

Victoria gaped at him "8am? On a Saturday morning, after a night like this?" She groaned, imagining how she, and everyone else in the village, was not going to be on their best form.

"Yep, there's a team comes in here at 6am and get's it all shipshape for 10am when the public starts coming in. All runs like clockwork, don't you worry!"

"I don't think I'll be shipshape at 8am tomorrow morning!"

"Oh yes you will young lady, as you'll be hand delivering YOUR cake for the judging."

She stuck her tongue out at him and poured another glass of fizz. "Cheers!" they said in unison.

People were getting up to dance, while some others were going round selling raffle tickets. "Lots of great prizes!" said a woman who Victoria vaguely recognised from the shop. She appeared to be dressed as a sheep. "Great, I'll have a strip of tickets then," she said, starting to feel distinctly merry. Albert also bought tickets, and they fell to chatting to their neighbours, a man dressed as a policeman (Victoria assumed he wasn't a real one, although his uniform looked authentic) and a woman who seemed to be a medieval damsel, complete with conical hat and laced bodice. Victoria was glad that her abbess costume was so loose fitting; if she'd been laced into a bodice she felt she might have exploded by now, given the amount of lasagne she'd eaten.

"Watcha! Victoria! Oi, Albert! Over 'ere!" cried the all-too-familiar Essex tones of Kev. Victoria and Albert turned to see not the erstwhile builder-cum-plumber, but instead were confronted by what looked like a moving greengrocer's stall and a woman-sized pink-and-white cupcake.

"Good grief!" Victoria was almost lost for words. The pile of fruit and veg came over and said, "How's it going then? Let me introduce my missus Kelly."

The cupcake quivered and waved and, from beneath a bubbly pink wig, came a girlie voice. "Hiya! Nice to meet you Victoria. 'Ello

Albert! Cor you look hunky in that get-up!" Albert laughed and managed to plant a kiss on her pink-and-white sparkling cheek.

Kev's fruit and veg bobbed about and he said, "Give us a twirl then Victoria!" Emboldened by too much wine, she duly tottered to her feet and did a quick pirouette. "Cor blimey love! That'd upset the Pope and no mistake – know what I mean!"

"Let me guess," said Victoria. "You're going for the topical entry and you're seven portions of fruit and veg versus the evils of sugar?"

"Got it in one!" said Kev, evidently delighted by the success of their costumes. "We've won it three years on the trot so we're pretty keen to make it four," rubbing his hands together in eager anticipation and looking over towards what Victoria guessed was the judges' table to the side of the dance floor.

"I reckon you're in with a good chance!" said Albert. "Good luck, we'll be cheering you on. Come on Victoria, I need a bit of fresh air after that walloping great dinner, and we need to be back in to see you being judged." He nodded at Kelly as she and Kev made their way onto the dance floor to make sure the judges had time to view their outfits.

Albert took her hand, threading a course through the tables and chairs. Victoria teetered on her heels, apologising and giggling as she tripped over chair legs. Just as they reached the exit, she pulled him to a stop.

"Look at that!" she cried. Lined up on the edge of the dance floor stood three familiar figures, all dressed in white, each one wearing sunglasses, with whiskers painted on their whitened cheeks and big white ears protruding from their grey hair. "Brilliant!" she said and they waved at the triplets, who waved back in unison. The Three Blind Mice turned and made their way slowly – Victoria guessed they could hardly see a thing through their dark lenses –

towards the judges' table. As they turned around, their long white tails could be seen, each one sporting fake blood and a big bandage about halfway down where the farmer's wife had cut them off and they'd been stuck back on!

"Well, I've seen everything now!" laughed Victoria as she and Albert stumbled into the cool darkness outside, away from the heat and noise. "Three Blind Mice, what a brilliantly simple idea! That Lavender is not as daft as she looks. Oops!" Victoria tripped and Albert caught her arm. "Goodness!" She took a deep breath. "That fresh air has made the wine rush straight to my head!"

"You hold on to me and we'll just walk for a couple of minutes and get some air," said Albert, as they strolled around the outside of the marquee. As they turned a corner, they heard a muffled giggle and then a deep male voice and a chuckle. Albert stopped abruptly and seemed to be listening intently. "Oh, Charlie!" said a breathy woman's voice.

Before Victoria could ask what was wrong Albert said, "Carol? Is that you?"

There was a sound of rustling and some muffled exchanges and then out of the shadows emerged two figures. "Albert Moreton, what are you doing round here?" said Charlie Weston, hastily brushing his hair back into place.

"Was about to ask you the same thing," snapped Albert. From behind Charlie stepped the blonde woman Victoria recognised both from the pub and the incriminating photos taken by prying Percy. "Carol, is that you?"

"What if it is?" barked Charlie. "Free country." Both men seemed to be framing up to each other and, through a haze of alcohol, Victoria felt a slight frisson of alarm.

"Hello Albert," said Carol in her slightly drawling accent. "You alright, my lover?" Victoria reminded herself that this was merely a general term of endearment in Devon and there was no need to launch herself at the woman and box her ears, although she did feel quite tempted.

"I'm fine. What about you?" said Albert, tight-lipped and still standing very tall and straight.

"I'm very fine, very fine indeed!" said Carol, taking Charlie's arm and snuggling into him. "Aren't I Charlie?"

"Yes," said Charlie. "We're both very fine." Victoria wanted to laugh, but suspected it was not the right thing to do just at that moment.

"Charlie and me, well we're – can I tell him Charlie? Or will you." She peered up at him with an exaggerated wide-eyed look. Victoria felt even more inclined to box her ears for such pathetic simpering.

Charlie puffed out his chest and, looking smug, put his arm around Carol. "Carol and I are getting engaged."

"Isn't that nice?" said Carol, still gazing up at Charlie like a moonstruck cow.

"Well, as long as you know what you're doing Carol," said Albert.

Victoria snorted – of course the woman knew what she was doing! She managed to turn the snort into a cough, and then cleared her throat. "I'm sure she does, congratulations to you both," she said, putting her arm around Albert, determined not to be outdone.

"Thank you! Victoria, isn't it?" said Carol, peering at her through the darkness.

"Yes, that's me! Anyway, come along Albert, we need to get back inside and see if the meat and two veg come out on top in the fancy dress!" She hauled Albert round and they set off back the way they'd come.

"Meat and two veg?" muttered Albert. "I reckon you're tiddled Miss West."

"I reckon you're right," she giggled. "Oh dear, meat and two veg – that's a bit rude, isn't it!"

They both started giggling. When they got to the entrance to the marquee, someone was saying "Testing, testing, one, two, three!" loudly into a microphone and there was a burst of howling feedback. Albert pulled her past and on around the further corner of the marquee. "We'll miss the judging!' she cried.

"Shush Victoria," he put his finger to her lips. "Look, we almost came to grief a few weeks back through a misunderstanding and some of that was about Carol and well, I just want you to know that, you see, I don't care about her in any romantic way, sort of thing." He scratched his ear. "But I care about her generally, see?" Victoria nodded. "I just wanted to be sure she was alright and that bleddy Weston wasn't taking advantage of her."

"A bit late for that!" chirruped Victoria, before she could stop herself. Wine always made her lippy.

"Yes, I know," said Albert grinning. "She's no innocent, but she's had a tough time and, well… you know." He scratched his ear again. "If he's going to marry her then, that's fine. She'll have some security again. He's a plonker, but he's well off and he's not a nasty man, I reckon he'll treat her well." He sighed and Victoria watched a series of emotions flit across his face. "I just wanted you to understand that I don't care for her in that way."

She looked up at him, enjoying seeing him struggling to express himself. "And what way is that?"

His ear got a further scratching. "Don't be contrary now, you know what way I mean."

"Do I?"

"Yes," he said quietly. "The way I feel about you."

Chapter 13

Victoria opened one eye slowly, and listened. Silence – no, not silence – birdsong. Very loud birdsong, actually. There must be a blackbird or a sparrow sitting in the climbing rose near her open window. It seemed much louder than it usually did; the bird was positively shouting or – maybe – using a loud hailer. Victoria moved her head and groaned. No, the bird wasn't shouting: she had a hangover.

"Victoria! Time to get up, wakey wakey!"

She closed her eyes again. The room was full of early-morning sunshine and much too bright, and she tried to work out where the voice was coming from. Again she realised it must have been coming through the open bedroom window.

"Victoria!" shouted a slightly more urgent voice.

She groaned again and tried to lift her head off the pillow. It felt like lead. She managed to get her legs over the side of the bed and tried raising her head again but now, for some inexplicable reason, the room itself was moving… and not in a helpful way.

"Right, that's it maid, I'm using my key, just giving you fair warning!"

There was a pause. She tried to get up again but just sank back onto the mattress. Heavy footfalls were coming up the stairs.

"Now look maid, this is not the time to be lazing in bed, we're due to get the cake to the show in thirty minutes. Look lively!"

Alfred appeared at the bedroom door, bright, breezy and very loud. He snorted at the sight of her and shook his head. "Lord sakes, you're a lightweight drinker you are, miss. Plenty had a lot more than you during the evening and look at you."

"I think you should know that I may never be able to get up again," said Victoria feebly. "Ever."

"Tough love needed here then," replied Albert. He whipped off the duvet and sat near enough to get his arms under her neck and shoulders and pulled her up to a sitting position.

"Albert, I think I hate you," she said, still holding one side of her head.

"No you don't. Now come on, up you get, cold water followed by strong coffee, we'll soon have you fit to go. Do you need a hand to get through to the bathroom? Cold water has great powers – I could even help you shower!"

She could feel Albert tense as he waited for her to slap him but she couldn't raise the energy.

"You are a horrid man." She got shakily to her feet and, mustering what little dignity she had left, said, "I can manage perfectly well thank you, now be off to the kitchen and make the coffee – that will be much more useful!"

Victoria smiled to herself, but even that small action hurt. She stood for a while in the almost finished bathroom, wavering slightly as if in a breeze, waiting for the water to heat up a little before she braved the shower; she didn't think a cold drenching was really needed. Completing the decoration wouldn't take much longer and she could already use her dream power shower – and this was exactly the sort of moment when she knew she would enjoy it to the full.

Well, perhaps 'enjoying' was a little strong as, once she stepped under the pounding cascade of water, she wished she were back in bed. What had been a wondrous power shower the day before now felt like a million small hammers raining down on her head. She turned the setting to normal (no power, no extra strength) and had just a quick shower to help wake herself up before climbing out and rubbing herself dry, very gently.

"Victoria!" Albert shouted from downstairs. "Stir yerself, it's time to leave! You'll have to try and drink your coffee on the way."

Victoria looked at herself in the mirror and hoped she didn't really look as dire as she thought. Bags under her eyes – come to that bloodshot eyes – and wet hair... wow! She was a real beauty. She brushed her hair gingerly up into a ponytail and pulled on her yoga pants (not used since she'd moved to Devon) and a T-shirt. Perhaps she'd get away with a sporty 'just out of the shower after a run' look.

She walked slowly into the kitchen and Albert grabbed her arm in quite an agitated way. "Lass, c'mon, time's running out, cake has to be there before eight!" She looked up at him and thought she saw a glimmer of a smile that was swiftly repressed. "Buck up now – here – you carry the cake and I'll bring the staging bits."

"Staging bits?"

"Yes staging bits, make sure the chocolate curls are just so on the top, extra if needed, extra doily, wipes to make sure there are no marks, that sort of thing, c'mon move it!"

Victoria took the cake just as Moss realised she was going out and he hadn't yet given her his morning licks and greetings. He jumped out of his bed and launched himself at her, and the cake wobbled and almost slipped. Albert swore loudly, which shocked both Victoria and Moss into cowed silence.

"Sorry," said Albert quietly, "but I thought the cake was a gonner then."

"Goodness, I'm sorry, I thought so too," said Victoria, feeling very wobbly herself. "Poor Moss, you were just being friendly... come on boy, you can come to the show too."

The jolt of the near-cake-disaster had sobered Victoria far more effectively than any strong cup of coffee might, and she took another deep breath as they walked towards the car parked outside the back door. Moss jumped gleefully into the back and settled down, his tail thumping on the seat with excitement.

Victoria held the cake very, very carefully and barely talked as they made their way to the showground. It was a gorgeous sunny summer's day and everywhere looked fresh and bright. She wished she'd picked up her sunglasses.

"Here, I'll take the dog – you go and deliver the cake and don't forget to find your entry number. Check how it looks once you have set it up, as I said, more curls, new doily – all those bits if needed are in this tin." He tapped it pointedly.

"I'd really rather you came too Albert." She felt ill prepared and rather panicky, cross with herself for being in such a state.

"We can't do that Victoria. They won't want the pup in there and it wouldn't do for folks to get suspicious if I knew what to with the chocolate and things."

Victoria sighed and felt more than ever that this whole subterfuge seemed ridiculous, but she must finish what she'd started.

She carried the cake carefully into the marquee and searched along the bench for her number. Forty-two was the number she had been allocated. She doubted there could be forty-two entries but apparently there were, more in fact as the numbers seemed to go up to about fifty.

She laid out the cake, prettied up the curls on the top that had slid a little when she nearly dropped it, and added a few more for effect on the large white doily it sat on. She remembered all Albert's instructions: check for smears or marks, make sure it's showing its best face, and then stop fiddling.

Feeling very relieved that she could indeed stop fiddling, Victoria collected up all her bits and pieces and packed them back into the tin. At the last moment, she got out her phone and took a quick photo to show Albert, waiting anxiously outside. She checked again that the cake was shown to its best possible advantage, then turned and almost fled from the tent with relief.

"All done, you happy?" said Albert as she got back to him.

"Yes," she replied, "the best that I could do anyway. Look, I took this shot. Does this look OK to you?"

Albert squinted at the phone and then nodded, lips pursed. "I reckon that's about spot on," he said, and let out a long breath.

She looked at his worried expression and touched his arm. "Oh Albert, this really matters to you, doesn't it?"

He scratched his head. "Yes maid, it does. As daft as it is, it's become a bit of a 'thing' with me. Your aunt understood. She used to get right competitive about it." He looked off into the middle distance and smiled. "Ah well... end of the day if we don't win, it's not the end of the world."

Moss was tugging at the lead. "Right," said Albert briskly, "dog classes then?"

"What now?"

"No you daft whatsit, we've got to enter him for this afternoon!"

"Oh right, yes I think I could manage that."

They wandered over to another small tent that was apparently the central admin office for all the classes. Albert ducked his head in and spoke to one of the officials sitting inside. He came out waving a piece of white paper.

"Here's the options, what do you want to enter?"

"Oh goodness," said Victoria. "I don't know – what do you think?"

"Well no point in entering dog that looks most like his owner, Joe Witchell has that sewn up, wins every year – he and his bulldog will never be beaten for that trophy, you can barely tell 'em apart!"

"Oh here, how about this, most endearing puppy. Oh, or how about dog with the waggiest tail. He's pretty good at that!"

"Sounds just right to me, let's enter him in the both of them."

They moved into the admin tent and there stood Bunty. She smiled broadly at them. "What ho you two, come to enter young Moss into the obedience class? Yes of course you have!" She waved at the paper Albert was holding. "Don't worry – I'll fill the forms in for you, bit of a line forming here, no need for you to wait."

"Oh but we, I mean, I was thinking of dog with the waggiest tail?"

"Good idea Victoria, let him have some fun as well as the proper stuff, not a problem. I'll sort it all for you, three o'clock then for your first entry."

Standing tall and business-like in her best tweed, Bunty gave them a 'good that's all sorted' smile and Victoria felt far too intimidated to object and merely simpered as they backed out of the tent. Albert grinned at her and took her arm. "C'mon Moss, off we go, time for breakfast."

Victoria started to shake her head in an 'I don't believe it' sort of way but then stopped as her headache reminded her it was still in residence. She looked around the field and saw that people were coming and going, almost as if on autopilot. Heads down, large armfuls of flowers and vast vegetables, bags full of potatoes and baskets of strawberries, all heading towards the produce tent. She noticed several pairs of glassy eyes and pale complexions, so she reckoned she wasn't the only one feeling rather shabby the morning after the dance.

Albert was looking around too and, as if reading her mind,

said. "Well you can spot the ones that was at the dance last night. Not a pretty sight, eh?" He laughed and Moss looked up at him and wagged his tail. "You save your wagging young man, you're going to need that later!"

Two of the triplets passed close by with baskets of flowers and a closed tin. "Morning Victoria, a bit of a headache I expect!" trilled Daphne. "You seemed to have lots of fun though."

Victoria smiled at them, then hesitated and felt a niggle of disquiet. "Albert, was there anything really untoward that I did last night that my brain has conveniently edited?"

"Well I'm not so sure your aunt, bless her, would have danced on the table with the habit being quite so short, but all the chaps seemed to enjoy it. I also thought your version of 'Climb Every Mountain' sounded quite different to hers, but still, we all appreciated it!"

Albert cut off a chuckle and Victoria narrowed her eyes. "Albert Moreton – you are deliberately winding me up! As if I would dance on the table!"

They passed Trudy on their way back to the car park and she greeted them with a huge smile.

"Morning you two lovebirds." Then she turned to Victoria and, nudging her quite sharply, hissed, "You're going to have to tell me where you got that underwear from, my Roger was quite excited when you were dancing up on those tables. You'll have to tell all when you come in for that special meal you won, I have some wonderful plans."

"Oh, I..." Victoria broke off and felt the worst flush of embarrassment she had suffered in ages. She averted her eyes, brushing strands of escaping hair back behind her ears. "I really, yes, well..." With that she pulled Albert and Moss off towards the car and kept her head down. "What is she talking about?" she hissed.

"Did try to tell you," said Albert with a wry smile.

"No… tell me I didn't… no, no… It's too embarrassing; I can't ever go into the pub again. But what was all that about a special meal and wonderful plans?"

"Why – you won the raffle, romantic meal for two down at the Swaddle Arms, to be taken any time over the next two months, but not on a Thursday as that's the pensioners' special and not on a Sunday lunch as it's the carvery," Albert said, doing a passable impression of Trudy.

"Won the raffle? Goodness – I have no memory of that at all."

"That'll be why you don't remember going up to collect the prize and singing 'Congratulations' once you got to the microphone then." He paused. "That was just before you danced on the table."

"Well that's it – I'll never be able to go anywhere in the village again. I'll have to move!"

"Don't be daft! You did a grand job and there was many a smiling gent watching."

"Oh stop it, I can't take any more! Oh God – I need coffee and a dark corner to hide in."

"You don't need to hide – the village loves a bit of fun at the dance, only point in putting the damn thing on in my way of thinking – you should have seen the Reverend shaking his stuff on the dance floor, had everyone in fits of laughter. There were plenty of others letting their hair down too, not just you!"

Once they were safely home, Albert made a large pot of coffee and a mountain of buttered toast, of which she managed one slice and he demolished at least four. While she was sipping her coffee and deciding whether she felt better or not, her phone rang.

"Just let them leave a message," said Albert. "You need to concentrate on coffee." Victoria loved it when Albert got all protective. It made life a lot easier to know someone cared for you.

After she'd downed her coffee, she picked up her phone and frowned. "It's an Exeter number, it might be the prison. I wonder if Sam's OK?"

Albert, wiping his lips free of butter, gave a small shrug. "Well, you'd better have a listen then." To make sure he didn't think she was being at all precious about it, she put it on speakerphone.

"Hello Victoria, this is Sam, I er… I was just wondering if you had found out anything, had any news. It's pretty bleak in here and nobody seems to want to come and visit me apart from some padre the other day which rather made me feel as if I was on death row."

Victoria looked over at Albert. Neither of them spoke.

Sam took a deep breath, and continued. "So anyway, if you have got time, maybe you could come and visit again or write to me with news, anything really, it would just be nice to hear from you… someone. There has to be some way to get me out of here. Bye."

Albert was the first to speak. "Look maid, there's nothing you can do today. We may yet find something out, but there's nothing much to tell just yet, is there. Just you forget it for the next few hours and enjoy your day." He patted her hand.

Victoria felt immediately depressed. Yes, they'd made some headway and had even written up a list of suspects, but nothing definite. But then she wasn't the police and, of course, it was really down to them, and she wasn't even Sam's family. But somehow she still felt guilty. She sighed. She knew Albert was right; she couldn't change anything today. Her headache was receding and she realised she felt considerably more human than she had earlier.

"Could you give me half an hour or so to check on the cows and then we'll think about heading back to the show to see if you've won?"

"OK, that will give me time to brush my hair and attempt to put my 'normal' face on – and some more appropriate clothes, too."

After a while, she heard him return. "Is that you Albert?"

"Certainly is maid, you ready to go?"

Victoria appeared at the top of the stairs in a red summer dress with a full skirt. She'd bought it for a friend's parents' golden wedding ages ago and hadn't worn it since. In her hands she held the wide-brimmed straw hat decorated with imitation flowers that she'd found in the spare room cupboard. "Will this do?" she asked.

Albert looked up and she saw his eyes soften. "I should say so maid. You look a proper picture!" He met her at the bottom of the stairs and examined the hat. "I recognise that, I think I remember your aunt wearing it, would be a few years ago now."

"I found it in the cupboard with the nun's outfit, no idea why the mouse hadn't eaten it. It's rather pretty, isn't it?" She perched it on her head.

"It is too," smiled Albert. "There's only one problem."

"Oh dear – what?" Victoria's hands flew to her hair, her face – what could be wrong – had she got mascara all over the place or something?

He grinned and lifted the hat slightly. "Damned tricky to give you a kiss under that enormous brim!"

Two policemen were directing the traffic as they approached the show field and Victoria was amazed at how busy it was. They parked at the front of the field, near the main showring, Albert seemingly able to thread his way past queues of cars and charm officials with a few winks and nods.

As Victoria neared the marquee she felt quite nervous. Would Albert blame her if she hadn't won? They'd always won when her aunt had played the game with him. Did she arrange the cake properly? Oh – why had she drunk too much the night before!

They entered the hushed atmosphere of the tent, passing tables covered in the most amazing arrays of vegetables of enormous magnitude and stunning floral displays and jewel-like jars of produce, until, finally, cakes came into view. With trepidation they edged along the line, Albert's eyes scanning the entries quickly. Victoria spotted a highly commended and a second place... yes, and a third... and then, at last, they reached number 42. There it was in all its glory – a certificate bearing a gold star and the words 'First Prize' emblazoned across its middle.

"Wow – we did it!" squeaked Victoria, jumping up and down with excitement.

"Yes indeed you did!!" said Albert, with a stern 'don't blow it now' look on his face.

"They must have liked it a lot, look there's barely half left," Victoria said, trying to cover her near faux pas, but nobody around them seemed to have heard anything.

Bunty came bustling past. "Good to see you have inherited some skills from dear Edith," she said, and gave a nod towards the certificate. "See you at three. Let's see if your little fellow can cover himself in glory too!"

Victoria gave a faint smile and repressed the urge to 'sit' that she often felt in Bunty's presence. "What do I do now?" she whispered to Albert.

"Nothing yet maid, cups are all presented late afternoon. You never know – Moss might have earned himself a trophy too, even if it is just for the waggiest tail! Now let's get going over to the clay pigeons, I always enters that; never win but it's a laugh trying to beat 'em. So many round here are crack shots!"

They tramped across the field and noticed the show was getting really busy. The big marquee where she had obviously had such a whale of a time the night before was now packed with people queuing for the bar and settling down to cream teas. Victoria spotted Jean talking animatedly with her sister over scones and jam and she thought she spotted Kev's highlighted spikes somewhere near the bar. Roger and Trudy were rushed off their feet and Victoria wondered at their stamina, considering they'd run the bar at the dance as well.

In the field itself, commercial stalls had been set up selling everything from leather bags to jewellery and even kitchenalia. There were ice-cream vans, hot-dog and burger vans and, much to Victoria's delight, an old-fashioned sweet stall, where they stopped so she could buy some honeycomb. She had strong memories of Edith serving honeycomb in a little cut-glass bowl on the kitchen table; strange how such memories could suddenly come back so vividly, she thought. Another stall sold toffee apples and candyfloss, the smell of both instantly transporting her back to childhood.

Albert was looking at some of the other stalls. Apart from the usual tombola and coconut shy, Victoria grinned at the 'welly-wanging' competition and an elaborate contraption along the lines of old-fashioned stocks. The game seemed to consist of no more than paying for the privilege of hurling wet sponges at someone in the stocks, something a group of young boy scouts were energetically paying up to do to their scout master.

A small tent at the edge of the main ring was a hive of activity and at its centre was the Reverend Ruminant. He was dressed completely in khaki and looked rather like an overgrown boy scout himself. He was handing out bits of paper and waving his arms about, but everything seemed quite good humoured. He looked up and waved at Victoria and Albert then picked up the microphone to announce the start of the tug-of-war, or at least Victoria thought he did. It came out through the speakers sounding very odd, with the same sound quality that she'd witnessed many times at London railway stations.

They wandered on, threading their way past families enjoying picnics and gaggles of over-excited children and numerous dogs. Eventually at the far edge of the field they reached a roped-off area well away from most of the stalls where a line of people stood, waiting patiently.

"Goodness – are all these here for the clay pigeon shooting?" asked Victoria.

"Yup, always busy like this, that's why I wanted to sign up early. One of the most popular events I reckon."

"Well I don't approve. I know they aren't real birds, but that's not the point."

"Oh I think that's very much the point," replied Albert, "no birds hurt, just testing your skill."

"But round here people do shoot real birds don't they? And furry things."

Albert sighed. "'Tis the country for goodness sakes, yes of course we shoots things, helps keep thing in balance."

"Well I don't see how killing things keeps anything balanced. I really had no idea I'd come across more guns down here in Devon than ever I did up in London. Never even saw a gun in London and look at all these!" She waved her hand at an array of shotguns all neatly lined up against some straw bales that had been arranged to make a sort of shooting gallery near the hedge, some twenty yards away.

"You go two at a time, see, standing over there in those spaces, called stands, and that metal contraption over there, that's a trap, that fires the clays and you have to shoot 'em and hit more than your opponent and with fewer shots."

Victoria scowled. "I sincerely hope my headache has gone by then as I expect it's very noisy!"

"'Tis a bit," agreed Albert as he moved forward in the queue. Moss pulled on his lead, eager to make friends with the various

Labradors and spaniels that were passing by in a near-constant stream. Victoria didn't think she'd ever seen so many dogs in one place, and she was amazed there hadn't been any fights. "Why don't you have a wander round the stalls while I sign up here, no point in you just standing about," said Albert. "I reckon it'll take a good ten minutes."

"OK, I'll have a wander. I'll keep going along the edge of the field – see you later." She set off along the nearest line of stalls that, not surprisingly, sold gun-related products. There were plastic ducks, long wading boots and a wonderful thing that you blew down to make noise just like a duck quacking. Victoria was drawn to a rather natty line of shooting clothes and quite fancied herself in tweed breeches and a deerstalker, until she looked at the price tags.

Next, she came across more dog-related items and found all sorts of lovely things she could buy for Moss including a wax jacket of his own and a clever zip-up fleece bag that you could stick your muddy and wet dog in to both protect the back of your car and result in a dry dog by the time you got home. Victoria made a mental note to buy one of those once Moss had finished growing.

She was enjoying picking her way through a stall of leather bags and wallets and belts when Albert caught up with her. "Bought anything yet?"

"No I haven't. I was expecting it all to be local stuff that would be a bargain – but it's just like shopping in any high street really."

"Yes, you could say that, although they do usually have some show offers running. Anyway, now all the excitement's over let's go and have a proper look in the produce tent, and then maybe grab a pint?"

Victoria grimaced. "Well, perhaps not the last item, but yes to everything else."

"Hair of the dog, you know what they say!" laughed Albert. As they walked across the show field the public address system was blaring away, and Edwin was asking for people to come and take part in various races in between bursts of feedback and hissing sounds. It's just like school sports day, thought Victoria, as she heard entrants being called for the three-legged race, followed by the egg and spoon.

She bought one of the programmes she had herself designed, and checked the timing of the events. Albert read it over her shoulder, but the brim of her hat was in the way, so she slipped it off. He pointed to the programme. "Terrier racing! We ought to see that – it's a riot!" he said. "It's at two o'clock, that should work out OK." He glanced at his watch, "Almost noon now. Moss is performing at three, and my shooting is at four. Plenty of time to have a good look around."

Victoria was enchanted by the produce tent. The immaculate displays of matching vegetables, the enormous onions and carrots – how on earth did they grow them so large? There were plenty of other gorgeous cakes on show, including some amazing themed ones made by children. Jams and pickles of every flavour and hue were on display, and she snapped away with her phone camera as a reminder to enter the various classes next year. "Oh damn! I meant to do the six matching eggs!" she cried, stopping in front of an array of perfect eggs, all neatly nestling in sand on individual paper plates. "I forgot all about it with everything that's been going on lately."

"Hardly surprising," said Albert. "Next year you can plan what you want to do – you'll have more time and you'll know what to expect after seeing all this. And, as the Reverend is bound to require your services again, you'll know all the classes well in advance too!"

She sighed. Oh dear – country life really wasn't all plain sailing. After admiring the entries for the photo competition (she'd meant to enter that too) and the scarecrows, they moved on to the feather and fur section and "ooh-ed" and "ahh-ed" over chickens and ducks of every shape, colour and size, plus rabbits and, to Victoria's horror, fancy rats. She clutched Albert's arm and hissed, "Rats! Huge rats – ugh!"

He laughed. "They're wonderful intelligent beasts you know – I had a pet rat when I was a lad, went everywhere with me it did."

"Oh God, please don't get another one," she shuddered. "It would mean a very abrupt end to our relationship!"

He squeezed her hand. "Oh well, if you mind that much, maybe I won't."

A trip to the bar, negotiating a seething mass of farmers, local youngsters and very pink people who'd spent too long in the sun, was followed by a more sedate cream tea. Wiping her mouth with a paper napkin and furtively feeding half her scone to Moss, Victoria said, "Would you mind if I had some candy floss?"

"Mind? Course not! I might have to have a toffee apple myself!"

To walk off their cream tea, they first did a circuit of the craft tent and saw woodturning, weaving and felt work. "Now that's where I'd spend my money," said Victoria. "Something handmade and unique, such lovely things!" She was stroking a felt hat decorated with leaves in soft autumnal shades.

It was lovely to wander about the stalls, enjoying the colour and the sounds – a local brass band was playing outside the bar – and Victoria felt, not for the first time since she'd moved to Devon, that she was living in a bygone era. "This is such fun!" she said, getting candyfloss all around her mouth.

"Here, Victoria, you'd better have a go at this!" Albert was steering her towards the welly-wanging stall. Their garage mechanic friend Tufty was running it.

"Hello you two! All the money raised here goes to the scouts so come and flex your biceps!" he said, rubbing his hands together in eager anticipation. Albert paid up and grabbed hold of the men's wellington boot – and threw it.

"Ooh!" cried Victoria, "That was good!"

"Not bad Albert, but Bill Bramley's got about ten feet on you!"

"I'm not surprised, the size of him!" snorted Albert.

"Victoria, you having a go?"

"Oh alright, I expect I shall be useless." She grasped the women's welly. "Gosh, it's actually quite hard to grip, isn't it?"

"Don't chuck it underarm like, it'll just go upwards and probably land behind you, try and sort of 'bowl' it," advised Tufty.

Victoria got a tight grip, stepped back a few paces and then gave it her all. The wellington sailed through the air and landed with a satisfying rubbery splat. Albert and Tufty exchanged surprised looks. "Blimey Victoria, you're in the lead!" said Tufty, awestruck. "You've just gone ahead of Madeleine Trusscott!"

Victoria looked nonchalant. "Well, there you are you see, hidden talents. I used to be good at shot-put at school."

"Shot-put? But you'm not hefty enough for that!" spluttered Albert.

"Why thank you for the compliment, but it's not just about heft, it's about speed across the circle!" She pretended to dust off her hands and took Moss's lead back from Albert. "Well come on then, don't just stand there gawping! Let's go and see these terriers racing."

They strolled off, and Victoria said, "So Madeleine is here. I haven't seen her or any of the Ansome clan yet."

"Oh you can be sure they're here. Most probably all in the beer tent somewhere. Except Madeleine – she'll be keeping a clear head for the shooting."

"Oh of course, she does a bit of that, doesn't she?"

Albert nodded and scratched his chin. "Yes, she certainly does."

As predicted by Albert, the terrier racing was indeed a riot. While owners struggled to hang on to their dogs at the starting line, a horrid, chewed bit of old fur, the lure, was waved in front of them, driving them into a frenzy of excitement. Just about every dog in the area, including Moss, started high-pitched hysterical barking. Once the terriers were at fever pitch, the lure was attached to a pulley that shot up the grassy track when, on a signal, the owners released their dogs that set off in hot pursuit. Half the terriers started fighting, a few more shot off in the wrong direction while the rest actually ran after the lure. The winner caught the lure and sank its teeth in – with no intention of ever letting go. There was then at least five minutes of owners trying to break up fights, find their dogs and separate the winner from its 'prize' before the next race could begin. As almost half the population seemed to own a Jack Russell there were plenty of dog races.

Albert and Victoria wiped tears of laughter from their eyes and wandered off to sit on a straw bale by the edge of the main ring. "Oh my goodness! That was hilarious," said Victoria, removing her hat and running her fingers through her hair.

"Told you it wasn't one to miss," agreed Albert.

In one corner of the field Victoria could see a birds-of-prey demonstration, while in another a disconsolate line of children in fancy dress was being scrutinised by judges. "Amazing," said Victoria. "I had no idea days like this still happened in the twenty-first century."

"Well, as you can see, it's pretty popular. All us locals still support it and, of course, the tourists love it too. It raises money for local good causes, keeps traditions alive and brings everyone together, so it's pretty important in my eyes." He glanced at his watch. "I reckon it's time for you and that young pup to get in the obedience class."

"Oh dear, it's really not what I wanted to do – and Moss got terribly over-excited watching the terriers."

"I reckon all the puppies will be in the same state. Just have a go maid, it doesn't matter, just have fun!" He patted Moss and pushed them both in the direction of the ring.

"Here – look after my hat please, I'd better not wear it in the ring." Albert took it and plonked it on his own head momentarily.

After a rather hesitant start, Moss performed well and Victoria was thrilled to come away with a third-place rosette. "Look Albert! I haven't won a rosette since I rode in a donkey derby when I was eight! How fantastic is that! Moss, you clever, clever dog!" She picked him up and hugged him, and the pup licked her chin and wriggled with pleasure. Bunty had winked at her when awarding the rosette and had been lavish in her praise.

To their surprise, Moss fared less well in the waggiest tail competition as two terriers and a spaniel wagged their short tails so fast they were a blur, and they came away empty-handed. "Well, Moss's tail was the most handsome and definitely had the best 'thump'," Victoria said.

"Not that you're competitive or anything," said Albert, grinning at her. "We'd better start wandering towards the far side of the field for the shooting."

Victoria wrinkled her nose. "I want to see you compete, but I'll hate the noise. And what about Moss?"

"Sooner he gets used to it the better maid, he'll be hearing it often enough in these parts. Anyway, he comes from a farm where they shoot, so I expect he's used to it."

As they walked past the produce tent, people were emerging with vegetables under their arms and cakes in bags. "Oh, can we buy some produce then?" asked Victoria.

"If you're quick, most of it will have gone. Some people sell it, but lots of the competitors take it back home with them. Look, I'll hang on here with the pup while you go and look." Albert took Moss's lead and made him sit.

Inside the marquee, now stuffy with the afternoon heat, Victoria realised she had left it late, but she managed to buy some beetroot – poetic justice, she thought – and a rather fine cabbage, the size of a football. Albert adored cabbage and all types of greens, so she thought this would go down well. The beetroot was in a plastic bag and could fit safely in her shoulder bag, but the cabbage was another matter. She emerged from the tent pink and flustered and rather regretting her purchase. Albert was walking towards her from the craft tent with a bag of his own.

"Good God Victoria! What are you going to do with that?"

"You like cabbage, don't you?"

"Well yes, but that's huge, and now we've got to lug it around with us for the rest of the afternoon."

She sighed. "Sorry, I just got a bit carried away. There was hardly anything left and, well…"

He grinned. "Here, give it to me, swap it for your hat, let's get going or I'll miss the start of the shooting." He tucked his own purchase from the craft tent inside her shoulder bag. "There, you can look after that," he said, and patted it.

"What is it?" But he had walked on ahead and didn't seem to hear her.

The crowds were starting to thin a little and fractious children, sunburnt matrons and slightly inebriated farmers were straggling back to their cars.

There was a crowd of fifty or so people around the clay-pigeon-shooting area. Victoria spotted Bill Bramley, king of the welly wanging, Tufty and also Madeleine Trusscott, all waiting to take their turns. Partly hidden, she spotted Charlie Weston and Roger

Mudge – was there no one in the place who didn't shoot? Bunty's husband, Kenneth, appeared to be in charge. Away from his wife and in his own area of expertise, he cut a much more impressive figure.

"First up, Farmer Bramley and Miss M. Trusscott!" he barked. They walked across to the stalls and took up their positions. Madeleine looked keyed up, but stood stock-still. Bill, a powerhouse of a man, looked relaxed, but less sharp. The first shots rang out and Victoria winced. Moss looked up at her and then wagged his tail before lying down next to her. She knew not to make a fuss of him as that would make him anxious.

It was a brief encounter with Madeleine wining easily, hitting every clay first time and with lightning speed. Bill missed one, and took two shots at most of them. He shrugged as he walked past Albert. "Trust me to draw Mad Madeleine," he said. "Hope you fare better..." Albert patted his broad back and waited his turn.

"Blimey, she's scarily good," whispered Victoria, as Madeleine walked to the side to watch the other competitors, her eyes darting.

"Yep," said Albert, "I reckon she'll win if she keeps that up."

Victoria saw Albert watching Madeleine as she fidgeted, licking her lips and twiddling a strand of hair. She looked really pumped up and yet, when in the stand, she'd been steady as a rock.

A few more pairs took their turns and then Kenneth Beacham-Brown called: "Farmer Moreton and Farmer Weston to the stands please."

Albert turned to Victoria and handed her the cabbage with a smile and a shrug. She stood holding it in both hands with her hat balanced on top in the front row of the crowd, feeling like an idiot.

Albert and Charlie walked across to their stands and eyed each other a little warily, Victoria thought. She found her heart was pounding and she desperately wanted Albert to win. She suddenly thought of jousting knights and felt she should fling down a scarf or, whatever it was called, her colours, or something and he should fight for her honour – although she realised it was a bit late for that. Shots rang out and she stopped daydreaming and paid attention. Albert won, but only by a few shots; it had been pretty evenly matched. At the end, the two men exchanged curt nods.

"Miserable bugger," said Albert out of the side of his mouth. "Still sulking about us discovering him last night I reckon."

Victoria frowned. Discovering him last night, what did he mean? And then she remembered, through a haze of wine, Charlie and Carol in a clinch. She grinned to herself, and squeezed Albert's arm. "Well done!"

"How's the pup?"

Victoria looked down at Moss, who was asleep on her foot. "Seems pretty bored by the whole thing," she said in amazement.

Madeleine shot again, with the same frightening accuracy, and trounced her opponent. Albert also won through, this time against a younger man Victoria didn't know. Tufty was shooting well too, but Roger Mudge was knocked out.

They were down to the last eight. Tufty beat a very round little man with glasses and Victoria overheard a fellow bystander muttering that he was 'from up country', so it was obviously good news he'd been knocked out. Albert only just beat a young chap with tattoos and they shook hands amicably at the end. Madeleine demolished her opponent and another woman with red hair won the other contest.

In what Victoria assumed was the semi-final, Tufty was drawn against Madeleine, while Albert faced the redheaded woman. Everyone shook hands. Tufty rolled his eyes and turned to Victoria. "That's the end of me then! No chance in this match." He was right.

Albert and the redhead slugged it out to the last clay, with

Albert just clinching it. The woman smiled and accepted defeat graciously and there was a round of applause.

"Quiet please! In five minutes the final between Miss Madeleine Trusscott and Farmer Albert Moreton will take place!" bellowed Kenneth, by now rather red in the face.

"Well, this is exciting!" said Victoria, clutching Albert's arm.

"You reckon? Well, don't expect me to win maid – I'm nowhere near as good a shot as her. You still nursing that damned cabbage?" He said, laughing as she jiggled the heavy vegetable into a more comfy position under her arm.

"When I put it down just now, a passing Labrador tried to cock its leg on it, so I'm keeping a tight hold on it for now." She was also still holding her hat. She feared if she put it on no one behind her would be able to see what was going on – the brim was so wide. Thank goodness Moss was behaving so well or she wouldn't be able to cope.

Madeleine was stalking around over by the stands. Victoria thought she looked drawn and immensely tense, but then some people were like that under pressure. She noticed that Albert was watching her with a rather inscrutable look on his face. "Everything OK?" she asked him quietly.

"Hmmm, I'm not sure. We'll have to see how it pans out I think..." He gave her a quick grin and then walked over to Kenneth who was looking businesslike and studying a clipboard.

In the background the public address system was burbling incoherently as if Edwin was partly underwater, but Victoria did manage to decipher the words "Final" and "Clay pigeon contest," and she watched as more people drifted across the field to swell the audience. She realised she felt quite nervous and gave Moss a pat. He seemed unperturbed and was wagging his tail and sniffing happily at other dogs and people nearby. Damn this cabbage, why had she brought it? She shifted it under her other arm.

Albert and Madeleine stood side by side as scorecards were readied and people drew closer to watch the final showdown. Victoria could see Albert say a few words to his opponent and she looked up at him sharply.

They moved across to their stands and the contest began. Albert shot well at first, but then Madeleine began to draw ahead. Then there was a delay as one of the traps jammed. "Stand down shooters please, stand down," said Kenneth very formally. Madeleine and Albert wandered back over towards the crowd and stopped, just in front of Victoria and Moss, both still cradling their shotguns.

"Well, here we are then," said Albert casually. "This'll be the final icing on the cake when you win this, won't it?"

Madeleine looked at him. "What?"

"Well, looks like everything's set fair for you now, what with George out the way – he was never going to give you a loan, so he had to go." Victoria's mouth fell open – what was he saying? Madeleine had turned to face him now, her expression blank, and her face white. "And dopey Sam's been blamed, clever move, ideal scapegoat, so money's no longer going to be a problem for you, is it?"

In a split second Madeleine whipped up the gun barrel and held it rock steady, inches from Albert's face. There was a collective intake of breath from the assembled crowd. Victoria felt herself go cold. Albert remained where he was, his eyes fixed on Madeleine. "Were you this close when you shot George? Takes some doing Madeleine, to see the fear in the man's eyes and then pull the trigger." She was breathing heavily, every muscle tensed. "You had us all fooled over that Nosy Parker Percy too, didn't you?"

"Just shut it," hissed Madeleine through gritted teeth.

"He'd been ruining your sales on eBay with his negative feedback, losing you sales, costing you money… so you dealt with him! What amazing luck that the gargoyle landed on him just afterwards so no one noticed you'd already bashed him over the head."

"Stupid old gits, the pair of them. Who'll miss them, eh? No one. Waste of space. And you're next."

As Madeleine's trigger finger twitched Victoria yelled and the cabbage sailed through the air. It hit Madeleine full in the face with such force that she was upended, her legs flipping up in the air and her shotgun discharging harmlessly skywards. People screamed and some ducked; Kenneth and Tufty had the presence of mind to leap on Madeleine and keep her pinned to the ground. Blood was pouring from her nose and she was struggling and swearing into the grass.

"Blimey Victoria," said Albert, wiping his brow, "I'm mighty glad you did like shot-put at school."

Victoria burst into tears and hugged him hard. "You stupid man! What were you doing? She almost killed you!"

"Well, I must admit, I didn't think she'd take on so, but it just seemed like the right moment."

She beat his chest with her fists. "The right moment? What were you thinking? It couldn't have been a worse moment! Oh Albert, I could kill you!"

"Not you and all!" he said, patting her gently on the back. "Come on now maid, it's all OK." Moss was yapping and jumping up, clearly as excited and upset as everyone else. Albert handed Victoria his handkerchief, and she blew her nose.

There was a lot of jostling and noise and the two policemen who'd been on traffic duty pushed their way to the front of the crowd.

"Arrest that woman!" said Victoria, pointing at Madeleine who was still writhing on the ground. Gosh, she'd always wanted to say that – just how much more exciting could life get?

Chapter 14

The evening sun was reflected in the gleaming silver trophy sitting proudly in the middle of the kitchen table with 'Best speciality cake, Swaddlecombe Show' engraved on its base. Victoria admired it and thought about Aunt Edith. Was she looking down and smiling her approval? The base of the cup was crowded with the names of previous winners and her aunt's name dominated for the past decade or so. Well, now her name would be added to the list, and although it was all a bit of a cheeky con she still felt a sense of family pride!

"What you thinking maid?" said Albert.

"Oh, just smiling at the thought of all the years you and Aunt Edith won this trophy. I think she would be happy that we've won it again, even if it isn't exactly a proud and honest family tradition."

"Not at all maid, 'tis the cake that won, not the person. And it's a damned good cake, even if I says it myself."

"I suppose so, if you want to look at it that way!"

There was a faint snoring sound from the corner of the kitchen. Victoria looked up and laughed as she saw Moss asleep with his paws in the air, jerking madly. "It looks like Moss is dreaming of rabbits!"

"Well I reckons any little pup that's won his first-ever rosette deserves a few rabbit dreams!" Albert nodded at the large rosette pinned to the puppy crate. "He did well that boy. Mind you, I reckon I'd do almost anything if that Bunty woman yelled at me, frightens the life out of me she does!"

"Oh Albert, you are rotten. Bunty means well... she's just... how can I put it... rather commanding."

Albert sipped his tea and looked thoughtful. "D'you know, I can't say that I'm sorry it's all over. Not an afternoon I would want to live through again."

"You don't want to live through it again? Good grief, I have never been so scared in my life! When Madeleine had that gun just inches from your face I thought I was going to have a heart attack, I was terrified."

"Can't say that I felt too calm myself," said Albert with a wry smile.

"Well, you hid it well, you looked steely calm to me! Most impressive."

He snorted. "Maybe, but it was my cabbage-throwing heroine who saved the day."

"I can't imagine what made you confront her like that, not your best idea – you were so lucky she hesitated. But look, what I am itching to know is what made you think that Percy had been murdered rather than accidentally killed by that gargoyle? And when did you start to think it was Madeleine, and why didn't you tell me and..."

"Hey, steady on maid, calm down! This is meant to be a nice soothing cuppa after all those police questions – don't you start on at me too."

"But please, just explain to me."

"Well it was a bit of a lucky punt really. She were acting a bit odd all afternoon and that tension somehow just crystallised an idea that had been mooching around in my head and then, suddenly, it all sort of came together. There was the negative feedback on her eBay account – now that all came from a punter that called himself 'Peashooter' and that made me pause and think of Percy – you see Percy Shooter is also P. Shooter and…"

"Yes Albert, I do get it, you can carry on."

"Then, you mentioned the inquest being adjourned and I started thinking hmmm… maybe they'd found something had already happened to Percy before that walloping great gargoyle smashed onto his head and they needed more time to check.

"Course, I knew Madeleine was really short of money as I could see how bad she was at paying her debts and even messing us about with your bits of kitchenalia. And then I remembered the pictures Percy took of George yelling at some woman and I was sure it was her, and I realised it must have been when she'd asked him to loan her money and he'd refused. Spoilt brat that one, not a good person to say no to!"

"She's June and Len's only child isn't she? I guess they just said 'yes' to her too many times. I always thought it was odd how easily Sam was condemned by his own family and they did nothing to try and save him. They must all have known it was Madeleine and decided Sam should be the scapegoat." Victoria shook her head, thinking about how unfairly the family had treated him. "But both June and Len – they must have known. When she went home after shooting George, she must have reacted, had blood on her clothes. How could they do that to Sam? And what about May too! The whole family closing ranks."

"Well, sweet soul though May is, she has scrubbed and cleaned for both the brothers for many years without so much as a thank you – and certainly no share of the money. George was a tight old cuss at times – well no, all the time, and Sam never thought to be grateful for anything, so there wasn't much love lost there. So when June told her to say nothing, that's just what she did. Faithful old

May," said Albert.

"As for how could they do that, I reckon a great many people would have done the same thing, don't you? Think about it, maid. Surely most mothers would have covered for their children. Both brothers had been a bit tough on June and Len, in George's case by refusing Len his workshop and never treating June really well. In Sam's case he never bothered about anyone but himself, so he was never popular with anybody really. He was a damned convenient scapegoat at the end of the day."

"Yes I suppose so. Tufty said he saw the police arresting all three of them at the show yesterday. Apparently poor May was sobbing, but the other two looked pretty calm in the circumstances."

"Well I 'spect June has done her crying, when she found out what her daughter had done, she must have been devastated. Can't be easy to find out your daughter is a murderer, let alone the murderer of your own brother, not an easy thing." Albert nodded thoughtfully.

"Not easy, but makes them just as guilty," added Victoria. "I guess they'll be prosecuted for aiding and abetting or association or something?"

"Oh I don't know all that legal stuff, but I reckon they'll have their time in court. Strangely, the only person in the family who isn't guilty of anything is Sam, which feels like a rum state of affairs!"

Victoria sighed. "I suppose so, but that seems a bit harsh, Albert – he's not that bad, just a rather weak character. But talking about rum things, something I haven't quite fitted into place is all that business about Charlie Weston's car that Sam said he heard – what was that all about?"

Albert laughed. "Ha, the only rum thing Charlie was up to was carrying on with Carol. Why they felt they had to keep their whole affair secret with an early morning rendezvous parked up in the lane near Ansomes and furtive trysts and turning the whole thing into a game of espionage is quite beyond me. Maybe they found it more exciting, but damned if I know!"

Victoria looked at him. "You aren't jealous of Charlie – about Carol I mean – since she used to be your girlfriend?"

Albert sighed. "Now, that's a tough one... let me think... which would I prefer?" He scratched his head and frowned theatrically. "A nice lady that's daft enough to fancy Charlie Weston or a lovely, intelligent woman who lights up my life every time she walks into the room?"

"Oh Albert, now I feel all embarrassed. Thank you, that's a lovely thing to say." Victoria fanned her face as she realised she was turning pink.

"More cake, that's the answer to that!" Albert reached over and cut two large pieces of cake, put one on his own plate and passed a plate to her. "Cake's the answer to most things, I reckon!"

"Well – if I carry on eating this much I may not even be able to get through the front door!" laughed Victoria. "I must have eaten more cake in the last six months than I have in my entire life."

"And very good cake it has been too," said Albert as he took her hand. "Ah, I almost forgot." He reached across and rummaged in her shoulder bag and brought out a paper bag. "I bought this for you at the show. Close your eyes."

Victoria did, clasping her hands together in childlike anticipation. "Ooh, What is it?"

She felt something soft and warm placed lightly on her head. Keeping her eyes tight shut she lifted her hands to feel. "Oh I know what it is, it's that adorable felt hat that I was admiring!" She opened her eyes and removed the hat to study it. "It's lovely Albert, you are thoughtful, thank you." She fingered the soft felt and admired the handiwork. Laughing, she placed it on his head and pulled him close.

They both jumped as there was a firm rap on the back door and, without waiting for a response, in came the Reverend Ruminant clutching a bottle of something that looked suspiciously like champagne.

"What ho dear friends! I just thought I'd pop in and share a toast to the dear departed, who will, I think, be looking down on us and feeling very grateful to the pair of you. Been quite a day, eh?"

"Edwin, thank you so much – come on in and let's raise a glass," said Victoria as she reached into a cupboard for some flutes. "I think you may have to have some obligatory cake to go with it though, as Albert hates to eat alone!"

Edwin paused and seemed to think about this idea. "Well, it would be rude to refuse, don't you think?"

Victoria raised her eyebrows at Albert as she slid her untouched slice of cake towards the chair into which Edwin was lowering himself.

"Nice to see you Reverend, been a hell of a day one way and t'other."

Edwin studied Albert's headgear with a puzzled expression. "Yes Albert, lots of hellish components crept into today, but brave actions on your part and that of dear Victoria here. Quite the heroes of the village!" Edwin tucked in enthusiastically.

"It's good to have everything sorted out," replied Victoria, as she watched Albert grapple with the champagne cork. "All so unfair on poor Sam."

"Absolutely," Edwin nodded furiously as he swallowed his mouthful of cake. "No man should be abandoned by his family and left to carry the can when he is innocent. I can tell you, I was shocked. Deeply." He shook his head and slumped a little over his plate. He must be exhausted himself, thought Victoria, poor chap. She patted his hand lightly and he looked up and smiled at her.

Albert popped the cork and began pouring the champagne.

"But anyway, let's have a toast," continued Edwin with deliberate cheerfulness. "Here's to cake trophies and, judging by the rosette on the little's pup's abode, success in the dog field too!" They clinked glasses.

Moss had woken up now and was very keen to greet the vicar, so Victoria let him out of his crate and he leapt enthusiastically over and sat beautifully in front of the Reverend's feet, head cocked to one side. "Now that's what I call a welcome!" laughed Edwin.

Victoria and Albert shared a look, and she smiled. "Actually Edwin, it's not entirely welcoming, it's slightly influenced by the fact that you are sitting on his favourite cuddly toy."

The Revered got up and looked on the seat of the chair and indeed, there lay a flat furry squirrel – which had been well chewed and was now minus most of its stuffing.

"Oh my apologies dear dog, here's your toy." Edwin bent down and gave the strange-looking item to Moss, who grabbed it and raced out of the back door. "Nothing like a puppy to show you the things that matter in life, eh? I meant to say, I assume this wonderful confection I am eating was THE winning cake, chocolate and beetroot wasn't it?"

"It is indeed," smiled Albert. "Well, what's left of it."

"Excellent recipe, well-deserved win." As Albert beamed, the Reverend winked in Victoria's direction.

"And now," he said as he swallowed the last mouthful of cake followed by the dregs of his champagne, "I must be on my way, plenty of lady villagers to go and comfort about their failure to win the cake contest!" He laughed and the other two joined in.

"Well, thank you for coming round, Reverend," said Albert seriously.

"I just wanted to check you two were alright, pretty frightening happenings this afternoon. I would prescribe an early night if I were a doctor, but I am not. But still…" Smiling at them again he waved cheerily and left.

"He's a very caring man, isn't he?" said Victoria. "I assume all the joviality was just a cover for checking how we were holding up?"

"I reckon, always liked him even if I'm not a regular churchgoer." Albert took the flutes over to the sink together with the cake plates. "Talks a lot of sense too – I think an early night would be just what the doctor ordered, you look all in maid."

Victoria pulled a face at him. "Well thanks, you certainly know how to give a girl a compliment! But talking of looking tired, I think you're pretty much in need of an early night too. Would you do me a huge favour?"

Albert looked puzzled. "Of course, if I can."

"Would you mind terribly if I asked you to sleep here tonight? Only somehow, after what happened this afternoon I sort of don't want to let you out of my sight. I think I'd feel safer if I knew you were here."

"Oh do you now," laughed Albert. "Never have I heard such a lot of nonsense!"

Victoria slapped him playfully and smiled. "I'm only half teasing, but I really would like you to stay."

"Oh alright then, if I must. Meanwhile, let's take the pup round the farm for a quick constitutional before bed and then call it a day, eh?"

"Are you going to keep that hat on then?" she asked. "It looks quite rakish on you!"

"Eh? Oh, I'd forgotten about it, it's so light. Here you are!" Albert laughed and gave it back to Victoria. He took her hand and, calling Moss, the three of them set off into the dusk.

The following morning Victoria woke to the sound of her mobile ringing. She rolled onto her back and was instantly aware that she was alone, although there was still a faint trace of warmth from where Albert had lain. Groaning as the phone continued to ring she felt blindly under her pillow, then scrabbled on the bedside table, and eventually realised it must still be in the pocket of her jeans. Opening her eyes a little she rummaged in the pile of clothes on the floor and found it. "Hello?"

"Victoria?" said a male voice.

"Um yes?" She rubbed her eyes and tried to cudgel her woolly brain into life.

"It's me, Sam."

She sat bolt upright. "Sam! How are you? I mean you've heard... of course you must! I mean..."

He interrupted her rambling. "Yes, of course I know. That's why I'm ringing. It seems my entire family is under arrest – well, everyone except me. And now I'm being released and there's no one I can ask to drive me home."

Victoria thought she head his voice crack. "Oh Sam, I'm sorry, look I'll come and pick you up. Don't worry."

"Thank you Victoria, I knew I could rely on you," he paused. "You've been a true friend to me throughout all this, I don't know what I'd have done if..." Again he faltered and Victoria cut in quickly.

"Look, it's nothing, really. I'd like to think anyone decent would have done the same thing."

"Not many decent people around then."

"Well, perhaps not in the immediate vicinity of the nursery, no, but still..."

She heard him clear his throat. "Well look, when I'm back and settled in, maybe we could, you know..."

Victoria pulled her knees to her chest and felt guilty for no real reason. "Sam, let's talk about it later – you must have things to sort out, and lots to think about. What time will you be ready?"

"About midday they reckon."

"Alright, that's fine, I'll see you then." She ended the call and hugged her knees. Poor chap – she felt bad not being there for him as he obviously wanted her to be. But she knew she was just doing her usual trick of siding with the underdog and taking on everyone else's troubles. She had helped him and she had done her best for him, but she had Albert now and that was all that mattered.

As if on cue, he appeared in the doorway with a mug of coffee and what looked suspiciously like a thick bacon sandwich on a tray.

"You alright?"

She nodded. "Yes, I think so. I just had Sam on the phone wanting me to go and pick him up when he's released about midday today."

"Do you want me to drive you?"

She hesitated, knowing it would not be what Sam envisaged, but also knowing it was the right thing to do. "I think it might be best, don't you?"

He nodded, put the tray on the dressing table and sat next to her. "Best to get these things sorted from the outset I always think, less painful in the long run." He looked at her closely, and smoothed a strand of hair off her cheek. "You still look tired maid. I left you to sleep in, but it's gone nine o'clock now and I thought you probably ought to be getting yourself a bit shipshape. Hope the coffee and the bacon do the trick. I've walked the pup, so you go and enjoy your weird shower thing," he waved a hand in the direction of her bathroom, "and I'll see you in the barn about eleven-thirty and we can go and get young Sam."

"Thank you Albert. You are wonderful."

"I know," he said with a grin and, getting up, walked off downstairs.

The drive to the prison in Albert's old but reliable Volvo was largely silent. They parked up five minutes early and Victoria chewed her thumbnail. "Stop that," said Albert gently. "Just you go and wait for him over there, I'll stay here by the car. Alright?"

Victoria nodded and walked the fifty yards to the forbidding prison gate. Somehow, she was more nervous now that he was about to be released than she had ever been when she'd known he was being held safely inside. She wandered back and forth with her hands stuffed into her jacket pockets. Out of the corner of her eye she was aware of Albert leaning against the bonnet of the car and pretending to read a motoring magazine.

She jumped as she heard the sound of locks and bolts opening and the small door within the large old gate swung open and Sam stepped out, blinking, into the sunshine. He looked tired and thin, and noticeably older. He met her eyes and smiled. "Victoria!" He embraced her warmly and she hugged him back, trying to relax and not let him feel her hesitation. "Thanks so much for coming to meet me! It is so good to see you and to be here in the sunshine, a free man!" he sighed, his face buried in her hair, still holding her. "I've thought about you a lot. About the future... well if I was going to have a future which I doubted for a while there... and whether we could have another go at things... I mean..."

Victoria pulled away gently, but before she could speak saw his eyes focus on something in the distance over her shoulder, and she knew he'd spotted Albert. She turned and saw the tall figure, arms folded, resting against the front wing of the Volvo, looking back at them both steadily.

"Albert drove me over. In fact he's brought me over every time I've visited, and it was actually him who worked out that Madeleine was the murderer."

Sam nodded slowly. "Ah, I see." He looked from Albert to Victoria, and back again. "So I owe Mr Moreton something of a thank you," he smiled ruefully. "That's rather ironic in the circumstances, don't you think?"

Victoria shrugged a little. "Perhaps, but I think once the dust has settled, we'll all see that it's for the best, won't we?" She held his gaze and he smiled at her and nodded.

"I guess you're right."

He picked up his bag, a tatty plastic carrier containing a few meagre items, and they walked across the car park. He and Albert shook hands and they all got in the car. The journey back was as quiet as the earlier one and Victoria was relieved when they reached Ansome Nurseries. But on arriving, her heart sank. The place was deserted and a 'Closed' sign hung on the gate.

"I'll wait here," said Albert, trying to be tactful. "You get yourself settled in, Sam, and I'll see you around soon!" he called cheerfully as Sam and Victoria walked through the gate.

"Well, not much of a homecoming," said Sam, his shoulders slumping as he looked around the silent nursery, the empty polytunnels and the abandoned plants.

"Maybe so just now, but look ahead Sam. Now you can have a fresh start. You can make a go of all your eco-projects and I'm sure there are lots of people around who would like to get involved." Victoria carefully crossed her fingers behind her back as she went on. "And, while you may not think it now, I've heard plenty of locals say they couldn't believe you'd been involved in George's death, so I'm sure you'll find you've got allies out there."

He nodded and looked around. She could see his mind starting to work, and he seemed to look less haggard. "I would like to get the eco-holidays off the ground, and I've got all sorts of plans and," he paused and smiled, "I can even get myself those damned chickens now!"

Victoria squeezed his arm. "Why don't you start with them? They'll give you a real focus and, take it from me, they're great fun and will give you hours of entertainment!"

"OK, I will. I might even need to come and ask your advice."

"Any time – but the real expert around here is the Reverend Ruminant, he's a proper fowl fancier."

"Is he? Right, I'll remember that."

"Meanwhile, to get things back on track, why don't you go and look out the details of some of the regular staff you normally have here? They'll want to know what's happening. Give them a call and ask them all to come in and resume work next Monday, then you can open up and earn some money and you'll soon find things feel more settled."

He nodded. "You're right. I need to focus on the future and not dwell on the past. I really don't want to think about any of that at the moment, it's all still too raw,"

Victoria nodded. "I'm sure. Look, keep me posted on how you get on. The article I wrote will be out soon and you should pick up some business from that." She didn't want to think about the fact that it featured George at its centre. "I may well want to come back and write about your eco-holidays too once you are up and running."

"That would be great, thanks Victoria."

"Look, I'd better go, Albert's sitting outside, and…"

"Yes, yes, of course. Thank him for me, will you?"

She nodded. "You take care of yourself Sam."

He gave her another hug, but this time she sensed he was ready to let go and already thinking about what the future might hold. Victoria closed the gate behind her and sank into the Volvo's comfy passenger seat. "Phew," she said, leaning back against the headrest. "I'm glad that's over."

"Not difficult was it?" asked Albert, concern in his voice, as he turned the car round and headed off down the narrow lane.

"No, not really, just lots of emotions and undercurrents and stuff. He'll be alright eventually and I think I managed to get him to look to the future, but I think the trial and the gossip will be a big test for him to get through. I might need to keep a watching brief."

Albert tutted as he turned left and narrowly avoided a rabbit. "Just like your damned aunt!' Stop worryin' about everyone else and look after yourself for a change!"

They bounded along the lanes, the old car floating along effortlessly. Victoria was beginning to feel drowsy when they pulled to a stop. She opened her eyes to see they were in Swaddlecombe's main street and parked outside the shop.

"Just need to get a few bits and pieces," said Albert, opening the driver's door.

She sighed. "Oh not more cake ingredients – please!"

"No, just some bread and milk and the like. You coming in?"

Never able to resist the lure of the quirky triplets she smiled. "Of course, I wouldn't miss it for the world."

They paused outside the door and looked at Lavender's bargain box. It seemed to be full of cabbages and fresh beetroots, with small pots of violas dotted in between. "Good heavens, what's all that about?" said Victoria, frowning.

"I'm not entirely sure, but I've got my suspicions," muttered Albert as he pushed open the door. The tinkling of the shop bell was almost drowned out by the round of applause and a general "oohing" and "aahing" that rose from the cluster of customers, mostly ladies of a certain age, who were milling around the shop.

"Well I'll be damned," said Albert, smiling benignly at the

twittering mass before him.

Victoria overheard snatches of conversation.

"And they said she threw it so hard it broke her nose!"

"Serves her bleddy right!"

"Oh, he's so brave, and so handsome!"

"You know they reckon a wedding's on the cards!"

At this last comment Victoria gave a start. She glanced at Albert and he looked equally panic-stricken. "Blimey," he muttered. "Stay close to me and we might just get out of here alive!"

They advanced towards the counter and the mass of womankind parted like the biblical Red Sea to let them through. "Hello Daphne – all I wanted was a few bits and pieces, but it seems like we've called at an inappropriate moment," he said.

"Oh no dear, far from it. These ladies have just come back from the WI lunch club and it will round off their day nicely to say that they bumped into you two in the shop!"

"Yes, it's the real icing on the cake!" said a woman in a headscarf. "That'll be the chocolate and beetroot cake!" chipped in another, and they all laughed heartily at her joke.

"Victoria, I warn you, I may bolt at any minute!" said Albert out of the corner of his mouth.

"Don't you dare!" she muttered, gripping his arm tightly. "Daphne, all we need is a loaf and some cheese," she added, trying to sound businesslike. "Oh, and some smoked salmon if you have any."

"Smoked salmon!" Victoria heard the sibilance as this item of great extravagance was whispered from WI member to WI member.

"Fancy!" said a very short woman with a squint. "Smoked salmon, and on a weekday too!"

"Do you want your usual Cheddar dear?" asked Iris, getting in on the act.

"Only if you have it," Victoria wasn't going to fall into that trap again. "If not, any tasty cheese will do."

"Right you are dear." The two sisters busied themselves with the shopping.

Victoria picked up some tomatoes and handed those over for weighing. "Oh and milk please, skimmed if you have it."

"Skimmed!" Once again the word hissed its way around the shop and eyebrows were raised and some even shuddered at the thought of such a healthy option.

As they paid and prepared to leave Lavender appeared from the back of the shop. She looked solemn. "Hello Lavender. Are you alright?" Victoria was slightly worried by the woman's expression.

Lavender nodded. "Did you see it?"

"Your display? Yes, we did." Now Victoria was stumped – what on earth could she say next?

Albert cleared his throat. "A nice tribute I thought. Symbolic."

Lavender's face cleared and she positively beamed. "Really?"

Albert nodded. "Yes, very nice Lavender, very... poignant."

There was a collective sigh from the assembled ladies. Victoria never ceased to be amazed by Albert's perception, often in the strangest situations. She looked at him now and smiled; he was rather marvellous. They gathered up their shopping and beat a hasty retreat to the car. Albert drove off at speed.

"You are such a creep sometimes, Albert Moreton!" Victoria laughed.

"I'd say anything to get out of there!" he shuddered. "All they women all looking at you – t'was like a nest of vipers waiting to strike!" He grinned. "Only joking. That Lavender, her's a funny maid, but I can sort of see where she's coming from."

"I'm glad you could, because I couldn't."

"That's because you can never see the wood for the trees!"

He swung the Volvo into the driveway and they bounced over the potholes and arrived in a cloud of dust in the barn.

"Oh it's good to be home," she sighed.

"Come on then, I can hear a small dog barking and it seems to be coming from your kitchen!"

They sat at the kitchen table and drank tea, the afternoon sun streaming in the window and Moss lying contentedly between them, his tail beating a tattoo. "Now, all that's missing from this scene of domestic bliss is a nice piece of cake," said Albert.

"There's some left in the tin I think."

Albert opened it up and peered inside. "Barely!"

"You have it, I really don't need any more."

"Alright then, I don't need much persuading." He grinned and squeezed her hand. "After all Miss West, I am a man who likes to have his cake, and eat it!"

Victoria sighed and glanced at the latest copy of the parish magazine that lay on the table. Turning her head to read something on the front page, she said, "Hmmm, now that could be interesting."

"What's that?" said Albert, through a mouthful of cake.

"There's a company advertising Devon cream teas by post."

"Eh? Why would you want that when I can bake you the best scones in the county and quite possibly make some of the best jam and…"

"No, not to eat, you boastful beast! I was thinking it might make an interesting rural business feature for my next article."

Albert gave a theatrical sigh. "Poor beggars."

Victoria looked affronted. "Whatever do you mean? Most people would be delighted to get free publicity in a national magazine."

"Well, I'm not saying you're jinxed or anything, but you do seem to make a habit of stumbling across bodies in the course of your journalistic endeavours."

Victoria opened and closed her mouth, unable to think of a retort. It was true: the founder of the very first company she'd featured had been murdered, and then poor old George had been killed too. She hadn't thought of it like that.

"Ah well, I'm sure it's just coincidence, maid," grinned Albert, wiping crumbs from his mouth.

"Well, I'm shocked, now you put it like that. Goodness, maybe I am jinxed – how awful!" She looked bereft.

"For heaven's sake Victoria, I was joking! You go and interview them, I'll even come with you and be your official scone taster if you like!"

"Oh alright, but you are rotten. And you must promise not to be rude about their scones if they don't come up to your exacting standards."

He patted her hand. "It's a deal. Anyway, if there are going to be any more bodies lying around, you're going to need me on hand to help you solve the mystery."

Victoria glared at him. "Albert Moreton, you get more boastful by the minute! But we do seem to be quite a good detecting duo, I must admit."

Albert grinned. "Holmes and Watson?"

"Hardly, more like Miss Marple and her knitting – and I'm the knitting!"

"That's a bit harsh, even for you," said Albert. "Morse and Lewis!"

"Oh do shut up and give me a kiss!"

About the Authors

Joanna Sheen has published over 40 non–fiction books and 'A Violet Death' is her second novel.

Joanna is better known for her presence in the craft world and regularly appears on Create and Craft TV demonstrating cardmaking and more. Having run her multi award-winning company for 36 years she now feels able to follow her dream and focus on writing as well.

Joanna lives in Devon with her husband, and has two lovely daughters who have perfected the art of rolling their eyes at their impossible mother.

Julia Wherrell is a professional writer, designer and photographer. When she is not writing novels, she writes copy for websites, blogs and magazine articles. She has attended numerous creative writing courses (usually with Joanna) and has written many thousands of words of fiction – all of them good, but not necessarily in the right order.

She lives on Dartmoor with her dog, chickens and long-suffering partner. She grows her own vegetables, makes things out of willow and goes to tango classes. She has also been known to go rock climbing.

The Swaddlecombe Mysteries:
A Sticky End • A Violet Death

Both novels are available on Kindle and in paperback.

If you'd like to find out more about Victoria and Albert and the residents of Swaddlecombe, go to: www.swaddlecombe.co.uk or follow Swaddlecombe on Facebook